DAUGHTER OF THE VALKYRIE

REAPER'S CALL

PART I

KEVIN SAUL

Tritale Books

tritale.ca
daughterofthevalkyrie.com

daughterofthevalkyrie.com Copyright © 2024 by Kevin Saul
tritale.ca Copyright © 2024 by Kevin Saul

Edited by Sarah Berti

Cover design by Steve Coleman and Kevin Saul

First Edition: June 2024

ISBN (softcover print) 978-1-7383733-0-7
ISBN (hardcover print) 978-1-7383733-2-1
ISBN (digital) 978-1-7383733-1-4

A special thank you to all of the people who made this possible, including:

Linda Shantz
Sarah Berti
Matthew Guillemette
Matthew Nichols
Gary Pererra
Steve Coleman
Nyla Martin
Larissa Smith
The incredible Launch Team
My amazing family, friends, and community who supported me through my entire process and never once said, "Why is it taking so long?"
Thank you.

For my Valkyrie and our daughter

CONTENTS

Characters and Notes

Thorkil – Gudrun and Siv's father, Odd's brother, Hildegunn's husband. He is campaigning in Albion with Chief Gudbrand's army.

Gudrun Thorkildatter – young hunter from a Norse family (known as an *ätt*) who was forced out of her home, the village of Lutvin, and she has given up trying to fit in.   Father: Thorkil   Mother: Tove

Siv Thorkildatter – Gudrun's younger sister who boldly turns heads wherever she goes. Off the farm people trip over themselves for her attention.   Father: Thorkil   Mother: Hildegunn

Odd – Lutvin's senior *völur* – a woman with the extraordinary gift of conjuring with *seidr*. Aunt to: Gudrun, Siv.   Brother: Thorkil

Jarl Ulfer ätt Wylfling – King of Vargr and the surrounding lands, including Hoddlund in the West, and the Silver Mountains in the East.

Frue Frigga – Queen of Vargr. Spouse: Jarl Ulfer.   Sons: Prince Ormer, Prince Hamund.

Gudbrand – Chieftain of Lutvin, currently campaigning in Albion. He wields ätt Lutvin's battle spear, *Skera-Brynja*, a weapon of great power and mystery.

Vigdis – Chieftess of Lutvin while her husband, Gudbrand, is campaigning

Grima – Chieftess Vigdis' most trusted advisor

Dreng – a raider and a pest, forget about him

Erich The Dane – A handsome, muscular Danish timberman wielding a large axe. He is the man of Gudrun's dreams.

Mista – a völur who lives with Odd and their two apprentices

Sangrida – Odd's apprentice

Haldana – Mista's apprentice

Ranvieg – weaver and healer in Lutvin

Bestla – hunter from Lutvin

Britta – mushroom collector from Lutvin

Greip the Warloga – a grotesque creature of unspeakable power, who will make a deal with anyone willing to pay the fiend's ghoulish price.

Seidr – a mystical power discovered by the Vanier gods. Freya is the most talented god with seidr, and taught her husband, Odin, how to use its power. Of the Aisir gods, Odin is the best with seidr. Some gifted women known as völur conjure with seidr more powerfully than the gods. The dwarves use seidr to craft the greatest items in the universe, such as Thor's hammer, Mjölnir. Others use seidr to shapeshift into animals, such as bears and wolves.

Yggdrisil – The Tree of Life which contains the entire universe of nine realms: Asgard, of the Aesir gods; Vanaheim, of the Vanir gods; Álfheim, elven realm; Niðavellir, dwarven realm; Midgard, human realm; Jötunheim, of the giants; Niflheim, of the Frost Giants; Muspelheim of the Fire Giants; Helheim, realm of the dishonourable dead.

CHAPTER ONE

Homecoming

More of the ocean stretched out in front of her from the clifftop. It beckoned to her, whispering to her heart. The ship was much further away, headed West, to Albion. *Another one gone without you,* Gudrun thought. If that one was the last to sail from Vestrijóborg this year, then she was stuck until after winter. Gudrun couldn't bring herself to look down the coast at the harbour. Already, smoke belched up from the tar-pit fires in the lumber camp, staining the wooden buildings a darker black. *I gotta get out of this sty.*

She touched the carved stone pendant under her tunic, the one mama had worn until she died. *Mama help me.* Papa had put it around Gudrun's neck before he left and swore he'd replace it with another of gold. Gudrun vowed she'd die before she'd take it off, even if papa made good on his promise.

A raven's shrill caw in Gudrun's ear sent a teeth clenching jolt up her spine, like the alarm of smashing glass. The bird was the size of an eagle, perched on a hopelessly thin pine bowed over under its weight, flapping its wings and rasping louder than a mule.

"Skadti's Branch, you tar-dipped overgrown hen! Can't you be quiet for even a moment? Why do you keep pestering me?" For days now! Each morning she'd wake and there it would be, perched on a branch, staring. Then it would follow her around and caw, incessantly. All day. Since Jarmond's Crook.

"Three days hunting, gone! Do you know how much silver that was? *Gone!* Because of you!" She looked around for something to throw, until the same question that had plagued her mind since she'd found the bird begged to be asked, one last time.

"Why didn't I just leave you to those wolves? Another winter wasted in this skitrhole. And you still make me pay for my kindness!" She drew her bow and aimed at the raven's chest. "You're too close and too fat to miss, bird." The raven twitched its head to the side. "And so lucky I've run out of arrows."

Gudrun took a deep breath and relaxed her bow. Her gaze fell upon the hunter's snare dangling from the raven's leg and bobbing in the wind.

"Stupid bird," she muttered. "Don't even know when you're being saved." Her hand still pulsed where the raven had jabbed its thick beak into her flesh while she'd been cutting it free from the trap. The bird nipped at the snare cuffed to its ankle.

"Yes, it would have been better to let me help you, huh? *Bah!* Hel take you! I've more important things to think about." She turned back to find the ship, now just a pebble on the horizon.

Orange leaves gave shape to a cold morning gust as it swept and swirled them from the trees. Last night's storm still had more to give today, judging by the dark clouds piling over the ocean's edge. Gulls cried as they glided inland on the bitter autumn wind.

Strange, Gudrun thought. The pebble was getting larger. *Have they turned back around, or is it another ship coming in?*

She bundled up in her coat to sit and wait. Her hand lingered on the pendant. *Is this one theirs, mama?* The ship would need to pass closer before sailing on to Vestrijóborg. If it had any markings on the sail, she'd see them from here. Not since the summer thaw had unlocked the Western coast months ago had she missed a single morning on that ridge, well before the trees were budding in the surrounding forest.

Since, those buds had grown and summered, and now lay as a thick blanket of orange, yellow, and red leaves smothering the ground. No one sails in or out of here in winter. If the men didn't return soon the deadly winter sea would lock them out until the next spring. It was foolhardy to try in winter, as the tides would mercilessly smash any ship against the fjord cliffs. *That would be two winters since they'd left.* She'd be locked in and they'd be locked out.

The morning sky was darkening. Gudrun clasped her hands together and touched them to her forehead. *I pray to you, Rán and Ægir, gods of the ocean, and Njord, god of ships: give them a good sea with a strong wind, and a steady hand at the tiller.*

The shape of the vessel became clearer and Gudrun's pulse raced. It wasn't just one ship, but two! One had a symbol on the sail, though shrouded in darkness and at an obscure angle. *Please be a black crossed hammer and axe.* Chieftain Gudbrand's banner. When she squinted she saw crossed slashes... or the sail was patchwork. "Sigurd and papa could be on one of those ships." And if they weren't? *Then this time, I'll be on one of them and leave with it.*

But, suddenly anything was possible. *If the men are back!* The harvest could be finished before the first snow; they would all be rich with treasures: gold and silver, cattle, goats, thrall...

"And mead!" Oh gods, it had been a long time since she could afford a good mead-drunk. Music, dancing... She stood on her toes, maybe she could see the ship's crew. Still too far. Though, even from that distance she noticed one ship was listing. *Taking on water?*

The raven startled her with another sharp *Krra!*

Gudrun sneered at it. "I'm sick of you, *fowl!* One arrow — Skadti's Branch for an arrow! Clearly, it's listing from unbalanced cargo." She squinted at the listing ship again.

The sail languished to the stear-board side. Was misshapen, too, as though the rigging were tangled or snapped. Oars undulated and clashed like a caterpillar with broken legs. Gudrun grimaced at their poor seamanship. *Exhaustion?*

The ships were about to cross out of sight behind a cliff when one of their sails shifted and the crossed hammer and axe became clear. Gudrun's heart leapt. "*Skoool!*" she yelled, arms raised in triumph.

Out of nowhere, the raven streaked past, cawing as its wing-tip brushed Gudrun's forehead. The bird's tail swirled behind it as though made of mist. Amid smokey tendrils the veil which lays between the mortal and the unseen realms parted, and the ships were revealed to Gudrun through a spirit's eyes.

Everything else, including the raven, stopped.

A dark, murmuring chant surged in a rhythm. In and on the water around the vessels, serpents swam and animals charged alongside the ships, led by a hound and a bear. All were dingy and ashen, corrupted *fylgja* — spirit animals.

Screams of death.

Roaring fire.

An ocean of blood.

Gudrun coughed and wretched as the mystical smoke choked her. "No! *Stop!*"

She pushed against it, closed her eyes and turned away. The raven flew past and the world rushed back in behind it. A sudden drop in the pit of Gudrun's stomach made her wretch and snap her eyes open again.

The mists closed, the vision faded.

Her throat soothed and she blinked away tears, as the ocean and sky settled back to dim-morning normal.

Gudrun sparked with rage. "What did you do to me?" she snarled. "Why show me this?"

The raven glided to a holly tree, cawing as it landed.

She stabbed her finger at it. "Don't do that again, bird! Be you either spirit or demon, I care not, but I know your vision was conjured from... from apparition! And, deceit! Tricks and illusions, questions and no answers."

Gudrun was no stranger to the mystical arts of *seidr* — the source of power in the universe that even the gods fought each other over. She knew better than to trust this bird. Ravens were known to be clever tricksters, but this one was obviously a master.

The raven flinched its head around as it watched her.

"Those have to be Chief Gudbrand's boats. I saw his crest on the sail! That is real, not your trickery," Gudrun said. The raven preened out a loose, greyed feather from under its wing.

What am I doing? Arguing with a bird? She threw a pebble at it. "Peck that!" The raven heaved itself into the air and the stone clattered off the waggling branch.

Gudrun looked back at the ships, just as they sailed out of sight.

Normal.

No animals or chants or fire; just ships heading to port ahead of a storm. *Not just any ships, Sigurd's ships!* A grin twitched on her lips thinking of her brother. *I can get to the harbour before them!*

She dashed off of the winding path, making a shortcut through the thick forest of heady fir, leaping down hills and over streams, and scrambling up a cliff. Luxurious evergreen branches swayed in the wind and stretched in every direction.

Mesmerised by her own stride and breath, Gudrun's thoughts drifted. How would Sigurd look a year later? More a man, she was sure, perhaps with a sailor's beard, scruffy and thick. Her brother was cursed with a baby face, but a beard would hide it easily. And papa. She could see him standing tall and stoic, as the day they left. Same beard and hair, maybe new streaks of grey. She'd missed papa, too, but it was different. Somehow she'd thought — or, perhaps she'd expected — that papa wouldn't return. That he'd become more of a seeker of Odin's paradise than a man who still needed to raise his family. His children were all grown.

Sigurd had too much life in him. Too much laughter to seek Odin's glory, yet. Gudrun laughed as she pushed through the trees. The vision of Lutvin's Hall in full celebration, stuffed with the entire village, made her heart ache. So hot from the yule fires it would melt the snow around the building and make a path for the children to run around. Roasted ham, boiled beef. *And duck! This'll be a yuletide to mark!* Not like the last—

She stumbled when she thought of who she'd lost to the winter plague. The thought clung to her like a thin, black shroud, neither revealing nor hiding the corpse beneath. *This yule will be different.*

Each breath was autumn pine and sea-salt. The smoke from Vestrijóborg became more pungent as she jogged closer to the logging camp. Her legs felt powerful, dashing out of the treeline. The evergreens stopped in a neat row before a stark field of wide stumps and cast-off pine branches. It was all that remained of the old woods in a one hundred yard clearing surrounding Vestrijóborg. Vestrijóborg had what her little village of Lutvin did not: a Western port deep enough to connect the Jarldom of Hoddlund to the world.

A dingy cloud of white smoke billowed from the tar-fires burning unseasoned pine, before the wind dragged it into the woods. It stung her nose and made her hide coat feel tacky.

She rejoined the path, through the east gate and into the camp's logging yard. On the other side of the camp lay the track to the main town, and the harbour.

The logging yard was long and wide enough that teams of horses could work four abreast, dragging logs or skids of wood between the buildings that stood end-to-end. Young boys heaved against creaking oak doors of the flat-roofed saw mills and chimneyed smithies.

This was how the camp started every morning, performed with near-ritualistic observance. Men and boys fetched wood and searched for supplies and misplaced tools, scuttling to-and-fro, like crabs snatching up dross in the current to inspect, only to cast it off again. They swore and cussed at each other. Gudrun knew all too well that for most of them, it helped cool the anger simmering just below a hangover that begged for the comfort of a noose.

The camp was tense as tempers wore thin. More so this year than last; at the cook-tent line, at the stables and the livery, men shouted and shoved each other over who was next or who'd taken what and how much. Only one bright-moon remained until winter and the camp's shut down. The end of this year's dismal 'silver-season' loomed and Gudrun knew at least three millers who would be working right up until the Yule trees were felled, just to break even.

The smoking tar-pit fires and the euphoric vapours from the tarring hall gripped her senses. She'd made good time getting into camp. *Before I go to the harbour I'll need to get the fight money Bodolf owes me. Stupid raven.*

She jogged to the furthest outbuilding in the camp, the pay office, where a dozen women holding baskets of laundry had gathered, banging their fists on the door.

Already geese waiting. Gudrun had seen some of the women around camp, though she only knew a couple by name. One of them grabbed the handle and shook it.

"We know you're hiding in there! No more laundry 'til we're paid!"

Gudrun rolled her eyes. *Bodolf. What a useless ass!* She peered toward the harbour. She didn't want to miss the ship, but... *I'll be in and out, nothing to do with their wages.*

"Move, I'll try," Gudrun said, sauntering toward them.

The laundrywomen sneered, blocking her path with their baskets planted against their hips. One gave Gudrun a sideways glance.

"Whadda you think *you'll* be able to do, hag? Scare it open?" The women snickered.

"I scare you, do I?" Gudrun glowered, towering over them.

"No!" the woman said, jutting out her chin with her fist on her hip. Gudrun pushed her to the side and strode to the door, parting the group like a wave off a ship's bow.

"*Bodolf!*" Gudrun pounded her fist on the wood until it shuddered and creaked like a stick snapping.

No reply. The women twittered.

"Bodolf isn't here anymore, he left two days ago. Bjorn is the paymaster now," one of the women snorted.

"What? Bodolf owes me money!" Gudrun said.

The women laughed. "He owes everybody money. You'll have to wait until he comes back, in the Spring." They laughed again.

"Why'd he leave? That *ass!*"

"He went home to get married."

"Married? Then who runs the fighting ring now?"

One of them chuckled through the look of disgust on her face. "Ander," she said, and spit in the dirt. The women groaned.

Gudrun rolled her eyes. *Anyone but Ander.* "Where is that hearthstone now?"

"Ha ha! Pimping at the Main Gate," another one sneered. Gudrun knew this woman. *Unne. Anna? Hela! Edda?* She didn't like what's-her-name. "I saw him there just a little while ago with a pretty little blonde. Poor girl. Very pretty. She looked familiar somehow... Wait! I know now! She's your sister!" The women laughed and chorused with surprised *"ohh'*s as Gudrun turned purple.

"What? You lying bitch! You don't know my sister. Why would she be here in Vestrijóborg?"

"I remember her from Gudbrand's farewell," What's-her-name said. "Siv is her name, I will never forget. She had more than a few men tripping over themselves to catch her attention that day."

"Oh yes," Gudrun chuckled. "I remember. Your fiancé was one of them. Didn't he fall off the pier?"

"Well," the woman snapped, "I'm sure by now Ander's found some disgusting place to bend her over and really let her experience what kind of a royal skitrhead he is."

Fire flashed in Gudrun's stomach. "Keep your mouth shut!" *What if she's telling the truth?* Gudrun pushed past them and marched across the yard, through the horse and cart traffic, toward the gate. The women made rude curses and gestures at her before turning to pound on the door again.

Gudrun rounded the corner to the main gate.

She was telling the truth!

From across the paddock Gudrun could see Siv's clean brown dress and blue smock. Her platinum hair was braided and covered by a white kerchief. She stood beside the gate, besieged by Ander and two other men. They towered over her, doing their very best to convince her to loosen her morals, offering strong liquor and smoke. Weary prostitutes in well-used frilly dresses ringed a brazier behind them.

Beside Siv, Ander and the men appeared even more filthy than usual. The trollops continued chatting as they warmed their hands, ignoring Siv's harassment from their pimps.

Ander leaned one pudgy arm against the post behind Siv and chuckled with a sneer, his eyes locked on her chest.

"*Ander!* You swine!" Gudrun said. "Get away from her and give me my silver, or I'll cut it from the fattest part of your ass."

One of the prostitutes snickered.

"Shut up, whore!" Ander glowered at the woman. He turned to Gudrun, then threw his head back and laughed. "Oh, it's just you! Come back later tonight. I've got someone who'll give you a good ass whipping in the ring." The men laughed and slapped Ander's shoulder, then turned their attention back to Siv. She tried ducking away, but Ander grabbed her arm. "You're not going anywhere!" He pulled her back in, trapping her between them.

"Let go of my sister, or she's the last woman you ever touch," Gudrun said, one finger pointed between Ander's eyes.

"*Your* sister?" Ander looked from Siv to Gudrun. He whistled and slapped his forehead. "How can one blossom into such a sweet flower, while the other becomes a withered stem in manure, sprouting only thorns?"

Gudrun whistled as though calling a dog. "Go on, boy! Go get my silver."

Ander's eyes flashed as he clenched his fists. "You bitch! No woman talks to me that way! All I owe you is this!" He slapped Gudrun's face, hitting her nose with his palm, the force twisting her head to the side.

She turned back, grinning, and shrugged. "That's it? Come on Siv, let's go."

She reached out for Siv's hand but Ander jabbed her shoulder and scowled, "*Hey—*"

Gudrun launched an uppercut into his jaw, snapping his head back. Ander went limp and hit the ground hard. The other two pimps gawked, while the prostitutes gasped and slapped their hands over their mouths, choking on laughter.

Gudrun chuckled at the men. "Eyes wide as goose eggs." She pushed past them and grabbed Siv's arm to pull her away.

"Wow! That was…" Siv gushed.

Ander lay in the mud, moaning.

Gudrun tore open his coat, and one of the pimps stepped forward to protest.

"I seen her fight before," one of the women shouted. "That weren't nothin'!" The women burst out laughing.

The other man grabbed the first pimp's arm and pulled him back, shaking his head. They leaned back against the fence, watching Gudrun like vultures overseeing a wolf's fresh kill.

Ander had a filthy brown pouch tied to his belt. Gudrun snapped the frayed cord and held the pouch's satisfying weight. The cheerful jangle of coins made her rip it open and pour out a hand-full.

"Hey!" One of the pimps leapt at her.

"That should do it," Gudrun said. She tossed the rest to the prostitutes. "I'm sure he owes you at least that." The thugs watched helplessly as the bag lobbed through the air and spilled open at the women's feet.

"*Aaaieee!*" They all scrambled to grab silver with fist-fulls of mud. The pimps shouted and hip-checked some women over, and they retaliated with piercing screams, punching and kicking for their cut. A passing worker grabbed up a coin which tumbled between his feet, exclaiming, "Praise Loki for answering my prayers!"

"Hey!" one of the pimps yelled and chased after him.

"Come on." Gudrun grabbed Siv's wrist and pulled her toward

the tent rows. Her nose was bleeding and she held her sleeve up to stem the flow.

"Gudrun, wait!" Siv struggled to twist out of her sister's iron grasp.

Gudrun didn't stop, and dragged Siv behind her for another three rows. "What are you doing here, Siv? Did you actually come by yourself? He didn't hurt you, did he?"

"No, but you are! Stop! My wrist!"

Gudrun let her go with an exasperated flick and continued on, storming down one of the tent corridors, leaving Siv to trot to keep up.

"Why are you here, Siv? Vestrijóborg isn't like Lutvin, nestled away in the fjord. Life moves fast here and snakes like Ander hide under every rock. I can't play the big sister and look after you here."

Siv's face went blank. "We need help bringing the sheep in. It's just mama and me now, and even with Ingunn and her kids, there aren't enough of us. You need to come home."

"No. I can't just leave. What about Frau Andred's boys?" Gudrun tilted her head back to let the blood drain down her throat.

"They'll help, but they're not shepherds. We need your experience, Gudrun."

"Hildegunn asked you to get me? I find that very hard to believe."

Siv paused. "She's your mama, too, Gudrun. You know I hate it when you call her 'Hildegunn'."

Gudrun bit her lip and continued walking between the tents toward the Yard Gate. *But, she's not my mother.*

"Gudrun! Stop!"

Gudrun looked back over her shoulder at Siv. Her younger sister stood exactly how Hildegunn would whenever Gudrun was really in trouble. Arms crossed, brow furrowed.

Gudrun stopped.

They were quiet for a few moments. Siv shuffled her feet in the dirt and Gudrun checked the blood on her sleeve before returning her wrist to her nose.

"Mama thinks I'm at Ivor Jomann's ranch, looking for help from his boys," Siv said.

"So why aren't you there?" Gudrun put a hand on her hip.

"I was, but they're too busy with the horse drive. I went along with Garrett and Kirk's crew when they drove a hundred from their ranch to Vestrijóborg. We arrived late last night and I stayed with them at their uncle's."

"When they go back you can return with them, I need to stay here."

"Why? There is hunting in Lutvin, and you have the bow of a hunter. And yet, the fists of a brawler. Is that it? You want to stay until someone here bashes your skull in? Gudrun, you have to help. It's just mama and me. Old-man Ketil does what he can around the farm, but it's not enough. We need—"

"*Shh!* Wait! I hear footsteps." Gudrun held up her hand. She cocked her head to the side. Someone was running toward them. *Ander? That pig!* She ducked her head out and saw a tall man waving.

"Gudrun! Wait!" he shouted. His worn leather coat swayed as he ran, along with the blonde braid down his back.

"Skadti's Branch, it's Erich! Siv, he can't see me like this," Gudrun hissed. She ducked behind a tent, leaving Siv standing alone. Gudrun glanced down at a dark splotch of blood on her tunic. *Of all the times for him to show up!* She weaved through the corridors until she found a secluded spot.

Between the tents she could see him, smiling and talking. Erich 'The Dane', Thor on earth. A divine chisel, wielded by the god Brage himself, carved this demigod from head to foot. A blonde beard spun from silk framed a mouth that Gudrun ached to have on hers. Under his coat he wore a thick wool sweater which had shrunk drying too close to a fire, and his bulging chest stretched in all the right places. He leaned against a large axe with a pack slung over his shoulder, laughing with Siv.

Wait! Erich with Siv? Gudrun's heart shuttered. Her younger sister, a goddess herself, smiled and thrust her breasts out at the man of Gudrun's dreams. The thought of what their god-touched children would look like terrified her. She balled her fists. *Must you nod and smile at* everything *he says?* She winced each time they laughed. *Get away from him!* They spoke for a few more moments, and Erich nodded enthusiastically. Then they waved goodbye and parted.

Siv strutted toward her, grinning.

Gudrun stepped out once Erich was out of sight, one hand on her hip. She wanted to grab Siv's skinny little neck and choke the smile off her face. She narrowed her eyes and aimed a single finger at her sister's nose, ready to smash it.

"What," Gudrun cocked her head, " —is that my pack?" Siv was carrying a green bundle on one shoulder.

"Yes. You left it back at the gate and Erich returned it." She dumped it into Gudrun's arms as she strode past. "He is the only real man I've seen in this place so far."

"There are plenty here!" Gudrun snapped. "And more coming into harbour every day!" Gudrun suddenly stopped, a realisation slapping her even harder.

"The harbour! Siv! I saw a ship this morning with a crossed hammer and axe on its sail, just like papa and Sigurd's!"

"Really? Here, at the port?" Siv squealed. She grabbed Gudrun's hand and they ran down the lane to Vestrijóborg.

The harbour sprawled before them, wide open to the ocean. Only a shoal-like group of islands within bow-shot of the shore blocked the view of the horizon.

Siv gasped. "The sea looks so huge here! It must burst with orange when the sun goes down! And so many buildings. Lutvin seems so small. Just a simple little fishing bay tucked in among the fjord's cliffs." She clasped her hands to her cheek.

Gudrun frowned. "Just stay close to me."

Fishermen manoeuvred their boats, draped with nets, plying oars and poles to secure berths. They would wait out the coming storm tied together in the harbour.

Otherwise, there weren't any ships. Not any the size that Gudrun had seen.

"It's not here," she said. Her shoulders slumped under the weight of her disappointment. She double checked.

Siv pulled Gudrun's hand. "Let's go down and have a closer look. We'll go through the market."

They ran around the horse paddock, where the rancher's herds were being wrangled into the selection hall. A dirt road had been packed hard by years of herding cattle and horses back and forth from the harbour.

The wind blew colder, encouraging buyers to rush their haggling. The market barely contained the heady throng who pulled animals and baskets of trade-goods around with them to each stall. Vibrant blue, red, and orange cloth snapped in the wind and tinted the cobbles and the wares. Glossy, exotic pottery in open crates and packed with straw and hessian, had vignettes painted on them of Byzantine lords and ladies; other stalls overflowed with bins of dried and cured meats, alluring foods and bizarre sundries.

Vendors sang out their wares. *"Spices! Salt! Local and exotic! Eastern spices!" "Dates! Sweet and large! Drives out gut-demons!" "Hemp rope! Sisal! Flax!"*

A piquant aroma rode the wind, of curious spices from open baskets and frying fish. Gudrun's mouth watered. Stalls and carts teemed with greeny-brown cod, silver and gold trout, crabs, shellfish, urchins, and Gudrun's favourite: kveite, the fish of the gods.

Gulls and crows hovered on the wind, making ready to besiege yelling fishmongers, and challenged each other for the discarded fish tails and guts that lay at the men's feet. The fishermen smoked pipes as they cleaned and filleted the morning's catch. Gudrun could see that the old men kept a cautious eye on the horizon. They sliced faster with their deft knives as the clouds darkened.

Gudrun frowned. "We should head back— "

"Please, no! I promise we'll be quick! Let's see if any merchants have brought any fine Eastern silks with them." Siv laughed and dug her heels in as she pulled Gudrun's wrist.

"Ha! Fine cloth from Araby to make a dress for the 'Princess of Lutvin'?" Gudrun rolled her eyes and smirked. "Ugh! Let's be quick!" Siv's enthusiasm was too infectious for Gudrun to resist. And her adorable, dimply laugh? Fatal.

Siv navigated them to the dry goods area of the market, on the wharf's edge. A headwind off the ocean flapped the cloth labyrinth of stalls. Buyers clamoured to trade silver and commodities for goods as men packed their wares away against the coming storm. Thin streamers whipped overhead, darting green, blue, and red, like snakes with their tails caught, desperate to escape.

Gudrun turned to say something, when a sudden, uninvited image of Erich and Siv laughing together burned away her thoughts and branded her memory.

"Siv, I—"

"Here we are!" Siv announced.

Within the jungle of stalls, crouched one with bolts of fine, imported cloth jutting out over top of a short cloth merchant. An old hemp cargo net held a bulging stack that creaked and whined against thin, frayed ropes. Cool ocean blues of indigo and woad, sensual weaves of delicate yellows and pinks and rich fiery reds—

Gudrun's head spun. The colours and patterns were already too much. She hadn't even seen the striped cloths, or the bunches of buto-teardrop leaves and flowers, yet.

"We could spend a fortune!" Siv gushed, her face alight.

"*We* don't have a fortune to spend."

"Oh, come now! Ander can afford a penny for a strip of cloth." Siv gasped. "Oh, Gudrun! I'll help you make a dress for Yule!"

"Why would you waste your time? I'm not going back to Lutvin, Siv. I can't be cooped up all winter in that tiny house, with you and Hilde— uh mama..." They both looked down and shuffled their feet. Gudrun felt queasy. *Every time I call her 'mama'. Every single time!*

Crows glided out from packs of swirling sea birds to claim positions on tent peaks, croaking arguments about the weather, ever searching for food. A large raven with a hunter's snare dangling from one foot scattered all the birds when it flew in to perch on the cloth merchant's tent peak.

The thin dark-skinned man stood within a small space below the precarious cargo net, wearing a shaggy wool coat that went to the knees of his thin legs. He reminded Gudrun of a sheep. His head poked out from the middle of the coat and he greeted them by touching the colourful *takiyah* he wore and bowing. He gestured to the sky with a sour face in silent apology for the weather. An old woman, as wrinkled as the pile of blankets she'd bundled herself under, sat upon a rolled up sleeping mat at a small table at the back. She poured hot wax in patterned lines onto undyed cloth. She looked up at Gudrun and smiled, exposing toothless gums. Her smile made sense of the deep wrinkles cut into her happy, round face. Gudrun guessed the two merchants lived there, in the tent. A small clay stove in the corner confirmed it to her.

The man offered three bolts of cloth to Siv, like platters to whet her appetite for a feast. He beamed as she gushed and chattered, caressing the fabrics, each one a muse for her inspiration. "Oh my! This one is just..!"

Gudrun stared at the mountainous bundles of cloth, but couldn't see them beyond the unshakable image of Erich laughing with Siv. A question burned within, too hot in the moment not to be quenched. She had to ask.

"You and Erich spoke for quite a while. A much longer conversation than 'I haven't seen Gudrun. Good day'. What did you two talk about?"

Siv waggled her fingers at two green bolts and the woolly man pulled them out with a flourish, chattering lovingly in an Eastern tongue.

24

"He wanted to return your pack." Siv hadn't taken her eyes off of the cloth. "Oh, yes, this one! Such rich, even tones in the colour," she cooed, holding the cloth like a baby, swaying and caressing it against her cheek. The man nodded his hat off, then laughed as he picked it up.

"*And?*" Gudrun crossed her arms.

"And, he wanted to know if you are going to work in the tar hall until Yule." Siv selected two needles and some thread from a basket.

"Not a chance!" Gudrun made a sour face and shuddered. "I can work a fishing boat, hunt seal, harvest whale, but tar sails? *Bleh!* Black *dreck* under my fingernails until *next* Yule? No, not for me."

"I told him as much."

"What did he say?"

"He looked sad."

"Really?" Gudrun perked up. "How sad?"

"Sad for home. He's so far away from his family, so..." Siv reached for another cloth and Gudrun grabbed her hand.

"So? What?" Gudrun squeezed Siv's wrist, imagining it was her throat.

"So, I asked him to stay at the farm for Yule."

Gudrun's jaw dropped, "You *what?!*"

The old raven rasped. Siv smiled sweetly as she rubbed the exquisite cloth on Gudrun's hand. "This one is so fine! Much finer than the others, don't you agree?" She beamed at the merchant, while pointing to the darker green. His eyes went wide and he held up a single finger, "Ahhh!" He ducked down, then reemerged with another bolt.

"Siv!" Gudrun had turned purple. "*You* invited Erich — Erich the Dane! — to stay at our house for the entire Yule celebration?" She couldn't keep shrillness from her voice. She raised her hands and shook as though Siv's spindly little neck was hers to crush. "*Why?* Why don't we just make the dress in *your* favourite colour? To *your* size? Whose bed will he sleep in, I wonder?"

Siv stiffened in shock as though her sister had plunged her into ice-water.

"Gudrun! I—"

"*Bah!*" Gudrun shoved her aside and stormed off.

"No! Wait, Gudrun!" Siv dashed after her.

"Whenever you're around, everyone else becomes invisible. Everyone, but me! I become the whipping girl, unable to be missed. We all know that Hildegunn is going to pass the household keys to you, not to me, not to father's eldest daughter. So, I have no dowry and no farm. Skadti's Branch! What I would do if that farm were mine!"

Siv stared at Gudrun intently and leaned in. "What *would* you do?"

Gudrun paused. She couldn't bear to face her sister at that moment. She didn't have enough courage to tell her she'd sell it. Get rid of it all. The animals, the tools, the house, the memories. She'd leave. But, she couldn't say that out loud. Sell the family home? Even the very thought crossed a hard line that would rip through the heart Siv wore on her sleeve. It would be easier to strangle her than break her heart. Gudrun shook her head. "You should ask papa what he would do."

She turned away from Siv's intense look burning with questions. She was so young, innocent, unprepared for the responsibility Hildegunn would soon place upon her. Gudrun could see to the horizon between the tents, flapping in the prestorm wind. Her heart suddenly leapt into her throat.

"*Siv!* There it is! Their ship! It's sailing into the harbour!"

They dashed around the tents to the water's edge to see. Siv gasped and grabbed Gudrun's arm. Out across the harbour of fishing boats, a single ship drove toward them from the small patch of islands just off shore. The ship's sail was full, displaying Chief Gudbrand's mark sewn onto it in black: the crossed hammer and axe.

CHAPTER TWO

Hoddholm

Gudrun and Siv watched as the ship sailed toward the harbour on the strong storm wind that felt fresh on their faces. Gudrun loved seeing the wash it ploughed to the sides. "Like a dog with a bone in its teeth", was the expression mariners used for a fast ship with a large wash.

It is listing. She thought. *A campaign returning with no oarsmen rowing and sail full? Are they in trouble?* The brooding storm clouds behind it suddenly felt ominous. A whiff of smoke made her pause.

"There's only one ship," she said.

"No. There should be another behind it, isn't there?" Siv stood on her toes for a better view. "They've left the serpent's head on the prow. It'll scare the *landvættir*[1] and curse us!" She clutched her chest and pointed at the dragon's head on the prow. They were never left on when sailing to port, only when on the attack to terrify and drive out the spirits in enemy lands.

One of the lookouts upon the palisade wall was shouting and waving his arms.

"Look. Smoke," Gudrun said, pointing. Yellow tendrils of fire flicked dark smoke up off the deck. Up and down the seawall

---

[1] Earth/land spirits

guards shouted the alarm, but the wind took their voices and the buyers and sellers continued their transactions, unaware.

"The ship is going to hit the harbour," Gudrun said. From the deepest part of herself, Gudrun knew and dreaded the worst. *Are we under attack?*

An alarm gong made Siv jump and grab Gudrun's arm.

"What's happening? Is papa's ship on fire?"

The raven cried out, its grating call like a shout tearing at Gudrun's focus.

A flash of colour made her spin to see the thin merchant jogging up from behind, a grimace on his face and his hand out for his silver. The gong prompted a different concern, and he stopped once he saw the burning ship barrelling toward them. His jaw dropped even though his hand hadn't.

Most on the wharf were still unaware of the danger, but the gong had them anxious to know the source of the alarm. Somehow, they hadn't seen the ship yet, sailing closer, as fast as the wind could carry her. Smoke from its deck thickened, blown into a haze over the harbour as blazing orange flames climbed the mast.

On the wharf and jetties they stopped and pointed. Sailors yelled to one another as they scrambled to row their boats clear. Someone finally shouted *"Fire!"* and the alarm was repeated throughout the harbour.

Men pushed through the stunned crowd to find buckets and containers for water as the burning ship careened on a path toward destruction. Others grabbed their families and pulled them away from the edge of the wharf, but the crowd churned to a halt as panic prevented them from deciding what to do next.

"We need to leave, now." Gudrun grabbed Siv by the shoulders as the nervous crowd tentatively backed away from the shore wall directly in the ship's path. It lurched into the harbour and smashed through a slow trawler. Fishermen dove into the water, forced to abandon their boats or be crushed under the ship's flaming prow. The crowd screamed, powerless to stop the ship from crashing into them, bearing down at full speed on the waterside market.

"Run Siv!" The crowd burst into a stampede, suddenly shoving and clawing to get away from the danger. They twisted, pushed, and pulled, driving the sisters apart, but Gudrun grabbed Siv's smock in her fist. Fleeing marketeers kicked and elbowed each other in their desperation to escape.

A deafening wallop rocked the flagstones when the ship ran aground and smashed the wharf. The cloth merchant screamed as his stall, along with the ones beside, catapulted into the air with his wife still inside. They shattered onto the stone like a tidal wave of fabric and goods. The ship launched up and twisted sideways, spilling flaming pitch across the market square, which stuck to and consumed everything within its reach, structure, stone, or flesh. A mountain of black smoke and flame erupted into the sky as the city caught fire.

"A fire-ship!" Gudrun gasped. She yanked Siv to her side. "We need to get out! Follow me through the fish market."

She fought through the panicked crowd while dragging Siv behind her. Gudrun caught a glimpse of one of the guards stationed on the wall as he collapsed and fell. *What?* Then another fell, then a third. *Gods, no! Please, it can't be true...*

A stunning wave of shrieking attackers surged over the palisade.

"Vestrijóborg is under attack!" Gudrun shouted.

The guards were overwhelmed by an army of savage men swinging clubs and thrusting sharpened sticks, wearing scraps for clothes. They pounced on anything that moved without prejudice, human or animal, pummelling and hacking everything and everyone down, impaling fleeing citizens in the back with spears. Men and women throwing buckets of water to fight the blaze were slaughtered before they'd realised the second threat.

"Do *not* let go of my hand! No matter what," Gudrun yelled.

She pulled Siv through the fish market, running and dodging through the crowd, across the square, between rows of stalls.

Wild attackers continued to surge over the palisade and across the harbour, hacking and stabbing shrieking villagers. The crowd surged to the exit gate and choked off the corridors to escape. The raiders had taken the harbour. Gudrun and Siv were trapped in between.

"Who are they?" Siv shouted, clutching Gudrun's arm. A man leapt out in front of them and roared, blood splattered across his face like a hand grabbing his jaw. He raised a gory axe up to cut Siv in two. She screamed and threw her arms up as he brought the axe down.

Gudrun lunged to catch the axe's handle and punched his windpipe. He grabbed his throat and fell backward, writhing and choking for air.

"Whoever they are, they've got the market. We need to find a way out now, before the whole city is overrun," Gudrun said. Siv buried her face into Gudrun's shoulder.

Over the shrieking of the panicked crowd a raspy thought came to Gudrun: *This way.*

She shook her head. "What?"

The greying raven, perched above on a tent, flapped its wings and thrust out its enormous chest. The hunter's snare still hung from its foot, like a thin finger pointing to the dark corridor between the tents below. The raven jabbed its beak toward the corridor, to emphasise the point.

That raven again! "Still trying to trick me? We're going that way, Siv," She pointed in the opposite direction, to a door in a stable. Gudrun picked up the axe and they sprinted to the building, leaving the raven flapping.

The storm driven wind whipped the fire across the harbour and choked the paddock with smoke. The horses had already kicked and trampled themselves free and the sisters were alone in the abandoned stable. Nearly.

Siv stared at a stable boy's corpse, laying in a pool of blood. She'd turned white and stammered as she pointed. "Is— is he...?"

Gudrun pulled her along and ran to the other end. "We'll get out this way." She unbarred the door and it creaked loudly as she pulled it open. A group of ten raiders, kicking at doors in an alley, all looked at her.

Gudrun blinked. She slammed and barred the door shut again, just before the raiders crashed into it from the other side. Siv screamed when they hacked it with axes.

The raven cawed from an opening in the loft. *Follow!*

"Shut up!" Gudrun snarled.

"What?" Siv was beside herself with terror.

"Never mind. Drop the cloth and follow me this way." *The raven was right, we should have left through the tents.* Gudrun led them back through the smoke, past the boy's corpse and out the way they'd come. Siv hugged the bolt of green cloth as she struggled to keep up.

"Doesn't this take us back to the market?"

"Yes, but there's an alley we can go through, if we hurry. There it is!"

They ran through the fish market, now deserted, to the corridor the raven had shown her.

Suddenly, a dozen raiders descended from around the corner, waiving axes and machetes and crying out for blood. Gudrun's heart leapt into her throat and Siv screamed.

"Get behind me!" Gudrun yanked her back and held her axe at the ready.

The men stopped and snarled, their weapons already dripping with gore.

Thor, give me strength! I beg you to protect Siv, if I should die.

The hateful squad took a step toward them, frothing and salivating, fury in their eyes.

Gudrun raised the axe and growled. "Come on, you goat buggers!"

One of the men turned to the side and ran, dropping his spear to clatter across the stones. Then another dashed off, and three more and then ten, until they were all racing away. The men abandoned

31

their weapons and crashed into stalls of fruits and vegetables at the other end, overturning carts and fighting each other in a frenzy.

"They're starved," Siv said. Another three ravagers sprinted past before a fourth grabbed Siv's arm. Gudrun's axe flashed and chopped through his wrist. He shrieked and grabbed the bloody stump, then stumbled and fell.

"Oh! Thor, protect us!" Siv flailed and slapped the severed hand away.

"Starved for more than just food, let's go!" Gudrun dashed on, between the tents and stalls, but Siv couldn't keep up.

"Siv! Drop that stupid cloth!"

Siv hugged it tighter. "They're butchering people, Gudrun! What are we going to do?"

Run, the thought rasped.

"Shut up, I know!" Gudrun snapped at the intrusive voice in her head.

"Then tell me!"

"We run, Siv! We get far away. If they catch us they *will* kill us and much, much worse before that. We're nearly at the wall. Once we're over, we can hide in the woods."

They dashed around outbuildings and through a dark alley. The stench of rotting fish and urine made Gudrun's eyes water. Siv gagged, the reek even worse than the acrid smoke covering the city. They dashed past the splintered remains of crates overgrown with long, decaying weeds. At the end was the log wall standing in mouldy piles of dross.

"*Dead end?*" Siv squeaked in horror, slapping the wall with both hands.

Gudrun pushed her aside and twisted out a loose, broken board. Light jumped through into the alley from the hole, revealing insect-ridden filth dangling across the opening, much worse than Siv could have imagined.

"In you go," Gudrun said. Siv looked at the small gap, laden with spiderwebs.

"I won't fit in there! This is your plan? To trap ourselves in the filthiest lane you could find?"

"*Shhh!*" Gudrun held up her hands. "Trust me, I know what I'm doing."

Siv jumped when a wave of screams crashed in from behind. Thicker smoke stung away the fetor of rot.

"We need to move Siv, the fire's spreading. Drop the cloth and get through!" Gudrun grabbed the bolt, but Siv pulled it away and stamped her foot.

"*No!* I'm taking the cloth!" Siv tossed the bolt through the gap and reached in to climb after it. "Eeww!"

"Hurry up!" Gudrun glanced behind just in time to see a man's greasy face peer in at them from between the stalls.

"Wha's dis?" he hissed. A nasty grin spread across his cracked and blistered lips. He glanced behind before stealing into the alley. He cackled as he drew a dull seax from his belt. He slowly waved it around as he slinked toward Gudrun.

"Cam 'ere, girly."

Siv was through to her torso, but her skirt caught keeping her from lifting her knee high enough. Gudrun reached back, grabbed Siv's leg and gave her a shove. Siv disappeared through the gap with a yelp.

The greasy man sauntered toward Gudrun with an obscene thrust in his hips, "Hoo hoo hoo! A *biiig* 'oman. Mmmm… You'll b' tastier dan col' fish. Warmer, too!" He licked his lips as he crept in. He made a couple of playful swipes with the blade, laughing and grinning, exposing what he had left of his yellow, rotting teeth. He reached out to grab Gudrun's arm.

"Not today," she said and thrust the handle of her axe into his nose with a dull thud. He threw his arms up too late and stumbled back with a grunt. Gudrun spun and shoved her weapons and pack in the gap, then dived through.

Siv was still brushing dirt off herself when Gudrun rolled out.

"You know, that wasn't—"

"You're welcome. Run!"

Beyond the wall, the clearing around Vestrijóborg was a long dash to the woods. They ran to the cover of the trees and within moments, they spotted others fleeing from the city to the woods. Half a dozen raiders came over the wall, shouting as they fanned out to search, black smoke billowing from the city, belching into the sky behind them.

"They're determined." Gudrun smirked.

Siv wasn't impressed. "Where do we go now?"

Gudrun scanned the woods. They were hidden, but too close to the city. Others were crashing through the woods, either to escape or to run down escapees. "This place is going to be crawling with them. We need to get to the beach."

Dense pine trees stood sentinel before the freedom of the open ground beyond. Thick wet branches slapped their faces as the sisters pushed through until they burst out the other side. The beach lay beyond a browning field, open to a fjord rolling out to the ocean.

"Now where?"

The men tracked just behind in the woods.

"To the beach or the cliffs?" *Which way? Come on, Gudrun, think! Can't risk fighting with Siv here, I can't let her get hurt.* She looked toward the cliffs. The trilling of the raven flying low over them grabbed her attention. It glided across the field toward the ocean.

Gudrun!

"What?" she snapped. Siv made a sour face.

"You didn't hear that? The raven calling my name?" Gudrun said.

Siv blinked, confused, then shook her head. "Just tell me which way we need to go!"

Gudrun. Follow.

"This better not be a trick, bird," Gudrun said.

"You're talking to the birds?" Siv was incredulous, her brow furrowed as though she would scream. She frantically shot glances between Gudrun, the bird, and the woods.

34

Gudrun ignored her, gripped by a fascination with the raven. It hopped toward the beach. *Follow.*

A snapping branch startled them.

"They're close! This way!" Gudrun hissed.

They sprinted across the field, the raven flying ahead of them. It landed and waited at the sand until they'd caught up.

"I need… to catch… my breath!" Siv huffed.

"You'll have to breathe later, here they come!"

The raven took off again, winging onward.

Gudrun jumped up and chased after it, leaving Siv to breathlessly haul herself up and run behind them.

One at a time the raiders broke through the woods into the field.

"There! I found two!" one shouted, pointing, and the men took up the chase.

"Gudrun! There's five of them!"

"With more behind— Siv, will you get rid of that cloth?!"

The raven cawed out. *Follow!*

"Keep up or we'll never lose them," Gudrun shouted over her shoulder, as she chased after the bird.

A grassy strip faded into a sandy beach with bitter, crashing waves. Across the water spread the cliff-face of a fjord, a small island at its mouth which stood before the open ocean.

The raven glided toward the water, then landed on a long white stone laying in the sand, like a small, beached whale. Otherwise, the beach was barren.

"We can't stay here, they'll run us down!" Siv said.

Gudrun looked along the exposed coastline. *Stupid!* she thought. *How could I have thought to follow that fucking bird?*

The raven cawed from on top of the stone, bobbing its head as it screamed at them.

"Your bird, Gudrun. It found something. We can hide behind the boulder." Siv took a few steps toward it.

"No, Siv, stay beside me!"

"Look!" Siv pointed at the raven then started running toward it.

The raven flapped its wings and cawed harder.

"Gudrun! It's a boat! The raven brought us to a boat!"

Gudrun cocked her head to the side. She couldn't recognize it.

The raven flew off when Siv pounded on the hull with her fist and it made a deep boom that could only come from hollow wood.

"A rowboat?" Gudrun gasped. She dashed over.

An old fishing boat big enough for two was half buried in the sand. They dug down to grab the rail, then heaved it over.

"'Upon the wings of birds are brought the whispers of gods'," Gudrun said, recounting Aunt Odd's words.

They scanned the inside.

"No sail or mast, but the oars are here. It better float or we won't get far," Siv said.

"Has the raven ever let us down before?" Gudrun grinned.

"Get them! Don't let them escape!" The shouts of the men across the field made Siv tense. They were already charging over the grass, brandishing their spears and axes, crying out for death.

"Siv, push!" Gudrun got behind the boat and the two of them heaved against it. The boat lurched over the wet sand. They strained against it, feet churning the sand, and it slowly picked up momentum. The men were now running across the sand.

"They'll reach us before we reach the water," Gudrun shouted. "Keep pushing as far as you can, I'll hold them off." She gave the boat one final shove and turned to face the men with her axe in hand. *Five against one,* Gudrun thought. *This is going to be something.*

She moved to line them up as best as possible and readied herself to swing at the first charging raider. He held his spear up to strike, the advantage of reach clearly with him as he thrust the spear at Gudrun's chest.

But, then he fell at her feet, blood spraying from his throat. Gudrun snapped her head around to see Siv reloading a sling for another shot.

"That's my girl!" Gudrun shouted.

The next man was already on Gudrun. He flailed his spear

wildly, like the cruel look in his eyes. He let loose a murderous cry and leaped to strike. Gudrun stepped back as he thrust, then forward again, swinging her axe. The blade smashed through the bones of his arm and his spear jammed into the sand. His forehead hit the shaft's end, knocking him unconscious before he could feel the agony of his severed arm.

"Small mercies." Gudrun shrugged.

She yanked his spear from the ground and readied to throw.

Another man fell to Siv's sling stone, leaving him doubled over and gasping for breath. Gudrun threw the spear, it punched into a fourth man's ribs and he dropped forward, driving the shaft deeper. He gasped for his last breath, the wound frothing as it huffed and sucked at the blade that had pierced his lung.

The last man scrambled to a halt. He abandoned his weapon and fled back to the woods.

"Woo! That's all of them!" Siv cheered.

"There'll be more. We need to hurry. Load the boat with anything useful."

Gudrun kicked one corpse over and yanked the spear from his deflating chest.

"Who are they?" Siv asked, searching the beach for more sling-stones.

"This one looks to be from the East… I don't know… Kvenland? And, that one could be from Albion. I can't believe any of them are from Noregr. Maybe from the Danelaw, but these are not our countrymen."

"They're so thin, sickly. As though they sailed to meet with Hel."

The raven cawed, facing the sea as it hovered on the wind. It was pointed at the island just beyond the mouth of the fjord.

Follow.

Gudrun watched the bird, for the first time awed by its strength and stillness; powerful wings which held it up on the wind with delicate, ebony feathers.

For a flash of a moment, everything around her stopped.

37

Gudrun became enthralled by the animal, no ordinary bird anymore. Something about it was… unearthly, sublime. The raven turned its head and looked at her with one, glossy, black eye. Gudrun was ensnared. She took a step forward, but couldn't turn her gaze away and its eye grew larger until it swallowed up the entire world. Gudrun fell into its abyss, as though it were a dark pool, locked in an infinite gaze with the divine, a binding which felt intimate… more akin to a mother's embrace. Her mind had fallen into the black iridescence of its eye, as the world around her disappeared into an infinite sky of ebony feathers.

Her body fell away and she soared through a world of swirling black and flitting shadow. Faster and faster she flew, then was all at once standing before the great, divine raven Huginn — known as Thought, one of Odin's messengers.

The herald turned its head slowly to face her and it spoke with a voice that moved through the Tree of Life, Yggdrasil:

Could your destiny await on the island?

Gudrun shuddered. She was immediately thrust back into her body, on the beach with Siv, and the shouts of more men coming from the trees crashed in on her.

" …Gudrun! *Gudrun!* What is happening with you?" Siv shouted.

Gudrun shook her head to clear it. Thunder rolled in the distance.

"We'll row to Hoddholm Island." She pointed to the mouth of the fjord and the island there. "There's a cove where we can wait out the storm." Beyond the island, white caps grew under heavy, black clouds weighing upon the sea.

They tossed weapons and their things into the boat, as haggard villagers stumbled toward the beach, exhausted from their escape. Another wave of men burst through the pines. They charged over the grass after the fleeing villagers, swinging their weapons, screaming and gnashing their teeth.

"They don't look happy. And, there are more of them this time." Gudrun got a good grip on the front. "Push, Siv! Unless you want to invite them for Yule."

Siv shot her a dirty look as she got behind and leaned in. "Just push!"

The rowboat inched forward, scraping toward freedom. Gudrun kept a wary eye on the raiders. They'd been spotted.

"Push Siv! They're coming!"

Savage warriors sprinted at them. *They're already on the sand. I don't think we'll make it.* Gudrun shook her head. *Focus! Get this thing in the water!*

Her legs burned.

"They're almost on us!" Siv shrieked.

Gudrun whipped her head around to check the distance. *I just need to pull harder!* But, Siv was so exposed. She dropped the bow of the boat and grabbed for a spear. The lead man was within range, but she couldn't fight them all. *We need to get on the water.*

Just as the raiders were steps away from them, the raven dived at the men, breaking their momentum. It flew at them again and again, taunting and slowing them into swinging wildly to fight it off, buying the women precious moments. Gudrun threw the spear and it hit the lead's thigh, dropping him. She pulled on the boat again.

Thank you, Odin, for sending Huginn to protect us!

A couple of the men broke away just as Gudrun's feet were drenched by the cold waves rolling along the beach.

"Jump in, Siv!"

Siv climbed over the side. Gudrun noticed, too late, one of the raiders had made it within a few paces. She lunged to grab a spear from the boat, but he was one step ahead and thrust with his own spear at her exposed side. A blurred flash of black streaked past and the pirate snapped his head back with a shriek, allowing Gudrun to raise a spear and pierce his gut. His fall wrenched the spear from her grasp and he thrashed in the surf, grabbing at the blade lodged in his stomach.

"Get in!" Siv screamed, her oars slipping from the locks as she thrashed at the water.

39

Gudrun heaved the boat further into the surf with a glance at the raven. It already beat its wings toward Hoddholm Island. She leaped in the boat as the men charged in to cut off their escape. The sisters pulled their oars along with the tide, an instinct found in those born on the water.

The first of the men reached out to grab the boat, but the receding flow grabbed it first, and sped it into deeper water. The man lunged for the stern and landed in the surf, the others just a step behind him.

The sisters rowed toward a rolling barricade of waves; the final bastion guarding the open sea. The raiders stopped, stumbling into knee-deep surf. They threw spears and loosed arrows against the wind, which tossed the missiles aside to drown in the swell.

The boat ramped against the building wave.

"Pull harder!" Gudrun shouted, muscles bulging with the strain. The tide did its best to throw them back to the shore, but the women had found their rhythm, synchronous with the heart of the sea, making it impossible for the ocean to resist welcoming them.

Arrows buzzed past, some cracking into the hull, most shot into the water. The women pulled harder to get up the wall of seawater, and the boat lurched before popping over the top. The bow dropped and they were on the other side.

"Keep going, Siv! We're almost away!" *Huginn, where are you?*

More arrows screamed at them. Siv yelped when the gunnel splintered beside her as one drove through. Another pierced the hull between Gudrun's feet with a sharp crack!

Gudrun bit her lip, water droplets fattening around the plank's wound as it seeped through. The boat sped forward, down the other side of the swell, ahead of another volley of arrows falling harmlessly short.

Most of the men gave up and turned to chase other villagers down.

"Leave them," one of the raiders shouted. "Magnor will get them!"

Gudrun heard the words clearly, even over the crashing surf. "Magnor? Who's Magnor?" *Or what?* She glanced at the black water below their tiny boat and her heart raced. She snapped her eyes shut. *Just get to the island,* she thought. Seawater and tears stung her eyes. When she opened them, again, the men had cleared off of the beach. Black smoke billowed up over the trees from Vestrijóborg, staining the sky.

The salty air was dense, in her nose and swelling her tongue, gritty on her skin. Her muscles burned as they rowed on the steely ocean.

The wind shifted to blow with them. It was fresh in Gudrun's face and cooling down her sweaty hide-leather coat. *This boat isn't wide, but it's so slow.* She turned to see how Siv was doing.

She was rummaging.

"Why aren't you rowing?" Gudrun yelled.

Siv mumbled. She had the needle, thread, and cloth she'd taken from the market across her lap and concentrated on careful stitches.

"You're making a dress?!" Gudrun smacked the water with an oar and splashed her.

"Stop it! I am making a sail," Siv said.

"No! We keep rowing. You can't make a sail. Not here, in the fjord. In this little boat. *Stop it!*"

Siv bit off the end of a thread. She slipped the shaft of a spear through the loop she'd made, then lashed the shaft to the boat's gunnel. She did the same to the other side, then stretched the cloth between the two spears.

The wind grabbed the green dress cloth and jerked the boat forward. Siv braced her feet against the spears' shafts and pulled the cloth tighter. The boat shushed through the water as it picked up speed.

"Clever girl!" Gudrun grinned. She turned forward and used one oar to steer.

Gulls floated on the wind and laughed at the coming storm as the boat raced toward the island. Waves battered the isle's cliff walls, which stood like the ruins of some once-mighty fortress, perhaps built by Rán, goddess of the ocean.

Scrubby bushes clung where they could to the tall cliff, blasted by a relentless wind. On one end jagged rocks jutted up like grotesque teeth, splintered from the island's cliffs long ago. They frothed white from heaving, crashing waves.

Gudrun felt good sailing along the rolling water, the violence of the market and the beach forgotten for a fleeting moment. Up the side of one wave and then down the other, again and again, until they were close to the snarling rocks. They sped toward them, unforgiving sentinels which could easily tear any boat in two and chew up the pieces that were left. They crested one last swell and the wind filled the sail with a crack, catapulting them over the wave's crest. They plummeted down the other side through a spray of brine.

"We just need to get around to the other side, where the cove sits."

They sailed toward a peninsula which pointed to the vast ocean. As they came around the bend, the cove opened up to them.

What the cove held made their hearts stop.

The sail fell from Siv's hands and Gudrun's mouth dropped open.

A shipwreck languished on the rocky shore. The cove hugged what was left of a two-hundred seat dragon boat; a once fearsome Kracken-hunter.

It now lay on its side, a mangled pile of timbers and rope, smashed and stranded on the rocks. The sails and rigging had torn away and were tangled around a splintered stump... all that was left of the mast. Waves lapped mournfully at the swamped stern and tossed bits of wooden flotsam at the rocks.

A bright fork of lightning flashed out on the ocean and thunder cracked moments later.

"We need to find shelter," Gudrun said.

"But, where?" Siv said. They scanned the cove.

The raven, Huginn, glided down and landed on a part of the wreck's stern jutting out of the rolling waves. The bird bobbed its head and cawed.

Come here!

CHAPTER THREE

Journey Through Fire

Frigga could not keep from selfishly thinking of her eldest son, Hamund. Her mourning period was over now, a year after they'd lit his pyre. It had been a felicitous cremation for the crown prince, on a ship crafted by masters, laden with his inheritance, three servants, and his sword and shield across his chest. More than some jarls had been sent to the afterlife with. She could still see the funeral ship burning in her mind: deep red flames, like the bloom of a tulip, smoke rising majestically in a straight column to the gods. Four eagles had circled overhead. A good omen, she'd been told.

Yes. Hamund had been well provided for in the afterlife.

But, her youngest, and last child, Ormer... *If only Hamund were still alive.* Frigga's heart grew heavy. She dropped her hands and the end of the banner she was stitching into her lap. It was painful for her to take the deep breath she needed while still remaining silent. The other women in her chambers hadn't noticed her brooding. *Good. They've seen me shed enough tears for Hamund to flood the ocean.* Perhaps it was true, what the old women said, that the sea was made of the tears of mourning mothers praying to Ægir and Rán, begging the ocean gods to return their sons from the depths. Frigga had been no different, having risen the ocean with her own grief. She contemplated pricking her finger with the sewing needle, just to feel something different, as one more tear dropped onto the banner cloth.

The other women in the room were young. Three ladies-in-waiting and the rest handmaidens, the oldest not even fifteen winters yet. They each sewed a banner for the Autumn Feast, to replace the ones Frigga had ripped from the rafters in her grief a year ago. Frigga really had no care for the ladies-in-waiting: her cousin's daughter, Acanta, and two others, Rinda and Eldrid. Frigga thought them horrid, but as Frue she was expected to have an entourage of young noblewomen in her wake, training them to become nobility, possibly future queens themselves. She couldn't see it in these ladies, though. They were too childish, too concerned with clothing and embroidery, and boys. She thought them too prissy to get their hands dirty, like she had for Ormer to ensure he'd be the future king. "No queen has clean hands, no matter how much they're washed," her mother had told her. That was the night before Ulfer had taken her from her home to be married. She'd finally understood what it meant, many years later.

Would any of these girls plunge their hand into a pot of boiling water to see their son on the throne? She looked at her hands. She could do it. She could do far worse. Already had.

* * *

The old firekeeper dropped an armload of wood against the stone wall. He straightened his stiff back with a groan. "I am a lot older than I used to be," he chuckled, looking at the cook.

Her chest and belly shook as she slammed and punched a ball of dough, lost in thoughts of violence. The grimace on her face made the old man's smile drop.

"I am done here," he said, rubbing the sweat off the back of his neck with a sleeve.

"You're done when *I* say you're done!" the cook snapped. She wiped her hands by slapping them on her apron and craned her neck to look at wood piles beside the ovens. All three had wood stocked up to the cross beams. "What of the pit?" She jabbed a doughy thumb at the centre of the hall.

"All three hearths there are full—"

"They need enough to roast a bull each!" she shouted.

The old man nodded. "Aye, and they surely do. I have instructed the boys to keep the coals low until tonight," he said. The firekeeper had always known the cook to be a demanding woman, but she was more agitated than usual. He was patient with her. It wasn't his ability she was weighing. After all, he'd kept Jarl Ulfer's fires since well before she was born. In fact, he'd kept the fire at her birthing, and her daughters'. The Autumn Feast was a monumental event which normally stretched the kitchen, but preparing this year's feast proved overwhelming. An expected announcement from the jarl was bringing a large number of distinguished guests, all ätt chieftains and their entourages.

"Braziers?"

"All done. Front doors and cattle doors; the far ten, near ten, and court ten."

"Court hearth?"

"Done."

"Chambers?"

"My last stop."

"Get to it!" she snapped and waved him away. He nodded and reached for the strap of his pack.

"Wait," she said, softening. "When you're finished, come back. I might have some stew left for you."

He smiled and nodded, then heaved the pack onto his shoulder. He trundled across the great hall, toward the court. The woody smells of heather, thyme and sweet lingonberry delicately hung in the air as servants raised garlands to hang from the second level. A group of women scrubbed the floor stones, chatting about how aggravating their grown children were. "... fishing all day, drunk on sour wine, his chores *still* undone in the barn..."

The firekeeper skirted around them to get to the Jarl's court. More servants there, cleaning, arranging, laying festive decorations.

The jarl's manservant and herald — a short, round man with a thin, meticulously shaped beard and a floppy hat — could be heard bawling at a slave near the cattle doors. He beat the man with his cane of office, because of the smell of manure wafting into the court. "Useless *thrall!* The jarl's throne might as well be set in a barn!" Thin Beard's face was a deep red from screaming. He spit his words at the man grovelling before him, his arms protecting his head from the blows of the hearald's cane. "Close those doors and get the cattle into the far pen! I told you, *only horses* here!"

The firekeeper felt it in his gut: the need to stop the beating, yet without any station the old man risked becoming enthralled himself. Or executed. Thin Beard was unpredictable and cruel, and had the ear of the Jarl.

"Master Herald!" the firekeeper said.

Thin Beard stopped, mid-swing, startled by the weight of the old man's booming voice. The slave escaped to the cattle doors as Thin Beard stooped over to catch his breath, leaning heavily on his cane.

"My mistake, Master Herald: I hadn't a clear view of the brazier, but my old eyes see the flames now. Apologies, master." The firekeeper bowed and continued on to the court. Thin Beard scowled, straightened his clothing and scanned around the room, sniffing for the stench of manure.

The old man walked around the noble's tables — set and decorated with linens, dried peonies and beach roses, and bunches of basil and lavender to repel insects — then on to the back rooms, where the Jarl's and Frue's bedchambers were. Much cooler there, away from the kitchen's fires.

He knocked on a door.

Jarl Hall, in Vargr, was reputed to celebrate more feast days than any hall in Midgard.

"You will find a better feast only in Valhal!" Jarl Ulfer of ätt Wylfling would proudly proclaim — yet always careful to never boast blasphemously in public. Then he'd double over with laughter. He never missed an opportunity to raise a goblet to the gods. He was a strict follower of Odin's diet, preferring wine over food. It had obvious effects on his sobriety. His court never saw this as a problem, as the jarl's endless supply of wine had its obvious effects on their sobriety, too.

Yet, the coming Autumn feast would be the first the hall had enjoyed for over a year.

Grief over their son's death had twisted the Jarl and Frue apart and thrown them into different corners of Jarlhalla. Frigga had become disgusted with Ulfer, her love for him poisoned by his drunkenness. Even as the mourning period ended, she still spent most of her days in her chambers.

Ulfer spent most of his, either drinking on his throne — not far from pandering sycophants — or drinking while hunting. Where he spent his nights… Frigga no longer cared. Her only concern was for their youngest and last living child, Ormer. She sighed as a mother does when she yearns for the child whom she loves to be different in many ways. She shook her head. That wasn't it. No, she yearned for the world to be different, but the child was much easier to bend into shape.

She'd always been careful to play the dutiful wife, at least to the limits of what the law required. Truth be told, she enjoyed all of the privilege and status she wielded as Frue. Though, from the moment her marriage to Ulfer had been arranged, she'd realised the role and title confined her. She'd found herself in the unusual position of being able to change things she could not see, and unable to change the things she could.

Her niece Acanta's eyes flashed at her. The girl whispered something to the other young ladies that made the girls lean in.

They stifled giggles. Frigga closed her eyes and rubbed her temples. *Now stuck with these wool-headed… children! Ulfer be damned! And the drunkards in his council!* Happier to be fat and lazy, spending Ormer's inheritance on drink, rather than listening to any of her plans of expansion, ventures all "too ridiculous, too difficult, too much". *Too far away from a whore's bed— Freyer's prick! Missed a stitch.*

She dropped the banner in her lap, frustrated.

I'm a free woman! The Frue! Still forced to be dependent on the men around her, and too easily dismissed by them, her ideas smothered by wine-soaked hubris.

"I swear, I'll leave these idiots behind, sail to an island, build a hut and weave silver," she muttered. She was much more ambitious than Ulfer could ever handle, or even understand. It was her father who'd instilled that in her: brutal ambition, drive, determination. She was bowing to fools. *Yet, I will endure, and they will see.*

Her son Hamund — Ulfer's protege — was now feasting in Valhalla (Odin be praised), instead of grooming for the throne. And their youngest, Ormer, was groomed all too well for a comfortable seat beside the throne, to his detriment. Her plans of a noble woman's graceful repose as council and mother to the jarl-in-waiting had become enshrouded by the Shifting Mists, once Hamund died. The jarldom, their bloodline, her future as a noblewoman, would all too soon rest upon Ormer. *He's still a boy.* They'd only just shaved the back of his neck a year ago — a symbol of a boy's life-pledge to his jarl, after his thirteenth winter, as customary. Ulfer had been too distracted by drunken grief to remember, until a week ago. Even in death Hamund still robbed his younger brother of their father's pride.

Without her husband, or one of her sons on the throne Frigga would never be safe. It was her quick action against Ulfer's nephew, Gunlaug, which kept Ormer's place in line for his father's throne. *It had to be done. It was a cruel joke the Norns[2] played on Gunlaug, born*

---

[2] Norns — three mythical beings — Past, Present, and Future — who weave the tapestry of destiny.

after Hamund and before Ormer... She was doing the right thing, wasn't she? *A sign, please Freyja! Give me a sign to show my son will become—*

She was startled by a knock at the door.

One of the handmaidens rose to answer it, and the rest of the young women did their best to feign disinterest.

"Keep to your stitching, ladies," Frigga chided. She kept a hawkish eye on the door. It issued a haunting groan as the handmaiden opened it wide.

"The hearth, miss," Frigga heard an old man's voice. The girl nodded and stepped aside to let him in.

"It's the firekeeper, Frue," she said, with a small, graceless bow, then returned to her seat.

The old man had been in the room many times before, keeping the hearth-fire burning. It was his habit to keep his eyes and attention on either the fire or the floor while in the presence of the frue, or her company.

The frue and her handmaidens, on the other hand, couldn't help but stare at him. Though he was just another servant to them, they were in an agitated state more deadly than lean winter wolves who'd caught the scent of blood; the pampered women were bored.

"Frue," Acanta spoke up in a haughty voice, "I've been told the firekeeper gazes into the flames and can divine secrets from the Norns." The other women jilted their needlepoint and gawked at the old man, a lust for entertainment in their eyes. "A washerwoman at the well said the firekeeper had cast into the fire at her son's birth, and everything he prophesied had come to pass."

"Show us!" the young women chorused, laughing and clapping with excitement. "I want to know!" They squealed in their eagerness for amusement. "We want to know the Norn's secrets!", "Will we be able to see them?"

"Firekeeper!" The frue's commanding voice silenced the girls, and they jolted upright in their seats. The old man took off his red and white cap, and fidgeted with the wool.

"Yes, Frue?" he said, with a mildly pained expression.

"Speak the truth, old man, have you the woman's gift of seidr? Can you glean secrets from the Keepers of Yggdrasil? We all know it is shameful for a man to have this feminine ability."

The old man winced. "Yes, Frue, I have cast my eye into the flames and have seen the Weave which spills from the Norns' loom at the root of the World Tree."

"How do I know you will not deceive me, by virtue of the seidr lessening your virility? Will you not use their Weave as a spider uses hers?"

"There is no matter of deception, Frue. Even were my heart black with evil, the fire's teachings purge all inequity to ash and leave only a bloom of purity."

"Then build up the flames and let us evaluate your seidr-craft." *This is it!* Frigga thought. *Freyja, my goddess! Do you answer my prayer, even before I ask?*

"This is no fortune teller's ruse, Frue," the firekeeper said, glancing at the youngest in the room. "The powers at play will consume an undisciplined mind."

"Do you mock me?" Frigga snapped. "Do not presume to speak to *me* of power! You are my servant, and I commanded you to build the flames, firekeeper!" She spit the words at him like bitter seeds. The younger women stifled giggles and twittered rudely among themselves.

Frigga gathered herself with a deep breath, then continued with a calmer tone.

"Bring your seats to the hearth, ladies. The firekeeper is going to tell my fortune."

"*Wheee!*" The young women squealed with delight and clapped. They danced about the room, as the handmaidens dragged chairs to the hearth.

Frigga straightened to her full height and sauntered forward, looking down her nose at the old man. Her handmaiden trundled ahead, dragging the frue's solid oak chair to the fireside.

51

The old man bowed with a quiet sigh, then shuffled to the hearth.

The ladies plunked themselves on their seats and chattered inanely, swinging their feet like children.

The old man heaved the pack off his shoulders, as though it contained boulders. He prodded the cherry coals with a poker.

"If you truly wish to know of that which must remain unknown, and commit yourself to your destiny, though your knowledge wails in anguish, then a token must be surrendered; a focus for the Norns to recognize who's threads from the Weave they scry. Something which is close to your heart," the firekeeper said.

Frigga cocked her head to the side and screwed up her face as she digested his words. She darted her eyes about the room, searching for an answer.

"Your broach!" Acanta blurted. She beamed as she pointed at the frue's silver cloak pin. "It's close to your heart." The ladies giggled again, and even Frigga smirked.

"Bring it to me."

Acanta skipped across the floor to the frue's cloak. She unclipped the broach and danced back to the frue.

Frigga looked at it briefly. She'd forgotten from where she'd gotten this trinket, and didn't care about the welded silver disks, nor the swirls carved into them. She held the jewellery out for the firekeeper, then hesitated when he looked her directly in the eye.

She lifted her chin and looked down on him. *What is he doing?*

He narrowed his eyes. "I see the fire within you, Frue. With this token that you freely give, you have asked thrice to know the weave of your destiny. By Tyr's law, none can claim you have been fooled or coerced. Such defences are bitter wine offered to the gods. Know this: I will tell of what I see, but not of how to understand it. My vision is but a moment's delving into the madness of another realm. I give warning, not just of this, but also of the insatiable hunger for understanding's nourishment, capable of consuming one's bones, thereafter."

Frigga lifted an eyebrow and snorted. "Get on with it," she

growled, and slapped the broach into his palm.

He nodded, placed the trinket on the hearth and knelt before it. He moved with a solemnity that he'd refined through patient meditation. He chose each stick with great care, deliberately arranging them on the hot ashes, until smoke curled from the dry tinder.

The younger ladies shuffled closer, craning themselves to investigate and observe his techniques, as though compiling a much anticipated critique of a court entertainer. They mustered all of the skills they'd learned on their stay.

"Get back! Give me room!" Frigga snarled. She pulled her chair forward, bumping it into the young women until they retreated. "I will seat myself right next to him, to see the very flames *he* does. Perhaps I will catch a peek of the Norns myself." Her tone was flat and lacklustre, as not to betray her wild curiosity.

With his breath resigned the firekeeper resurrected flames from the coals, as though he were blowing fire from his lips to ignite the wood. The flames quickened and he added more wood to turn the ashen coals into a healthy, crackling blaze.

"He has the breath of a dragon," the youngest gushed. They all clapped and chattered with glee, bouncing on their chairs.

"Ladies!" Frigga snapped. "Keep your asses still in your seats, or I'll have them whipped until you are forced to stand! Let the womanly man work!" The young women stopped laughing and they froze under the Frigga's gorgonish stare.

The flames engulfed the wood completely, within a heartbeat, the heat already making their brows sweat. Frigga shifted in her seat as she watched the firekeeper build the blaze higher. One of the women shuffled her seat away from the oppressive heat, still, the firekeeper added more wood.

Freyja be with me! Frigga thought. Her dress felt molten, and a sickening pain slithered up to cluster as an ache in her head. *Too much, I must pull back, just a breath*. Her skin was burning. She thought of Hamund, on his pyre. Could she last through the fire's test? *Can Ormer?* She gritted her teeth and stayed where she was, determined to endure the blaze as an example to the young women.

Orange and yellow flames cast undulating shadows throughout the room, snapping and cracking the dry wood to burst with red sparks. The firekeeper stared at the blaze with an intensity that could have squelched the rage of two spring bulls, jealous and anxious to mount the same cow. The women were stunned. When he swayed his head, the flames turned with him.

He whispered to the fire, words that were strange to their ears, yet the power his voice commanded was evident as the flames sprang higher, or shrank down as he willed. He spit into the palm of his hand, then added soot and ash, mixing it together with his fingers until it became a paste. He rubbed the paste onto his fingers and drew three diagonal lines on the stones.

"Three for the past," he muttered, then drew three more, crossing the first like an 'X'. "Three for the future." Then more lines down through the centre. "Three for the present. Nine lines the Norns weave into the Net of Destiny." The firekeeper placed the broach into the centre of the Net.

He fell into a trance, moaning a guttural chant. The fire grew hotter and larger, flames reaching out, woofing and huffing for more wood, more to burn.

"The fire is too big!" the youngest bawled. "It will climb to the roof!"

"What if it burns down the hall! With us in it!" another wailed.

"Stay quiet!" The firekeeper's voice boomed up through the rafters.

The young women dashed behind their chairs and huddled together to weep.

Beads of sweat ran down the old man's face, orange flames roasting his skin red. He kept his focus in the face of the searing heat.

"The journey through the fire is a test of endurance requiring mind and spirit — the *hugr*[3] — to be harder than steel. This is the path of the gods, through the centre of the inferno that purifies the soul. What cannot be purified will be consumed by these unforgiving flames." His voice was no longer his own. It droned and choresed, joined in unison by other voices from unseen realms.

To travel through the fire required him to leave his body, moving with his hugr only; a journey more real for him than any other that he might have ever undertaken in his physical body.

Within the searing flames he could sense a portal opening; a breach within the firestorm of orange and yellow. He moved his hugr toward it, steadfastly keeping to the centre, within a gap the size of a needle's point. *The centre opens the path, the centre opens the path...*

The inferno raged and consumed everything his hugr carried within his heart; every pain, every anger, every gladness and joy. The firestorm swirled around him, fuelled by this baggage, cleansing his spirit until his mind was broiled to perfect coherence. The purifying flames seethed until all parts of him had burned and the ash flaked away. Without warning, his hugr slipped through the gate.

The other side was beyond any in Midgard; the centre of the cosmos, the place where the roots of Yggdrasil were nourished by the Norns from the sacred well, *Urðarbrunnr*. The Norn, three giants from the realm of *Jötunheim*, were the maidens who drew water in a white, gold-edged pitcher, large enough to hold an entire lake's worth. They sang as they poured the pitcher out over the Tree's roots. So high, they were, that the water fell as rain and quenched the land and the wood of the Tree.

They each took their turn with the pitcher, and each upon the Loom where they spun destiny. Not even the gods were exempt from the unsettling mysteries of the Loom. Their own threads were interwoven into the tapestry of fate along with man's, even well

---

[3]   One of the four parts that make up a human spirit, in Norse belief.

before Odin had breathed life into the first humans.

The Norn's song unfolded with such harmonies never to be heard in Midgard. The firekeeper could smell and taste the song, felt it within and saw it in vibrant colours. It was an ancient song, in the seidr-language of the *Vanier*, so potent with life that a wellspring bubbled up within his hugr. The Norn Urther sang of that which had been; Verthandi of that which now shall be; Skuld of that which yet needs be. Singing together, their opera wove destiny, filling their bodies and guiding their hands upon the Loom of Fate, where destiny was weaved.

The wellspring within the old man continued to rise up, and even as the Norn's song filled him, it did not quench the fire. In fact, the blaze grew feverish within his hugr.

As much as she tried, Frigga couldn't see anything within the fire, blazing an oppressive heat. Still, the power emanating from it, and from the old man, was undeniable, palpable, like a blazing shield advancing against her.

The old man was silent, his body still as the fire's light dashed across his face. Even his breath seemed to have stopped. Frigga suddenly had a terrible thought: *What if he's died?* He hadn't moved for a while. Had it been too long? She tried to casually glance at him, but the scraggly hair that grew sideways from his head in all directions blocked his face. The bald patch on top made it look as though he were wreathed in a snowy nest. She tentatively leaned forward for a better look.

Stinging heat raked the side of her head. The unfocused glow of the firelight reflected off the old man's cheek, making his weathered and pocked skin appear red and sinister. Frigga leaned out further, the heat blazing against her hair, until she could finally see one eye. She stiffened with horror.

The eye held the red-orange glow of the fire, like a creature from the underworld. Frigga yelped, recoiling and made a sign against evil. She pressed against the back of her chair and snapped her eyes forward. *I should not have done that.*

The other women peeked out from between the chairs and saw the frue's panic. They, too, made signs against evil, weeping and huddling closer.

Then, the fire sprang up to the ceiling in a column and the women screamed. The firekeeper broke his silence with a raspy voice combined with his own and of those from other worlds, feminine and yet as deep as the Tree's roots.

From him came the song of the Norns:

"The Grey Wolf in its den does laze
As a western shadow blankets the sun.
All the king gives, a prince's sum
Repaid with blood and shallow graves.

"Beauty is plain, as plain as yearning
Revealing no truth, nor a champion's name
He chases wild, or follows tame
Leaving the weaver's tables turning.

"Logs grow ice beneath their pyres
On overgrown roads, deathfeeders lament
Their nest doth burn, though the crows are content
When a stronger bird rises from out of those fires."

The blaze suddenly died to coals and the firekeeper slumped to the side with a groan.

"The bond is broken," he whispered. An eerie wave of cold washed over all of them. A chill breeze moaned through the rafters. Their clothing was drenched with sweat and the women began to shiver as cold rushed in to claim the room.

The youngest were curled into balls on the floor, hugging their shins and weeping into their knees. The others were huddled in a group and moaned as the chill shook them.

Frigga's mind was clouded by the cryptic words, unable to think of anything else. Pain crushed in, searing from inside her skull. The firekeeper's prophecy was indelibly etched into her memory, burned into her mind.

This was not prophesy, she realised. It was more than that. She did understand that it was prophetic, but it was shrouded in a darkness that made it much heavier than prophecy. Like a fist of ice reaching up from her stomach and crushing her throat, terror gripped her. *This is an oath!*

Frigga swayed, mouthing the words that shone from every corner of her mind, "The Grey Wolf in its den does laze. The Grey Wolf in its den does laze… "

The firekeeper sat up. He looked about in a daze, taking a moment to catch his breath. He wiped the sweat from his brow with his sleeve. The horror carved into the frue's face as she stared at him was startling.

"The… the…" she stammered.

The firekeeper's nod was solemn. He gently placed Frigga's broach onto the mantle, then added three more pieces of wood and stoked the coals to rekindle the fire. Frigga watched his every move, desperate to say something, *anything*, to him. "The…"

He stood, hauled the pack up and onto his shoulder, then lumbered to the exit. The women gawked at him, unable to speak.

Frigga fell from her chair. She needed to shout, to *scream!* Her raised, trembling hand — the hand of a queen, the frue; the hand of sovereignty which, with a wave, had subjugated and swept away the lives of men like so much chaff — proved powerless to stop him from pulling the door open.

"What does it mean?" She struggled to breathe words past her lips; the whisper an assault on withering vitality.

Yet, he had already gone and the door closed to her, transforming her chambers into a stark, sealed tomb: cold, stale, and vacuous.

CHAPTER FOUR

Shipwrecks

G udrun and Siv landed the rowboat on the island's rocky shore, near a copse of thin maples wedged between cracks in the stone. Neither of them could take their eyes off of the wreck as they got out of the rowboat. The broken ship lay upon a whale of a rock which stretched across the entire cove, worn smooth through the ages by the constant lapping of waves.

For a hundred paces, no other trees or shrubs grew, only dark patches of moss on top of the whale-rock. Beyond, a silent forest of thick pines and brilliant red maples took over. The natural crescent wall surrounding the island shielded the trees and water from the worst of the blasting ocean winds.

They squatted quietly, their attention locked on the twisted ship. Its crushed fore languished on the rock. Jagged finger-like splinters clutched at the drowned stern as it bobbed in the sea. It moaned and creaked with the tide.

"Let's pull the rowboat out. We can shelter underneath it from the rain," Gudrun said.

"What do you suppose is in that thing? Do you think there are dead sailors?" Siv shuddered.

"You've never seen a body before?" Gudrun grinned.

"I don't want to go looking for them!" Siv snapped. Gudrun grunted. They picked up the rowboat and pulled it up as far as they could, then flipped it onto the rocks.

Huginn cawed from the stern of the broken ship, flapping and bobbing. *Here! Hurry! Hurry!*

"The raven really wants attention," Siv said.

Gudrun furrowed her brow. "I'm not sure I wanna know why." She let out a deep sigh. Siv stood with the rowboat between her and the wreck. She'd locked her eyes onto the black, gaping hole in the ship's side and wrung her hands. Gudrun pointed to the trees.

"See if you can find some dry firewood. I'll go see what Huginn wants."

A gust through the trees hammered branches together. A large branch cracked and smashed into the underbrush.

Gudrun frowned. "Would you rather come check out the wreck?"

"No! I am *very* happy to collect wood." Siv hopped over puddles on the whale-rock to hunt for dry driftwood.

"Alright. Just, stay in sight."

Siv straightened and grinned, eyes wide. "Freyja take witness! You sound more like mama than mama does!" She snickered at Gudrun's scowl.

"I've changed my mind. I hope you get crushed by a tree." Gudrun dismissed Siv with a wave and turned toward the wreck. It was good to hear Siv laughing, it gave Gudrun hope.

Gudrun navigated slick stones that were revealed when the waves fell. They grew thick, hairy algae that squished under her feet. She imagined shaggy troll's heads.

Wood debris in the water bumped with a hollow thump against the whale-rock. Gudrun reached in and rescued the dragon-head prow, charred and drowned, broken off at the neck. Its colours had faded to grey and the broken jaw was missing. She hauled it onto the rock.

The ship had been torn in two, just ahead of the mast. Long

splintered boards jutted out like the teeth of some horrid creature from the depths. A storm had smashed the ship onto the rock which now served as its grave stone.

It's been in a fierce battle. Arrows bristled from the side, stuck firmly into the timbers. Black scorches scarred the wood and splintered, missing chunks left bright gashes in the weathered boards. Gudrun pulled a few splinters out. *The damage is new. Did this ship wreck in last night's storm?*

Huginn jounced and cawed, *Hurry! Come!*

A mangled canvas shelter was wrapped around the prow which once held aloft the mighty dragon's head, now a shattered piece of driftwood. Gudrun walked to the railing, wary of what she might find within the wreckage.

"Anyone there?" She called, peering in.

Flotsam in the flooded stern swayed gently with the tide. A tangle of rope and tattered sailcloth had caught around the mast stump and stretched out over the side of the ship, trailing into the water. The rest of the ship was empty.

"Abandoned," Gudrun said, surprised by her disappointment. Thunder clapped, startling her. Her heart raced. She felt small beside the wreck. It was eerie to see it laying on its side.

She climbed over the railing and picked her way over the slanted, broken deck.

Huginn cawed from the top of the stern-post jutting out of the waves, his beak skimming the water in the swamped rear deck. Gudrun climbed along the broken boards and waded through debris to get to the stern.

A flash of silver caught Gudrun's eye, just below where Huginn bobbed and called. The water's rippling surface distorted the metallic shape, making it appear to waggle. *It glints, even in shadow!* She reached in and felt around until she found the smooth shaft of a tool secured under one of the benches. She pushed it forward and it slid, until she could pull it out of the water. It was a spear! Its haft was blackened with runes painted in red. The head of the weapon looked sharp and strong, scarred from battle and inlaid with more runes and knotwork decoration. Gudrun *knew* this spear!

"Skera-Brynja!" Gudrun gasped, her breath caught in her chest. She couldn't believe that in her hands she held Chief Gudbrand's great war-spear, *Skera-Brynja* — Mail-Piercer.

"But— if this is Chief Gudbrand's spear, then this must be his ship!" Gudrun looked back at the obliterated ship. *There's no way anyone survived this!* Gudrun began to panic. She checked to see where Siv was; still collecting wood. *Were Sigurd and papa on this ship?* She frantically looked about for a clue, or a mark, some sort of message left behind. Something. *Anything?!* She stood and nearly dropped the spear. Then, realising her irreverence, she held the legendary weapon respectfully, with both hands.

The spear. Skera-Brynja is their message!

The chieftains of Hoddlund had passed the spear to their sons for three generations before Chief Gudbrand had inherited it. Its legend, too, had been passed from generation to generation, just as papa had passed it on to Gudrun and her brothers. She loved the story. Perhaps, more than that, she loved papa's telling of it.

Forged by King Eitri — the dwarven Weapons Master who'd been tricked by Loki into forging and giving up Thor's glorious hammer, *Mjollnir* — the spear was said to have powers that even the gods envied. The legend said that whomever wielded the spear could not be defeated in battle, that it held a mysterious power enabling its wielder to command men.

Then, what evil happened here? Gudrun thought. Her heart raced. She looked up and down the wreck. *Was this … Chief Gudbrand's ship?* Huginn flew overhead and landed on the tangled sail. He pecked at the cloth.

Siv dropped an armload of driftwood at the rowboat. "Is everything alright, Gudrun?"

"Yes, I'm good! There's nothing here." Gudrun waved and Siv went back to collecting wood. Gudrun's hands shook as she held Skera-Brynja. *I can't tell Siv that this might have been papa's ship!* She took a few deep breaths to calm herself. She waded back to the mast deck, holding the sacred spear in earnest, ensuring not to bump it or dip it in the water. Thunder clapped and rumbled and a fat raindrop splattered onto Gudrun's hand. The sky would burst, soon; the scent of rain off the ocean was savoury and brisk.

Gudrun cleared the rail with a light hop onto the rock. Another rumble. She turned back to look at the deck once more and froze. The sail. White, with a black symbol sewn into it, too tangled for her to identify. *Could it be a crossed hammer and axe?*

Gudrun gingerly climbed back over the railing and the wood groaned and creaked under her weight. She crawled up the inclined deck to reach the sail and lifted the cloth to spread it out. She gasped.

The body of a young man — a boy, really — lay as twisted and broken as the wreckage itself, in a pool of water-thinned blood. His sickly-grey face was covered in gore. He flinched as Gudrun lifted the tarp off of him.

"Gods have mercy!" She knelt beside him. The boy coughed blood and cried out when his body jolted. Sobering pain unmercifully kept him conscious. Both of his legs were broken and twisted and blood had soaked through his coat. Gudrun gently opened his tunic to find some of his rib bones had pierced out of his chest. His body shuddered as he laboured and wheezed for breath.

"Gils? Butcher Lodmund's son?" Gudrun's jaw dropped. Gils' hair and face were so dirty and screwed up from pain she found it hard to believe this was the same boy she'd hugged goodbye over a year ago.

"Gils, it's Gudrun, Thorkil's daughter. What happened? Where is my father?"

"Gudrun Thorkildatter... of course it's you." Gils wheezed the words, slow and deliberate. "Odin told me you would come... I didn't believe—" He wept, clenching his eyes shut against his tears.

"Did any of them...?" Gudrun trailed off. She already knew the answer and regretted asking.

"No," Gils croaked. "No."

The word hit Gudrun like a hammer slamming into her ribs. The tiny word lodged into her chest like hot iron. "No." She inhaled, but couldn't find breath. No.

"Are you sure?" She barely managed a whisper. "Even Sigurd? Gils, is my brother dead? And Hermund and Aren and Garet?" Gudrun's head spun, remembering the men along with Sigurd and papa whom she'd known her whole life.

Gils shivered. "Betrayed... by... by Magnor."

"Magnor! The men on the beach said that name. Said 'Magnor will take care of them'." Gudrun's voice was hollow. Her chest pulled tighter than the skin of a drum. She was flattened by the weight of the world upon her, keeping her from taking a breath. She closed her eyes. Then opened them again. Open or closed made no difference, she was unravelling. Her knuckles turned white from clenching the handle of her seax in its sheathe. *Merciful Freyja, bring the darkness. Take my pain. End my sorrow with sweet destruction!*

The vision of Gils' face would not move or fade from her mind. She wanted to smash it, wanted him to be lying. She wanted to trade Gils' life for her brother's. Even as the fragile boy struggled for life and breath, shuddering on the splintered deck boards, she wanted to choke it from him.

"Murder..." she whispered. Rage became her, for she would not surrender to grief.

Gils settled his gaze upon her and held it there. Gudrun burned with rage, but Gils simply stared into her eyes.

"You're angry," he whispered. Tears streamed down his face. "Me too."

Gudrun recoiled at the intimacy of the moment. She fought the urge to look away, but something in the boy's fading eyes, that she'd never seen anywhere before, held her. A tenderness. Her rage faltered and she softened. As though a boulder split beneath her ribs, she was able to pull in a full breath with a forced gasp. Her anger diminished. She could see the broken, dying boy before her.

A rumble rolled over the island.

Gils coughed and the movement made him wince. It brought Gudrun back to the stark reality of the situation and his grisly wounds. "Hurry..." he whispered, as he gasped for air.

"What does Magnor look like?" Gudrun asked.

"Blue cloak... gold broach... "

"Gils," Gudrun checked on Siv. "I can't take you back with me—"

"I know," he stopped her, "Magnor... he searches... " Gils winced through clenched teeth. It was a long moment before he could hiss a breath out.

"What is Magnor searching for?"

"Lutvin," Gils whispered. His head went limp when he slipped out of consciousness, then back in again with a shudder. "His ship! Patchwork sails... Cutthroats! Murderers!" He fired the words out.

"What do they want in Lutvin?" Gudrun asked.

Gils strained to form a single word: "Gold."

Gudrun furrowed her brow, confused. She waited, expecting Gils to say more.

"I don't understand. There's no gold in Lutvin, only sheep and fish, and misery," Gudrun muttered.

She checked over her shoulder at Siv again. Siv was looking out at the ocean, and began waving her arms. "Gudrun! A ship!" Siv pointed at the horizon.

The prow of a dragon ship was pushing through the water where the ocean met the fjord's cliffs. A square, patchwork sail clung to its mast, little more than tatters tied with string. Yet, the ship hove forward, driven by a full wind. It was clear the boat had been ravaged by the previous night's storm, judging by how low she ran in the water.

"That's got to be Magnor's ship," Gudrun said. "We can't stay on the island, we're too exposed." *They're bound to explore the wreck and it wouldn't take long for them to track us down and find us. How do we bring Gils?*

Huginn leapt into the air and cawed as he flew away. *Must go!*

Gils wheezed, sobered by fresh pain. He grabbed Gudrun's arm. "Please, I die! Too slowly…" he panted, "a last mercy…"

Gils gave Gudrun a look, a pleading from the depths of his being. He touched the longknife on her belt, sending a chill down her spine. She hadn't expected that.

"Oh, Gils," she whispered, dropping her head. She understood, and her heart broke.

The boy was going to die, they weren't going to save Gils' life. That desire fell away until she could only feel the excruciating weight of his final request. But, he was right. *I can't sacrifice Siv's life for his.*

Gudrun nodded with deliberate solemnity. She gripped the handle of her seax, a knife as familiar as a limb, yet in that moment its grip was awkward, foreign to her hand. She squirmed inside. *Just like a deer, a sacrifice to Odin,* she told herself. She pulled the keen blade from its sheath.

Now, Gudrun! Now! Huginn rasped.

Gudrun's heart jolted against her chest, surging the blood in her veins. She brought the blade to Gils' throat. The boy's eyes were as two black coals set in a bed of ash, his skin grey and clammy. She cradled his head with gentle fingers; it was light and fragile in her hand.

Huginn was incensed, *Must go! Must go!*

Gils surrendered completely to Gudrun's mercy. His trust melted away the grimace he'd held under his blond hair, matted with blood and filth.

"Valkyrie," Gudrun prayed, "take this son of Odin into the Great Hall, to be welcomed and celebrated for his honourable deeds." Her words were hollow to her; she knew it would not be so.

"Goodbye, Gils," she said, and gave him a gentle kiss. Then, she pushed the blade down and across his throat. She pulled back and Gils let out a gurgled gasp, but barely struggled.

He shuddered once, then was still.

Siv was struggling to flip the rowboat. "Come on, Gudrun, hurry!"

Gudrun pulled Gils' broken body from the wreckage and carried him across the rock to the water. Her heart raced as she lowered Gils into the ocean. "Daughters of Rán, protect him," she said and pushed his body out into the waves.

Without a second glance, she dashed to the wreck to grab Skera-Brynja, then sprinted to the rowboat.

"Are those the raiders?" Siv shouted, eyes locked on the ship.

"I don't want to find out," Gudrun said. "We're not safe here." Gudrun slipped Skera-Brynja in with the other spears and helped Siv push. They shoved the boat across the rock to the water. Siv jumped in and clamoured to set her oars, as Gudrun set at the stern.

They rowed with all their might, surging the boat toward the cove's mouth.

Gudrun could see Gils' body bobbing in the waves. *How do I tell Siv?* The unmistakable shape of his corpse in the water and the smashed ship upon the rock made a haunting vision.

The sisters rowed toward the open sea, racing to get out. Gudrun knew it wasn't right to leave his body in the water. Guilt and regret sat heavy in her stomach.

I vow to you, Gils, to leave an offering for you to have in the afterlife, Gudrun thought. His mother suddenly came to her mind. *How do I tell her? Do I tell her?*

"Siv, there's something I need to—"

A horn from the raider's ship blared a dreadful, tinny sound and men began to shout orders. The ship lurched toward them. Gudrun's heart leapt into her throat.

"They know we're here, now. Row as hard as you can. As soon as we're out of the cove and with the wind, you set up your sail," Gudrun said.

Siv nodded. It was a race to the mouth of the cove.

The women leaned into their oars with their backs, legs braced strong against the hull. The wind was against them, though, trying to push the boat back to the wreck, while driving the dragon ship faster, closing the small gap the sisters had to escape.

"Go! Go! Go! Or we'll be trapped!" Gudrun shouted. She metered out the cadence and their boat surged through the water; a sleek, wooden dolphin, rising, cresting and plunging with every stroke. "Almost there!"

A quick glance back. The dragon ship was so much closer, looking twice the size it was a moment before. Its crew slowly set their oars.

"Once they start rowing they'll pick up speed very quickly. They'll catch us, unless the crew's asleep!" *Huginn, where are you?* Gudrun scanned the clouds. She fumbled her oar and it splashed her. *Stupid!* She shook her head and shut off her mind to focus.

Pains pierced through, then melted away. New aches came and went, swallowed up by the dull, numbing, repetition of the task. The wind hit her back and she pulled harder against it.

...pull lifttwist, push twistdip, both arms together, back arms legs, pull lifttwist, push twistdip...

The women drove through the water, the rhythm of their bodies at one with the boat, their oars at one with the ocean. Gudrun focused on their wake to keep their line straight. The wind carried the frustrated shouts from the sailors, but Gudrun was lost in her rhythm.

"Steerboard!" Siv called. Gudrun snapped her head right. She plunged an oar into the foaming water and their boat swung to port. The barnacled dragon ship was nearly upon them, only two lengths away, as the rowboat left the inlet. The cross-wind hit them and Siv scrambled to set up the makeshift sail.

The men's shouts were clear on the wind, their cadence clumsy.

Siv grimaced. "They sound terrible!" she said. "Are they drunk?"

The dragon ship's oars knocked into each other, until a furious man shouting set the rowers straight. A deep drum began to beat a cadence.

Siv pulled the green cloth tight across the spear shafts. The wind caught the sail and their boat picked up speed.

"I'm going to steer as close to the island as I can," Gudrun shouted over her shoulder. She continued to row.

"The rocks—!"

"I know! I want to lead them to the rocks. They'll smash their ship," Gudrun shouted.

"But not ours?" Siv said.

"If we're caught in open water on the fjord we'll have no chance at all. Their ship is too fast. The rocks at the other end of the island are our only chance. We'll get as close to them as we can and trap the dragon boat." *I hope. Not sure how we can get through the rocks, though.* "If the gods will it, and the Norns have it in their weave, we'll get through!"

Gudrun refocused. The gods would take care of their part, she and Siv already had enough to handle. Gudrun's heart pounded and her muscles burned. Back, arms, legs and lungs.

The rocks were a stretch away yet, still hidden by the curve of the island's natural wall. *If we're too early, they'll turn the ship away from the trap. But, if we're too late...* Gudrun shuddered at the thought of being captured.

The ocean splashed her back as they crashed through the waves... salty brine, sticky and rough on her skin. The ship's prow surged after them, pumping up and down like the jaw of a mammoth serpent, buffeting the waves aside.

A drum boomed from the dragon boat, keeping the oarsmen in a rhythm which had the ship gain momentum. It grew louder as the boat surged closer. Its hull listed like the fireship that had crashed the harbour, low to the surface as it ploughed through the rough sea.

The patchwork sail, made of cast-off cloth, bulged where it was poorly sewn together and fluttered where the storm had torn through. Rigging was stretched and tangled around the mast and beams. No shields hung on the sides, making the ship look emaciated. Cresting certain waves Gudrun could see the entire crew, heads bobbing as they rowed. The ship was a mess. These men were not sailors, not by trade.

A group of them pointed and jeered at the women. Their words were lost to the stormy wind, and they waved and mockingly beckoned for the women to come aboard. One began thrusting his hips in grotesque gyrations. He held his tongue out and the others laughed. His own laughter eventually prevented him from continuing. The men each took their turn jeering.

"It's a shame we can't hear them," Gudrun sneered. "It's always satisfying to hear how stupid a man is from his bluster."

The men stiffened to attention and shuffled away from the railing when two others came up from behind. One was a giant who towered over the rest, and the other was clean and polished, thin and regal.

Gudrun narrowed her eyes on the broach the smaller one wore, in the shape of a skull. *Blue cloak, gold broach. Magnor!*

He rested one shining, leather boot on the railing and leaned on his knee. Even as the waves bucked the boats, Gudrun could see disdain in Magnor's eyes.

"There's really no need for all of this effort, ladies." He stroked his beard.

Gudrun found it surprisingly easy to immediately hate him. "I am Gudrun Thorkildatter, and I will see you dead!" she shouted. The men laughed.

"Gudrun! Shut up!" Siv pleaded.

"I am pleased to know, Gudrun, that I am already loved here as much as I am in Albion. Such spirit! But, let us not waste the day. I am Magnor Iversen of the Danelaw, and I extend my hand in greeting to you women. It is always pleasant to meet the natives, and to learn what I am working with. What I need is a guide to this untamed land, and what you need is an opportunity. So, *I* will give you that opportunity, to save your lives, and in return you will provide *me* with an opportunity, too. One might say, a *golden* one." They all snickered.

Gudrun's stomach turned.

"Lutvin!" Magnor leaned in. "Do you know it?"

"You won't find gold in Lutvin!" Gudrun blurted. Magnor straightened and his eyes went wide.

Why did I just say that? Gudrun bit her lip.

"That's where you're wrong! I know there is gold in Lutvin. You are only the first people I asked, and you know of the place, and the gold. Excellent! *Ha ha!*" Magnor clapped his hands. "You see, Roar? I told you. This is my destiny."

Roar sniffed at the air as he lumbered to the railing. The parts of his face not overgrown by his orange beard were covered in tattoos. Green, swirling lines and dots gave him the appearance of a savage beast, but he winced whenever the boat dropped over a wave's crest and shuddered against the sea, like a frightened child. A thick, grizzly-fur hide lay across his broad shoulders as a cloak, and a wild, tangled mane of orange hair radiated out from his head like fire. He held the rail with an iron grip, as Magnor laughed.

Like a pet at his master's side, Gudrun thought.

The prow rose and fell only a few feet from their rowboat and a gaunt, wiry man climbed onto it and leaned precariously out over the water, swinging a lasso.

"Come on, girlies! We won't harm you," he said, then exploded into a fit of laughter.

"Speak for yourself, Dreng! I plan to do a lot of harm!" a man hollered, followed by sneers and raucous laughter from the rest.

"I can see you're not from around here," Gudrun shouted, compelled to outdo their bravado. "Your boat is a disgrace! Did you steal it from someone's grave?"

"Gudrun!" Siv hissed. "Don't provoke them. They'll kill us!"

"They don't want to kill us. They want to fill us with terror. *Not a chance!* Not for these skitrheads!" Gudrun glowered at Magnor.

He shrugged and laughed. Then, his smile vanished and he leaned over the railing for a closer look. "What is...? Is that—? The spear! *How* did you find that spear?" Magnor pounded the railing with his fists. "Capture them alive! Do not sink their boat, I want that spear!"

The sailors shouted and whipped the rowers until the ship began to gain on the rowboat.

CHAPTER FIVE

Daughters of Rán

The men turned to the women, snapping whips as they shouted obscenities at them, licking their lips and panting like starved dogs. They laughed and boasted about rape and pain and their insatiable need to inflict both. The oarsmen received their fair share of the lash and were rebuked to row harder.

Gudrun and Siv strained to keep pace with the ship in their small fishing boat. Siv pulled with all of her strength on the improvised sail as Gudrun rowed. The dragon ship's barnacled hull trenched low through the water as though it dragged Rán herself across the ocean floor.

Siv strained against the wind, feet braced against the spears, the cloth wrapped around her hands for better grip.

The waves reached higher up on the rock face as the two boats chased each other around the island across an ever roughening sea.

Not more than a good twenty strokes from the rocks, Gudrun figured. The temptation arose to ease off, in case they saw the trap too early, but Gudrun continued her strong pace. *Nineteen.*

Despite its appearance and the damage, the dragon boat gained on them. The prow rose and fell on the waves like a hammer, inching closer to smashing the little rowboat. *Eighteen.* Gudrun prayed to the waves — the Nine Daughters of the gods of the ocean:

Rán and Ægir.

"Horron! Unnr! Dúfa! Gather your sisters and lift our boat high over the rocks, that these pigs may be smashed upon them!"

Seventeen. "Praise to you, wave maidens, who cradle our ships in your bosom and bless us with your bounty. Command the wind against these defilers, send them to the edge of the sea." *Sixteen.*

They crested a wave and sped down then up the other side to the crest of the next, an oceanborne chariot charging across valleys of water. *Fifteen.* The dragon boat barreled on after them, smashing through the waves, sending shudders through its timbers.

"Gudrun! The sail's slipping from my grip!" Siv strained to pull the cloth taught. Both her legs were braced against the spearshafts in the gunnels as the wind did its best to tear the cloth from her hands.

"We're almost there, Siv!" *Fourteen.*

 The men relished the chase, ready to pounce. It excited and aroused them. The ship's bow loomed over the women, only a few feet away, its wash surging with each stroke of the galley's oars. *Thirteen.*

"They're going to smash us! We're sunk!" Siv cried out, as splash from the prow's wash rained over the side of their little boat, soaking Gudrun's legs. *Twelve.*

The rowboat jerked forward, hit from behind, sending the women scrambling for balance.

"They rammed us!"

Gudrun momentarily lost her rhythm and when she set again, she caught the glimpse of a woman's form within the waves. The woman moved alongside them like a dolphin, but she wasn't human, not made of flesh, rather formed from the sea itself. The woman surged forward and shoved the rowboat, propelling it ahead of the prow's wash. Then another woman appeared in the water, and another. They materialised and vanished in the spray and the foam, their bodies revealed by the lines of the waves.

"They're wave maidens, Siv! Rán's daughters heard my prayer!"

The wave maidens pushed in between the rowboat and the dragon boat's hull. They held the little boat just ahead of Magnor's ship and kept the wash from swamping them. Gudrun set her oars again.

On the prow, Dreng hooted and shouted at Siv as he swung the rope beside his head. *Eleven.* He was filthy. His patchwork clothing blended in perfectly with the shabby boat. He wore a fur vest, wet and slicked by the ocean, giving him the look of a rat. *Ten.* His black hair was pulled back in long, greasy locks and his chin could support no more than thin wisps of a patchy beard. He dangled one bare foot over the side in the wash, with the long toes of his other foot gripping the wood of the prow. *Nine.*

"Hey! Hey! I know which one I want!" Dreng shouted back to the crew. He pointed at Siv. His patchy beard was lost in greasy smears of dirt on his face. *Eight.* "But the rest of you can share the sow I am about to string up!"

Jeers and laughter.

He swung the loop of rope over his head and threw it out at Gudrun. She ducked the rope, but knew even if he missed he could still slow them down or capsize their boat if the lasso caught a part of it. *Seven.* He flicked it back to try again.

The women were running out of room. The ship was nearly upon them again, with nowhere for them to escape to.

"This isn't going to work!" Siv shouted.

"Hold on! We're almost there!"

The wave maidens jumped and dived in the surf and pushed the rowboat faster until the two boats kept pace with each other. *Six. Now or never!*

"Can you see the rocks, Siv?"

"I see them!"

Five.

Dreng threw and roped Gudrun around the neck. "I got one!" He yanked hard and pulled Gudrun to her feet, making her grasp desperately for the spears.

With another sharp yank her head slammed into the side of the prow. She saw stars and barely felt a spear's shaft with her fingertips. Dreng snaked a greasy, sinewy arm around her neck and heaved to pull her onto the ship.

"Come here bitch! I have you now!" he said, as he adjusted to wrestle her on board. He cackled in her ear, his breath foul with the stench of hunger and his armpits rank. "You're mine, girl!"

"Ugh! You stink! Here, have *this*." Gudrun swung a spear at his head. He dodged and she pulled the blade down across his bicep. In one deft slash the spear cut his flesh to the bone, half severing his arm. Blood sprayed Gudrun's face before Dreng yelped and jerked his arm away.

He wailed in fury, dropping Gudrun and the rope, then fell from the prow and tumbled into the sea.

Gudrun's feet found the bottom of the rowboat again, when the waves shifted and for an instant their boat came level with the ship. A gap was opened to the perfect shot at Magnor's golden skull and the spear itched in Gudrun's hand. She launched it like a harpoon.

It bolted straight at Magnor's throat, slicing the air with death on its blade. Magnor twisted and dived and the spear severed his ear. He rolled across the deck as the spear streaked past and found a home in the tillerman's chest, driving through to the haft. Two men beside the tiller leapt back in terror, shock slapped on their faces as the pinned man shook and coughed up blood in spasms.

"Get her!" Magnor shrieked, sprawled on his ass with a hand clamped on his bloody ear.

Gudrun dropped into her seat but her oars were gone. "Skadti's Branch! Siv, give me yours!"

The dead tillerman slumped onto the bar and the ship yawed toward the island. Men slipped and sprawled across the deck as the prow swung to port. Men fell on their oars which flailed and smashed against the rowboat. One caught the sail and tore it from Siv's hands.

"The sail!" She dived under her seat as the oars raked across the

76

boat.

Gudrun dodged and snatched up another spear. She leapt onto the ship's oars and climbed them to the railing.

"*Hidthrwyrd!*" she shouted to Siv — a shepherd's command given to a dog that it should run to the back of the herd — then vaulted over the railing onto the ship.

"I'm trapped!" Siv screamed, on her back.

Gudrun focused as she landed on a sprawled pile of sailors and overturned benchchests. A man looked up at her from between the bodies pinning him. His mouth and eyes gaped wide. "Buh— buh—!" was all he could manage before Gudrun speared him through the neck. She leapt forward onto the deck, leaving him gurgling blood from the gash in his throat. Her hand tingled on the haft of the spear.

Blood

The ship careened toward the stone wall and Gudrun lost her footing on the scummy deck boards. Frayed ropes, scraps of cloth, and smashed wood were littered everywhere. She gagged and faltered when the stench of rotten food and vomit from the galley punched her in the stomach. "*Ulp!* Skadti's branch!"

Two young men tumbled to their feet, eyes locked on her. They lunged, left and right. Gudrun speared through the side of one's gut and twisted the blade to bash the other's nose with the haft. With a shove she sent them screaming and tumbling back.

A swift kick folded another coming from the side before she twirled the spear, slashing its razor edge through thin clothes and slicing flesh. Four more dropped to writhe or die. Blood sprayed into the bilge and the rest backed away.

More blood

A wide man with a thick leather vest lunged at her from behind the mast. He grabbed at her tunic and she dodged, leaping toward the stern. He had one eye scarred shut, though he deftly matched her footwork, then coiled to pounce. Gudrun cracked his jaw on his blind side with the butt of the spear, foiling his leap, but he took the hit without pausing and cut off her escape with his arms out wide. "Ho! C'mon gurly!"

His belly was exposed, aching to be split. She slashed, but was grabbed from behind before the blade could slice. Gudrun thrashed and kicked and her assailant stumbled off balance and collapsed under her weight.

His head cracked off of the deck, yet his grip held her fast. The other man punched Gudrun's ribs. She shot one foot up, shattering his jaw and smashing teeth out, sending him tumbling away after them.

Two more bleak raiders took his place, their clubs raised to murder.

One stepped in to smash Gudrun's skull, when a shadow streaked across from out of the aether. The man screamed and thrashed, twisting as though on fire. The shadow formed into the raven, flapping and clawing the pirate's face. The man behind him swung his club and it passed through Huginn when the bird turned itself into a mist. The blow shattered his friend's cheek with a clear *snap!* and a spray of blood.

Gudrun threw her head back to smash her captor's nose, two, three times until his grip slackened and she could burst free. He writhed double when she drove her heel into his balls to help herself stand on the rolling deck, then dashed toward the stern. *If I can destroy the steerboard...*

The sailors lurched to control the ship before it crashed into the island's wall. Gudrun slid to a stop; three sailors recovered the tiller before she could get there. She scanned ahead for the rock trap. *Just a bit more!*

Then she saw Magnor at the fore, stabbing a spear over the side.

"I'll take that pretty golden head off your shoulders!" he yelled at Siv, veins bulging purple in his neck.

The ship jerked away from the rock wall. Huginn cawed and flew to the yard arm. Gudrun cocked her arm back to throw at Magnor, when she felt a jolt from the spear.

Command them

It was a thought, strong and sure, but definitely not the raven. She flinched. *What is happening to me?*

The men closed in. She dodged a club, but slammed into Roar and his treelike arms clamped around her from behind.

Again?!

He lifted her off her feet.

No one's ever— "Ughh!" She kicked and bucked, driving her heels into his shins, over and over and over. Roar's arms constricted. Despite Gudrun's punishing blows that would have broken a lesser man, he crushed her lungs with her elbows pinned to her sides. She slammed her head back and walloped his face. The huge man shook her like a sack of grain, impervious to her blows.

Magnor continued thrusting his spear at Siv. She screamed with an unearthly terror, and Gudrun's blood boiled.

The sailors were now locked onto Gudrun. Half a dozen cried out as they clawed and leapt onto her. Roar stumbled under their weight and they pulled the two of them down onto the deck. The sailors piled on top and yanked the spear from Gudrun's hand.

Their crushing weight stalled her breath. Siv's screams of desperation pierced through into Gudrun's mind, along with Magnor's laugh, clear and sharp. The way he said 'bitch' made Gudrun want to tear his head off. The lasso was yanked tight around her throat and squeezed away what little breath she could take in. She used Magnor's voice as an anchor, fettered by a desire for vengeance, to keep herself from sliding into unconsciousness.

Without warning, the ship convulsed with a *Boom!* The deck lurched like a catapult, as though struck by Mjölnir itself. For a moment everything — the men, benches, sewage, all of it — floated in the air, then walloped down onto the solid deck, breaking bones and teeth, fracturing skulls. Gudrun landed on top of Roar. With a groan he released her and she scrambled away.

Gudrun's heart stopped. *The rocks!*

The ship had glanced off of one and she watched in horror as they sailed past the rest. *I need to get off this ship and get to Siv!* The deck was littered with debris and woozy men, slowly recovering from having the wind knocked out of them.

In her search for an escape route she was stunned by what lay on the deck only a few feet away. It was, unmistakably, the spear fate had thrust into her hand when earlier she'd blindly grabbed for a weapon from the rowboat.

Skera-Brynja! Gudrun dived for it and wrestled it into her grasp.

"Steer away from the island!" Magnor bellowed. He hung from the rail by his fingernails, struggling to climb back onboard. Most of the men were still shaking off their stupor.

Gudrun glanced at the spear and a shudder ran through her body.

Command them

"What?" *Did I hear that? Or... feel it, maybe?*

Command the men

"Skadti's branch!" The voice had come from the spear! Skera-Brynja had spoken to her! *The Raven has driven me mad, now everything lectures me!*

The men were closing in, bloodthirsty pirates on all sides, cutting off her escape.

If I don't leave, they'll tear me apart!

The Raven called to her from on top of the yard — the beam tangled in rigging, yet still holding the top of the tattered sail to the mast in the full wind.

The ship brushed the island, twisting and breaking oars, and a yard line snapped, making the sail shudder.

Caw! Caw! The yardarm 'see-sawed' for a moment until the gust pushed the sail into a new position, spilling wind.

Siv was frantic; men shouted, ready to pounce; the Raven—

"I don't understand!" Gudrun shouted.

The bird pecked the mast, flapping its wings.

Command them

"Shut up!" Gudrun screamed, grabbing the sides of her head to crush away the madness.

Sailors scrambled to regain control of the ship and a group closed in on Gudrun from the front, forcing her to retreat to the stern. One cackled as he moved in on her. Behind him, Roar pointed at her as he reached to pull on his hood.

Command them

"No!" Gudrun threw Skera-Brynja and it streaked at Roar. He dodged and the spear sliced his neck, tearing the hood from his hand. The weapon hit the mast and plunged deep into the wood. With a deafening crack the timber split to the top and the ship shuddered. The sailors flinched and with one long stride Gudrun dashed onto the gunnel of the ship. She leaped over the oars and dived in the water.

Gudrun swam toward the rowboat, as Siv sculled to get clear.

Another loud crack split the air and the yard crashed down. It smashed into the gunnels, crushing the pirates' heads. The sail and tangles of rigging flopped down along with it.

"*Yes!*" Siv cheered, throwing her arms into the air.

The ship lurched and threw the crew down once more. Men moaned and cried out in pain as the ship drifted; the patchwork sail fluttering uselessly on top of their heads. Those who hadn't been smashed by the yard timber or tangled by the sail, used their knives to cut ropes and cloth to free others from the broken rigging.

Waves hit against the crippled ship, turning it sideways, and the current dragged them back toward the island.

"They're being pushed back into the rocks!" Siv said. Gudrun swam to the rowboat and held a hand up for Siv to pull her out.

Men scrambled over the deck to set their oars, but it was too late. The ship was on a collision course with the island. It was heaved by the foamed sea, timbers groaning and screeching as it tore between two large monoliths. *BOOM!* The ship cocked upward and men were tossed into the sea. Crew and cargo were smashed upon unforgiving stone and others became whimsy for crushing waves.

"That's what you deserve!" Siv cheered. She helped Gudrun out of the water, then grabbed her in a bear-hug. They laughed and shook through heavy tears. The raven circled above the doomed ship and cackled.

Gudrun and Siv sailed back to the mainland. They watched the pirates scramble and swim for their lives as the waves broke their ship apart against the rocks.

Siv laughed as their boat nosed onto the beach.

"From here it looks kind of funny. Like they're water bugs." She stopped when she saw Gudrun's furrowed brow. "What's the matter?"

Gudrun couldn't take her eyes off of the ship. *How could I?* "I had it, Siv." Gudrun dropped her chin to her chest and her shoulders slumped.

"Had what?"

Gudrun looked at Siv. She wanted to tell her everything, about Gils, the spear, the men... but she couldn't. The words were like stones locked in her chest.

"Nothing. I just wish..." Gudrun trailed off and looked at her feet. *I threw it away. It spoke to me. Skera-Brynja spoke to me! In my hand I held the power to stop them, but I was so... afraid, I just threw it away and fled. I'm a coward!* She shuddered, trying to keep herself from wailing her sorrow.

"We were lucky to escape, Gudrun. You saved us *and* sank their ship!" Tears streamed down Siv's cheeks as she beamed with pride at her sister. "You're a hero."

Siv's gushing enthusiasm couldn't break Gudrun's brooding. *I need to prove I'm no coward. Huginn said I'd find my destiny on that island. Skera-Brynja is my destiny, and I'm going to get it back!*

They jumped over the side and dragged the rowboat onto the beach. Siv flopped on the sand and stretched her arms out as far as she could to embrace the earth. "Thank-you thank-you thank-you!"

The lasso still hung around Gudrun's neck. She pulled it off and threw it. Her throat was raw, inside and out, and bled where rope had cut her. Her body ached, and she could already picture the bruises she had. She gingerly lowered herself down beside Siv to catch her breath.

They watched the blackened clouds.

"For a moment... I didn't think we'd make it," Siv said. She sat up and leaned over, giving Gudrun a hug. "When that asshole got you around the neck I thought he had you for sure."

Gudrun stiffened, not used to that level of affection, but slowly put her arms around Siv, too.

Gulls soared past on the wind, looking to find shelter as the storm rolled in. For a moment, the sisters quietly watched the pirates' doomed ship. Waves shoved what was left of it against the rocks and the distant sounds of the hull cracking could be heard even from where they were on the beach; its timbers protesting as they were twisted and bent over the rocks under the weight of the pummelling sea.

Smoke from the fires burning Vestrijóborg blew over the forest Gudrun had been running through that morning, leaving a brown haze in the air.

"Come on, we have to get back to Lutvin," Gudrun said, letting go of Siv. "We'll carry the rowboat to the fjord cliffs. There's a spot where we can launch it back into the water. It's out of sight of the island, in case any of Magnor's rats are watching. We'll be able to sail halfway to Lutvin, near Ivor Bondi's ranch."

Siv nodded.

They dragged the boat toward the fjord over slick grass, up a slope to the top of the cliff, where they stopped and looked back over the ocean. Hoddholm island looked so small from up there, the trapped ship like a child's toy, nicely wedged into the rocks. The pirates were gone, scattered to the ocean.

"We did a good job," Siv beamed, catching her breath. Then a thought suddenly hit her. "We just stopped an invasion!"

"They still have the port," Gudrun said.

Huginn hovered on the wind. *He has the spear*, the raven's voice grated in Gudrun's head. His words hit Gudrun like a slap to the face.

"Do you mock me?" she yelled at him.

Siv gave her a questioning glance, but didn't say a word.

Gudrun hadn't expected to feel so strongly about such a simple thing, but now that the spear was gone it made her feel as though their father was even further away. *He would have known what to do. Known exactly what to do.*

"I need to go back," Gudrun said, not taking her eyes off of the churning wreck.

"Good. So, you're coming home with me," Siv said, a quizzical look on her face.

"No. You go home. I'm going back down there." She stood up.

"*What?* No, Gudrun! You and I need to go home together. Why would you need to go back down?"

Gudrun stared at her feet. She hadn't been prepared for Siv to demand the reason. "There's just something I need to do," she said, her voice nearly a whisper.

"You want to kill him, don't you? And how will you do that? Swim over and wrestle him with your bare hands? No, our duty is clear: we need to return to Lutvin and inform the Chieftess. We need an army, and she can raise one. I can't do this alone and neither can you. I need your help, Gudrun."

Gudrun looked at Siv, who stared back with a blank expression. A knot tightened in Gudrun's stomach. She could hear echoes of Skera-Brynja's voice in her mind. An emptiness grew within her and filled with shame when she thought of how quickly she'd thrown away the ätt's heirloom and all the legends with it: the defeat of King Vili, the miracle of Karlman shore, the battle of East Ridge. Her guts twisted tighter.

How could any of this have come to pass? The legend was clear: as long as a member of their ätt held the spear they'd be unmatched in battle. *What happened, father? How could Magnor have defeated Gudbrand?* Too many restless thoughts ran through her head;

Sigurd, papa, Gils. The spear had spoken to her! *Will it speak to Magnor, too?* Gudrun took a deep breath. She made a silent vow that she would take Skera-Brynja back, no matter what.

"Siv," Gudrun said, her eyes downcast, "papa and Sigurd..."

Siv nodded. "I know," she said quietly. "In my heart I can feel they are gone."

The storm front was on them and without another word they hauled the boat in the rain, sliding it over the slick ground to continue down to the water.

CHAPTER SIX

Tales of a Fisherman's Corpse

The path was hard and cold under Mista's bare feet as she ran through the forest. *How could I forget?* She spared another glance behind to be sure she wasn't being followed, but she knew it to be true. The cottage wasn't far; Odd would know what to do.

A thunderous flash over the lake turned the darkness of night into day and Mista caught a glimpse of the world beyond the veil. The twisting shapes of writhing spirits over the water were revealed to her völur's eyes, before the darkness rushed back in like a turbulent vengeful sea to hide the unseen world from her seidr-sight once more.

"No!" she pleaded with the wind. "Not yet! Freyja, have mercy!" She ran faster.

The storm was coming and it was well beyond her power to stop it. She knew that something else came along with it, from the lake; something not of the world of Midgard. Something that should have never been summoned.

The hair on her neck stood on end and she whipped around to look down the path, like a deer aware of a hunter. Her heart raced. *It is following me!* She couldn't see it, not yet, but she felt it with her seidr, searching in the darkness along the path.

At least she'd sent Sinmora home in the rowboat with her husband's corpse; *it* wouldn't pursue Sinmora, not while she carried the protection of the Widow's Necklace. Mista had placed the necklace around Sinmora's neck, made from a sow's ear and imbued with Frayja's power.

But now, Mista could feel *it* coming for *her*; an infectious, creeping mist of death and corruption. Terror whipped her to hurdle herself toward the cottage.

The wind rushed at her off of the water, fluttering and billowing her robe, sending a chill up her spine; her stained white robes were still wet with the dead fisherman's blood.

The 'Western Wolf' inside her rose up and threw its head back to howl praises to the gods. *He is close. Smell him on the wind.*

Mista stumbled and fell, yelping at a stubbed toe. "Quiet!" she yelled at the Wolf as she cradled her bleeding foot. "I do *not* want to know who you smell! Oh! Why, Freyja? Why did I forget?" She knew she was being punished for her mistake, though not nearly enough for what she'd done.

She scrambled to her feet and hobbled toward the cabin. *I must get back before the storm lets loose!*

Sitting beneath a hanging corpse was the best way to speak with the dead, but Mista could not rid her mind of one word the fisherman's corpse had repeatedly offered: *war.*

She'd tried knocking on an elm, blowing into a stone, tying a strip of cloth to a frog; nothing her master had taught her would release the word from her mind or cleanse it from her aura. The corpse had said one other thing, but the word 'war' pulsed in her brain.

She caught a fresh, anxious smell in the air. New rain. Stronger as a memory than a scent. Trees trembled on the far shore, a roar carried by the wind, increasing as a heavy gust blew across the dark lake.

"Freyja's cats!" *Next gust brings the storm and sparks the spell! I'm doomed!*

She stumbled along the dark path, oblivious to the long grasses brushing her legs, cold and wet. The wind picked up again, howling louder as it flew across Nifel lake. She braced herself against the tempest, heavy with rain, and the storm crashed down upon her. Sheets of rain slashed in waves, the torrent soaking her and carving gullies through parched mud with snaking streams. The flawed spell was activated.

Whatever thing had come through the veil was here now, unable to stop or be stopped. *It* turned toward her and shambled along the path. Mista struggled in the dark to keep her feet from slipping, her toes clenching sharp stones and mud to find grip.

Boom! Thor's fire illuminated the world in its true form once more and revealed the silhouette of the small cottage, so close that Mista could almost touch it. Death pushed toward her through the forest from behind.

Mista put her head down and shouldered against the blowing rain swirling her robes. Ignoring the pain in her foot she dashed to the cottage. The Western Wolf licked its lips.

The door flew open, pulled from Mista's grasp. A cruel, cold gust slipped across the floor toward the fire. It wrestled with candle flames and hanging trinkets, knocking over a precariously placed jar before casting its icy breath at Odd and Sangrida. It rose goosebumps where it brushed bare legs under dresses and blankets.

"Close the door!" they yelled in unison, quavering from the chill. Odd pulled her cat fur shawl tighter around her waist.

Haldana helped Mista push the door closed against the blustering storm. The wind hammered against the door to get in, forcing the women to lean their full weight against it. Mista fumbled with shaking hands to secure the latch. Thunder cracked and shuddered through the log walls, making hanging fetishes and delicate metal trinkets dance and clink.

"Praise Thor!" Sangrida said, rosy cheeks bright like a child's.

"You finally came home, Mista! We thought you had died, too," Odd said, not looking up from her weaving. The other two chuckled.

"Welcome back," Haldana said, handing Mista a cloth. Mista flinched from it, surprising Haldana. Mista's dishevelled hair stuck out in every direction, and she pressed flat against the door, chest heaving.

"Mista, are you well?" Haldana asked, head cocked to the side. "You seem to have lost your breath."

Across the room, Odd sat weaving impossible hypnotic patterns into a shimmering cloth. A thick candle bathed her in golden light.

"Völur," Mista squeaked, her words dry and scratchy in her throat.

"She probably saw the *vættir* of that dead forest cat again," Odd teased. Mista was known to see spirits.

"Völur."

"She only sees that thing when she's tending the herbs," Sangrida laughed. "And once on the shore collecting shells. And, mushroom picking in the woods. Climbing that elm tree under the new moon." Sangrida furrowed her brow. "I'd like to see one once."

"Völur!"

Odd chuckled. "Three days sitting under a fisherman's corpse can make one's mind begin to unravel. Did Herrick give you an answer for Sinmora?" Thunder crashed. Odd looked up. Mista was pressed against the door, her mouth working hard to birth the words she struggled to carry.

"Mistress!" Mista cried.

Odd sprung up, sending her shuttle skittering across the floor, and dashed to Mista's side. It had been many years since Mista had called Odd 'mistress'.

"What have you done, woman?" Odd held Mista's face in her hands and inspected her, like a bear with her cub. Her wooden bangles clashed as she waved a hand over Mista's head.

"Some darkness hangs over her. Haldana! Fetch the sage from the black clay pot." She looked deep into Mista's eyes. "What did Herrick's ghost say to you?" Odd plucked invisible webs off the terrified völur and flung them to the ground.

"*He comes for you.*"

"What?"

"*He comes for you.* He told me only one other word, and he told me often: 'war'."

"For three days?"

"Yes. But that is not—" Mista took a deep breath. "The beacon…" She squeaked the words, tears brimming. "It failed. I—I placed the staff, sang to Hel, left a hare as the sacrifice, but *it went right past.*" Mista gave a great sigh then went limp. Her head banged when she slumped against the door.

"It?" Sangrida said.

"Bring mead and broth," Odd ordered. "Her eyes are so sunken. Mista! Stay awake. Where is that sage, Haldana?" Odd grabbed a rattle and shook it over Mista's head while intoning a chant.

The younger völur's eyes fluttered open.

"Here! I have the sage," Haldana said, dashing in. She handed Odd the clay pot, along with a smaller copper one holding a lit coal. "What's happening to her, völur? What does she mean by a 'beacon'?"

Odd blew on the coal until it was bright enough to make her face glow orange. "When opening a portal to speak with the dead, some innocent vættir will slip through. That is fine, but evil vættir, like *draugar* or *haugbui*, can slip past, too. They will try to consume the one who summoned them." She sprinkled crumbled sage over the ember. It crackled and burned, until a thick plume of white smoke drifted up. "The beacon attracts all of those spirits, like moths to a candle, so the völur can concentrate on her spell without having to deal with all of those vættir. Once the portal is closed the vættir fade, cut off from the seidr that holds their form together in this realm." Haldana handed her a large fan made from an eagle owl's wing, and Odd used it to wave the incense over Mista.

"Do the evil vættir fade, too?"

"Yes, but sometimes they become agitated and stay, or are trapped here, like the *huldra* in the marsh."

"The huldra!" Haldana gasped, shuddering.

Mista twitched and pulled away from the incense, wrinkling her nose and screwing up her face at the smoke.

"Strange for someone so familiar with cleansing vapours," Odd said. She reached out to Mista with her seidr. A heavy darkness surrounding the younger woman swirled. Odd's eyes went wide. "Mista! You foolish *krona!* You cast the beacon spell upon *yourself!* Do it right, or don't do it, woman!"

Thunder crashed, so close it rang their ears and rained droplets down from the thatch. Another struck, then another. Wind howled through the cabin, creaking the old wooden beams. Hanging loops of garlic and dried cod swayed on the rafters like corpses from a gallows. The ceiling writhed and dripped.

"I hope the roof isn't going to crash down on us!" Haldana cried, eyeing the thatched ceiling.

Three more claps thundered over top, threatening to smash the timbers and split the cottage in two.

Then, one more crashed *Boom!* and their world went silent.

The storm stopped.

Nothing moved.

Odd thought she'd gone deaf. Sangrida let out a squeak before she clamped her hands over her mouth.

"I can still hear, that's good," Odd said, the buzz in her ears fading. They looked about in wonder. The roof no longer dripped and the fish had stopped swinging. Terrifying silence pressed in on them. The soft sound of the crackling fire eventually trickled in.

Haldana's eyes were wide. "Völur, have you ever...?"

"No, this is new," Odd said. "The fire continues to burn, but the weather is still."

The hairs on the back of Odd's neck stood on end and she locked her eyes on the door. Death lurked just outside, as near as the threshold, yet an entire world away. The comfort of home instantly decomposed into that of a frigid, isolated crypt.

A pounding startled yelps from them and threatened to smash

the door from the frame.

"Everyone around the hearth, *now!*" Odd said.

Haldana and Sangrida dashed to help Odd drag Mista to the fire. "What's out there, völur?"

"Pay attention here! Make the spirit-ring, ladies. We must remove the beacon spell from her," Odd instructed.

They stood over Mista and held hands.

"Sangrida, you start and Haldana will follow." Odd's firm, gentle voice reassured them, yet the younger women flinched when the door was hammered again. Odd stood unwavering. "We are right in the face of this evil, alone before the eyes of the gods who see our deeds and hear our valiant voices! Sing, ladies! *Sing!*"

Sangrida closed her eyes and began to hum a low melody, her voice shaking. Haldana took a breath and harmonised. Their voices grew stronger and more confident together.

Another pounding made the door shudder. It wouldn't hold out for long. Done right, their spell would protect them and remove the beacon from Mista.

"No matter what happens, continue weaving the spell or it will fail. Dig deep, sisters, and let it flow," Odd said.

Sangrida chanted a mournful song from her heart's sorrow of loss of family and love. Haldana from her soul's rapture of spiritual surrender. Odd could feel the beacon lifting, and Mista, too, found the strength to join in their hymn, intoning the body's longing for comfort.

A few points of light appeared and floated in the air around them. Curious spirits flitted in and out between them.

"It's working!" Odd said.

Odd closed her eyes and inhaled deeply. She scattered a handful of sage onto the fire like seeds in a farmer's field, then sang:

"Thor be with us! Arrive with the lightning!

We welcome you, lord protector, swift be your arrival.

Praise to you, God of Thunder, your servants await you!"

The crumbled herb crackled, creating a thousand pricks of orange light as it burned up instantly in the coal's heat. Another handful of sacred herbs was tossed in, the leaves and twigs smoking and warping before bursting into flames, filling the room with sweet, aromatic smoke.

The door crashed in with a boom and clattered onto the floor. Odd gripped the young women's hands to hold them there. Yet, already their eyes were closed, lost in the euphoria of the seidr they collectively wove, and continued the song. The strength of their conviction to weave the spell kept the spirits from fleeing, too. Wisps of light flitted around Mista, each one loosening the magical beacon bit by bit as it passed.

The thump of a heavy foot at the doorway hit the floor. Odd dared not look, not yet.

"Spirits give us your knowledge, tell us how to protect and cleanse our sister."

Odd signed sigils of protection over Mista. "Freyja, Lady of the völur, Valkyrie of Fölkvangr, protect her; Lady of love, guide her; Lady of seidr, give her strength. Teach us what you taught Odin: the secrets of the Vanier; the mystical seidr."

Odd opened her eyes enough to see the silhouette of a warrior so large it filled the splintered door frame entirely. *A haugbui!*

"Freyja be with us! Odin protect us! The corpse of a restless warrior stalks our sister, Mista!"

The haugbui swayed and landed a heavy step inside the cottage. Then, it dragged its feet as though they were chained to slabs of rock. Each step made its armour jangle, and water splash onto the floor. It let out a gurgling moan and water gushed from its mouth.

The women sang louder, the pitch raised with urgency. Odd's heart raced. She'd expected the spirits to have melted away back to their realm when the undead warrior had entered, but they stayed. She could hear tears in Sangrida's voice as the warrior thunked another laborious step closer. A quiver rose in Odd's stomach, making her body tense compelling her to continue weaving the spell, to not give in to her primal instinct to desert.

The temptation to flee, to run from danger, was visceral, like a cord tugging at her hips. She felt it in the other women, too, as they pulled away from her. She firmed her grip.

The beacon was fading, she could sense it. Just another moment and the malign spell would be removed from Mista's aura.

Then the warrior was there at the hearth, looming, water still pouring off him like a spilling bucket. The cold water cascaded onto them. He began to suck in a deep breath, when the tension snapped like a ship's rope frayed by gale winds.

The spirits fled, liberating Mista's spell as they dissolved.

Sangrida snatched up a long-knife and faced the haugbui. "Keep away, *beast!*"

"Sangrida, stop!" Odd yelled.

The stiff warrior turned with great effort, and locked eyes with Sangrida. Odd didn't know what the young woman saw within the dead soul's windows, but Sandgrida turned white as snow and shuddered as though the blood in her veins turned to ice. The young woman yelped and lunged at the warrior's breast. The blade sliced through his armour and Sangrida was sprayed with saltwater.

"What evil—?" She lifted her blade and lunged again.

"Sangrida, no!" Odd shouted. "It's Thorkil!"

Sangrida backpedalled on the wet floor and fell on her rump to pull her blade from the strike.

"Thorkil! I'm sorry! I—"

The women looked from Odd to the warrior, mouths agape and brows furrowed.

"Your brother?" Haldana whispered, confused. "This monster is not your brother, völur! Thorkil is with Chief Gudbrand, viking in Albion. You are mistaken, mistress."

Odd straightened herself with refined grace and walked to him. She shuddered at the numbing cold when she took him by the arm.

"Thorkil," she said softly, admiring his pale, grey face. Ice water flowed over his bloated, leathery skin from some unseen source. His gnarly beard had great chunks torn from it, and was tangled with strands of kelp. His cheeks and throat were puffed as though too much food were stuffed in.

Odd turned to the women and smiled. "This is my brother's ghost," she said, as though introducing an old friend. "See the jagged scar on his cheek? You got that defending my honour, didn't you, my beloved?"

Mista recognized it. "But, völur! That means..."

Odd nodded, tears filling her eyes. "Thorkil will not be returning," she said. "What stands before us now is no longer of this realm, no longer of Midgard. This is not truly Thorkil, but a shadow of his former self. A mindless shell, shambled up from the sea. Still, he is a guest in my house and we will make him comfortable, ladies. Sangrida. Haldana. Fetch our guest some food. Come, brother, you've had a long journey, warm yourself by our fire." Odd put a stool next to the hearth for him.

Thorkil lumbered to it with slow and arduous movements. He swayed from left to right as though being pushed and pulled by ocean waves. His soaked hair flowed down around his face and swayed with an invisible current. Water splashed off of him constantly, spilling onto the floor. He sat and put his hands to the fire to warm them, dribbling water to fizzle and pop into steam over the hot stones and coals. Three fingers from one hand had been slashed off in a fight.

Sangrida placed a tray beside him with a bowl of stew and a cup of ale.

The women sat and watched in silence through the hearth, gathered together across from him.

He sat for a long while, rubbing his outstretched hands over the fire. His wrinkled skin constantly dripped. The floor was already wet from the leaky roof, but this was something altogether different; water flowed from him. His hair, beard, armour, everything dripped as though he were the water's source.

Odd shifted in her seat.

Sangrida and Haldana held each other like giddy children.

"A ghost!" Sangrida whispered. "An actual ghost at our hearth!"

Thorkil opened his mouth wide and water gushed out, cascading off his beard and onto the stone. He reached deep inside his mouth until his whole fist had fit in.

"Oh! No, that's not..." Haldana said, grimacing.

Sangrida clapped both hands over her mouth, and Mista turned away. Still, they remained, their curiosity more powerful than their revulsion.

The haugbui's cheeks puffed out as he twisted his head back and forth, struggling to pull his fist back out again. With a hard yank and a spray of water, his jaw cracked and out popped his hand, holding a pearl the size of an apple.

"I am going to be ill!" Mista cried and clamped a hand over her mouth.

He slowly leaned forward, holding the pearl over the stone of the low hearth. Then, he spun it like a top. It bounced once on the stone and rang out a clear *ping* which reverberated through the rafters. The sound continued as a high pitch while the spinning pearl swayed over the stone.

The women leaned in, enraptured by the iridescent sphere as it spun. Across its surface beautiful scenes of the ocean world appeared.

Suspended within a deep blue, a kaleidoscope of shapes and colours were projected onto the walls of the cabin and unfolded all around them, becoming schools of fish that drifted past. The wooden walls gently morphed into coral and flowing sea plants; the furniture transforming into barnacled boulders resting on a floor of fine sand. The women gently lifted from their seats and were suspended in the water, to frolic with the Waves — the nine daughters of Rán, goddess of the sea. Floating around the spinning pearl, the women were captivated by this new world.

Odd knew this magic.

The pearl had been created using powerful seidr, designed to fool and trap the unprepared, the unwise. She could see beyond the impressive conjure and recognized the illusion. She focused all of her attention on the present moment — held precariously within the glamour — and the surface of the pearl revealed itself to her. Ignoring its hypnotic sway, she searched, until— *There!*

Along the blurred, iridescent surface, she'd found a thin crack. In her mind she held a small, sharp tool to pick at the crack and chip away at the veneer. The crack widened, but not enough. She needed to get a wedge in, to break it open.

She conjured the pick into a chisel. *Still too small.*

A spear. *That will do!* She drove the point down, but it skated off the surface. *I require something more… creative.*

Odd dismissed the spear and unsheathed the ritual blade she kept on her belt. She rested its keen edge across her palm. A quick pull and a sharp sting were followed by a dribble of crimson. *This will either break the spell, or…*

"Divine goddess, use your light and the life this blood gives to reveal what is hidden."

She clenched her fist over the pearl and let her blood dribble onto it. The pearl pulled the sanguine fluid in until its surface turned a shimmering crimson. A crackle. Then a crack spider-webbed across the surface, and it split like the shell of an egg.

An iridescent veneer crumbled away to show another layer beneath. *Plain truth will not be revealed here, merely another perspective of it*, Odd predicted.

The other women remained entranced by the pearl's ocean illusion, believing they swam like fish among the waves. Yet, Odd bore witness to a very different scene, one brought from a grave within the corruption.

A land arose from the sea, beyond this one, where soldiers hacked each other apart, battling under a storm of arrows, knee-deep in mud and gore. Smoke from a burning town choked and blinded them, and one army was trampled and churned under a poisoned earth, like wheat stocks being tilled into feted soil. Plants sprang up, bearing children as fruit. They grew in an instant, ripened into men and women, who toiled in the killing fields the moment their feet touched the earth. Soldiers slaughtered them, too, though the plants grew and sprouted new fruit in an unceasing harvest.

When the soldiers had their fill of murder, they burned the land before mounting warships, axes and armour dripping gore, and the ships sailed into the rising sun.

Tears streamed down Odd's cheeks as the vision unfolded before her. She understood, she knew: war was coming to Lutvin, and there would be no help, no one coming to save them.

The pearl pulled the younger women in as it grasped at their minds and permeated their thoughts, dragging them deeper into the illusion. Odd could feel the cull upon them.

Give this to her, Thorkil said, and runes formed in Odd's mind into a single word.

"Geirahöd," Odd read. The other three were drooling in dumbfounded rapture, their noses nearly touching the pearl. Before it trapped them forever, Odd smashed her fist on the gyrating pearl.

The water suddenly collapsed beneath them, as though a wave had crashed onto the floor. A thunder clap shook the cabin and the sounds of the storm ravaged them, again, as though a giant bubble had burst. A frigid gust howled through the door.

The women fell over, thrust back into their senses, as the illusory ocean disappeared under the walls.

"What was...?" Haldana said, blinking in confusion.

"Fishies?" Sangrida asked, searching for more ocean creatures.

They all gawked at the room and each other.

They were alone. Thorkil's haugbui was gone. Only the soaked, wooden stool he'd sat on remained, set within in a large puddle. Haldana and Mista lifted the door and braced it back into place.

Odd contemplated what she'd witnessed. *Geirahöd means "Spear of Battle". "Give this to her." Give her a battle spear? Who? I don't understand.*

"Völur!" Sangrida cried, "what does it all mean?"

Odd inhaled, and slowly let her breath out.

"War is coming. And more horror, I fear. I must consult with the spirits, to get clearer sight. Then, I will speak with the chieftess." Odd was pensive. *'Give this to her.'* She thought. *Geirahöd. Who am I to give this to?*

Her gaze fell upon the timber posts framing the front door and the lines carved into them that kept the memory of a growing child's height.

"I will seek out my brother's daughter," Odd said, understanding at last.

"Do you think Siv will be able to help, völur? She seems to be a curious choice," Mista said. She had the pained look of apprehension in her eyes.

"No, not Siv. His eldest daughter."

The other three stiffened. Mista shook her head.

"No. I don't want her here. You said war is coming, and we need help. She doesn't help, she only brings destruction! You can not mean to say—"

"What I *mean* to say," Odd said, hissing the words, "is that I will seek out my niece, Gudrun."

"Look! I still have the scar where she bit me!" Mista pulled up her sleeve and showed off the white crescent dotting her forearm.

"She was three."

"She was impossible!"

"Stop it, Mista!" Odd snapped "My mind is set. Destiny is woven! Everything is in play, now. There will be no other help! The gods have called and we must answer, and if Gudrun doesn't, then she will lose what is left of her family to war. We all will."

CHAPTER SEVEN

A Burned Out Port

agnor hacked through dripping underbrush toward Vestrijóborg, further soaking the waterlogged leather of his boots until it squelched between his frozen toes. *That pestilent woman!*

The rain had let up and steam hung off his cloak like a phantom. Water sprayed from the sleeves of his overcoat with every slash at the stubborn thicket. His knuckles were pressed white from strangling the shaft of the spear. *I want to feel the bones of her neck snap as I choke the life from her!* A wet branch slapped his face.

"Gahhh!" He thrust the spear, along with his frustrations, into the trunk of a tree refusing to be easily limbed. Wrestling the weapon out again made him stop to catch his breath.

"Cut a hole through this crap!" he snapped.

Roar stepped up from behind and swung a long-bladed cleaver to make quick work of the bushy pines.

Magnor's shoulders heaved as he panted and trembled with fury, glaring at the spear clenched in his hands. That very weapon had destroyed his ship with one blow. Ironically, it was the sail that saved him; kept him from flying into the water. Unlike most of the others. It had taken all of his strength to wrest the spear from the split mast and nearly cost him his life as the ship was dragging him down.

How? How! he thought, unable to comprehend the speed at which the situation had turned on him. *How could one woman defeat an entire army?* A champion of the gods? The small blonde had called her Gudrun.

"Gudrun." Her name was bilious in his mouth, and spitting it out would not clear his palate. *I will find you and your Lutvin. I will dig up every corner of every home, I will find your gold, and I will bury your corpse there.* Then, he'd buy his way back into Albion. *Not before burning Lutvin to the ground.*

Roar cut a path through the brush, bringing them to the clearing around Vestrijóborg's wall. The gate was sealed, with raiders guarding on top. Once recognized, the men shouted down to open it for Magnor.

One end of the city was smouldering. Magnor's men had rounded up the people and kept them packed together in the burned out market square. They sat bound together in two groups; men on one side, women and children on the other. Half of them had been beaten into unconsciousness, and lay on the wet, blackened paving stones.

Magnor strode to a pile of scorched timbers and began removing his wet clothes.

"Captain Brokk!" he shouted.

One of the raiders, Egil, recognized him and ran to his side.

"Magnor! We hadn't expected you so late. The town is secured, and we're gathering prisoners."

"Where's the Captain? Have any of the other men returned?"

"Captain's dead." Egil nodded toward a pile of corpses at the end of the wharf. "One of your men was picked up off the shore, needing to be stitched."

"Just one?" Magnor grimaced. He scowled at the prisoners. "I want to know where Lutvin is."

"Most of these donkeys are caravan merchants who babble in some language none of us understand. The Northmen here understand, but they're as tough and stubborn as asses."

"And, probably just as stupid," Magnor said. He pointed at a shelter attached to the side of one building. "Set a table under that overhang. Get a chopping block and find a volunteer with an axe. Then bring three of them. They will loosen their tongues or I'll remove their heads. Let the Northmen know that once we've chopped our way through them, we'll start cleaving their women. And, bring us some food and drink. *Now!*" Magnor dismissed Egil with a wave, then strode toward the building. Egil barked Magnor's orders at the men, prompting them to run and shout at the prisoners as they hauled three to their feet.

Within minutes Magnor was under the shelter, leaning back on a chair behind a table with a bowl of food and a mug of ale. Roar hunched over the table, shovelling food into his mouth with his hands, spitting what he didn't like to a pack of dogs that had gathered. Two merchants stood before them in the rain. Clearly, neither of them had understood the question Magnor had asked.

He was fascinated by their horror. They couldn't take their eyes off the third merchant, struggling against the men holding his head down against a fresh block of wood. The man bawled and gnawed at the leather gag they'd cinched between his teeth. Rain splattered off the back of his neck that the guards held exposed.

A fourth, one of Magnor's, and much younger than the other three, stood beside the block. The rain rinsed blood from his tattered tunic and trousers, running dark down his bare legs and feet. He stared at the merchant's bare neck and gripped a wide-bladed axe above his head, eager to chop.

Magnor dropped a fat chunk of pickled herring into his mouth and enthusiastically smacked his lips.

"*Mmmm!* So good!" He scooped up another hunk of silver fish, then looked each prisoner in the eye. "Tell me where Lutvin is."

The man on the chopping block wailed.

"*Uhh!* What is he babbling in, Greek? Grates on the ears." Magnor grimaced and nodded at the axeman.

The youth flexed and slammed the axe down, splitting the merchant's neck with a brilliant spray of sanguine. The head thunked to the flagstones and tumbled in front of the other condemned men. Their faces screwed up in horror and they fell to their knees, wailing prayers, alternating between Magnor and the sky. The executioner looked at them and sneered as he kicked the decapitated body aside.

Magnor couldn't understand the merchant's words, but he'd heard men grovel for their lives many times before.

"There is a weakness here, Roar. It requires cleansing. These are not men! They're less than those grovelling dogs. They beg to be made slaves, believing that will save them from inevitable death. They slobber and moan for mercy, promising the lives of their wives and children in exchange, like sacrificial goats or gambling silver. They're too blinded by fear to see that I already own their children. Their wives are mine to be bought and sold as I please, like the cheap goods these swindling cowards once hawked in this skitrhole market."

The guards dragged the next merchant, screaming and thrashing, to the block.

"*No, kurios! No!*" he wailed. They beat him until they could force his head down onto the bloody stump.

"These men know nothing. They are only useful for impressing the others that I mean business. Kill these ones and bring two Northmen and another skag."

Magnor finished off what was left in his bowl as two more heads fell. The dogs lapped up the blood bathing the stones.

The guards returned, wrestling three more men before Magnor. The extrinsic man became agitated at the sight of the decapitated bodies, and wailed as they dragged him to the bloody chopping block. The other two remained silent.

Magnor swirled his ale, picked out and flicked away a blob of dirt, then threw back the last mouthful. "*Ahh!* Weak ale, but the best I have had in months. Now, can anyone in this dung pile understand what I'm saying?" He wiped his mouth with the back of his hand. He reached over to an ale keg and dunked his mug in, up to his wrist.

One of the Northmen spat in the keg. A guard was quick to crack his skull with a truncheon, and the other guards took it upon themselves to club all three of them.

The doomed man on the block clasped his hands together and shook them, weeping for mercy.

"Another Greek," Magnor said, annoyance overriding the disappointment in his voice. He waved his hand and the crying man was held to the block. The axe swung and added a fourth to the growing collection of heads.

"You two don't look like the other merchants. You look like Northmen. Can either of you tell me where Lutvin is?"

"I can," one said. "One of my women lives there."

Magnor perked up. "Now we're getting somewhere. How do I get there?"

"Sail up the *Njörðrfingr* fjord."

"Ah! Do you see that, Roar? Easy! Except, we don't have any boats." Magnor pointed at what was left of the ship's smoking hull, blackened and smouldering in the harbour.

"Put him on the block," Magnor said.

They muscled him over the decapitated corpses and held him to the butcher board.

"I have women!" the man shouted. "They're willing and you can have them!" He thrashed and kicked the two pulling him to his death.

"I already have your whores," Magnor said. "There's only one woman I want, so I can mount her head on a spike. I already have all of the others," Magnor said with a shrug.

"Who?! Who is the woman you want?"

"You idiot!" Magnor yelled. "I want *Lutvin!* The woman I'll find after I've taken the village."

A guard punched the prisoner in the gut, doubling him over with a wretch. They wrestled him onto his knees and piled on his back, forcing his face against the gory wood with all of their weight.

"I can take you there!" the prisoner screamed.

"Shut up. Kill him."

"I know the area! I know about the seidr protecting it, I swear to you! There are völur there who keep a monster trapped in the swamp, and protect Lutvin with the help of spirits and wights. That land is haunted."

The executioner chortled and raised his axe.

"I can show you how to avoid the landvættir! Without a guide the spirits will never let you find Lutvin!" The prisoner huffed through clenched teeth, each breath spraying the pool of blood away from flowing into his mouth. The young man looked at Magnor for the signal, unaware that the raised axe dripped blood onto his hair.

Magnor studied the prisoner for a few moments longer, then held up a hand. He narrowed his eyes and flicked his fingers, and the guards rolled off of the man and yanked him to his feet.

The prisoner panted as though he'd just run miles, blood trailing down his neck from his face.

"What do they call you, slave?"

"Ander Boarhead."

"The pretty woman called her Gudrun," Magnor said.

"Oh, yes. I know Gudrun, alright," Ander laughed.

"Shut your mouth!" the other prisoner yelled, and thrashed an arm free. He lunged at Ander, but the guards beat him and tackled him to the ground.

"No one could miss her," Ander said, with a wry glance at the Northman. "Fist like a hammer and the face of a brawler; broken nose, front tooth missing. Mother was a giant, some say. Aye, I know the Gudrun you speak of. A thief and a murderer, that one. And a sister who men would slit their wife's throat for."

Magnor stiffened. "Alright, Ander Boarhead, I'll give you one chance." Magnor looked at the executioner. "Give him the axe."

The young man snapped his head around in surprise. "S-sir?"

"Ander will take the next prisoner's head." He pointed at the other Northman.

They cut the rope binding Ander's wrists, and the executioner shoved the axe into his hands.

"Good weight for chopping," the young man snarled. His eyes were wide, feral and black, peering out from behind wicked splatters and smears of crimson across his witless face.

Ander took the axe and looked at the Northman pressed to the ground by a scrum of guards.

"I know this man. They call him Erich the Dane. I'll take his head with pleasure. Get him on his feet," Ander said with a smirk. He checked the edge of the axe with his thumb. "His neck is thick. For his sake I hope it doesn't take more than one chop."

Erich glanced at the corpses. "*Pwah!* Are you going to send me to the afterlife following these pathetic fools? Bah! They'll lead me astray to Hel! I'm destined to seek Odin!"

The guards muscled Erich to the block.

"At least hold my hair away from the axe," Erich said. "There is a lot of it, and I would hate for you to ruin it, or it get in the way and make you hack." He remained on his feet and bent over to expose his neck, his dishevelled braid dropping down off his shoulder.

Roar belched forth a laugh that shook his entire body, exposing his filed teeth with a mad smile. He pulled a fistful of his own hair tight, and growled and barked.

Magnor guffawed. "Your hair? *Ha ha!* Fine," Magnor laughed. "Hold his hair back. I want to see his head swinging in your hands."

The young executioner grabbed Erich's braid and pulled it away from the doomed man's neck.

"Hold it tight, boy," Erich said. "It will be a lot of extra work if he has to chop through this mane."

They all chuckled at the bizarre joke.

Ander spit into his hands and rubbed them together, then lifted the axe high and waited for the signal. Magnor stared at Ander until the axe began to shake in his hands, yet Ander's eyes showed he was unwavering.

"Do it," Magnor said, and gave the nod.

Ander grunted and swung with all of his strength, bearing the axe down on Erich's neck. With a mighty pull Erich jerked his head back, hauling the young man forward. The axe smashed through the man's forearms, severing both hands. Erich tumbled backward and Ander yelped when he realised what he'd done.

Even before the blood began gushing and the young man wailed, Roar and Magnor had fallen over with laughter, holding their sides. The other men dropped to their knees in fits, the hilarity leaving them gasping for breath, as the young executioner flailed until he collapsed.

Erich bounded for the edge of the pier, dodging and body checking pirates who scrambled to recapture him. He leapt off the pier and crashed into the water.

Men rushed to the edge and fired arrows at him as he twisted himself to bring his bound hands out from behind, and thrashed his legs to swim toward the sea.

"Let him go!" Magnor shouted, through his laughter. "That was the most amusing entertainment I have had in a very, very long time!" He doubled over again, thinking about the expression of surprise on the young man's face when he was yanked forward. Magnor nodded. "Erich the Dane will rest in Valhalla, of this I have no doubt. To show such bravery and wit before one's death… that is the kind of man we need, Roar. I regret not having known him."

The wind burst at them from the ocean and the storm let loose. The pirates hauled their prisoners into the paddock and tied them all together, leaving them outdoors under guard.

Magnor snatched the axe from Ander. He stepped in close with a finger pointed in Ander's face.

"Take me to Lutvin, cur. Bring Gudrun to me. Erich's stunt was funny, but it was your hand on the axe that chopped my soldier's arms. Try something like that again and I will have Roar crush your skull like *that*," he said, with a snap of his fingers.

"I will bring you to Lutvin," Ander said. "You will stand in Chieftain's Hall within the week, I promise you." Ander held Magnor's hateful glare, turning aside when the scorn became unbearable.

Thunder cracked, rattling the awning as a wall of white driving rain roared down, the deafening bluster of quenching fires now consuming the city.

"If not," Magnor sneered, "I will bring *you* there, sliced thin in a butcher's basket. I promise that to *you*."

CHAPTER EIGHT

Embla

The sisters sailed up Gunnlaug fjord and abandoned the boat on the shore, near Ivor Jomann's ranch. It had been many years since Gudrun had visited the horse farm, but even in the bewitching light of dusk she saw it hadn't changed much. The gnarled old willow that had cascaded over the yard was gone, though the cedar fence was longer.

"You two look exhausted," Erica Jomann said. She welcomed Gudrun and Siv with tight hugs. "Sit and eat. I'll fetch you some dry clothes."

"We haven't stopped since this morning," Gudrun said between bites of pork stew and oat bread. "But, we need to keep moving."

"Vestrijóborg has been attacked," Siv said. "Taken by pirates, led by an outlaw named Magnor. We need to report to Chieftess Vigdis."

"Vestrijóborg attacked?" Ivor put his arm around Erica and pulled her in tight.

"They think there's gold buried in Lutvin," Siv said.

"Every crazy farmer with a shovel has delusions of finding gold in Hoddlund. I've seen them diving under waterfalls, hoping to catch nixies or other watervættir by surprise and steal their treasure. Such nonsense!"

"And Vestrijóborg is burning because of that nonsense," Gudrun said, into her bowl. *Sigurd died, papa died, Gudbrand and all the rest died, because of that nonsense.* "Magnor is coming and there's no use haggling with a man selling nonsense. Magnor will only stop when there's an army to stop him."

"And with Gudbrand gone we have no army to stop Magnor," Ivor said. He looked at Erica. Gudrun could see on his face his heart breaking with his next thought. Erica put a finger to his lips before he could speak.

"Do not say another word, husband. There's too much work to be done. You and the boys gather the stables. Have Mullen bring a cart to the front and I'll start packing the house."

Ivor pulled Erica off her feet and kissed her. She touched down lightly again and they squeezed each other tight.

"The gods sent you to me, Erica, you poor, unfortunate woman," Ivor said, with a grin.

Erica laughed and shook her head at him, then Ivor turned to the sisters.

"My boys and I will ride out tonight and spread the word. You two finish up, change and before you leave, come see me in the yard," he said. He nodded once, then left for the stables.

Erica shooed her daughters off to pack up clothes and beds, then turned back to Gudrun and Siv. She sighed deeply and leaned against a timber post. "I hope there will be something to come back to." Her hand lingered on the wood's smooth surface — well worn after years of her children chasing each other around the hearth. Gudrun could see the love this family shared, and it made her squirm.

Gudrun and Siv finished eating and Erica stopped them from clearing the table. "I will take care of this, you need to be on your way," she said, drying her hands on her apron.

Siv was still munching on a carrot and gave her a hug. "Thank you, Erica, you have been so kind to us."

"You are always welcome, no matter where our home is. Your

parents took us in for a year after our first house burned down. It was the same year your brother Audin was born. I will never forget it. We have such fond memories of them. I don't think any of us in this room would be here if it hadn't been for them." Erica quickly wiped her eyes with her sleeve. "Well, enough of that."

One of their boys, Mullen, came in from the rain carrying two grey oilcoats, woven from thinly spun wool rubbed with seal blubber. "Raining harder now," he said, with a smile. "But, these will keep you dry." He blushed when Siv smiled at him, then ducked away as the women put their coats on.

They left into the rain and spotted Ivor coming out of the stable. He entered the yard leading a pretty, dapple grey mare, with one front leg stocking. She was tall and lean, more so than the draft horses the Bondi's bred.

"This mare is set to be slaughtered. She's too fast and spirited, and refuses to pull a plough. Some horses like to work; some like to be eaten. I will give her this: she's the most curious and perhaps the bravest horse I've ever owned. I think she'll be perfect for getting you two home quickly," Ivor said.

He held the reins out for Gudrun.

She put up her hands. "This is too much, Ivor! Thank you, but we cannot accept her."

"Yes, you will accept her! It's the least we can do," he said.

Erica had come up beside him and nodded in agreement. She held a hooded lantern which steamed in the rain. "Her name is Embla."

"Embla! I love that name," Siv gushed. She gave Embla the rest of her carrot and stroked her muzzle.

"Thank you," Gudrun said. She shook Ivor's hand, then offered it to Erica.

"Ha!" Erica pushed her hand aside and threw her arms around Gudrun's neck, who nearly fell over in surprise. Erica gave her a hard squeeze before letting go, and smiled at Gudrun. She looked deep into her eyes, then caressed Gudrun's cheek with a mother's

111

loving touch.

Gudrun smiled sheepishly and bowed her head, then took the reins from Ivor.

Embla pulled away and tried to jerk them out of her hand.

"Hey!" Gudrun gave a sharp pull, and Embla stiffened. Gudrun carefully moved to Embla's side, then sprang onto her back. Embla snorted and side-stepped as Gudrun twisted and kicked to gain control.

"Hey! Hey Amber!" Gudrun called.

"It's Embla!" Siv shouted.

Embla dashed forward and Gudrun's feet went shooting into the air. She was sent rolling back, onto Embla's rump. Embla bucked and threw Gudrun forward again.

Ivor pulled Erica back with a protective arm up in front of her, to give them room. "Easy. Easy! Siv, get back!"

Embla snorted and bucked, and Gudrun dug her heels in.

"Come on, you—"

Embla pinned her ears back and shrieked a rolling scream as she stomped about the yard.

"Come on, Amber!" Gudrun shouted, doing her best to hold on.

Mullen dashed in to help just as Embla reared. Gudrun was tossed and landed in the mud, flat on her back. Embla trotted away, snorting, shaking her head as she sneezed in triumph.

"Are you hurt?" They all dashed forward to help Gudrun up.

"Yes, I'm fine. But I know now why you were set to slaughter her. She's unrideable."

"I'm sorry," Ivor said, "I should not have given you this horse. I thought she would be a good match for you, but perhaps she is too hardheaded."

Siv was already approaching Embla.

"Siv, don't…" Gudrun started to protest and shook her head.

Siv cooed to Embla as she approached beside her. She carefully reached out to stroke Embla's muzzle.

She was nearly hugging the mare one moment, and then the next,

112

was up on her back.

Gudrun's jaw dropped.

"That's how to do it!" Ivor shouted.

Embla stayed still. Siv clucked and Embla casually walked back to the other end of the yard, as though the two of them had been doing this together all of their lives.

"How?" Gudrun said, gobsmacked.

"I think she's a fine horse," Siv said, stroking Embla's shoulder. "Thank you, Ivor, Erica. She is a very precious gift."

"The dawn will come too soon," Erica said. "Take her and be on your way, with all the gods' speed."

"We will get word out to the other homesteads," Ivor said, "but you must leave now, we will soon be behind you. May Odin go with you, and his horse, *Sleipnir*, with this hag!"

"We will not forget your kindness," Siv said, smiling with her hand over her heart.

Ivor held Embla's bridal while Gudrun mounted behind Siv.

"Sit back on her haunches," Erica said, "and she will take the weight of the two of you more easily." Embla was calm as the women adjusted themselves for the long ride.

They said their final goodbyes, then rode off into the dark and the rain, leaving the Jomanns to pack their lives onto a cart.

* * *

Britta's mother had a dream that night which rattled her. By some miracle, it healed her chronic hip long enough for her to pull her daughter out of bed well before the sun — in the hour of *ótta*. She sent Britta into the rain with a basket of seidr-mushrooms for the völur, in exchange for consultation.

The demon promptly returned to her mother's hip once Britta was dressed. "You'll need to walk the distance for me," her mother said as she closed the door. Britta had never seen her mother so agitated.

113

Britta adjusted the unwieldy basket on her arm and sloshed along the cold, muddy track to Nifel lake. *I hope they don't get ruined*, she thought, with a dubious glance at the wet basket.

Mother insists that Völur Odd will know why the dream afflicts her so. Perhaps an angry vættir, or a fox put the vision in her head? She popped another dried mushroom cap into her mouth and chewed it slowly, relishing its meaty yield with her teeth. She'd never been to see the völur without her mother, which made her nervous. *Völur Odd will know what to do*, she soothed herself.

The rain didn't bother Britta so much as the damp. The rain fed the mushrooms and made them fat, and rolled off her wool cape. But, the damp seeped into everything, locked in the chill. She shivered. Water was pooling on the basket's hide cover, surely dripping through. *I hope they don't get ruined.* She brushed the water puddles off the cover..

The seidr within the precious red-caps was more delicate than flakes of snow, but just as powerful as… as…

"*A winter storm!*" she shouted, giddy with the thought as it swirled and tumbled inside her head.

The mushroom she'd eaten before she left was beginning to make her feet warm. She tucked the basket under her cape and quickened her pace. Her mind was already wandering as the mushroom's seidr walked through her head then onto the path before her. The muddy track skirted the lake through the trees, up the hill to the völur's cottage. The path already showed signs of high traffic; cart ruts and footprints.

They looked so surreal to her. *Were those made by people? More likely, elves shaped them in the mud with little sticks.* She giggled at the idea of elves sitting in the mire with trowels and twigs, making tracks and footprints…

They must be from people. She was proud she'd figured it out. *But already? They gather to sit with the völur this early?* The stormy, dawn sky was fading into a blue glow, just enough to make the trees into fuzzy silhouettes. Britta expected Odd's yard would be crowded.

She adjusted the basket on her arm. *I hope they're not ruined.*

Her thighs began to buzz, and shadows in the woods swayed as the mushroom's seidr took her over. She laughed after she'd slipped and fallen to her knees in the soft mud, then managed to slip every few steps after, until her long green skirt was covered in muck up to her waist. Her bare feet were numb to the freezing mire, the mushrooms doing their trick. She shivered, though, which made her laugh. It would still be another month before Britta would even think about putting on footwear. Even then, only when she was in the snow, or absolutely forced to. She loved the feeling of the ooze between her bare toes as she squelched along the path, and the fiery pricks of sharp twigs and stones poking her toes and the soles of her feet.

Odd's cottage came into view as Britta climbed the hill. It seemed extremely funny to her, and she stopped to laugh. She continued laughing until it was bright enough to see some of the faces of the people waiting in front of the völur's door.

The wooden house overlooked lake Nifel, the water grey from the rain. The lake was always shrouded in mist. Most believed the mists to be the result of powerful seidr used to hold open doorways between the nine realms held on the branches of the tree of life, *Yggdrasil.* Britta certainly believed it.

Some believed the völur who resided here — Odd and Mysta — conjured the mist, with the intent of travelling between realms. Others believed this was a place of great evil but profound healing, to be avoided unless absolutely necessary. All of the stories seemed true.

But, Britta knew why the völur were really here. The mushrooms had told her. The women stood guard, their cottage a bastion against an evil living in the marshes. They prevented dark spirits from escaping and capturing mortals to drag away and endure unspeakable horrors. Sometimes into other realms.

Some didn't know what to believe in that regard, but everyone in Lutvin kept far away from the marshes, the domain of the huldra.

One thing was clear to all who held an opinion of the völur: they possessed powers beyond the understanding of most mortals and gods alike.

I was right, Britta thought, as she approached the crowd of people. Deeper in the woods, others were camped in shelters made of cloth, hides, or evergreen branches. All around the cottage people danced, and sang, juggled or played instruments. *Too much rain for fire breathers,* Britta giggled.

A man ranted prophecies, his eyes rolled back in his head. A few others rolled around in the mud, wrestling and laughing, vomiting, crying. Britta smiled. She could recognize when someone had eaten a mushroom that planted one foot in the spirit realm; twitching, drooling, shaking, the effects of body and spirit being pulled in two directions.

Someone shook jingles and another drummed on a tambour. Others thrummed and shimmied instruments as they danced and sang suggestively in the fine rain, seducing others to join with them.

The greatest majority sat where they were, sleeping or moaning in pain, as they waited to be seen by the völur.

Sangrida stood on the top of a ladder, stuffing thatch reeds into the roof, dripping wet and miserable.

"Hey! Sangrida," Britta waved. She tried ignoring the rainbowy trails her hand left behind. "What are you doing? Trying to keep faeries out, or trap them in?"

Sangrida gave Britta a curious look. "No faeries. Rain. Out."

Britta stiffened. "Did I say that out loud?" Sangrida gave her a sideways glance. "I need to stop doing that," Britta mumbled.

"Odd will be happy to see you," Sangrida said. Britta was wandering down toward the lake. She paused, allowing a giggling, half dressed woman to run past, who was being chased by a naked man wearing a bull mask.

"Oh? My mother had a dream and wanted me to tell the Völur..." Britta lost her train of thought. "I... I hope your mistress will be happy with what I've brought. It's all we have, and the best ones hide from mortal eyes when it rains." *I hope they're not ruined.* She walked into the lake up to her knees, then squatted to rub the mud out of her skirt and the grime from between her toes. The rain made the water cold, but it felt silky on her skin.

She looked up and spotted a silhouette moving through the woods, on the other side of the narrow lake. She couldn't tell if it was really a horse carrying two riders, fast along the shore, or...

Britta stared. She suddenly stood and picked up the covered basket, then strode toward the cabin. She wove her way through the throng of people sprawled out across the yard, to the door, then pounded on it.

"Völur Odd!" she shouted, thumping her fist.

"Are you alright?" Sangrida said, leaning back to check on her.

Britta turned back to find the riders.

The heavy oak door swung open to reveal Odd, nude, her skin painted with ash paste.

"I said to wait until— *Oh!* Britta! I was expecting your mother. I assume she got my message," Odd said.

"Your message? No, I came because... my mother had a vision..." Britta's thoughts jammed up, like sticks damming a creek.

"Yes, I know," Odd said. "Come in."

Britta blinked at her and her mouth fell open. "You were the one who...?"

Odd smiled. Her long, black and grey, elf-locked hair fell down to her knees. Feathers and bones stuck out where they'd been tied and twisted into it, and the greyish black ash paste had been painted onto most of her naked body in patterns which swirled and swooped over her skin. Britta glanced back across the lake once more at the riders. Odd poked her head out of the door.

"What are you looking at?"

"Oh, it's nothing. I just wanted to know if those are two riders on a horse, or a three headed centaur," Britta said, pointing at the hazy silhouette in the mist. They were nearly out of sight by then and had never been close enough for Britta to see them clearly.

Odd stepped out onto the spongy, wet grass. She squinted against the rain.

The runes 'Geirahöd' flashed in her mind. "Yes, of course," she whispered, under her breath.

The rain was rinsing her skin, making the thick ash paint stream down her body, into the grass.

"Yes, Britta, they're real. Come in, we haven't a moment to lose." Odd motioned to the door for Britta to get in out of the rain. "Warm yourself by the fire and get dry. You know Völur Mista. She will help apprentices Haldana and Sangrida choose what is needed. I must leave to meet with the Chieftess."

An old woman stepped forward, her hands on her hips, ready to protest. But, Odd held up her hand and stopped her.

"It's not a good day!" Odd said. She sniffed at the air with concern and squinted into the grey. "The gods hide from the mists. There will not be any messages from the gods today!" she announced.

"Oh no!" the old woman grumbled, along with some of the others. "What of the ache in my bones?" she pleaded, holding her twisted hands out.

"And my tooth?" a man said, five grandchildren with him.

Odd gave the woman a stern look. "Willow leaves," she said, "boil them and drink the broth. Then, sacrifice a goose to Freyja, boil it, too, and eat it. Grida! Come down from the roof and help Ottar the Elder with the pain in his tooth."

Britta stepped past Odd into the cabin. The cabin's warmth embraced her immediately. Mista was kneeling by the hearth, also nude and painted with ash paste. Britta couldn't have known both völur had been engaged in ritual since their visitor from the previous night. Mista tapped on a frame drum, her eyes closed as she hummed. The cottage smelled of honeysuckle incense, smoke, and raw fish.

"Haldana. Fetch Britta some drink, then fill a skin for me," Odd said. She turned to the grumbling crowd. "Go home! Collect your families and bring them to the hall. I predict there will be an important announcement this evening."

Odd stepped inside and closed the door. She grabbed her hair up into a great, wet bundle and pinned it up to dress.

"I must leave for Lutvin," she said, as she pulled on her finer robes.

"Now?" Mista said.

"Yes, the spirits were clear. I go to consult with Vigdis. And with Gudrun. My brother, too, needs tools to fight his battle to escape Rán's kingdom. Grida, hand me the Ulfberth seax."

On her way to the hearth Britta caught sight of the kitchen, half of its floor submerged in water.

"That's convenient. You can catch fish in the kitchen," she said. It made so much sense to her.

Haldana smirked as she carefully straddled the water, stretching precariously toward a shelf for some cups.

Britta seated herself by the fire, after examining a three-legged stool and determining it was, indeed, real.

Odd made a final adjustment to the drape of her cloak, then joined Britta, who was hunched over, giggling into her basket which sat between her feet. She rummaged through the contents: a harvest of mushrooms, henbane, and angelikarot herb.

"They're not ruined! You've all been worrying for nothing," Britta announced, with a laugh of relief. She knew the rest of them could now relax their concern over the leaky basket.

The mushrooms glowed their happiness at her, and she felt an ache in her heart. "Like children," she cooed, beaming with pride.

Haldana tread carefully from the kitchen, balancing four full cups of cider and a drinking skin in her hands. Each of the women took a cup.

"Skoll!" They toasted, then drank deeply of the tangy alcohol. "Good journey, Odd!"

"Thank you for coming, Britta. Mista knows what we need, and I think this will be everything that you need: for the mushrooms and for your mother's hip." Odd handed Britta a nugget of silver and a small pouch of herbs.

"Yes, völur, thank you!"

"I take my leave. I'll return when I can." Odd slung the drinking skin and the seax, then pulled her oiled cloak on. She stopped at the door, took one more look around, and nodded. Then she left, banging the heavy door shut behind her.

Britta turned to Mista. "So, what is it you need?" she asked, then took another drink from her cup.

"We are going to make an elixir, brewed with primal seidr."

"Oh! In order to be able to understand Asgardian and speak with the gods?" Britta asked, bouncing with excitement.

"No," Mista said, flatly. "We're going to brew *berzerkaul*."

"You're going to make berzerkers?" Britta's smile dropped and her eyes went wide. She swallowed hard, then pushed the basket toward Mista. The völur carefully studied the trove of magical treasures within.

CHAPTER NINE

Dark night of the soul

The Autumn Feast celebrated the summer's harvest, held before Slaughter Month: the beginning of winter. This would be the second Autumn Feast without Chief Gudbrand, nearly two years since he'd set foot in his own hall. The Chieftess remembered it well, the campaign feast that sent him off, marching to Vestrijóborg to board the dragon ships that took them viking to Albion.

Chieftess Vigdis watched the rain through her window. She missed him dearly.

Did I forget a sacrifice? Maybe not enough? Freyja, show me a sign that Gudbrand returns!

The bustle within the hall faded as *dagmal* — the morning meal — was cleared from the tables. The servants were quiet as they worked, making Gudbrand's absence even more pronounced by the resounding silence. His boisterous, commanding voice would fill the hall more than those of a hundred men. She'd heard it. Still did, when indulging in the memory.

Nearly half of the village's families lived in the hall now. So many had withered from sickness last winter that she'd moved them into the hall, at the time, to make treatments by the völur easier. Families moved in to care for their children and never left after they'd laid those children to rest. The elders had either succumbed, or left to relieve the burden they put on the village. The most noble of sacrifices. Vigdis fought off the heartbreaking thoughts she'd had so many times before. None under twelve winters survived, nor did any over thirty remain. She was the exception, along with Odd and Grima.

She imagined, instead, her mother's time, when everyone lived and worked together under one roof. They ate and slept, loved, birthed, taught and raised their children within the walls of one hall. It wasn't uncommon to have lived their entire lives around the village; most having been born, lived, and died on the same bed. The entire cycle of life happened within the walls of Chieftain's Hall, making the building a special part of their history.

She watched the rain, drinking nettle tea alone in her anteroom. Her dagmal plate was cold, barely touched. She went through a mental list of the tasks still needing to be completed before the Autumn Feast. Storms had already delayed the harvest, as well as fishing.

The last of the glorious days of summer lay well behind them, blown away last night by colder winds driving a deluge cast by dark clouds. After the feast they would still have a few days before the full moon and the Elf-Blessing — the feast of the hallowed 'Last Sheaf' of wheat left in the field for Odin. After, the fields would be left to the snows, hogs, goats, and spirits. *If the rain stops by tomorrow, we'll be ready.* She wrung her hands together. They had no other choice but to bring the harvest in tomorrow.

Through the door, she could hear people gathering in the hall. *Already.* She took another sip of tea. All of Lutvin flowed through and around the hall, as though it were the lungs and heart of the community. Nothing moved through Lutvin without first moving through the hall, and something was always moving through Lutvin.

The vendors had been moved out yesterday to give the hall a much needed cleaning in preparation for the feast. *Then, tomorrow we'll begin decorating*. Vigdis was looking forward to bringing some colour and vitality back into the dreary building. The village hadn't been the same since the men left. Vigdis had not been the same. She longed for her husband, as much as the other women longed for theirs.

Gudbrand had been viking with his army long enough for the women to forget about the difficulties of living with men in the village. Especially after their return from a campaign; disputes were different — both in their nature and how they were settled; priorities became skewed, and more often weighed in the men's favour. Not all of the women had forgotten, but for Vigdis, the worst parts of her husband were a distant memory.

She desperately wanted to keep the servants and hall ready to throw a victory feast to honour their return, the very moment they came marching around the southern ridge. The reality was more complicated, with resources stretched so thin. Yet, she knew she was not alone in wanting, so badly, to *properly* welcome their heroes home, and to Vigdis that could only start with one thing: a gluttonous feast, including zealous worship of Freyr, the god of fertility.

She imagined everyone gorging themselves and getting gloriously drunk, sharing the spoils and stories of the campaign. She longed to share in Gudbrand's glory... and share each of their sorrows. The realisation of how much heartache she held onto shocked her. A strong desire to mourn, with honour, those who had passed on to the Great Halls in Asgard this last year, was overwhelming. In Lutvin there had been many. Too many.

She suddenly felt alone, left with a staggering desire to have Gudbrand there with her. A yearning for him to carry her to their bed and wrestle in the furs as they made love burned within. To taste him, to feel his touch, his weight upon her, to squeeze his waist between her thighs. She closed her eyes and took a few deep breaths.

Loud voices from the hall pulled her from her fantasy.

She focused instead on the Autumn feast, which always gave an idea of how well the community would fare through the hungry months. She preferred Slaughter Month to end with a feast that was not too small and not too large. Either of those could eventually spell disaster.

No. Just enough for everyone is perfect. A good omen, thank Freyja. She looked at the cold food on her plate, frustrated at her lack of appetite.

The door opened and her servant, Audney, slipped in.

"Chieftess," she said, with a quick curtsy.

"What is it?"

"Chieftess, the Thorkildatters are here to see you. They say they've travelled from Vestrijóborg with grave news they would only tell to you."

"Thorkildaters. *Both* sisters?"

Audney nodded emphatically.

"I see," Vigdis said. *Thor give me strength!* She finished her tea, placed the cup on the table, then walked to the door.

"I will see them now, Audney. Have this table cleared."

"Yes, chieftess," Audney said, with a curtsy. She held the cloak of office up for Vigdis to slip into. Vigdis let Audney drape the cloak over her shoulders. The young woman then pinned it with a golden crescent brooch, and looked Vigdis over to make sure everything draped properly.

"It's fine, stop fussing and open the door," Vigdis said.

Audney pulled it open and Vigdis strode into the main hall with her head high, as regal as a Roman noblewoman.

Some of the servants paused their chores to watch and whisper.

Gudrun leaned against one of the main doors, and Siv paced with her hands on her hips, each of them still catching their breath.

Grima — Vigdis' vassal and most trusted confidant — stood by the door and announced, "Chieftess Vigdis!" She followed Vigdis to her chair at the front of the hall and took the seat beside the chieftess.

Siv faced Vigdis, then curtsied, low and graceful.

Gudrun remained at the threshold, refusing to enter the hall.

"What is this all about?" Vigdis demanded, trying to overlook Gudrun's rude behaviour. "I hear you have travelled across the breadth of Hoddlund to tell me important news." Vigdis picked a fluff off her cloak and flicked it away, then glowered at the sisters.

Siv scowled at Gudrun, screaming "get in here" with her eyes narrowed and nostrils flared.

"I have nothing to say to her," Gudrun sneared, looking down her nose at Vigdis.

"Mind your tongue!" Grima shouted.

"I will forgive your rude behaviour because of my love for your aunt, Odd," Chieftess Vigdis said to Gudrun. "Though, my patience will wear thin quickly, as I do not share that same love for you."

"It is true, Chieftess," Siv blurted. "We sailed up Gunnlaug from Vestrijóborg to Ivor Jomann's, and have ridden through the night to deliver you grave news. Raiders have taken Vestrijóborg, and make their way east, chieftess. They are determined to find Lutvin and will be here within days."

"Siv!" Hildegunn stormed past Gudrun into the hall, in a rare moment of dishevelled concern.

"Mama!" They dashed together and embraced. Hildegunn pulled a square of cloth from her sleeve, dabbed it on her tongue then began rubbing dirt from Siv's brow with her thumb, like a cat grooming her kitten.

"Why is *she* here?" Hildegunn snapped at Gudrun. "How has she cursed our family this time?"

Gudrun scowled at Hildegunn.

"Enough!" Grima scolded them. "You will respect the chieftess' court!"

"Gudrun saved my life," Siv said. "Without her I would've died in Vestrijóborg."

"What proof can you give us that Vestrijóborg has fallen?" Grima said, eyeing Gudrun sideways. Grima was a shrewd woman, to the point, her demeanour and advice always succinct and sober. She'd raised eight boys who couldn't stay out of trouble and her mind was always suspicious. Both she and Vigdis shared the opinion that healthy suspicion was a necessity in Grima's position as Acting Chief Advisor. Gudbrand had taken all of his advisors viking along with him.

"When we escaped, the town was still burning," Siv said. Her voice wavered. "They'd attacked swiftly, and ruthlessly slaughtered their way through the market. We were able to slip through the wall and get out, but they chased us to the ocean, where we found a boat and barely escaped their spears. They came in two ships from the west-lands. One they turned into a fire-ship and rammed it into Vestrijóborg's market. The other Gudrun waylaid at Hoddholm island. Their leader's name is Magnor, and he bragged about searching for Lutvin, believing there is a hoard of gold here to plunder."

"*Ha!* A likely story!" Grima snorted. Vigdis shot her a disapproving look. Grima stiffened. "The idea that raiders would come here, to Lutvin, in search of gold is laughable, Chieftess." She made a low curtsy to save face.

"Chieftess, it's all true," Gudrun said, sheepishly. "One of them got me around the neck with a rope and tried hanging me off the side of their ship. I have this to thank him for." She showed the wound she'd gotten from Dreng's lasso, scabbing and grinning from ear to ear.

"Did they hurt you?" Hildegunn said to Siv, horror in her eyes as she darted them over Siv's face and body, investigating for wounds.

Siv embraced her mother. "I'm fine, mama," she whispered.

More women crept into the hall, with others following in behind. They whispered behind their hands, curious to know why Thorkil's daughters had charged through the village on horseback — as though being chased by wolves — straight to Chieftain's Hall.

"Chieftess!" Odd called, as she breezed up to the open doors.

"Oh, here we go," Hildegunn muttered, shaking her head.

"Elflocks, my friend," Vigdis said, using the name she'd given Odd when they were children.

Odd spun and turned to Gudrun, her robes billowing with an impossible sheen, like moonlight, and she enveloped her niece in a tight hug.

"I knew you'd be here," Odd whispered. "You and I must speak after I meet with the chieftess. Do not leave without seeing me first, understand? I have much to tell you. Come in, you are welcome here."

Gudrun nodded, but didn't let her go. They held each other for a long moment. Gudrun could feel the sorrow her aunt carried.

"You know," Gudrun whispered, pulling away in surprise. Tears welled in her eyes. "You already know about papa."

Odd held a thin, mournful smile on her lips.

Gudrun caught Hildegunn's scowl, as her step mother pulled Siv in protectively to her side. Odd looked at Gudrun, nodded, then turned to the chieftess.

Vigdis stood with her arms wide to welcome her friend, but kept her dour expression.

"As always, you are where you are needed most. We are pleased to have your council."

Hildegunn scoffed.

"Your nieces speak of an army of raiders having overthrown Vestrijóborg, and who bear down upon us, seeking to take our gold, of all things. We may need your help in divining its location, before the pirates arrive."

Women in the hall snickered and twittered to one another, behind their hands.

"Vigdis," Odd interrupted, moving with the grace of a cat as she held up a single finger of warning. The women went silent. Odd let the chieftess' name hang in the air, like a word of power spoken within the temple. She crossed the hall and Grima stiffened, turning her head to look down her nose at one corner, unsure of what she should do with her hands.

Odd's eyes were fixed on Vigdis with an intensity that made the chieftess recoil. Her ability to catch others off guard with that look was unnerving. It terrified Gudrun.

"What is it you know, Völur?" Vigdis said.

Gudrun caught a glimpse of a smirk on Odd's lips, like a twitch. Her aunt prided herself in having a knowledge of things that she ought not know.

Odd's cloak flicked behind her as she slinked to the chieftess with the grace of a cat. She wove through the gathering of women with long strides. As she passed, they touched her cloak, hoping to receive a blessing; that their hugr might move into the völur's prophetic visions.

Odd swayed up to Vigdis, and her cloak swept around the chieftess when they embraced to hold each other as sisters. When Odd let go, her smile had faded.

"I see in your face the deep lines of a great burden," Vigdis said.

"You are wise, chieftess, as the tidings I bring are indeed the heaviest I have yet borne on this coil."

"Tell me." Vigdis eyes went wide. "Or, do I want to know?"

Odd shook her head. "I do not know which is more burdensome: the knowing, or the telling." She was pensive for a moment, then sighed. "War comes to Lutvin, my chieftess. It is sure. The spirits have shown me. Yet, within their visions of desolation I have seen seeds of hope. We have a chance, but you must act quickly. Send warriors to Vestrijóborg. The raiders can be stopped there."

"You know I have no warriors to send. Gudbrand took the best of them, and the rest have either gone on their own ships or died of plague. The men who are left are best for labour, not war."

"Then we must negotiate for the Jarl's protection."

"The Jarl will not give us his protection. He has not met with any of my envoys since Gudbrand's absence. I suspect we have fallen out of Jarl Ulfer's favour, especially since the death of his eldest son. Our only hope, now, is Gudbrand's return."

Odd cast her face down with grief.

"All that my nieces have told you is true, but this is not the worst of it, I fear. These raiders…" her voice trembled, "betrayed, attacked, and murdered chief Gudbrand and all of the men with him."

The hall was deathly still as shock blanketed them.

"*No!* How can this be?" Ashilda, the leather worker, cried, the first to digest Odd's words. The woman began to wail, a low moan that grew into a fit of grief. Ashilda's daughter fell on top of her and sobbed with her mother.

The rest of the women wrung their hands, or buried their faces in them. Their sounds of anguish filled the hall with the haunting wail of mourning.

"This can not be! *You are wrong!*" Vigdis screamed. She fell back into her chair, slumped as though she'd caught a spear in her chest.

Gudrun recoiled in horror. Grief pushed its way up from the pit of her stomach, like a boulder being forced up through her ribs. *Too much!* She gasped for breath and clenched her eyes tight. She needed to avoid, at all cost, seeing Gils' mother and sister or suffer being ripped apart by the mountain of anguish rising within. Gudrun was pregnant with grief, and needed to stuff it down with strong drink, or wormwood gall, or any kind of pain. *Gods, please, take my limbs! Strip me of my flesh! But do not make me tell Gil's mother I delivered her son to Valhalla!*

The warspear Skera-Brynja flashed in her mind, and she froze. *Even worse! Thor, I pray to you: strike me down!*

Vigdis gripped the arms of her chair until her knuckles turned white. She dug her nails into the wood as she pulled herself up to stand, but her shaking legs would not allow it. She'd turned a sickly white and couldn't stop her hands from shaking.

She stumbled from her chair, holding tables and posts to keep herself upright, made it to an open festive mead barrel and stopped to catch her breath. She regained enough composure to snatch up a goblet and plunged it into the alcohol. She gulped it down, spilling it over her face and neck as she drank. When the cup was empty, she plunged it again, and drained that, too.

"Freya be with us," Vigdis said into her cup, eyes closed. "We are not prepared. We have not yet healed this aged, jagged wound, now torn open once more! There's still so much..." she muttered. She swayed and steadied herself against the mead barrel.

Some of the women fled the hall, pulling their hair and tearing at their clothes. Vigdis despaired once she'd noticed their flight. She searched the faces of the others, her mouth agape, hoping for an answer. They gawked back, desperate for answers themselves. She plunged the goblet once more.

"A toast!" she cried out — a scream issued from the depths of her soul. It stopped the women short of the doors, and they all looked at her. Their chieftess held her cup high, tears and spittle streaming down her proud face, turned up toward the gods. "To our fallen!" Her voice cracked.

The women shambled in a daze to fill cups and drinking skoals, and echoed the toast.

"To the brave!" Vigdis continued. "Who have joined our brothers in Valhalla. May they look upon us now as we beseech Odin for his blessing: god of wisdom, give us your strength, share your knowledge, that we may defeat our enemies and avenge our families!"

"*Skoal!*" they cried out, and drank.

Vigdis returned to the chieftain's seat. She turned to Grima. "I am full of woe for the way this chair has come to me. Help me toast." She stood, with her cup raised, and Grima held her up.

"To our warriors! Our beautiful men... Hermund, Aren, Galm, Sigurdhr, Thormod..." Vigdis toasted each man by memory. "... and Gudbrand. My dear husband, Gudbrand. May I see you again, in Odin's hall, or Freyja's field. You were a good husband. Though I did not give you children, you loved me still and never forsook me as your wife. You were a fine chieftain, with a clever mind. I will make you proud, and honour you in this sorrowful seat of office."

Vigdis put the mead to her lips and drank.

Her shoulders slumped and she hung her head. "I must excuse myself," she said, then stood up with great effort, and retired to her antechamber.

The women mourned together, an observance that would last well into the night, holding each other, singing songs of valour and glory to give themselves strength, and remembrance for their fallen. They wept through mournful songs, drinking toasts and sharing memories of their beloved, brave men. Tears were also secretly shed for the freedom they'd been granted, and for the woe to come. They laid a stick on the fire for each man, with his rune carved into it. In this way, they sent their prayers with the smoke to honour the dead.

Odd eventually knocked on Vigdis' door and was bade enter. Vigdis' voice was faint and weary.

"You are not joining them?" Odd asked as she entered, genuinely curious. Vigdis was slumped in her seat at the head of the dining table in the anteroom. She could barely lift her hand.

The chieftess rubbed her temples. Grima closed the door behind Odd, then took her usual place beside Chieftess Vigdis.

"I've had enough, Elflocks," Vigdis sighed. "I feel so old and tired. I just want to lay down and die, too, to be with Gudbrand in the afterlife."

Odd took a deep breath and lay a hand on Vigdis' forearm, as she sat beside her cherished friend.

Vigdis put her hand on Odd's, as tears rolled down her cheeks. "This is their time to mourn. These women have been missing their husbands as much as I." She wiped the tears away with the back of her hand. "But, I can't mourn now, can I?"

"No," Odd said. "Your time will have to come later."

"This will now become my war table," Vidgis said, absently, as though she were seeing the table for the first time. Dark bags had already gathered under her eyes; this last hour had aged the chieftess ten years. "I need to have my head clear. We have much to discuss." She hauled herself up to sit straight.

"I advise you to send riders out as soon as we can. This morning, if possible," Odd said.

"Yes. I need to know more about what happened in Vestrijóborg. Grima, fetch Bestla. Tell her to get her hunter scouts ready to ride west."

CHAPTER TEN

Inheritance

Dreng trudged in the dark through the muddy field. *Is it made entirely of cow skitr?* His arm ached when the wind slapped the crudely stitched wound. He stiffened, hissing a sharp breath through his teeth. The throb had become more intense, touching a nerve that climbed up through his shoulder and stiffened his neck.

He squinted at the gloom to see the other two: Yot and Mar. *Stupid kids.* Likely conspiring to murder him and rob his corpse.

"Ol' Dreng's corpse ain't easy to rob," he muttered. He knew they all whispered about him. Nasty words, spoken when they thought he couldn't hear, like secret daggers shanked into his back. He smiled. *They don't know I know.*

A freezing gust buffeted him, cutting through the holes in his trousers.

"Arrrh! Miserable land!"

"Why d'ya not put on d'em trousers ya gone worked se 'ard to pull off d'old mahn?" Mar quipped.

"We watch yer back," Yot said. Dreng could hear dark mirth in his voice.

"I'm waitin' till we get there," Dreng grumbled.

"Suit yerself. Wind na gettin' warmer, ta."

Another cold gust flipped Dreng's collar down and splatted a wet leaf against his ear, dripping icy water down his neck.

"Stink on a stick!" he yelped. He ripped the slimy leaf away and looked at the other two to see if they had noticed.

"Y'alright, granmuddah?" Mar shook his head and chuckled.

"Why did I get on that cursed boat?" Dreng said. "Oh, to be back in Northumbria!"

"Qui' yer moanin'"

"The next boat I find I'm leaving this dung heap!"

"Swear an oath on it?"

Dreng spat on the ground, "I swear! You can have this skitr pile!"

Mar and Yot laughed, snide jocularity that prompted more whispering.

Dreng's feet and legs were frozen. He hung back on the flank, with the open field to his left. For a quick escape, should he need it. *You will*, he thought. The other two walked a few paces ahead on a grassy strip at the edge of the field. Some skitr on his boots was a small price to pay to have an escape. He scanned the field. *Only darkness and evil shapes.* He stumbled in the muck and turned his attention forward again.

He saw it, faint in the murky distance.

"A light!" he said. "Must be the farmhouse, like the old man said."

"Good!" Mar said. "I gon' t'ave supper an' a woman ta warm me tonight!" He and Yot laughed and jostled.

The throb jabbed up Dreng's arm and pulsed in his ear.

"Let's jus' get there," he muttered. Already out of breath and close to swooning, the muck caked on his boots dragged precious strength away. *Jus' need sleep ... Soon t'will come.* He focused on the smudge of light ahead, regretting his decision to trudge through the muddy, cow pat field.

This all better be worth it, he thought. He glanced at the other two with trepidation. They'd taken too much joy in killing the farmer and his son. He looked behind toward the cliff edge where they'd thrown the bodies over, into the sea.

"Wha'?" Mar demanded. "Why ya lookin' back?"

"No reason," Dreng shrugged. He winced from the movement.

"Den quidit! You try'n ta curse us?"

Dreng tripped on a clump of dirt, landing on his hands and knees in the mud. Hot pain tore through his arm and he felt sick thinking he'd done permanent damage to it.

"Miserable night!" Rain blew into his face and down his neck as he struggled to stand.

The gods hated him, he was sure of it. The day before they were under the leadership of Captain Brokk; a fair captain and a solid commander. He'd known and trusted Dreng. Now that Brokk was dead and Magnor was in charge, he'd been demoted to nothing more than a stooge, sent out by a stooge, to beat up and kill farmers. *Without sword, without ship; we're not even pirates.* It was miserable luck.

His entire arm ached through to the bone, so much so, he no longer noticed the wind cutting through his wet breeches. Of course it had to be his sword arm. Each movement — even the most careful — pulled tighter on the rough stitches holding his arm together and threatened to pop them out. It didn't help that the other two just laughed and kept walking.

He did his best to hide the pain from them, but the wound throbbed and ached to distraction. He couldn't adjust his arm anymore to the spot where he'd once found temporary relief. The amount he'd sweat in the cool night air told him something was terribly wrong. He forced himself to keep trudging forward, ploughing half of the field's mud along on one boot, and half on the other.

It would mean his death if they thought he couldn't pull his weight. He cradled his arm again. He hissed at a shooting pain up through his shoulder. *That can't be good.* This was taking forever. He was afraid if he didn't get to a healer soon, he'd lose the arm altogether. *The gods don' even exist, why do they hate me so much?* It made him angry to think about it, but he knew he had a right to be angry!

He despised his own helplessness, a shame that weighed on him enough to drive him into the ground. *What am I doing here?* He tried focusing ahead. The rough outline of the farmhouse came into view. *Nearly there.* It was a simple structure made from stacked dry stone, timbers, and a thick sod roof.

A dog was barking, standing by the front door. It was grey with a field of white around its muzzle and had a low bark. There was no growl left, due to its advanced age.

"Been 'round dogs all m'life. Dis one old, wit no teef t'hold de bark back," Yot said. He nodded for them to continue and they walked cautiously to the door.

Yot tossed a rabbit's foot and the dog sniffed it. It wagged its tail and lay down to chew. Yot let the dog sniff his hand before he scratched behind its ear. Mar banged on the door with the blunt of his axe and the dog gave him a few tail wagging barks.

The bar dragged away on the other side of the door.

"Lemme take care a this," Dreng said, and slipped under the lintel as the door opened.

Standing behind it was a short, tough looking woman. An undyed, beige smock covered her plain, brown work dress, and a bright blue kerchief with simple white stitching around the edge wrapped her head, making her eyes look cold and fierce. A long braid of blonde hair hung down from beneath it.

Typical farmer, Dreng thought.

"Yupi! Shut up!" she yelled. Dreng flinched. The lines on her face suggested she wore a permanent scowl. "Useless dog." Her grimace became more intense as she studied the men.

"Who are you? What is this about?" she demanded. She stood in the doorway with her fist on her hip, like a sentinel.

"Good evening, *Frau Bondi*—" Dreng began.

"I'm Thorhalla. Don't try to honey me, not at this dark hour! If you're looking for hospitality then come at a hospitable hour!"

Dreng casually leaned against the door frame. He stiffened when the wound twinged and lightheadedness overtook his concentration, but he forced a sweet smile and turned on what little charm he had.

"Sorry to disturb, Thorhalla. We've lost our way to a town called Lutvin, do you know of it?"

"Lutvin?" she snapped. Her face screwed up with a frown. She shook her head. "No Lutvin round here. Go north." She pushed the door closed, but Dreng planted his foot against it, holding it open.

Thorhalla snapped her head up in rage, mouth agape. With her eyes she bored holes into his.

Dreng raised an eyebrow and blinked in surprise, before he spread a smug grin. She took in a sharp breath to bawl them out—

"Thank you, Frau Thorhalla," Dreng said quickly, bowing his head with a pained grunt. "Could you do us one more kindness? We've been travelling for many days and would do well with a hot meal. Spare the *nattmal*[4] scraps in your pot?" He ducked his head to look inside, hoping to catch a glimpse of the hearth pot, then pushed his way in.

Thorhalla stumbled back a few steps, surrendering the doorway to him. She was bound by common law to provide hospitality to any who asked.

"Hey!" she yelled, pointing at his feet. "Take those off or you get nothing!"

Dreng gawked at the muck caked on his boots, and Thorhalla's clean shoes on her immaculate floor.

"But I—"

"*No!* You will take them off and leave them outside," Thorhalla said, hands on her hips. She pointed at the empty space beside the dog.

Dreng looked at Yot and Mar for help, but they simply grinned wide-eyed back at him. Mar lifted one clean booted foot up and

---

[4]   Evening meal

taunted Dreng by wiggling it.

Dreng grimaced. "This is stupid," he grumbled as he pulled his boots off outside the door.

Mar pushed past Dreng, into the door with Yot right behind.

The farmhouse had been built with a partition down the middle, separating the living quarters from the livestock. Four cattle were stabled inside, plus two goats. In winter the animals provided much needed heat and dairy throughout the brutally cold "hungry months". The ripe smell of cow dung hit Dreng full in the face when he stepped in. He could taste it in the back of his throat. It was all that he could do to keep from gagging on the bile coming up.

"Ho! That's a *stink!*" Mar coughed, "I 'ope dat's de cows and not yer cookin', woman!" The men burst into laughter. Mar and Yot strutted through Thorhalla's home, inspecting the interior with disgust.

Thorhalla's face turned a deep red, until Dreng thought her head would pop.

"*You filthy dogs!* You come into *my* house, tracking skitr in with you, and you complain about the smell in *here?* What in Odin's name were you three *ragr*[5] doing in the woods? Did you fokka each other because you couldn't find sheep? Keep away from my goat, you depraved perverts! My husband and son are due any moment, but I won't need their help to deal with you three! I'll tan your filthy hides!" Thorhalla grabbed at something behind the door.

She made Dreng so nervous he couldn't stop grinning. That kind of foul language was common on the ship, amongst men or whores, but he hadn't expected it from a plump country-born woman.

"Ho ho! I ken tell ya, frau," Mar said, "d'only ones ta fokka t'other out dere are yer ragr husband and son."

Yot chortled and pulled a wool cap out from under his coat.

"Yer 'usband about dis tall, wit' fat nose an' limp? An' yer son, 'ave patchy beard smeared wit' skitr?" Yot said, making Mar laugh.

---

[5] Perverted, effeminate man.

REAPER'S CALL

Yot put the cap on his head, and Thorhalla's eyes went wide.

"That's my husband's! I knit it for him! Where did you get it?"

They laughed harder.

"Lewk! 'Er face turnin' purple, jus' like 'er son's did!" Yot pointed and doubled over.

Dreng stood in his bare feet, a stupid grin hung between his ears. He'd thought it'd be a good moment to put on the trousers he took off the old farmer, and held them up.

"You filthy mongrels! Those are his!" In a flash, Thorhalla swung a hatchet at Dreng's head. Yot and Mar took a quick step back in surprise. Dreng yelped, wrenching his head away to avoid her axe, and smashed into the kitchen table. He lost his balance and fumbled to keep the table between himself and Thorhalla's fury. The other two drew their daggers.

"Easy now, woman," Mar said, in as calm a voice as he could muster. He backed away slowly from her, toward the larder. She'd placed herself in a defensible position close to the door, leaving it open for them to escape, should they be smart enough. A loud growl in Mar's stomach made him more interested in the larder.

Yot was closest to Thorhalla, near the fire. He flashed the seax in his hand at her.

"We'll 'ave some fun, yeah?" he taunted, a wicked grin smeared across his face. "C'mon, farmer's wife, show Yot whas under dat dress." He laughed, crouching low, making kissing noises as Mar rummaged.

"A hatch!" Mar said. "I'ma look fer food. Lemme know when's me turn wit 'er." He climbed down into the coldroom under the floor.

Suddenly, Yupi came to life, barking and snarling at Yot.

Yot was between Dreng and Thorhalla, his seax ready for an attack.

Thorhalla swung her axe at him and he leaped back in a comical, mocking fashion, just out of her reach. He laughed at her.

"Common! You wan' me, huh?" Yot thrust his hips out with his hands to the sides. Yupi jumped and snapped at him, pushing him off balance. Thorhalla swung the axe at Yot's ribs with all of her strength.

He parried with his seax, but she stabbed her apron knife full and deep into his belly.

"*Argh!* Bitch!" He swung his fist wildly and punched her nose. Thorhalla flew backward and landed hard on her head, sprawled unconscious on the floor. Yupi lunged and Yot stabbed the old dog in the throat, killing him instantly. Yot dropped the bloody weapon, then fell to his knees. He grabbed at the knife planted in his gut.

"De bitch stuck me!" he screamed.

Dreng stood beside the table, his mouth agape at the sudden turn of events. He carefully crept his way around the table.

"A-Are you alright, Yot?" he said, too trepidatious to get closer to the wounded man. Yot grabbed a hold of the knife protruding from his stomach and with a shrill yell, wrenched it out. A spurt of blood splattered onto the floor. He slumped sideways as he desperately clutched his abdomen, writhing in pain. The blood had soaked through Yot's coat.

Dreng's arm throbbed, his feverish head swam, and he felt nauseous. He lumbered to Yot and knelt beside him, but Yot put up his arm and pushed Dreng away.

"Don't touch me!" Yot screamed.

Thorhalla lay unconscious in a pool of blood, her nose clearly broken. Dreng could hear Mar banging around in the cellar.

"Mar!" he called out in desperation. "Get up here!"

"Tie tha' bish up," Yot slurred. His eyes began to droop from having lost so much blood.

Dreng used her bloody knife to hack strips of cloth from her dress, and tied her ankles together. Feverish and sweaty, he struggled to drag her over to the table by her heels. His head swam and he knew he wouldn't be able to lift her limp body onto the tabletop. He wiped his forehead with the back of his hand, shocked to find his skin burning with fever.

"No no no, I'm fine. Just... a headrush. I think I..." Bright blue spots squiggled before his eyes and darkness threatened to envelop him. He clenched his wounded arm as another throbbing pain shot up to his head. *Ignore it and it will pass.*

Dreng stumbled to his pile of cloth strips and snatched them up on clumsy, wobbly legs. Standing straight again nearly made him fall over.

Thorhalla sat up suddenly, her nose and lips caked with blood. Dreng yelped and lunged at her, trying to pin her to the floor in a bearhug.

"What are you—?" Thorhalla was still in a stupor, struggling against him. Dreng toppled on top of her, sobering her up, and her indignation quickly dissolved into rage.

"Get off of me, you *pig!*" She smashed her forehead into his nose. He shrieked as blinding pain engulfed his face and stumbled backward. She struggled to get her hand into her apron and pulled out a paring knife.

Dreng swayed, the pain in his nose fading slowly. Thorhalla sliced through the bindings with the precious moments she had, then jumped up and dashed toward the door. Through watering eyes Dreng saw the flash of her dress as she fled. He lunged and tackled her to the floor. They hit the floorboards hard, but Dreng kept his grip around her chest.

"Wha's goin' on up dere?" Mar called, through a mouthful of food, and banged on the floor from below.

Thorhalla couldn't move, but had one arm free below the elbow and she drove the knife down, plunging it into Dreng's thigh. He yelped, yet his grip held firm.

Thorhalla yanked the knife out and stabbed again. Dreng screamed, twisting to avoid having his leg butchered while keeping his weight on top of her.

She stabbed again and again, until he couldn't take any more. He rolled off her and she kicked him away. He grabbed his mangled leg as he screamed and writhed on the floor. Thorhalla scrambled to a chopping block near the hearth. A hatchet stood there, stuck into the wood, and she yanked it free, then turned to Dreng.

He was still screaming and clutching his leg, but saw she was about to charge at him with weapon in hand.

He turned himself around and got a toppled bench between them. She charged screaming, *"Die, you pig!"* She had the axe raised to strike and her bloodied face made a horrific visage.

Dreng kicked the bench at her and it caught her foot. She stumbled, hit the floor face down in front of him and the hatchet bounced into his hands. He rolled onto his good knee and brought it down hard onto the back of Thorhalla's exposed neck. The hatchet chopped through her spine with a sickening crunch, spraying Dreng with blood. He furiously chopped again and her head wobbled away from her shoulders.

He dropped the bloody hatchet and rolled over, wincing as he collapsed onto his back to catch his breath. *Come on! Breathe!*

The cellar ladder creaked and Mar poked his head up, munching on a strip of dried fish. He stopped chewing and swallowed hard.

"Wha' de fokka 'appen'd 'ere?" he shouted, eyes wide. "Look like t'was brawl in slaughterhouse. Yot dead, she dead. Even dog dead! Place are a disaster! An' look a' you. Pathetic fool! Bested by de milkmaid!"

Mar spat the words out, then laughed as he climbed up into the room.

"Tis quite funny, tha'. Was gonna kill ya anyway, an 'ere is ya crawlin' trew a pool o' blood. Not sure all tis yours, mind. Still, I's ta thank you, Frau Milkmaid, fer doin' me work easy." He nodded to her. "'Ad spected woman ta put up fight, but much better dan I's wot thought. Fook it! I's 'ave whats I's want." He held up two bulging hemp sacks of food. Mar carefully stepped over and around pools of blood, broken furniture, and smashed pottery on his way to the front door.

"What about me?" Dreng cried out. He winced as he rolled around and slid about in the sticky gore.

"Die!" Mar said with a bright smile. He stood there briefly, to really soak the moment in. Dreng could see the hatred in Mar's eyes.

"I'm cut bad, Mar!"

"I's tought you's weak coward *before,* an' proof 'ere shown to me own eyes."

"No! Please, help me!" Dreng begged. He did his best to crawl, but the pain from his injuries and loss of blood had already weakened him too much. A dark vignette encroached on Dreng's vision as his body was giving up on keeping him conscious. He could barely see the blurry image of Mar's large frame filling the door as he laughed.

Mar turned to leave, then stopped.

"Wha? Who you?" he said, startled to see a woman standing behind him. "Peace, woman."

"Help me," Dreng managed to say.

Without hesitation the woman thrust a spear through Mar's chest. Dreng was too weak to see the tip of her spear pierce the back of Mar's leather coat. But, he unmistakably witnessed Mar's lifeless body slump to the floor.

Dreng laid back and shook his head. *Captain Brokk wouldn't never'v made me a stooge,* he thought, before everything went dark.

CHAPTER ELEVEN

Curse for a Curse

The boy guiding Frigga's horse carried the oil lamp above his head, but it did little to cut through the inky dark. The frue couldn't see the narrow path they walked, snaking through the mountains. She pulled her cloak tighter against the cold and gripped the saddle as best she could. The thrall boy knew the way to the cave that Frigga swore she'd never visit again. Behind her horse walked his brother, leading a goat. He was an older boy of about twelve winters, though Frigga didn't care about his age. Her contempt for thrall wouldn't allow her to care about these disgusting boys in any way, so sickly and thin. As their frue, she expected only their service.

The light was too bright and painful for her to look at.

"You're holding the lamp wrong, it's blinding me!"

"Yes, Frue, forgive me!"

He lowered it, yet it still glared in her eyes, building an ache that pushed into her brain. Her annoyance was simmering, slowly condensing into rage.

"Stupid boy!" She raised her whip to lash him with, when the firekeeper's words flooded her mind, washing all other thoughts away.

The Grey Wolf in its den does laze—

"No!" She fought against the vision and shook her head defiantly, as though she were being forced to eat rotten flesh. But the vision bore down upon her, like an avalanche. Once started, the damned words — burned, not just into her mind, but into her very being — would continue until the janky poem's end. She shook as she fought against the depraved mysticism which had taken over her will. The vision surfaced, overwhelming her resistance and suffocated her under its crushing weight.

The Grey Wolf in its den does laze
As a western shadow blankets the sun.
All the king gives, a prince's sum
Repaid with blood and shallow graves.
Beauty is plain, as plain as yearning
Revealing no truth, nor a champion's name
He chases wild, or follows tame
Leaving the weaver's tables turning.
Logs grow ice beneath their pyres
On overgrown roads, death-feeders lament
Their nest doth burn, though the crows are content
When a stronger bird rises from out of those fires.

Frigga's chest was so tight it made her gasp and claw for breath. She was desperate to find a way to banish the unrelenting script from her mind. *The Grey Wolf in its den does laze... The Grey Wolf in its den does laze...* she tried repeating only the first line of it, hoping to create a cycle — though painful and relentless — that would obfuscate the entirety of the prophecy. Though, much like the lamp, it proved to be a tool whose uselessness was evident, though contemplating its abandonment was abhorrent. *TheGreyWolfinitsdentheGreyWolfinitsden!*

The words pressed against her mind and mashed against her skull, pummelling into an ache which had started when the firekeeper shackled her to the prophecy. The pain was worse than before, much worse. Fear consumed her completely, creeping into her mind through the muscles in her neck. She imagined it slowly twisting and crumpling her into an old hag, an unbearable horror that would only end with her death. She tried praying. *The Grey Wolf in its den. The Grey Wolf...*

"No!" Even prayer had become impossible, her thoughts no longer her own, usurped by the cursed prophecy.

"The warloga will know what to do. The warloga will know..." she muttered, over and over in an attempt to soothe herself.

The lamp's light was so garish, it seared through her eyes and into her inflamed brain.

"Hold that lamp— *Gaah!* Where is the warloga's cave, thrall?" Yelling sapped her strength.

"We here, lady," the younger boy said, his voice shrill. He stopped the horse and Frigga had to catch herself from falling off, the distraction so great. The cursed words had been etched by powerful seidr, obviously wielded against her by the firekeeper. Yet, even thoughts of vengeance had become impossible.

She reflexively looked around, though nothing could be seen in the inky dark. The oil lamp revealed a steep mountain cliff ascending into darkness on one side of the path, and descending into an ominous abyss on the other side. In front of her a natural archway of grey stone framed a black void, like the giant maw of a tormented soul. It gaped, forever frozen in terrible a scream; a warning to all who might consider entering.

"This is doorway to—" The boy hesitated and looked around nervously. He held a hand beside his mouth. "Warloga's lair, Frue," he whispered.

Frigga slid gracelessly from her horse. She pointed at the older boy.

"Bring the goat, and be careful with it! I do not want it to be harmed, do you understand me?"

The boy shuffled forward.

"Get up there!" She snapped, swatting the air. He scurried past with the goat trotting behind him. It bleated its displeasure. Frigga grabbed the lamp and wrenched it from the smaller boy's hand. He startled but dared not breathe, instead staring up at her, his eyes wide with fear.

Frigga's were thin slits, her nostrils flared.

"Watch the horse until I return, thrall. Should any harm come to it, I will have you and your brother flayed, do you understand?" She hissed the often repeated threat through clenched teeth.

The boy gulped and nodded vigorously, until Frigga thought his head might fall off. He gripped the lead rope and pulled the horse's muzzle closer. She stared daggers at the boy, forcing him to drop his eyes to the ground. She turned away before she could see the fat tears rolling off his cheeks, which would have only inflamed her wrath.

She looked back the way they'd come, searching the darkness for any signs they'd been followed.

The Grey Wolf in its den...

She grunted, then turned toward the cave's entrance. "Get moving!" she snapped, shooing the older boy ahead of her.

He swallowed hard. "B-But, Frue! Tis the den of the— Ugh! None have ever returned from there!"

The Grey Wolf in its den...

Frigga slapped the boy's cheek and he fell.

"Insolent fool! *I* have returned from the warloga's d-d..." Frigga wiped her mouth with her sleeve to hide her stumbling on the word. "I have all intentions of returning this time, as well. Now march! Or *I* will ensure you do not return. Would you like to see your family again? Your brother?" She pulled a thin dagger out and pointed it at him.

The boy shuddered and nodded.

"Then get up there! Make sure the path is clear for me."

Frigga knew the boy was right. No one but her had ever returned. All others found out too late the horrible bargain and terrible price the warloga demanded. But, she knew, and brought yet more this time.

Like a sheep leading a wolf into a mountain lion's den, the thrall boy crept into the cave with Frigga breathing down his neck. Stumbling on loose stones with shaky legs, he pulled the goat across the threshold of the cave, whispering prayers of mercy and protection.

Frigga was amazed that even then he still held on to naive hopes of salvation.

They carefully picked their way over rocks and debris, the putrid stench of rotten meat and mildew assaulting and choking them with every step. The foul air was moist, oily and sticky on Frigga's skin. The boy began to wretch. Frigga covered her nose with the perfumed nape of her cloak, though it gave little relief from the stench, alchemizing it into sweet sewage.

The damp walls glistened in the lamplight, and ominous silhouettes prowled along the dark hall, keeping outside of the lamplight. A chattering of insane whispers and the constant dripping of water all echoed through the chamber.

"Stay within the light, boy, or the shadows will drag you away. I do *not* want anything to happen to that goat, understand?"

It became increasingly colder as they stumbled their descent into the earth. The scattered detritus threatened to twist an ankle with any misstep. The boy tripped and fell hard on his hands and knees. He whimpered, too terrified to cry out his pain, and paused to collect himself before he would regain his footing on the harsh stone.

As Frigga caught up with the lamp, the dross he lay upon was revealed, made of gnawed and splintered bones; the skeletal remains of unfortunate creatures, small and large, strewn about the cave floor.

Directly in front of his nose lay a mouldering, fractured femur, large enough to have belonged to a full grown man. The boy clambered to his feet in panic, and clamped a filthy hand over his mouth. Frigga could only imagine what his thoughts were, of the wretched souls who'd become fodder for the horror lying in wait for them further down.

"Frue, I—"

"*Shhh!* Quiet, pest!"

He tried turning to run, but Frigga easily anticipated his rout and grabbed him by the scruff of his neck. She snatched him off his feet, and threw him roughly onto his rear.

"Do not test me, thrall," she spat. She yanked him up again and tossed him ahead of her like a doll.

He wept, hugging the goat's neck while cradling the lead rope close to his chest as they crept together, deeper into the blinding darkness. Worse than the void, were the shadows sliding through it just out of the light's reach; unfamiliar, gnarly shapes, darker than the empty nothingness.

The tunnel took them through the mountain side and spiralled down until it opened up into a large cavern. Throughout the subterrane, stalagmites stood like the jagged teeth of a leviathan.

"Frue! A light!" the boy said. She heard the relief in his voice and smiled at his misplaced comfort. Sure enough, a dim light from deeper within the cavity illuminated enough for them to see patches of the crude path ahead, as though it were floating in a sea of ink.

The goat bleated, just then, and the boy flinched. The beast's loud, warbled bleating echoed through the cavern. Something near the distant light shifted, and a monolithic, jagged shadow lumbered across the random folds of the cavern's wall. The boy froze, mouth agape unable to stifle his cry of surprise.

Frigga saw it, too. What appeared to have been a massive boulder was in fact the shoulders of a huge, squatting creature, and the goat had just announced their presence to it. She remained undeterred by the hellscape; Frigga knew with whom she had come to bargain, and was well aware of the price she'd need to pay. Would have gladly paid a hundred times more! No price was too high to unfetter her mind of the norn's prophecy.

The Wolf in its den— She recoiled from her thoughts, realising she'd had relief from them from the moment she'd entered the cave. This was why she was there, after all: to reckon with a devil for bitter salvation.

Do not resist the sooth, Jarl's woman, hissed a slow, beastly voice. It had forced its way into Frigga's head; a vile notion creeping alongside her own thoughts, with a frigid touch which stained hers coal black.

Come to Greip, Jarl's woman. Warm-fleshed oblation for Greip to slake the want, the voice slobbered. Its presence in her mind was a putrid slime oozing over top of her will, smothering it into submission.

She pulled a dark scarf from her cloak and tied it securely over the boy's eyes.

"This is for your protection. Do *not* take it off! One look at the warloga and it will turn you to stone," Frigga lied. The boy gasped.

She grabbed his arm and dragged him forward, until the warloga's den was in full view. The den was a refuse heap, scattered and stinking, with piles of bones and rot forming a crescent around a wide, smouldering fire pit.

The creature squatting in the middle of it all was Greip, the warloga. Hideously large and thin, with grey skin, scarred and afflicted with gangrenous pustules. Griep whispered to a rotten, decapitated head it held on a stick. Greip's own deformed head was much too large for its grotesquely sinewy body. Black, coarse hair sprouted in greasy wisps from its flaky scalp. More patches and strands grew across its back, like the bristles of a boar. One elongated ear pointed straight up, while the other was missing altogether, replaced by a thick, gnarly scar like a fleshy bubble. Black, beady eyes were set deep into its skull, and far too close together, pinching a massive, hooked nose. The nose dripped and ran with mucous, down puffy, wide lips, quivering like two slugs connected by tendrils of slime, flexing and spitting as Greip breathed through its gargantuan mouth. It kissed and nuzzled the shrunken head, whose tongue, swollen and blackened from rot, hung limp from its gaping jaw.

Frigga's more feral instinct was to keep her head low, but she knew not to take her eyes off the monster. She hauled the boy to where Greip squatted, dragging thrall and goat over the discarded bones and dross, accumulated over decades of lairing.

A grotesque, evil grin slithered across Greip's lips, and the creature quivered at the sight of Frigga's offering.

Greip stood and attempted to stretch out to its full height. Its bones and tendons cracked and snapped in protest, and a pronounced hunch kept it from straightening its bowed spine. Flies scattered when it moved and buzzed about its naked, filthy body. Rodents fled to find hiding places among the refuse.

Long, thickly matted hair sprouted from Greip's armpits and from between its legs. The warloga was easily twice the height of a man, even with the hunch.

Frigga tossed a bag of coins at Greip's feet.

It reached down with one clawed, sinuous hand to take the bag, and with the other plucked the goat, now screaming, off the ground, out of the startled boy's grasp. Greip squatted down again and curled its giant arms back in, like a vulture folding its wings to feast. It dropped the goat, then pressed it into the ground and crushed it down with its massive, clawed hands. The animal's scream was cut short with a sickening crunch.

Frigga blinked a few times at the abrupt violence, but dared not take her eyes off the warloga. The blindfolded boy covered his ears, startling at every noise, left to imagine what horror was happening around him.

Greip lifted the goat's fresh corpse and with a razor-sharp claw slit the animal's abdomen open. Its guts spilled out across the ground; Greip stirred the bloody offal with one clawed finger, and studied the mess of intestines with great interest. It whispered to the shrunken head, then listened for its reply.

The warloga let out a satisfied, grating sigh, happy with the head's report. Greip sat back on its haunches and idly poked holes into the dead goat's hide with its claws. Frigga was reminded of a child, absently playing with a toy. The goat's once white hair had quickly stained red.

"Speak, Jarl's woman!" Greip's deep voice boomed through the cavern. Frigga bristled. She loathed being referred to as a thing owned by her husband, like a horse or a thrall. She knew the creature's guile and the game it played to try and keep her off guard, to force her into making foolish mistakes. She was more cunning than that.

"Hail to you Greip, Warloga of the mountain," Frigga recited. "I come to ask for your aid."

"Again," Greip said and stared off into the distance, as the ambiguous word echoed back at them: *again, again, again...*

"Yes," she hissed. The simple word tasted bitter in her mouth. "I come to ask for your aid, *again.*"

Greip smiled with its eyes closed, savouring the moment with a groan of satisfaction.

"Yesss… again Jarl's woman come to Greip! The spider tangled in her web, for Greip to pull out, thread by thread. Thread by thread, spider web, hang you up until you dead! *Hahaha!*" Greip cackled and spit as it laughed and bobbed its head along with the childishly simple rhyme.

Greip suddenly plunged a clawed fist into the stinking pile, sending bones flying. Frigga and the boy started at the violent movement. Just as quickly, the warloga pulled out a fat, squealing rat the size of a small dog, squirming and twisting to get free. Greip bit the rodent's head off, crunching and chewing bones, gristle, and fur without prejudice. It moaned and licked gore off of its slimy lips with pleasure. Two more pulpy bites and the rat was gone.

Greip swallowed and smiled a sickening, gap-toothed grin. Bloody tendons and fur hung down like threads, trapped between decayed teeth, sharp and nasty, and as wide as flint arrowheads. Greip plunked a mortar made from a large, round stone between its feet, then began to carefully pick through the garbage and filth within its reach.

"Speak!" Greip bellowed. The arrogant word echoed through the cavern and pulsed in Frigga's mind as an ominous challenge.

Greip's grin had turned into a grimace, its gargantuan lips resembling the exaggerated expression of an angry catfish.

The wolf in its den— "I have been cursed!" Frigga blurted, shaking with fury. "A ragr firekeeper deceived me, using this!" She held up a small leather pouch.

"A clasp to bind," Greip said. It held the rotting head to its ear and nodded in consideration of the head's whispered council.

"He's inflicted a cruel punishment upon me!" Frigga said. "And my niece, my ladies-in-waiting, my servants! All had to be hidden away to keep their madness from infecting others. They speak no words other than the firekeeper's prophesy! Words that I-I..." They bubbled up in her mind again, torrential pain along with them. The foul air made her queasy and she started to swoon. *The Grey Wolf in its den does laze—* She did her best to hold everything in. "Ughh! No!"

"Speak it!" Greip demanded, leaning in hungrily as though it knew her thoughts. "She must say it!" It held its clawed hands out; a grotesque midwife zealous to deliver a stillbirth.

Frigga trembled and gasped for breath. Then, she let go; surrendering to the first time she'd spoken them out loud. A pang of the embarrassment of her affliction, such as she hadn't felt since childhood, was quickly trampled as the words of the prophecy stampeded over her:

"The Grey Wolf in its den does laze
As a western shadow blankets the sun.
All the king gives, a prince's sum
Repaid with blood and shallow graves.
Beauty is plain, as plain as yearning
Revealing no truth, nor a champion's name
He chases wild, or follows tame
Leaving the weaver's tables turning.
Logs grow ice beneath their pyres
On the overgrown road, death-feeders lament
Their nest doth burn, though the crows are content

When a stronger bird rises from out of those fires."

Frigga fell to her knees, like a marionette amputated of its strings.

Greip held the decapitated head to its ear, cooing as though a lover whispered seductive honey. The warloga shook with a malign chuckle which grew into a laughter that echoed throughout the caverns.

"Tell me what it means!" Frigga shrieked, no longer able to hide her desperation. "Do not mock me, warloga..." She trailed off, gasping to catch her breath. Fatigue had gripped her mind with its steely claws and filled her body with lead.

Greip continued to sneer as it scooped up a collection of filth from the ground and dropped it into a depression in the stone between its clawed feet. Satisfied, the warloga pounded and ground it all together with a stone pestle.

"Greip is know of this hex; this... fire-keep trick," it spat. "Best to Greip you came, Jarl's woman. Curse Greip can break, like children bones. Easy! But this not just curse-full be, no! Also warn for Jarl's woman. Warn from Norns. Warn from Weave!"

"Do not test me with riddles, warloga," Frigga said. She laboured to rise back up to her feet. "I know you are able to read the minds of women, but *not* the minds of men. Twenty of my best spear-men — each one loyal kin, mind — await my return at the entrance to your hole. I had no need to give them orders to hunt you down and kill you should I not return, for they are all more than willing to volunteer and would happily compete for the task. I am just as prepared to go and tell them to do the deed regardless!"

Greip let a large gob of spit drool down from its lips into the mortar, then continued grinding.

"Not mock, Jarl's woman. Greip speak how Greip can. A warn, is this curse. Yesss, Greip is know cure, make of cunning for Jarl's woman. Curse Greip make, for curse Greip take." Greip threw its head back with rasping laughter, then launched forward again with a violent coughing fit.

"Then tell me!" Frigga's words reverberated through the cavern, and spidery shadows crept closer along the walls. She flinched when something brushed her ankles, but dared not to look.

Greip whispered to the shrunken head, then put it to its ear to listen, nodding at the answers. "Beware the Autumn Feast! Your king is too trust of war-bringer who come from West, and trust is breaked into trap! A great price your Jarl will pay." Greip listened more.

"All the king gives," Frigga mumbled, " a prince's sum, repaid with blood and shallow graves..."

Greip nodded and giggled at the decapitated head's whispers. "He leaves for beautiful woman. *Hahaha!* She is lies! Still, he follows; to you hands kingdom, ruined!"

Frigga's eyes went wide as the prophecy's riddle unravelled, as though the warloga had turned a key and thrown open a chest to reveal the stock within. "Beauty is plain, as plain as yearning, revealing no truth, nor a champion's name, he chases wild, or follows tame, leaving the weaver's tables turning..." She shuddered against the tears breaking through her meticulously cultivated demeanour.

"There be death. None to carry, none to bury!" Greip licked its quivering lips as it listened to the grizzly storyteller.

"Logs grow ice beneath their pyres, on overgrown roads, death-feeders lament..." A tear ran down Frigga's cheek as she remembered Hamund's final voyage through purifying flames.

"But, stronger! Rise from ashes! Glorious and terrible!"

"A phoenix," Frigga whispered. She could see Ulfer rising up, more powerful than ever. Perhaps Hamund himself? "Tell me, Warloga! What is your council?" she said. "This prophecy is from the Norns, a destiny which is as fixed as a thread within the fabric of life! A thread which *cannot* simply be plucked from the loom. The Autumn Feast is but days away! Do I have every stranger arrested? The people will revolt. Ulfer will think me mad!"

"Leave! Divorce Jarl and leave!"

Frigga ground her teeth and shook, pressing her clenched fists against her sides.

"No! Ulfer is to choose brides for Ormer from the noble ätt, I *must* be there! I am Frue! To show disloyalty to Ulfer would be shameful and the nobles would see it as weakness within his house." She closed her eyes and forced a few breaths in and out.

The warloga nodded slowly, a grim smile growing on its barren face. "Ohhh! Ohohohohh! Leave you can not. Too much enemy. Too much dead. Jarl's nephew, no?" Greip snickered.

Frigga clamped her eyes tight, but the tears leaked past. "Please," she whispered, her voice pitiful, a limping repetition through the cavern.

Greip smiled and shook with excitement. "*Hahahahaaa!* Greip know! Hahaha! Yessss! Many comes to feassst. Praise Jarl, do they? Honour son as next jarl, do they? Scheme, do they. Profit, do they! Jarl know. Weak wolf never becoming grey. Jarl know. Know profit. Jarl's woman show Jarl better than profit, much better! Show lost. Lost gold have greatest price. Show Jarl war-bringer weak! Jarl's woman welcome is give! Pity is give! Honour is give, all to war-bringer!" Greip croaked, then cleared its sinuses with a snort which would have frightened a boar. It swallowed hard. "Toast is give, with wine, and wine is trap does Jarl's woman weave."

Greip picked up the goat's carcass and held it over the mortar and hummed to itself as blood dribbled into the depression in the stone, until it was to the brim. The carcass was tossed aside and Greip stirred the dross within the mortar with one claw, as it whispered and incanted. The air felt heavy and thick with a dark magik Frigga had only been in the presence of twice before, from the same creature: just after Ormer's birth, and then after Hamund's death.

"Clasp to bind," Greip said and held out its other clawed hand. Frigga opened the small pouch, then poured it into the warloga's claw. The broach the firekeeper had used fell out.

"A clasp to bind," she said.

Greip looked at the silver jewellery and grunted, then dropped it into the foul mixture and continued stirring. The warloga sat back on its haunches and closed its beady eyes. It whispered incantations of evil origins to the shrunken head. The voodoo crept like spiders from the warloga's festering lips and filled the head's rotten ear. Greip spoke in an evil, forbidden language; praising dark powers, making salacious promises, begging for hidden knowledge. This practice was one of the primordial magiks of the giants; not seidr, but pure, unbridled evil.

The slough continued to swirl on its own, stirred by an unseen hand. It transformed from an inky, sticky paste, into a crumbling dough, before settling into its final form.

The warloga croaked and opened its eyes. The mixture had become a smooth, glistening slab, resembling a cow's liver, shivering and undulating in the stone bowl. Greip scooped the thing out of the mortar and slapped it down with a loud *blat!* then tore through the putrid organ with its sharp claws.

The thing jiggled and shook, oozing filth and puss as Greip sliced through layers of fibrous membrane. Greip grunted at having found what it was looking for. With its claws together in a delicate grasp, Greip cooed as a mother would to her newborn and coaxed the small object out of the eviscerated offal. Greip held it up in front of Frigga's face, the jewellery dripping with mucus. It was her broach, though the silver had become obsidian and the veins of the carved inscriptions on the surface were stained a deep red.

The warloga cackled and dropped it onto a dirty rag, then grabbed up what was left of the oozing mess. It squeezed ichor from the unnatural organ to dribble into a small pot made from a dented helmet, then placed the pot onto the hot coals.

The warloga hummed as it gently shook the pot over the coals. A greenish vapour curled from it, and a reek that bit Frigga's nose as it crawled into her stomach to make her wretch. The boy vomited and Frigga slapped him.

"Control yourself —*ulp!*" She swallowed what she'd regurgitated.

Greip rummaged through the refuse again and pulled out a

bulbous dark green bottle, then carefully poured the steaming liquid into it. Then Greip jammed a cork in and shook the bottle. Once satisfied, the beast folded the cloth with the broach into a small bundle. It held the bundle up and looked Frigga in the eye. Frigga forced herself to stand straight and tall, fighting against her desire to run, to hide from the warloga's gaze, from its hypnotic, yellow, bloodshot eyes.

"This is 'a clasp to bind' for cloak. *Then*, little spider, war-bringer is in trap! Cloak become slave collar," Greip hissed.

Frigga swore she saw a twinkle in the monster's eye. Then, it held up the bottle. "This only for Jarl. A sweet wine will he taste, '*Exotic!*' Jarl's woman says, and fills his skol. He drinks, is a *gooood* on the tongue, but a fester in the belly. His anger it is — to rage and destroy! Freyja's voice her hears, a fester in the ear: "Odin gives call! Wage ever-war! More servants to battle! More warriors for Odin's hall!" A fester in the eye: ugly and wicked broach-wearer be, and Jarl sees only enemy! '*Thrrraaall!*'" Greip arched its back in an obscene manner as the word echoed throughout the cavern, again and again, like a foul tide.

The echo died and Greip wiped the dripping spittle from its mouth. "Wine turn Jarl to see evil in broach-wearing war-bringer. More powerful than seidr, is this. Jötnar magiks, is this! By word of Jarl war-bringer is made slave. Prophecy broken! Jarl's woman is save of kingdom. Sneaking hero of kingdom! *Power of kingdom!*" The giant held up its clawed fists in triumph, as its voice reverberated through the cavern.

Frigga reached for the bundle, and Greip pulled away, wagging its bony finger. "Ah ah aaahhh!"

Frigga got hot under her collar and shot the warloga a look of death.

"New magiks, new price," the warloga hissed. Before Frigga could protest it held up the bundle with the broach in one claw and the bottle in the other and waggled them like children's toys.

Controlling her rage, Frigga forced herself to look at the warloga.

She nodded. "Fine. What is your new price, then?"

An evil grin spread across Greip's lips as it turned its attention to the thrall. The young boy stood alone, blind and silent, shivering in the cold, too terrified to do any more. Greip salivated and Frigga could see the lust in the beast's eyes. Without another thought she nodded once, thrusting her hands toward the warloga. Greip cackled, then dropped the evil treasures into her hands.

Then the monster pounced on the boy.

"Nooo! Frue?!"

Frigga ignored his begging and shrieks of terror as Greip uncontrollably molested and ravished the child. She turned with her prizes and walked back along the passage. *The boy is only thrall, I have no more use for him,* she thought, as his screams reverberated through the hellhole. She held the lamp up higher and the creatures hiding in the dark scattered and shrank from the light.

The oil lamp burned itself out just as Frigga left the cave. She gasped in fresh air and collapsed to her knees. The lamp smashed as she caught herself, cutting her hand on the stone. *The Grey Wolf in its den does laze...* The pain had resumed. She clutched the treasures she'd bought with the thrall boy's life; a forlorn hope for the answer to her dread.

"Help me up!" she panted.

The young boy with the horse startled awake and dashed to help her to her feet. Frigga groaned and leaned heavily on the boy as she hobbled to the horse.

"Get down, I need to stand on your back."

He fell on his hands and knees so Frigga could use him as a stepping stool. She heaved herself onto the pony, hugging its neck and laying her face in its mane.

The boy rose up onto his knees, looked around and blinked.

"Where Aren?" he asked, his voice pitched with distress.

"He was just behind me, but got stuck. You need to go in and help him." Frigga spurred the horse.

"Aren!" he called, carefully picking his way through the dark, toward the mouth of the cave. "Where are you? I'm coming, Aren!"

It wasn't long before the clop of hooves drowned out the young boy's desperate cries. His family were thrall. They wouldn't dare to ask about the boys.

She lay on the horse, summoning all of her will to make it back home before she'd pass out. The bundle she tucked between her arm and the horse, and clung to the mane with the other hand.

The Grey Wolf in its den does laze…

Her salvation lay in a plan conjured within the mind of madness. She was committed by desperation to find liberation there.

CHAPTER TWELVE

The Call

O dd left the chieftess' quarters many hours later. The women were still in the hall, drinking and eating; a customary feast for the dead. Some had rubbed ash paste on their hands and face while in prayer, grief shawls and hoods covering their heads.

Gudrun sat at the back. Of all the people she could be thinking of — papa, Sigurd, mama, Erich — she couldn't stop thinking about Gils.

Odd stopped at the fire and said a prayer. She made an offering of dried herbs to the coals and waved the smoke over herself. She bowed, then walked over to Gudrun and sat beside her, placing a wool shawl over her nieces' shoulders.

Gudrun startled with a sharp breath. The soft blanket was warm.

"Thank-you, aunty."

"I'm glad you came back, my little *sæta*," Odd said. "I've missed you. I have some things for you."

Four women sang a haunting lament by the hearth and the hall was quiet as everyone took in their sorrowful harmonies. The fire burned low and they leaned on each other, as they'd done so many times already that year.

"Come with me," Odd whispered. She gestured for Gudrun to

follow her to a quiet corner, where they could talk alone.

Odd turned and swept Gudrun up in her arms. Gudrun startled, but as they remained quiet and held each other, she trembled with sorrow. Memories of Huginn's vision of the ship and the evil fylgja[6] on a blood-red ocean flashed in her mind. *He showed me, and I fought against it! What have I done?*

Odd gently shook Gudrun by the shoulders, "Hey! Where are you? Look upon my face. An unbalanced boat will tip and sink. Seidr is the river of mystical energies, sometimes a trickle, other times a torrent! Let go of your anchors; sail the tides."

Gudrun nodded.

"You pause. I understand." Odd sighed. "Your father came to see me last night."

"How? That's not possible," Gudrun gasped.

"As a haugbui, from Rán's ocean kingdom."

Gudrun turned away.

"He drowned," Gudrun whispered. She fidgeted with worn threads on her sleeve.

Odd was solemn.

"I have something for you." She pulled a rolled up blanket from her cloak, and placed it in Gudrun's arms.

"For your horse."

Gudrun opened it up. She'd never seen its like; black fabric that shimmered even in the dim light in their corner of the hall, with figures of horses that ran when the cloth moved.

"I-I don't have a horse."

"You mean, "Thank you Aunty, the blanket is beautiful," and yes you do have a horse, I saw you riding it."

"Oh, Embla. No, I don't want that horse."

Odd shrugged. "Then keep it as a sleeping blanket. It's better for a horse, though."

"Maybe I'll give it to Siv."

---

[6] The part of the spirit which is personified as an animal.

"No. This is my gift to *you*. I chose *you* to keep it."

"Oh. Well, thank you Aunty, the blanket is beautiful."

They hugged, then listened to the women sing a mournful song of resurrection, a reminder of the immortality awaiting in Valhall. It called back to life those who hadn't been chosen, that they may be able to do greater deeds and be chosen for Odin's hall in the next battle.

Odd took in a few deep breaths.

"Are you feeling ill?" Gudrun said.

"There's something else," Odd said. "Your father told me to give you a spear."

"Oh?" Gudrun stiffened. *She knows about Skera-Brynja!*

"I believe his intention was for you to have a battle spear." Odd paused. Gudrun's eyes darted between the floor and the doors.

Odd narrowed her eyes as she studied her niece with a quizzical expression. Odd had given her that look many times in the past, although Gudrun had only ever caught it in glimpses; yet again, she ducked her head to avoid it, choosing instead to focus on the blanket.

"Does the name 'Geirahöd' mean anything to you?" Odd said.

"No." Gudrun pursed her lips and shook her head. *What a fool I am! Why did I come back? Of course aunt Odd knows!*

"I see," Odd said. She gave Gudrun a small stick of bark with the runes scratched on the inside. "Those are the runes the haugbui showed me."

"Geir... spear... Spear of Battle? A woman."

Odd nodded. "He said "Give this to her". I don't know what it means, but... maybe you've already figured it out?"

Gudrun flinched away from her aunt's sly look. *What did she mean by that?*

"Here, take this." Odd gave her a dried sprig of oregano from her satchel. "Lay it on the fire with the questions on your heart. Your mind will cleanse, and answers will come."

Gudrun nodded and stood quickly, anxious to get away before

her aunt could draw up any more questions. She walked to the fire, holding the herb in both hands. Her head spun. *Does she or doesn't she know about Skera-Brynja? Aunt Odd is powerful. And, even papa knows I've failed! He must have told her—*

Gil's mother, Audhilde, sat on the floor comforting her daughters, one sleeping under each arm, exhausted from grief. Gudrun's breath caught in her chest. The handle of her seax, the way it felt when the blade sliced through Gils' throat, made her gut twist with guilt.

She shuddered and snapped her head forward. *Gods no, nonono!* She walked straight ahead to the fire. She teetered and stiffened to hide it. Her guilt was revealed with each wobbly step, she knew it. *How can I tell her? How can I not?! If I do, they'll find out I lost Skera-Brynja! They'll call me cursed, and then...* She knew what would happen next: she would be forced to endure one of the Trials of Innocence. Every one of them brought terror, pain, and death. *Fire. Always fire.*

She tripped on the hearth and caught her balance on one of the posts. If the dried sprig in her hand could have talked it would have been screaming. *The questions on my heart. What questions are on my heart? Does Odd know? Papa? Papa said 'Geirahöd', not 'Skera-Brynja'...* She laid the herb onto the hot coals and it curled and smoked before catching fire.

She took a deep breath. "Who is Geirahöd?" Gudrun said.

The name shot through the hall like a hammer on a bell. It rang in their ears and the room went dark. The women screamed.

"I'm blind!" "As am I!"

The fire and lanterns around the hall had been blanketed by some unnatural shadow.

"Stay calm!" Odd said, her voice strong above the rest.

A light grew from under Gudrun's tunic, until it shone bright enough as rays from between the weave of the cloth. *Mama's pendant!* She covered it with her hand and pulled her cloak tight.

A wind picked up and swirled about the room, growing strong

enough to smash goblets and dishes. The women yelped and covered their heads, veiling their faces from the swirling ash and dirt. Benches, chairs and tables skidded across the floor and slammed into the walls. The women screamed each time a bench smashed.

"What evil is this?", "Völur, what is happening?"

In the rafters a bright light flared up, blinding them. A ball of blue fire twisted, swirled and spun, growing larger and larger until an opening formed at its centre. The ball stretched into a burning, blue ring.

Within the ring they saw into another world: a turbulent red sky roiling over a blasted and burned land. Two armies clashed on a chaotic and grisly battlefield. Thousands upon thousands battled on each side.

"Ragnarok is upon us!"

The women cried out in terror.

If gods were to be considered great warriors, then the battle they witnessed was being fought by the greatest. Fierce, blue skinned dervishes spun and whirled with blades and spears, crashing against knights in brilliant armour, fighting with swords, axes, and shields, all of it flashing under a red sun.

One such knight suddenly appeared: a helmeted warrior goddess, streaking down from the firmament on strong, white wings.

"A Valkyrie, in flesh and steel!" Odd cried, and fell to her knees.

The Valkyrie pounced, like a lioness, with a piercing battle cry lashing the women's ears and slicing through their hearts. She struck with her battle-lance through the flames.

Within the span of a thought, the sublime weapon announced itself, with a terrifying celestial voice:

I, Heartseeker, holy lance, instrument of gods, pierce and cut the terrible hearts of my master's foes, without error; know of my glory and tremble before my might! For I am Heart Seeker, Harbinger of Death!

The Valkyrie's stunning shriek knocked them to the floor as she dived through the flaming ring. She thrust Heart Seeker down and it smashed into the hall's hearth, piercing through stones and timbers like rotten cloth. Hot coals and stone chips showered the air from its force, and the impact threw the women tumbling back.

Then, her shield announced itself:

All hail Adamant! Bastion against my master's foe; unwavering wall of might; "Hold fast the line!" is my cry, as my enemies are crushed against my bulwark!

The warrior dropped to the floor and the boards groaned under her weight. She stood, tall as a giant, the white comb atop her open-faced battle helm brushing the rafters. Her armour flashed and gleamed bright blue in the fire's light. Her wings folded into a brilliant cape made of swan feathers, which swept down to the floor. They shimmered and fluttered with every breeze.

Her plate armour spoke next:

I, Stoneskin, protect the divine. Pure of heart; font of courage. The arrow breaks upon my breast, the spear and sword turn, blunted against my plate. Beyond bravery, beyond pride, beyond fierce love is where I was claimed, and from such a station shall I forever be ready to serve!

The helm, with its white comb falling down to the Valkyrie's knees, announced itself then:

I am The Tear of Mourning. Tremble! For I am the last which my master dons; the warrior's crown; ready for battle and death. My visage rallies Her sisters to fight, and strikes fear into the hearts of the enemy; a demon, they see, and cry in terror, for the warrior before them: death's mistress.

The dust thinned and the Valkyrie pulled her spear, Heart Seeker, from the ruins of the hearth. She stood over the crater and looked about frantically.

"Görilf! *No!* How hast thou escaped my vengeance, scourge? What sorcerous evil be this trap thou hast devised?" She reached up to the flaming ring and it burned her hand.

"Cursed foil! Yet now, Odin's skill shall be tested. Lo! Even wings are clipped! Cunning magic. A trap not for death, yet doth syphon urgency, marking the likeness of a dungeon."

The immortal looked around the room with caution.

Something caught her eye.

She flipped a table over, exposing a huddled group of women. They shrieked in terror as she leaned in to examine them.

"Askr's lineage? How came I to Midgard? Am I chosen to harvest rotten fruit while I lead Odin's battle?"

She turned to see Gudrun, covering her chest.

"What be this here?" The Valkyrie took one large step, reaching Gudrun from across the hall. She stooped down and pulled open Gudrun's cloak. The pendant under her tunic shone with a bright white light.

Gudrun trembled. The silver and gold of the Valkyrie's armour gleamed in the eerie blue flames. A crimson sash trimmed with gold adorned her chest, like a blood-red gash raked from shoulder to waist.

The Valkyrie spoke directly into Gudrun's mind: *Twas thou, who hadst given the reaper's call? Stolen away mine glory? Thou hast turned the tide of battle to mine enemy's favour! Be thee a god? To wrench me from such a task — as set by Odin! Sanctified by Norns; honour-bound in blood— Oh, pray that thine divinity be set, wretched fool! That thy sacrifice doth please the—* The Valkyrie looked about the hall, just as confused as she was disgusted. *What evil be this?*

Gudrun fell to the side, withered and stunned by the demigoddess' wrath. The giant searched more intently. Around posts and under a table. She looked between her feet.

Where is the offering?

"I-I don't understand, Great Reaper," Gudrun said.

Odd stared at Gudrun, mouth and eyes wide.

My patience be not allied to thine cause, woman! The worthy champion. The corpse! Thou canst have summonsed me bereft of one who's been slain in battle! The offering, knave! Where hast thou slain it?

The Valkyrie stomped about the hall, sending the huddled women to scatter and get as far away from her as possible, some running from the building, screaming.

Gudrun was stunned and overwhelmed, a pain that ached away her resolve and made her want to crawl into a ball until it all went away. She prostrated herself before the Valkyrie.

"Forgive me, Lady of Judgement," she said. "I have no offering." Gudrun pressed her forehead to the floor, her body like lead.

"Gudrun!" Odd gawked at her.

Apologies do not spin gold in Asgard, fool! I shall render thy life forfeit! Sit up! Face punishment for thy blunder, oaf! I wouldst mark thy face and keep knowledge of thy rough and ugly features.

The words boomed and echoed in Gudrun's head. She swayed as they blasted her mind and sapped her strength. *I've got... to sit...* Her arms shook as she pushed herself upright.

Geirahöd held Heart Seeker's blade under Gudrun's chin. The Valkyrie's Cheshire grin shone in the evil blue light, stretching from ear to ear.

"No!" Odd screamed. The Valkyrie ignored her.

And, dost thou attempt to keep treasures hid beneath thine vestment? With a deft, surgical stroke of the Spear tip, Geirahöd flicked away the toggles of Gudrun's tunic. The pendant fell out as the toggles clattered to the floor.

Gudrun shivered, a convulsion from her neck down her spine, as though ice had dropped down her back.

Tis a curious trinket. The Valkyrie reached for the pendant.

Gudrun's hair stood on end and a tingling skittered across her skin. Sparks, like blue threads, leaped from the talisman, and an arch of lightning struck Geirahöd's hand. She yanked her arm back and struck the ceiling with her elbow.

"*Gaah!* Thou darest attack *me?!*" The building shook and the women cowered further. Geirahöd flexed her hand, and bored holes into Gudrun's skull with her eyes.

Speak thy name, girl! Geirahöd demanded, with Heart Seeker's blade under Gudrun's chin.

"Gudrun," she whispered, trembling. The blade hummed and

buzzed, crackling with a magical intensity Gudrun could feel pricking against her skin, like sparks off of burning wood, but... cold. Intensely cold. Gudrun closed her eyes and swallowed hard. *Can't turn away! Whatever I do,* she thought.

Speak it, troll! The curse thy father uttered at thy birth! Lest it be a shame that thy voice could ill afford to have land so offensively upon godly ears!

"Gudrun Thorkildatter of Lutvin!" Gudrun shouted defiantly, droplets of spit crackling off Heart Seeker's blade. She locked eyes with Geirahöd — the Valkyrie's black and primal like a shark's.

Geirahöd sneered. *Insolent fool! Gudrun Thorkildatter of Lutvin, Heart Seeker marks thy name. But naught a god's mercy wouldst halt its path. Low! Doth it pierce thy ribs! Low! Doth it freeze thy heart within thy breast! Mine aim fairs true, shouldst a knave's doubt fall upon this news, though neither folly nor pause for wisdom cull the Tree to its own task. And so the terrible arm shall flash, though just the once. Proof is blessed Heart Seeker's burden, and therein shall thine answer lay: truth upon cold earth, among consorts of death-feeders and a host of consolatory worms.*

Geirahöd looked at Odd and communicated directly to her. *Thou dost escape not the sight of Tyr, völur! Hadst thou eyes not over Skuld's weave to foretell of such calamity? Mayhap thine head hadst brimmed and sloshed from testing giddy broth and fairy sponges? A poor tutelage dost the blind master scourge upon apprentices of a mindful eye.*

"Forgive, goddess!" Odd prostrated herself with her forehead on the floor.

The Valkyrie blew into the air, creating another mighty gust of ethereal wind to howl through the hall and smash more furnishings.

A piercing, white light burst forth from the Valkyrie's otherwise lifeless, obsidian eyes, and a blinding column of light fired through the ceiling.

All of the women cowed on the floor, covering their heads to protect themselves from the flying objects and furniture. Then, the demigoddess' words penetrated the minds of all who were there:

Let it be known to thee: Gudrun Thorkildatter is branded outlaw and shall receive an outlaw's comfort, for as long as thou dost value peace in thy home. Who gives't an outlaw relief or aid, shall suffer likewise condemnation. Mark my words well, scribes, on vellum or in song, lest Lutvin burn!

In a final, blinding flash the hall went dark. The wind stopped and everything crashed to the floor. The women yelped then fell silent.

Everything was black, quiet.

"Is anyone hurt?"

A shout pierced the dark and started a spate as they fumbled about in the dark, their vision slowly coming back to them in the hall's dim light.

"What does this mean, völur?"

"The Valkyries are real! We all saw her with our eyes!"

Some of them crept to the blasted hearth, gripped by a euphoria of spiritual revelation.

"We've been chosen! Our men have been sacrificed that we may be Odin's chosen!"

They fell to their knees, intoning prayers, tearing at their clothing and smearing ash on their bodies. They touched the stones that had been rented apart, venerating them.

"Heart Seeker, Her holy blade, cut these rocks like a reaper's scythe slashing through wheat!"

Others were gripped with terror and stayed hidden under the furniture. Shock clouded all of their minds with confusion. They'd all heard the Valkyrie's words, clearly spoken into their minds, but to make sense of any of it seemed monumental.

They helped each other out from under the debris.

Vigdis burst into the room and froze, speechless. She gawked at the hearth, split in two, and the enraptured women kneeling there, crying, laughing, embracing anyone within reach.

The wreckage remained, though the demigoddess had vanished. So, too, had Gudrun.

CHAPTER THIRTEEN

For a spear

The snorting of a horse made Gudrun turn to see who it was coming up behind her on the dark, muddy track. She really didn't need to look, she already knew.

"So you got my message," she said.

Siv looked at her older sister thoughtfully from on top of Ivor Jomann's horse. Embla was taller than most, though smaller than those rumoured to run wild in Albion. Their silhouette cut a handsome pair. Siv was slight, and astride Embla the two were proportionate.

"No. What message?" Siv replied flatly, with a grimace.

"Then how did you find me? Did anyone follow you?" Gudrun said, scanning the darkness behind Siv.

"No. I ran home and saw you in the shadows, sneaking out toward the wall—"

"And through the gap?" Gudrun demanded, furious that Siv — anyone, really — had found her so easily. "But, how did you know which way I went?."

"I just followed you," Siv shrugged. "Which other way could you have gone?"

"You can't come with me," Gudrun said. She turned and continued walking. "I'm an outlaw now. The Valkyrie forbade you from helping me."

"She didn't say *me.*"

"Anyone from Lutvin, Siv! That includes you. You can't be thinking of turning me in."

"No. And, don't flatter yourself, I'm not going with you," Siv said, deadpan.

Gudrun stopped. "This isn't a joke! If you help me, the Valkyrie will kill you."

"Yes, I understand. That's fine, because I'm not helping you. *I* happen to be travelling this way, and you would be doing me a great service if you helped *me.* The Valkyrie did not say anything about you not being able to help others. We'll make a contract; I'll pay you by allowing you to ride with me." Siv smiled at Gudrun, a squinty-eyed grin from ear to ear.

Gudrun jerked her head back in surprise. "Siv, I—"

"And as a favour to you, I will allow you to help by collecting the firewood, cooking meals, and doing the washing," Siv said.

Gudrun crossed her arms across her chest. "Oh, very generous! And do I even want to know what you'll be doing?"

"I will take care of Embla, protecting my investment and your wages," Siv said, beaming.

Gudrun gave her a hard glare. "It's still Embla, is it? You know Hildegunn won't let you keep the horse. There's no hay to winter it. Ivor said she won't work, so she'll have to be sacrificed in *Gormánuður.*"

"Hey! Don't say that in front of her! And, you know I hate it when you call mama 'Hildegunn'," Siv said, pantomiming her mother's name with a sour face. "She's your mother too, not just mine, and if that's not enough to garner respect from you, I'll remind you that she's also papa's wife!"

"Not anymore," Gudrun grumbled.

Siv gasped. "Gudrun!"

"Forget it. It's just hunter's humour. Papa would have laughed."

Siv frowned as she picked at Embla's shaggy head and stroked her mane. Gudrun read her mind. She, too, did not want to think about Gormánuður — slaughter month. They were already in *Haustmánuður* — sheep-gather month — and Gormánuður was only the next full moon away.

"Are you coming with me or not?" Siv asked quietly.

Gudrun was studying the mud. Her feet were freezing. "I don't even know where you're going," she shrugged.

"Embla and I are going this way," Siv said. "Where are *you* going?"

"To Fellthorpe."

"Oh. Why there?"

"To get help. It's been many years but we still have kin there. A talented blacksmith lives in Fellthorpe who's said to have been raised by the black dwarves, the greatest smiths in all of Yggdrasil[7]. They taught him the secret wisdom of their craft and I'm going to get him to make me a new spear."

"By the gods!" Siv exclaimed. "That's the very place where I'm heading!" She smiled, a big grin that made her eyes sparkle. Gudrun shook her head. She didn't like this, but she also dreaded doing all this on her own.

"It's not going to be easy, Siv. I'm an outlaw in Lutvin. News travels fast, and I'll have to move faster. I could be attacked by anyone looking for a reward or to gain a slave."

Siv nodded enthusiastically. Gudrun frowned.

"Didn't you hear me? If you're with me, you'll be attacked, too."

Siv shrugged. "You'll protect me. You took out a whole ship! You summoned a Valkyrie! Who can touch us?"

Gudrun took a deep breath. "Siv, that was not— you don't understand. *I* don't understand!" All Gudrun could think about when she remembered the ship was having thrown Skera-Brynja away. It spoke, and she threw it away. *But, spears aren't supposed to speak.*

---

[7]   Tree of Life — the entire universe

Siv had that pleading look on her face which she'd cultivated since childhood.

"Fine. But, I'm in front." Papa couldn't resist that face, either.

"Yes!" Siv shouted. She slid off Embla's back and landed lightly on her toes.

As Gudrun walked to Embla's side the horse recoiled slightly. They didn't have a saddle so Gudrun laid the blanket Odd had given her over Embla's back.

"Oh! That's so beautiful!" Siv gushed. "The golden thread on the black cloth... this looks like one of Aunty Odd's."

Gudrun nodded. "She gave it to me in the hall."

Siv ran her hand over the cloth; black so deep that the weave could barely be seen. Images of Sleipnir[8] were stitched in gold thread all along the edges.

Gudrun put her hands on Embla to vault up, but she whinnied and pulled away.

"Not this game again," Gudrun said, through clenched teeth. She stayed with Embla as she sidestepped Gudrun's attempts to mount.

Siv grabbed the halter and cooed. "*Shhh shhh!*" She petted Embla's muzzle until the mare calmed.

"Huh," Gudrun grunted. She cautiously patted Embla's back and when she was satisfied that the horse would stay still, she vaulted up.

Embla shuffled, but remained calm in Siv's hands.

"Good!" Gudrun nodded and smiled at Siv, adjusting the reins in her hand. "You really do have a way with this nag." She laughed, then offered her hand to help Siv up.

As they rode, Siv chattered away. Gudrun just let her talk.

She could only admit to herself that she was glad to have Siv there, but was unable to say it out loud. Siv was so charismatic. She could speak in a crowd without fear or hesitation, something

---

[8]   Odin's grey eight legged horse, and one of Loki's children. The "best of all horses", Sleipnir translates to "Slippy" or "Slipper", indicating that he is very fast and can slip between the realms.

Gudrun was terrified of. Beyond fair, unconsciously graceful, Siv was extremely good at getting people to like her. *Just like papa,* Gudrun thought. She preferred the solitude of hunting, the quick action of the bow. She smirked. *Just like papa.*

Her thoughts kept collapsing back to him and the Valkyrie. Then, Magnor's ship and Skera-Brynja. She'd practically *given* it away! The spear that had protected the clan for more than a hundred years. She tried convincing herself she'd had good reason, but the excuse felt thin and flimsy. *And doesn't change that it's now in Magnor's hands.* She tried putting it out of her mind.

Travelling the road from Lutvin to Fellthorpe was miserable; muddy, cold, stark. Trade had waned between the two settlements after they'd been ravaged by disease. The neglected road had aged poorly; pot holed ruts and washed out banks, barely a cart track anymore. Even coming out of Lutvin it was narrow and rocky, terrain too rough for a wagon, the path straddled by deadwood. By the time they'd made it into the hills beyond the eastern pasture the two tracks had merged; one swallowed up by overgrown brush and long grasses.

Vestrijóborg had been settled no more than ten winters ago, able to receive seaborne trade goods from the south, and occasionally from Albion in the west. Fellthorpe was well supplied by Vargr, and the mountain route between Lutvin and Fellthorpe reflected the relationship between the villages; it had all but disappeared.

Vestrijóborg had opened Hoddlund up to the world.

Now it's gone. Along with my last chance to leave and start a new life.

Siv wouldn't stop chattering about the Valkyrie. The only answer that Gudrun had for her was, "I don't know, Siv."

She really didn't.

Eventually, Gudrun took the talisman out and moved it to her back. "Here. You can look at it, but I'm not taking it off."

Siv studied it quietly for a while.

"Geirahöd!" she shouted, enthusiastically.

"Don't do that!" Gudrun yelled, and snatched it back. They both looked expectantly up at the sky.

"Awww!" Siv groaned. "How come I can't do it?"

"You want to get us killed? Thank Odin you can't do it, because it *shouldn't be done!*"

Siv crossed her arms over her chest and sulked. "If I could summon a Valkyrie..." Siv grumbled.

"What?"

"I'd command her to defeat Magnor!"

"She can no more be commanded than the tide. That's a child's wish."

Siv quietly brooded.

The sky gradually lightened to grey as dawn broke, revealing more of the hills and the river, which could previously only be heard. Gudrun allowed herself to get lost in Embla's rhythmic sway and sighed, grateful for Siv's silence. Birds twittered and chased each other from pecking spots among the leaves.

"I wonder how Oskar and Erica fared," Gudrun said.

Siv was quiet.

They crossed the wooden bridge over the Kalder river, which marked the eastern end of the grazing fields. The track continued between the river and a stone wall that'd been built as a barrier to the marsh on the other side. *The huldra's home.* Odd's, too. They both stared at the wall as they rode past, trepidatious of the mould and lichen that grew on the stone. Naked branches hung over the top, like the spindly fingers of a creature clambering over.

Gudrun felt the soft, smooth cloth of the horse blanket and thought of her aunt. She caught sight of a movement by her foot and leaned to look. As the blanket moved with Embla's stride the golden images of Sleipnir appeared to glow, and gallop and jump through the treacherous landscape of the underworld.

Gudrun smiled and shook her head.

"Oh! This blanket is superb!" Siv said. She swished her hips back and forth. The blanket held them both securely on Embla's back, yet she trotted as though she were free of any burden. "Are we moving faster?"

"I believe so! Aunt Odd must have infused the weave of this blanket with seidr. This old nag has been blessed with the speed of Odin's godly mount!"

Embla ran east along the path, toward the Warg mountains.

They left the wall and the bog behind, travelling through sorrowful fields of brown grass that rolled on like a muddy ocean. A cool wind picked up at their back. It played with the wet grass, snaking through in waves. Few patches of trees dotted the countryside, but as they travelled closer to the mountain's foothills, granite boulders appeared in the hills, the ancestors of the land.

A fierce wind had worn them smooth over the ages. It still howled as it drove between the stones, huddled together in clusters on both sides of the river.

The river widened and quieted, allowing Gudrun's thoughts to turn to the last few days: the Valkyrie's terrifying gaze; Heart Seeker's lustful intensity; Magnor; the fire ship; Skera-Brynja—

"I'm glad you decided to ride with me," Siv said.

"Wha—?"

"It feels good to be out of the village for a while." She wrapped her arms around Gudrun's waist, startling her. Siv pulled away.

"Sorry, I—"

"No, it's fine!" Gudrun said. "I just... didn't expect it, is all."

Siv hugged her again and Gudrun adjusted her seat. Siv laid her head on Gudrun's back, and Gudrun let herself melt into calm.

The wind buffeted them along the path as it wove through the hills, but they kept each other warm. The track twisted around boulders and stone outcroppings which became larger the nearer they travelled to the Kaldr's source. It was an active river which tumbled from the mountains, down countless waterfalls where watervættir made their homes.

They rode through the morning, lost in the rhythm of Embla's hooves.

Dark clouds had gathered and the rain began just after midday.

They stopped to rest at Alfar, a waterfall which sat exactly halfway between Lutvin and Fellthorpe, and ate under the shelter of a thick cedar grove.

A shrine hut had been built there long ago, at the bottom of the falls in honour of the watervættir living in the cascading rapids. Stones had been placed in the shape of a 'C', with a crude roof made of two rough-hewn wooden planks.

The shrine's opening yawned at them with a cold stillness, making the hut seem tiny. A jawless skull lay between them and the stone hut, upper teeth planted, biting the gravel.

Gudrun and Siv stared at it; gaunt, mouldering bone and lifeless pits where eyes and a nose once dwelt. It laughed at her, Gudrun was sure of it.

The shrine was on the edge of the falls, once bright with candles and glittering fetishes, overflowing with ornaments and garlands. Now, the alcove was cast in dark shadow by the mountain. The offerings had long since withered and blown away.

Bones lay scattered about, a collection which, even with the skull, made an incomplete set. The last wretched soul who had tried to shelter in the watervættir's shrine. Tattered scraps of clothing did nothing to hide the remains strewn across the path.

Gudrun crouched and chewed on a stick of dried fish and gulped thin ale.

Siv crept in for a closer look. The tops of the bones, facing the sky, were ash white faded to grey, bleached only where the sun had been able to reach them. She counted five ribs, a hip, plus the skull, missing the jawbone, strewn about by animals. Wolves, most likely. A tattered woollen blanket was stretched out, a strip within the shrine, rotted and mouldy. Slimy brown grass and plants poked through the holes of the blanket's loose weave.

Siv closed her eyes and opened her arms to the waterfall in prayer.

Gudrun watched.

When Siv opened her eyes again, Gudrun nodded at her.

"Let's keep going. I hope to get to Fellthorpe before dark."

Siv blew kisses to the shine and the dead pilgrim.

They mounted Embla and continued into the hills.

"Do you remember going there with mama and the other children? The shrine covered in glittering candles?" Siv said.

Gudrun smiled. "Oh, yes. And the music, the odes… so beautiful. And the waterfall…" Gudrun shook her head at the memory and a shiver went through her.

The shrine was so different now, as though anything good which once resided there had been crushed down; grey, dull, and heavy with death.

"It's been too many summers since— *Torberta!*" Gudrun exclaimed.

"Since Torberta?" Siv chuckled in mild confusion.

"That was the name of the bitch in the logging camp."

"Do I know her?"

"No, well… in a way, you do," Gudrun said, chuckling. "At papa and Sigurd's sendoff Torberta's betrothed tripped and nearly drowned in the harbour trying to get your attention." Gudrun laughed.

"Really? I remember him falling into the water, but I didn't know it was because of me," Siv said. She laughed and shook her head.

"I suppose I should thank her," Gudrun said. "I wouldn't have found you at the gate, if not for her."

"Well, then," Siv said, "to Torberta. Skol!" She laughed but stopped suddenly when she saw Gudrun stayed quiet.

"Oh," Siv said. "I suppose she could have escaped."

That wasn't it. Gudrun could still picture Siv and Erich together, laughing and flirting. Though, this time she wasn't angry over it. It didn't matter anymore. Gudrun was an outlaw. *I wonder if he'd join me?* She shook her head. Erich had likely died in Vestrijóborg.

They rode quietly over the next few hours. The overcast daylight reluctantly seeped into dusk when they reached where the track widened. It led them through a valley between two great hills kneeling before the Warg mountains.

It was already nearly dark when the path left the Kaldr river behind and switched back up the hills. It led them in the dark to the final corner ahead of a bridge which crossed the mighty Juttal river. Fellthorpe's gates lay just beyond.

"Finally here," Gudrun said. "We'll stay in the hall tonight."

"I'm sure Frau Ingeborg will let us stay with her," Siv said.

"No, I don't want to be an imposition this late. There's always a bench to sleep on in the hall, and maybe some soup and ale."

The girls had met Ingeborg only once, years ago when the family travelled to Fellthorpe for the summer feast. Hildegunn spoke fondly of Ingeborg, and often. They'd been friends since childhood, even after Ingeborg's husband had taken her to Fellthorpe. Gudrun had been too young to remember.

"Gudrun, it'll be fine. Mama said Frau Ingeborg was there for my birth, and mama had helped her when she gave birth to her three children. Vegard... no, Hellgurd... and... two others. Anyway, she won't find it an imposition to put us up. I brought a gift. A fine blanket mama made years ago for Frau Ingeborg, but never had a chance to give it to her. Well worth its weight in silver."

"Fine, but you're going to help her around the house," Gudrun said. "And with chores and meals, am I clear?"

"You sound like mama," Siv said, smirking.

"Am I clear?" Gudrun put her hands on her hips and turned to see Siv's face.

"And what will you be doing?" Siv said.

"Negotiating with the blacksmith to make a spear. And, raising an army."

"Ha!" Siv snapped and chuckled. "You don't know how to raise an army. They don't grow from the ground like barley. Even if they did, you wouldn't know what to do with it."

Gudrun shoved Siv's shoulder with her elbow.

"Shut up! I'll speak to the chief. And, in the square, if I need to," she laughed.

"Do you even know who the chief is?"

Gudrun didn't.

"You can't even speak in front of Vigdis without losing your thoughts. We'll give Frau Ingeborg mama's blanket and I'll go with you to see Chief Eskor. We'll talk to him about raising an army. You get your spear from the blacksmith, and we'll *both* help Frau Ingeborg around the house. I even remember where their house is: on the river, near the mill."

"Well... fine. We'll do it your way, this time. We'll make Hildegunn proud—"

"Mama. We'll make *mama* proud. Of *both* her daughters."

Hildegunn wouldn't ever accept her girls being an imposition upon anyone. They were strong, capable, and independent, and she wouldn't have Ingeborg thinking that her daughters couldn't keep a house. *Well, one daughter*, Gudrun thought.

The Juttal river rumbled in the murky dark. Only the dim outline of the bridge could be seen, but something was strange.

"Why does the bridge look like that?" Siv asked.

The wooden bridge spanned at least twenty paces across a canyon which had been carved out over thousands of years by the fast mountain waters of the Juttal. But, the relentless rains of late had turned the river into a powerful spate. It was difficult for the girls to fully understand what they were seeing; the near darkness had melded shadows and silhouettes together and created unnatural shapes which undulated with the flooding river.

The bridge groaned and cracked, straining against the torrent, already flooding the banks of the canyon. Water gushed over top of the bridge and battered against the timbers.

"The river's going to wash the bridge out!" Gudrun had to yell above the roar of the water. They would more than likely be swept down the river if they tried crossing, nevermind the dark.

"Skadti's branch!" Gudrun shouted. 'I wanted to speak with the blacksmith tonight. We'll need to find a dry place to sleep, and continue in the morning." Dry was going to be a challenge.

"Look, Gudrun. There!" Siv pointed, and through the darkness Gudrun could make out a faint light. She spurred Embla to walk toward it. A tiny house, built into the side of a small hill, stood just beyond the track. The light of a candle peeked through the cracks of a shuttered window.

"Let's see if someone there will shelter us for the night," Gudrun said. "Tomorrow we'll need to find somewhere else to cross."

They dismounted in front of the small house, and Gudrun knocked on the door.

"Heya! Does anyone live here? We come in peace, and require shelter for the night!"

After a few moments, the door opened a crack, spilling warm firelight onto the ground. An old woman peeked out at them.

"Good health to you," she said, opening the door wider. She had a warm, toothless smile that shone on her wrinkled, squinting face. She was ancient; thin, white hair drawn up in a bun and a brown work dress made of sturdy, stiff cloth. She'd kept the dress together with patches and darning, but it was tidy and clean. Gudrun thought her face was made entirely of wrinkles, etched with her easy smile.

"Good health, wisemother. I am Siv and this is my sister, Gudrun. We've been travelling since sunup and were hoping to receive hospitality in Fellthorpe, but we dare not cross the bridge tonight, as it is."

"And see it as a boon, child," the old woman replied. "If the bridge had been sure, you'd have only found death in Fellthorpe. Who travels with you, heh?" She scanned behind them in the darkness to see if anyone else was there.

"Just the two of us, and our horse."

The woman grimaced. It rained harder.

"Well, you two and your horse are welcome enough. Whatever else is out there will have to remain outside. Here then, come! Get out of the rain. You will be my guests, heh? Get dry before you catch your death of cold. I'll bring food and drink for my happy guests. There's a shed in back to stable your horse." She left the door open and shuffled to the larder.

"I suppose I'll take care of Embla," Siv said.

"Well, that's our contract," Gudrun said, sneering.

Siv muttered to herself.

Gudrun ducked through the low doorway and entered the cottage. It was quaint and cosy and, best of all, warm. The thick scents of beeswax, apples, and cedar cut through the smoke from the hearth. The wood walls were dark with age, rafters nearly black from a lifetime of cooking fires. The floorboards groaned under Gudrun's feet. It gave her a strange, inexpressible comfort.

"I've always loved the sound of creaking floorboards," Gudrun said.

"Ha! Me too," the old woman nodded with a grin. "I like to imagine the cottage is speaking to me when it groans. Perhaps complaining that I am getting too heavy, heh?" The woman laughed and slapped her knee.

"The floor in the house I grew up in was stone and dirt, cold and hard," Gudrun said. Solid, but unyielding; lacking in voice and comfort.

Gudrun's wet clothes puddled on the floor. "Sorry for the mess! I'll clean it up," she said, doing her best to take off her soaked clothes and keep the water contained by the door.

"No no! Make no mind of it. You are my guest, heh! My eyes are too dim to see the floor anyway. Whatever mess is there is destined to be. But, you two will need dry clothes for the night." The old woman pointed her bony finger across the room at a dusty trunk tucked into a corner. "You should find something in there to wear. Stoke up the fire and hang your clothes to dry."

"Thank you, wisemother. We're in your debt," Gudrun said.

"Nonsense!" the old woman laughed. "It is my pleasure to have guests. Many a night I have spent with my own, lonely company, and it's a joy to have beautiful, youthful spirits haunting this house once more. Please, call me Tove." She chuckled and clucked to herself as she prepared a board of food.

"Oh! My mother's name was Tove. I love that name. So gentle and peaceful," Gudrun said, smiling. The simple, easy joy the old woman radiated touched Gudrun's heart.

She stripped down bare, hanging her wet clothes up on the myriad of hooks and pegs that stuck out in all directions from between the stones of the hearth. It wasn't common, even for strangers, to be modest about their naked bodies; it was seen as a reality that one may be exposed to another in the course of daily life. It would be nearly impossible to relax, and remain modest at the same time, while crowded into a small sauna with a group of naked people.

One had to be mindful, of course, not to flaunt oneself. But, occasional nudity in mixed company could be expected, even unavoidable sometimes. A great number of people still lived in longhouses with very little privacy for changing or bathing.

Gudrun padded across the floor to the trunk. She shivered as she rummaged through it. There were enough clothes for someone Siv's size, and she laid some aside for Siv, but almost everything was too small for her. On the very bottom she found a faded brown dress for herself. There were under-linens and a well worn brown tunic which had been made for a man, and she pulled them on. The dress was snug, but would do for the night.

The door opened and Siv came in. "Embla is set for the night. Thank you, frau, for taking us in. We are indebted to you."

"Ha ha! Your sister said the same, and I will respond the same to you: think nothing of it. It is my pleasure to have you as my guests. Now, get dressed in something dry and we'll eat."

Tove had the small kitchen table set with simple fare; vegetable stew, blackbread, cheese, and cider. Siv changed into the dry clothes, then the three of them sat on three-legged stools at the table and ate together.

"My, do those dresses bring back some memories, heh?" Tove said, sighing.

"You said it's a blessing that we can't cross the bridge. Why?" Gudrun asked.

"Well..." Tove went quiet and let out a sorrowful sigh. "The gods have abandoned Fellthorpe. Plague descended upon the village and took up residence there last winter. All have either left for the hills, or been left to feed crows and eagles."

The sisters exchanged shocked looks.

"The whole village?" Gudrun said.

"Yes. All have abandoned the cursed place."

"Frau Ingeborg, and her family, too? I..." Siv was aghast. Tove shook her head slowly.

"There goes my plan to find help here," Gudrun said.

"Illness had overcome my daughter's youngest boy," Tove said. "My husband visited them every day through the winter, until... My daughter found him collapsed outside of her door. They gave him a bed in her house, and one by one, they all succumbed." Tove hid her face in her hands.

The story was too familiar to the sisters. They could have told nearly the same thing about Lutvin. At least Lutvin hadn't been completely wiped out by the pox.

Tove composed herself. "I'm sorry, it was rude of me to burden you with grim memories."

"You haven't burdened us, Tove," Siv said. "We each have grim memories to mourn over."

They told her about the raiders at Vestrijóborg.

"Did you know the blacksmith who lived here in Fellthorpe?" Gudrun asked. "I can't remember his name, but do you know if he is still alive?"

"My husband knew him. Brokkr... uhh... *Oskar!* Yes, Oskar Brokkr was his name."

"Was?"

"He left with his family and went south. He was very skilled, as I understand; said to have learned his craft from the *dvergar* — the black dwarves of *Nidavellir*.[9]"

The dvergar. Dwarves who lived within the earth. Master crafters whose prizes — such as Thor's hammer, muljiner — were coveted by the gods.

Gudrun nodded, lost in her thoughts. Another village gone, abandoned by the gods. Her plan was ruined, too.

They retired for the night, soon after they'd finished eating. The girls laid out hides on the floor near the hearth and shared a large blanket. It was cosy, and warm enough, yet it took a long time for Gudrun and Siv to fall asleep. Once she had, Gudrun's dream was a vivid revelation which shook her.

---

[9] Realm of the dwarves

CHAPTER FOURTEEN

Landvættir

Smoke billowed from the burning farmhouse and Magnor rubbed his stinging eyes. The blood on his hands irritated them even more. He leaned heavily against the spear to sit on the soggy trunk of a fallen tree. A wave of exhaustion washed over him. He cleaned the blood off his sword with a tattered scrap of cloth he'd torn from a woman's dress, days ago. A drizzle of cold rain trickled down his face and forced a shiver. He clawed at the drip down his neck.

"Miserable land. Hel take you!" The men were sporadically walking into the pasture, carrying whatever meagre plunder they'd found in the house. One of them walked past pulling a goat behind him on a rope. The creature bleated at Magnor.

"Hel take you, too," Magnor said. His eye throbbed.

More men staggered from the farm into the woods, carrying sacks and barrels, before they collapsed to rest under the shelter of the trees. Everywhere was wet, everything soaked. Magnor's feet ached in his waterlogged boots.

He leaned the spear he'd wrenched from the split mast of his ship against a tree, sure to keep it within arms reach. He felt a longing for it, a calling to keep it close. It gave him comfort, somehow. *Show me. Guide my hand, point the way.* He could hear it, buzzing, like a nest of hornets. *Show me.* Show *me!*

"Look at this!" Ander dropped a small chest with a clank.

Magnor startled, and his blood boiled hot enough to steam away the rain.

"Where is Lutvin?" he snarled.

Ander crouched in front of the chest, digging his knife into the lock to break it.

"We're on the way. Just beyond those hills behind, through the cliffs, and the forest, valley— *Ahh!* There! It's open!" The chest was smaller than a loaf of bread. A fistful of silver coins and some simple jewellery spilled onto the grass.

Magnor leapt up and grabbed the spear. He jabbed it under the small chest and flipped it away, sending coins flying with a fury.

"Do you think I'm looking for *this?!* You think I'm content with *this?*"

"Hey!" Ander blinked at him, his mouth falling open. Magnor thrust the spear at the swollen lump in the shocked man's throat. Ander yelped and back-pedalled, like a crab, scrambling to keep Magnor from piercing the tip through his Adams apple.

"I am losing my patience with you, you simple *pimp!*" Magnor spat, slinking toward Ander, the razor's edge against his neck. "Three hundred men took that skitrhole of a harbour, and I've gained another fifty mercenaries, besides. A lot of men, wouldn't you agree? Yes. Yet, you can not find the very place you said you could take me. The *only* reason I let you keep your head is because you claimed to know where Lutvin is. But, it has become clearer to me, with every passing moment, that you have deceived me and have offered me no reason to keep you alive. You're happy to steal *pennies* from farmers and eat what little food we have, like a lame mule, you useless hearthstone! You have taken me no further than I could have come myself. You have given me a whore's promise; a thief's word. Take me to Lutvin, or I will take *you* there, packed into tiny, little penny cases, carried on a cart pulled by a jackass!"

Ander backed into a tree and pressed himself as flat against it as he could. Magnor closed in until their noses touched, with only the spear's blade between them, resting against Ander's throat.

"*No!*" Ander cried, unable to pull away further. He swallowed hard and the blade pressed into his skin, threatening to slit his throat. "Magnor, we're on the path, I swear it. It's just—"

"It's just *what?!*" Magnor swung the spear around and cracked Ander in the skull with the shaft. He hit the ground with a groan.

"That way!" Ander shrieked, dazed, pointing a wobbling finger at a track through the hills behind them. "The road to Lutvin is that way! Three days, I swear! B-but, Lutvin is protected by völur and landvættir. They confuse and mislead those who intend the village any evil. That is the road, but there are so many paths that lead off it. Take the wrong one and you'll be lost for weeks."

"Then you'd better take me down the right path. I'll be counting the turns. If we're not in Lutvin within three days, Roar takes a finger for every turn we have to take to get back to this spot. Once you've run out of fingers, I'll begin slicing toes, and work my way up until I reach your head. Do I make myself clear?"

"Yes," Ander nodded, "very clear."

"Three days."

Roar came up behind and grunted.

"Tie a rope around one of his feet and the other end to my horse," Magnor said. "And no food or water. He can eat and drink once we've reached Lutvin."

Roar nodded, then grabbed Ander by the scruff of his neck. He yelped when Roar pulled him up off his feet. The giant cocked his meaty fist back to punch.

"No! Magnor, please—"

Roar cracked his fist into Ander's jaw, knocking him out into a limp pile in the mud. Roar tied a rope around one of Ander's ankles, then dragged him to Magnor's horse.

"Get up, you lazy bastards! You're not done yet," Magnor shouted at his men, from the saddle. He thrust the spear into the air. "We march!"

A roll of thunder encouraged them to drag themselves to their feet and shuffle to the track. Roar tied the rope to Magnor's horse, and walked beside as Magnor rode, dragging Ander.

It didn't take long for Ander to come back around.

"Magnor! I can't — *ow!* My elbow! Magnor, please! I'm getting — *aah!* My nose!" His tunic had ridden up to his armpits, filling with mud, wet leaves, and fresh manure.

Magnor dragged Ander for another few miles along the road, when it dipped down between two sheer cliffs and continued along the floor of the crevasse, narrowing considerably.

The men crowded together, shuffling into a haphazard column as they marched along the narrow road. The crevasse turned a corner, revealing someone standing at the other end, where the crevasse left the hills a couple hundred feet away.

Magnor leaned forward and squinted. "Who is that?"

"Looks like a woman, m'lord."

She raised her arms and thrust a staff toward the sky.

"What is she doing? Bring her to me!"

"Yes, m'lord!"

A dozen men were ordered forward. Magnor watched as they closed in.

They were nearly upon her, when the woman collapsed and transformed into a black bird. She furiously beat her wings to climb higher.

"A witch! Kill her!"

The men threw spears, but the bird's wings created a magical wind which scattered them like sticks.

"Fools! Shoot the witch down!"

As archers drew their bows, the ground began to tremble.

Magnor's horse flared its ears, grumbled as it stamped its hooves.

"What is happening?" Magnor said, trying to keep control of his mount.

Pebbles rained down onto them from the cliffs. The men raised their shields with a shout, attempting to peer up and scan the ridges for the enemy. Small rocks and sand pelted their faces and eyes, forcing them further under cover.

Without warning, one of the cliffs at the end of the crevasse exploded out like a fist. It engulfed the dozen men in a billowing mass of dust and crushing rock.

Magnor's horse screamed and reared, sending Magnor tumbling backward to land on top of Ander. Roar swiped at the bridal, too late. The horse charged back out of the crevasse, dragging both men behind it, trampling anyone in its way. Magnor and Ander screamed just as loud as the panicked animal, as it charged out of the crevasse and back into the hills.

"*Roaaaaaarr!*" Magnor screamed, as he and Ander bounced behind the horse, across the rocky ground.

* * *

The wagon stopped.

"No, Ola, please! Just a little further," Lottie begged the horse. The old stallion favoured his back leg.

Lottie glanced around at the hills, concerned about the shadows moving through the shifting mists. She climbed down from the cart, and the baby began to cry. "Oh yes, one moment, Brokkr," Lottie muttered. Her breasts were sore.

"Mama, I have to pee," Lene announced.

Lottie didn't look up from Ola's back leg as Lene made the long climb down to the ground. "I can do it!" She slapped at her brother's hand when he grabbed the scruff of her coat.

"I'm the oldest, I need to take care of you," Oskar said, holding her coat.

Lottie lifted Ola's foot and cradled it between her knees to inspect the hoof.

"Ola isn't holding his leg up because he's tired, mama," Oskar said, letting Lene go.

"Mmmhmm." Lottie scraped at the dirt packed into the hoof with her paring knife. Ola grumbled with a shiver.

"Do you want to know why?" Oskar said, puffing out his chest.

"Why?" a gruff voice said, from behind.

They all startled and spun. Three men stood on the other side of the road. One held a chipped dagger and another a well used axe. The lead man stood between them, leaning against a heavy club torn from a tree branch. All of them had thin smiles on their lips, and violence in their eyes.

"B-because..." Oskar's eyes were wide.

Lottie could see an old, crimson splatter on the lead man's tunic.

"What do you want? We have nothing of value to you," she said, letting go of Ola's leg. She snatched Lene off the ground, and the three year old buried her face into Lottie's neck. Her child clung tight enough to choke her. "*Shhhshhhshhh*, we're fine," Lottie whispered.

"Oh, I wouldn't say that you have *nothing* of value," the lead snickered.

The other two men stared at the children.

"Take the cart and leave us. Oskar! Bring your brother to me!"

Oskar grabbed the screaming baby and scrambled across the bench. He jumped down, then ran to his mother. He handed baby Brokkr to Lottie, then stood in front of her and faced the men.

"Get behind me, *boy!*" Lottie hissed.

"*No! You* stay behind *me!*"

"Hoohoohoo! A little warrior!" the lead said. "Do you want a fight, boy?" He picked up his club, and the other men laughed.

"*No!* He doesn't want to fight! He's only nine winters! You have the cart, and we have the black death. Leave us be, and live a long life." She struggled to keep the waiver from her voice.

The men stopped. "Don't want no plague, Audof," the one with the knife said to the leader. They looked at Audolf, and shuffled nervously.

Lene bolted upright. "I'm not sick! Are you sick, mama?" the little girl shouted, tears welling.

"Ha! She's lying," Audolf said. He took a step toward them.

Oskar picked up a rock and threw it, hitting Audolf between the eyes.

"*Ow!* You little *skitr!* I'm gonna break yer hands for that!" He lunged at Oskar and grabbed him by his tunic.

"Excuse me!"

The men were startled by the voice of yet another man, walking up the road behind them.

He was tall, wearing a long leather coat that swished with his stride. Lottie couldn't take her eyes off his thick wool sweater, which was stretched across his chest in all the right places, and the blonde braid cascading down his back.

The men couldn't take their eyes off the huge Danish axe which looked childishly small slung over his massive shoulder.

"Woman," the Dane said, not stopping. "Do you know where Lutvin is?"

Everyone blinked and stared as he walked past, not breaking his determined stride.

Lottie nodded, as though in a trance. Panic suddenly pounced on her and her jaw dropped open. "*Help us!* These men mean to take us into bondage!"

Audolf struck her with the back of his hand. "Shut up!"

The blonde man stopped. "Is this true?"

Audolf scowled. "Mind your own business, boy!"

The Dane took the great axe off his shoulder. "I am Erich the Dane. There are many things which I will never abide by. Hitting a woman is one of them. The least of them is a man who tries to tell me my business. Another is being called a boy. You don't look as tough as my mother, so do it again and I'll take your head from your shoulders and jam it into your filthy crotch. You'll wander Hel's kingdom with your little prick in your mouth."

Oskar burst out laughing.

Audolf's face turned so red Lottie thought he'd burst.

"I'll kill you!" He ran at Erich, club raised.

Lottie gasped when the other two stepped toward Erich as well, their weapons held ready for murder.

Audolf screamed as he brought his club down to bash Erich's head, but the axe had already swung. It sliced through Audolf's neck, sending his head twirling off.

The others jumped at the shock of it, as the head spun through the air, then plopped on the ground just as the corpse hit the mud.

Erich whistled. He flipped the body over and tore off the pants. He grabbed the head in a fistful of hair, then slammed the head into the corpse's crotch.

"There," Erich said. "*Now* Audolf knows what a boy looks like."

He turned to the other two. "You have somewhere else to be."

They looked at Erich, the corpse, then each other. Without another thought, the two of them turned and ran back down the road.

"Huh," Erich said. "Didn't even look back."

Oskar whooped and leaped forward, yelling and throwing stones after them.

Erich wiped his axe on Audolf's funerary tunic.

"Now," Erich said. He leaned his axe against the cart. "Let's take a look at your horse."

Lottie ran to Erich and mashed her lips on his, with Lene squealing and the baby crying in her arms.

"Thank you! You saved us!"

Erich smiled. "You said you know the way to Lutvin?"

"Yes! We're heading there, too. But, Ola won't move because of his sore foot, and the bandits..." Lottie looked down the road to make sure the men were gone. "Oskar! Come back here, now!"

"There are a lot of bandits, it isn't safe to travel alone," Erich said.

"We were part of a caravan. Ola's foot became sore last night, and I thought we'd be able to catch up this morning, but..."

"Well, first let's get Ola ready to go. Then, I'll escort you to Lutvin. If... that's alright with you."

"Yes! Yes, of course," Lottie said, beaming. "We don't have much to give, but you're welcome to share our meagre supper."

"Thank you, I would enjoy that very much."

Erich lifted Ola's foot and picked away the packed dirt, then trimmed the hoof with his knife.

"What's waiting for you in Lutvin? Home? Work? A woman?"

"Yes, I hope so." He grinned.

Lottie' smile was cautious, "Oh, I see."

Lene cupped her hands around Lottie's ear.

"Mama," she whispered, "I still have to pee."

CHAPTER FIFTEEN

Old Friends

She pushed through an endless forest of pine branches, slapping her face and spraying cold wet down her neck and into her ears. Her knife was missing. She stopped to grope for it in the dark. A sharp movement and a snapped branch made her stomach drop. She tried to run, but her bare feet couldn't find grip in the icy mud. She gasped and held her breath. She'd surely fall if she ran.

Wood shrieked, torn by a grey paw that snapped through the trees and crushed them to the sides. A dire wolf's massive head wedged through, its body crashing the trees flat to the ground. Its snarling muzzle thrust jagged yellow fangs at her, black hackles raised like knives and spikes as the beast snapped its jaws.

The evil Fenrir! Her heart stopped.

She fell, scrambling to escape in mud, one moment too slippery to stand on, then too sticky to let her go. The wolf leapt and caught her in one bound, pinning her to the ground with one giant paw crushing her chest. The beast's snarl vibrated hate through its slobbering muzzle and the queasy stench of decay slammed her in the stomach and made her retch.

A rider clung to its back, hidden from view. Someone she knew? The wolf clashed its teeth together and nipped her ear.

"*Shhhhhh…*" a woman's sultry voice slid from the rider's lips. She was naked, rubbing the wolf's neck, sensually running her fingers through its fur. Her long blonde braid draped down to the ground as she cooed in the evil wolf's ear.

The wolf licked its chops, dripping froth, like venom, into his captive's eyes and on her mouth, clamped shut. Then the beast leapt off her, spraying mud as it loped south, along a wide river.

She sat up and wiped the slime from her face. She knew the rider, she was sure of it, but…

"Where are you going?" Her voice was swallowed by the wind.

The answer sunk its teeth into her thoughts as it pounced, growling, "*Vargr.*"

Gudrun startled awake, confused from sleep, unknowing of where she was.

It was dark.

The fire was down to ash.

Slivers of dim morning blue outlined shuttered windows. *The old woman's cabin. Tove.* Siv and the old woman were still asleep.

Gudrun yawned and stretched, then quietly climbed out of the fur pile. She felt drained, as though she hadn't slept at all. She thought of the dream. *A warning? Or a blessing?*

The cabin was chilled. She checked their clothes. Cold but dry.

She pulled hers on, then raked the ashes, exposing red pricks of light from hot coals hidden in the ashes.

Tove stirred and sat up. "Good morning," she yawned and stretched.

"Good morning," Gudrun said, laying sticks down to rekindle the fire.

Tove dressed and shuffled into the kitchen.

"Thank you for tending the hearth, child. Did you sleep well?"

Gudrun laid pieces of wood across the flames she'd cultivated and warmed her hands.

"I had a Mare on my chest who robbed me of sleep," she said.

She was cautious of mentioning Loki's child, the dire wolf Fenrir, from her dream.

"Burn some sage to be sure your Mare rides the smoke out through the roof. You must be hungry. I will prepare dagmal to break our night's fast." Tove pulled a sack from the larder.

Siv awoke too, and stretched with a loud yawn.

"Oh! You're up already," Gudrun said, a wry comment their father had often made.

"It's impossible for anyone to sleep in between two others who are not," Siv said through a yawn. "I had a horrible sleep,"

"Oh no!" Tove said, concerned that her guests were uncomfortable.

"All night long I thought I heard a ghost in the cabin, but it just turned out to be Gudrun's snoring." Siv dropped her jaw open wide to imitate a corpse, then snorted. Tove laughed, and Gudrun rolled her eyes.

"My snoring is better than your breath," Gudrun said.

"Uhh!" Siv clamped her mouth shut, her eyes wide in shock. They all laughed.

"It is good to start the day with mirth," Tove said. "It's been too long since this old cabin heard youthful laughter." She smiled and set a pot to boil over the newly kindled fire. Then, she fussed about in the kitchen, humming to herself.

Gudrun placed one last piece of wood on the flames, and satisfied they were burning well, went to help Siv fold the bedding furs.

"I'm going to Vargr," Gudrun said. "I'm going to seek out Oskar Brokkr, the blacksmith."

"You mean, *I'm* going to Vargr and you'd like to come with me," Siv said, pleased with herself. She liked this game.

"No, you're not. You're taking the horse back home. Hildegunn must be beside herself, looking for you."

Siv sighed. "I don't want to think about how angry mama is. I'm going to Vargr."

"Vargr, did you say?" Tove said. She laid the food out on her small table. "Then you will need a good breakfast. Come, eat! We'll have broth and tea when the water's boiled."

The sisters sat with Tove and ate the dagmal she'd laid out for them; black bread, cheese, apples, honey, and curds.

"Do you know anything about Vargr?" Gudrun asked Tove.

"That is where Jarl Ulfer and Frue Frigga live," Tove said. "Follow the Juttal river south for a day, perhaps a while longer, and you will come to a bridge called Biå. That is the crossing to Vargr. But heed my words; it is not a place in which to travel lightly. It is aptly named, for you must keep your wits about you while you are there, deep in the wolf's den. It is too late to plan your escape once the wolf has closed its jaws around your throat." She smiled and winked.

Gudrun shuddered, remembering her dream. *The rider saved me from Fenrir's jaws.*

The women ate quietly.

"You should be in time for the Autumn Feast," Tove said, uncomfortable with the silence. She stood and shuffled to her bed. "Here. This is for you, Siv." She held a kerchief out for Siv to take. "Wear this while you are there. A beautiful woman like you, without a husband or escort, in Vargr… you'll need to keep attention off you, I think."

Siv smiled and took the light cloth. "Thank you," she said. "The gods will remember your kindness, and Freya keeps a special place for you in The Field."

Siv and Gudrun each embraced Tove like she was their wisemother.

"You will forgive me if I do not stray too long from the fire. It has yet to seep into my bones. Get along, and Odin travel with you and protect you," Tove said, shuffling with them to the door.

The Raven called to them when the sisters stepped outside. It perched on the limb of an oak tree, whose unfallen leaves flickered yellow with a cold breeze. The cottage was draped by the shadow of the mountain, making the brisk morning seem colder.

Tove gasped. She grabbed Gudrun's arm and pointed at the raven.

"A sign of death! Do not go to Vargr," she pleaded, making a sign against evil. Huginn stretched its jet black wings wide and leapt into flight. Its feathers shimmered, even though they were untouched by the morning sun's rays. Huginn cawed as it flew south along the edge of the river gorge and disappeared into the trees.

"That's no evil omen, wisemother," Gudrun said.

Siv laughed. "Gudrun thinks that's Huginn."

Tove cocked one eyebrow and looked Gudrun in the eye. "Go home. Move your family from Lutvin, start a new life—"

"I can't!" Gudrun cut her off. "I can't return to Lutvin. I can't return home to my family. Not... yet. Not until I find a way to— I need to defeat Magnor. If I can do that, then I'll have the sacrifice required for—" Gudrun sighed. There was too much she was unwilling to explain. "I need a weapon to best him with. The blacksmith is my hope."

She lifted her head and met Tove's gaze. The intensity in her eyes made the old woman's eyes go wide. "The raiders are coming, Tove. They don't care that you're an old woman, they will hurt you. They need to be stopped and I need a weapon to stop them."

Tove let out the breath she was holding.

"I wish you all of the blessings of the gods, and may Loki be too busy with his lover, Angrboða, to stand in your way. Good health to you, and good journey." Tove made one more sign against evil before she shut the door against the cold.

The night had left a frost on the ground, a silken drape that shimmered in the growing dawn light. They wrapped their feet and shins with cloth scraps and leather hides to keep them dry. Siv draped Odd's blanket over Embla's back. It hung handsomely over her flanks. Siv smoothed it out with her hand, admiring the gold stitching. "Aunt Odd's seidr glows through the threads," she said.

They finished packing Embla, then walked her to the edge of the gorge.

The bridge looked much worse in the daylight — its timbers twisted and misshapen by relentless water. Deadwood had dammed up against it, flooding the opposite bank and forcing the river to course over the bridge's warped deck in a torrent. Muddy brown water sprayed down the other side, strangling groaning timbers in a kraken-like embrace — slowly smothering its prey while dragging it down to the fathomless depths.

Across the gorge stood Fellthorpe's empty gates, in among silvery hills, only a hundred paces from the bridge. It was too melancholic a sight for Siv, and she looked away. One gate stood ajar: a dark, foreboding entrance to the necropolis, haunted by memories of those who once delighted there.

"We need to leave," Siv said. They mounted Embla with Gudrun seated behind Siv this time. They headed south, down the river toward Vargr, the direction which Huginn had flown. An overgrown dirt road followed along the gorge's edge. Siv spurred Embla on and she leapt to the course with tremendous speed.

The river twisted through a great expanse of rock, contained within a fissure which had opened up long ago when these mountains were born. It stretched out for many miles through forests of spruce, pine and silver birch.

They travelled for the entire day, with only the ever present roar of the river to accompany them, and Huginn gliding just ahead as Embla raced along the fissure's edge as though she carried no riders at all. The seidr infused into Odd's blanket bore their weight.

They hadn't seen another traveller along the road, though shadowy figures hid among the trees, too wary of Huginn's presence to violate the travellers who rode alongside Odin's Thought.

A fog set in as the sun set, blanketing them with a foreboding mist, forcing them to slow Embla to a walk.

"I'm going to walk ahead," Gudrun said, and slipped down off of Embla's back. She held the bridle to guide them through the dark once the sun had set.

It was well over an hour before they finally saw a light: an eerie smudge of orange glowing in the distance.

"What is that?" Siv whispered. They both squinted at it.

"There! Another!" Gudrun pointed to a smaller, dimmer smudge further in the woods. It winked on and off as it moved through the trees.

"Look! More appear!"

Indeed, more lights winked and bobbed along through the trees.

"Are they vættir?" Siv said, her voice wavering.

Embla grunted and pulled at the bridal.

"*Tsshht!* Easy girl," Gudrun said, holding the bridal tight.

"She is spooked by the mist," an old man's voice startled the sisters from within the fog. A moment before they couldn't see him. He stood between the pull shafts of an apple cart on the side of the track, in place of an animal, smoking a pipe. He passed the pipe to his wife. She stood beside him holding the other shaft.

He chuckled gently. "My apologies, young maidens! I hadn't intended to spook *you*, as well."

His wife hit him in the chest with the back of her hand.

"Stop it, Bori! Keep pulling. We have enough trouble of our own."

"What troubles you, wisemother?" Siv asked.

"Our mule has run off, because of this useless hearthstone," the old woman snapped, jabbing an accusatory thumb at Bori. "The cart is too heavy for us to pull across the bridge."

"What bridge? We are looking for a bridge called Biå," Siv said.

"You near found it," Bori said. "Is just beyond, hidden in the mist. Can see the fire brazier at the guard post."

"Then we can help," Siv said.

"No we can't," Gudrun snapped.

"Yes, we can," Siv insisted. She slid off of Embla's back. "Our horse is strong, and more than capable of pulling your cart across the bridge."

"*Siv!*" Gudrun hissed. "What are you doing? We don't have time for this."

"These people need our help. It won't take us long."

Gudrun scowled. "It better not, or I'm leaving you to these people while I go find the blacksmith."

"Fine. Help me get Embla hitched up."

"Thank you, young maidens!" Bori said, beaming. "The gods smile on you for helping an old withered man and his grumpy wife. Isn't a big cart but much too heavy for the two of us. Mule got spooked by faye in the mists and bolted..." The old man chattered on about the misadventure that led them there, while Gudrun and Siv secured the straps around Embla's chest. The woman was quiet. She kept to herself, still smoking the pipe as the sisters strapped Embla in.

"There," Siv said. "Ready to go!"

"Climb on back, I'll drive," Bori said, helping his wife onto the cart. The sisters jumped aboard and Bori clashed the reigns. Embla pulled them forward with a quick jerk.

"Ho! Much faster than that stubborn mule!" the woman said.

Within a few moments Gudrun could see the black outline of the bridge against the brazier's light, in the darkness and fog.

A large group of people waited for the guards to let them cross. The people were dressed for a feast, in beautiful, colourful dresses and tunics. Some had animals with them; cows, goats, sheep and dogs on tethers, hens, roosters, and geese in wooden cages.

They sang and bantered as they waited for their turn to cross, exuberant and excited. Their lanterns flickered and glowed in the fog; fuzzy, like balls of wool, extending into the forest.

"Wisps in the trees," Siv beamed. Her eyes sparkled, even in the dark.

The old man chuckled. "The Autumn Feast brings folks from far and wide to Vargr. Must be why you're here, yes?" he asked, not really looking for an answer.

A group of guards were stationed on the bridge and were slowly letting people through. They had some stopped on the side and were questioning them.

"What are they looking for?" Gudrun asked.

"Bah! Who knows," Bori said, unable to hide his annoyance. "Protection for the jarl and frue, I should think. Looks like this will take a while."

Bori drove the cart toward the waiting crowd and made to turn toward the rear to wait for their turn to cross. Gudrun heard the cawing of the raven and turned to look up at the bird, perched and calling out from on top of the bridge.

"Huginn," she whispered, as though the bird could hear her from there.

As Embla started to move to the right, one of the guards stopped them and waved them on. "This way, old man! Bring the cart through."

Gudrun put up the hood of her cloak. "Siv, put on your kerchief," she whispered.

They hid their faces as the cart approached the guard post. Siv grabbed Gudrun's wrist and squeezed. People shuffled past the guards as they scrutinised the crowd for threats.

On one side of the bridge they'd detained several small groups of men who'd ridden in on horseback. *They're looking for someone,* Gudrun thought.

Bori steered Embla toward the guards.

We're here from Lutvin, for the Feast and for business, Gudrun practised, anticipating the guards' questions. Her heart raced as they drew nearer.

"Take your hands off of me!" a man on the bridge shouted, startling her. A horse neighed as the guards scuffled with him. Gudrun and Siv exchanged worried looks. They were coming up beside the young soldier who'd been waving them forward.

Gudrun turned, opened her mouth and drew in a breath as Bori brought the cart to a halt.

"Not looking for carts," an older guard behind the soldier

grumbled. He waved them through. Gudrun caught a glimpse of his eyes; bloodshot, tired, and dull. "Keep it moving. Go make your cider, old man. Lets not have the wheels fall off, here." He yawned as he spoke, then turned back to the waiting crowd.

"Ha! The gods smile on us again! It is because of you two," Bori laughed. He broke into song, even after his wife asked him not to. She crossed her arms and hunched down with her pipe.

They passed over the bridge, along with revellers playing instruments and singing, dancing as children skipped across the flagstones to get into the city.

One man playing a lute hopped onto the cart without missing a note, and continued his song as others walking laughed and clapped along. Bori took great delight in it and gave Embla an extra clash of the reins. By the time they'd reached the other side the cart was laden with people, laughing and singing.

Two nithing poles were put up on either side of the bridge in front of Vargr's main gate. They would ward off evil spirits and undead: haugbui and draugr.

Bori drove the cart through the gate and up a dirt street that ran between tall houses. They all stood packed together like sailors in a gale, one house built onto the wall of the next. Gudrun had never seen such houses, each with windows high up in the walls. *Are these houses for giants?* she thought.

The street split, and while Bori drove on to the right, the extra passengers leapt off to continue the other way, to the karl halls. They waved and thanked them for the ride, wishing them a good feast and continued on. Their singing could be heard well after they'd disappeared around the corner.

Bori drove them a little further then pulled on the reins to stop Embla.

"Here we are!" Bori said. "We won't keep you girls any more than you need. Unhitch your horse and be free, on your way." They all got off of the cart, and unhitched Embla from the harness.

"Our thanks to you, girls. We could not have made it here

without your help." Bori gave each of the sisters three apples, and one for Embla. The old woman shuffled to the door of one of the buildings and ducked inside, without saying a word.

"Do not mind her," Bori said.

"Where would we find a blacksmith?" Gudrun asked, putting the apples into her pack.

"Tonight? At one of the karl-halls, I should expect. But, you'll not get any work out of him now, not unless you are in silver." He rubbed two imaginary coins between his fingers. Then he pointed them toward the karl halls.

"I'll take you there," he said.

They followed him through the crowds toward the centre of the city. The houses and buildings were made of stone and thick timbers; sturdy and solid, not a single one misshapen or in need of repair. Doors and window shutters were decorated with swirly shapes and knots in brightly contrasting colours. Each building had a tall lantern lit that hung beside the door, to chase away the shadow of night. Closer to the central square the street was cobbled, and Siv enjoyed the beat of Embla's hooves as they clacked and echoed off of the stone walls. It went well with the music of the revelry, which she found delightful.

The road split, and the crowds split, too. Gudrun wanted to get around the throng; the crush made it hard to think. She was glad to have Bori guiding them. Huginn flew ahead and landed on the outcropping of a house and watched.

Bori led them down the crowded street to a Karlhall. Its doors were wide open with a drunken celebration spilling out onto the street. Huginn landed on the roof of a stable and preened one wing.

"I suppose we'll bring Embla there," Gudrun said, with a shrug.

Two stable boys sat on a wood pile drinking cider. Gudrun made a deal with them, and chopped a silver coin in half with a hatchet. She gave them one piece.

"You get the other half tomorrow." The boys nodded.

She rolled up the horse blanket and stowed it in her pack.

"Alright, let's see if we can find Osakr Brokkr, or someone who knows where he is," Gudrun said.

Bori took them into the hall. The free townspeople drank and feasted there; tradesmen and women and their families. The building was deep, with tight rows of long, solid tables and benches packed with people. Children squealed and screeched as they chased each other up and down the corridors, dodging and climbing over people as they gathered bowls of food and cups of ale. The smell of cooking fires, pork, and herring made Gudrun's stomach growl.

Children ran past them in a group, squealing. Siv stared at them with ardour in her eyes. "I'd almost forgotten what they sound like," she said.

Proud fathers showed off their children's wit and innocent wisdom to the other men. They would ask questions that the child would answer with pride and confidence, prompting great mirth and laughter, hair ruffling and wrestling hugs.

Delighted mothers did similarly, presenting their babies to the women, mothers and wisemothers, showing off dresses and coats, laughing over the antics of their child's adorable musings. Babies were passed from wisemother to aunt, friend and neighbour, each woman clamouring to hold wiggling, waddled infants. They inspected them thoroughly for weakness or stunt, until a mother interrupted to breastfeed or change a soiled linen.

When the adults had satisfied their adoration of the children, they'd set the kids free again, to play and run through the hall.

Three men at the centre of the hall enthusiastically played loud, bouncy music, but the conversations at the tables were what made it impossible to speak without shouting.

Bori spoke with a man sitting nearby. The man looked Gudrun and Siv up and down, then smiled and turned to another table. He yelled to a middle-aged man with long blonde hair that draped over a sleeveless leather coat. "Oskar... *Oskar!* This woman's asking for you."

Oskar had a muscular arm around a woman and sloshed a wooden drinking *skol*[10] of beer. The woman scowled at Gudrun.

Someone else at the table remarked, "Oh-oh!" and they all laughed with a suggestive "Oohh!" Oskar turned beet red, but shook his head and laughed along. "Naturally. They all eventually ask for me," he said, with a laugh.

The woman under his arm hit him in the chest. "You pig!" she sneered. He pulled her in close and gave her a kiss. Then he stood, wobbling to keep his balance. His friends snickered as they braced him up.

"I'm fine," he said, slapping at their hands. Then, he hit his fist against his chest, "*I* am Oskar. Who is it that is looking for me?"

Everyone at the table turned and looked at Gudrun.

Someone whistled.

Gudrun felt a pang of anxiety with all of their eyes on her. She remembered the timber camp's food hall and the men there; more bluster than bite, but who held no value in timidness. *These men are no different*, she thought. She took a deep breath.

"I am Gudrun Thorkildatter. This is my sister, Siv. I've heard of your smithing skills, from when you lived in Fellthorpe. I was told you might be found here in Vargr, and here you are. I've come to have you make a spear for me."

They all turned to Oskar.

"Where are you from that you heard of me in Fellthorpe?"

"Lutvin, in Hoddlund."

Oskar's face brightened. "Hoddlunders! We could be cousins! Come! Sit and drink with us. This is my wife, Elli, and these louts... well, they can go to Hel."

They laughed and shuffled closer together on the bench to make room for the sisters.

Gudrun hesitated. "So, will you forge me a spear?"

"Drink first! In the morning we'll talk about spears."

---

[10]   A bowl used for drinking.

"No, I need to know now. I have silver, and can pay now—"

"Why does a woman need a spear so badly?" a very large man at the table said. He leaned in closer and probed, "Is it a gift for your husband?"

They all laughed again, some shook their heads.

"Tiu just wants to know if you're married," one of the women quipped.

"Are you?" Tiu said, with a sheepish laugh.

Gudrun wasn't amused.

"Raiders have taken Vestrijóborg and are coming for Lutvin," she blurted.

They all looked at each other, stunned.

"Then... you'll need more than just one spear," one of the men said.

"Better to let the men fight," a woman said. They chuckled and cheered their skols enthusiastically.

"The men fight outside, we fight inside," Elli said, and the table burst into laughter. Doubled over, some laughed so hard, they cried.

"No. The men of Lutvin are all dea—"

"Better that you stay here and drink with us. *Skol!*" Someone interrupted. They laughed again and raised their skols.

"Better to get the raiders drunk and take *their* spears!" More laughter.

From the looks and shoulder slaps the men exchanged it became apparent to Gudrun that they were sharing an inside joke. She crossed her arms and frowned.

"I don't find this funny," she said.

Siv grabbed her elbow. "Let it go, Gudrun, it's a feast. They're drunk and just having some fun."

"We jest, cousins!" Oskar said. "Come and sit. Better to drink with us, now, while the kegs are still full!"

They all laughed and cheered their skols.

"So, then, after the kegs are empty?" Gudrun said.

209

"Then, we can all go and dip kegs of mead at Jarlhalla!" Oskar said.

They all cheered again.

"Come on, Gudrun." Siv grinned.

"Yes, join us," Oskar said, waving at the others to make room for the sisters. "Tomorrow, after breakfast, we'll see about your spear."

"Better to go to Jarlhalla and ask the jarl for an army to carry a hundred spears to Lutvin!" They laughed again.

"Is that possible?" Gudrun said.

"Well... you can ask—" They all chuckled.

"Gudrun, let's sit with them. They've offered a skol, it would be rude to refuse," Siv whispered.

"You and your sister can sit here, beside me," Tiu said.

Siv smiled and gently pulled Gudrun by the hand.

"Fine," Gudrun relented.

"Skol!"

They sat, mashed against each other on the bench.

Wooden skols of ale were passed to each of the sisters, which they drank quickly — customary, to show respect to the host — and belched as loud as they could — also customary.

Skols of ale and cider were filled and emptied, though the sisters took care to sip theirs slowly. They feasted on vegetables, roast pork, stone fried flatbread, and herring.

Gudrun began to relax. She hadn't felt this much at home since before her father had left. Yet, something one of the men had joked about earlier kept coming back to her mind and wouldn't let go, stalking her like a hunter's dog does fowl.

CHAPTER SIXTEEN
New Arrival

anvieg couldn't help herself. She searched the faces of the refugees limping into Lutvin, with bitter wonder; how many of them had come to genuinely exchange aid for shelter? Or were they only following beguiling rumours of hidden treasures? Staying only long enough to get their fists full of coins? They arrived by the dozen; dragging the evidence of Magnor's brutality and his raiders' thuggery with them. It grew even more apparent as the day faded into night. Ragged families had made their way east, mostly farmers and herdsmen (also labourers and bound men, sailors, hunters, tradesmen and their apprentices), seeking safety.

Ranvieg had no doubt they all needed refuge, and she was happy to provide it. Though the ones who stayed cast furtive glances at each house and into every corner of the village. She knew the look of desperation. Tales of hidden gold, maybe buried in pits or hidden in the rafters or under the fire. Rumours of gold cannot be easily dispelled with reason; more often it took proof, and when that wasn't enough, destruction inevitably ensued. She was already fed up with repeating that she didn't know of any hidden treasures. She decided to lose herself in work.

"But, it must be true!" most said. "Why would they attack if *nothing* was here?"

No one wanted to think their home had been burned for no good reason, or that they'd buried their children because of a fool's errand. Ranvieg dropped her head mournfully, knowing those were the people who'd come, with more following behind.

She decided it really didn't matter why they'd come, only that they *had* come. More people meant more defenders, more supplies, more hands to rebuild the crumbled defences. Most had some kind of simple weapon — an axe, a bow, knife, or staff. Some even had a shield or a helm. Few had any kind of armour to speak of, perhaps leather or a thick, padded coat. Still, more than what she had. *The village wall will be our breastplate*, she thought.

Currently, the weapons most needed were shovels and hammers. The repairs to the palisade's timbers would have to be completed before the trench could be properly finished. Even as the sun dipped well below the Sunset Oak at the West end of the field, work parties continued, dropping armloads of freshly cut wood into piles to be sorted for need: wall stakes, spears, pit spikes.

Ranvieg filled her basket again with sticks to make more arrows. The smell of churned earth made her feel warm. Even the shouts between the labourers was a comfort. She stood and stretched her aching back. The sun set grey clouds on fire with orange, red, and pink, and cast the Sunset Oak's shadow long across the field; well past the time to prepare *nachtmal* — the evening meal. The question of whether they would stop to eat hadn't come up. Not yet. Still too much work to be done.

Oxen protested under a driver's whip with their low, hollow voices, as they strained against their harnesses and struggled to pull a wagon through the muddy field. Red-faced men on either side yelled and pushed the wagon — axle deep in muck, weighed down by a tall pile of stone — which creaked and groaned under the load. The driver continued to holler at the oxen, goading them to pull harder *"Heppa! Heppa!"* He steered them toward one of three great heaps of stone near the wall, also being sorted by size.

Ranvieg walked toward the West Gate. Women carried torches and lanterns out to the field so the labourers could continue into the night. She nodded greeting as they passed, careful not to smile, or face judgement of her level of mourning.

She averted her eyes to the pool already forming in Erica and Ivor's field— *Well... not Ivor's,* Ranvieg thought. Not anymore. Ranvieg had already been reminded too many times that day, each reminder a slap to her face. So many of her friends had lost sons and husbands, men that they loved. They did their best to keep their grief at bay, but Ranvieg could see their burden. She wanted to comfort them, but she felt... guilty. Guilty for feeling happy. *They all want their's back, and I'm glad mine's gone.* She shook her head and walked on, gazing out over Erica's field.

It was shaped like a dish and flooding it had proved easy, from the swollen Kaldr river. The rains had helped a great deal. Everything was soaked. Even if Erica's field couldn't be turned into a pond, the sodden earth would do a good job of protecting the village's right flank.

Ranvieg made her way through the gate toward Truda's smithy. Truda had apprenticed under her father, Thurlow, who'd been the previous blacksmith, before he coughed himself to death. The clang of Truda's hammer shaping hot metal on the anvil rang through the village. Smoke from the forge rolled out of the open doors of the shop as Truda worked. Ranvieg admired her focus in the sweltering heat, as the blacksmith wrought iron and steel.

Ema — the one from the valley, not the shore — carried clay pots back into her house. She'd left them to cool under the lean-to in her yard that morning, after they'd been fired last night. Each trip out she carried a handful of broken pottery from the pieces that hadn't survived the kiln. She dropped the pieces onto a pile, then picked up another pot. Ranvieg could read the grief written on Ema's body; the way she moved and carried herself, gone the easy smile she normally kept on the edges of her lips. Her husband, Ottar, had been a good man. Their sons, too. All gone now. *I would've mourned a good man, also,* Ranvieg thought.

Ranvieg's house was beside Ema's, but she continued along the path toward the Chieftess' hall. She looked over to the back wall of Helja's house. *I still do that, every time,* she chided herself.

Helja's had been built beside Truda's shop a few years past. Ranvieg had been so used to walking between the smithy and the tannery, ever since she'd first come to Lutvin after getting married, and despite it having been years, she still looked in that direction. She could see it from her kitchen window.

When she closed her eyes she could still envision the house on the other side; the house that she'd always wanted... the man she'd always dreamed of.... She shook her head. *That's all over now.*

She continued and walked to where bondi Gilby's old barn once stood. They used the stone from its walls to build Helja's house. The barn would have collapsed on its own, had they not torn it down. Its timbers had become rotten and it was infested with mice and forest cats. Ever since the Gilby's barn came down the East Gate could be seen from Ema Valley's house.

From that gate Ranvieg could see the thin treeline that stood before the bog. It was haunted, as all bogs were. Odd's domain. A stewardship that the völur shared with the Lady of the Forest: the huldra. Ranvieg shivered and made a sign against evil. She'd never ventured near the bog, not on her own, and certainly not after dark. The women talked about it in the weaving huts, that no one ever escapes the huldra, that she traps them forever.

At least we are safe from attack on that side. She shivered again, thinking about the Lady of the Forest.

Even if the raiders were bold and clever enough to get away from the huldra's mystical charms — beauty paled only by her malign intentions — they'd fall prey to the völur's traps and protections. Yes, the huldra and völur made sure the village was well shielded on the left flank, too.

Only the centre remained, where the enemy could be channelled through missile fire toward the strongest part of the main wall, their best defensive position. Work still needed to be done to blockade both gates, and to close the wall along the shoreline. *With a little more help, and Freyr's blessing…* Ranvieg thought.

She carried the basket of shafts through the large doors of the hall to a table near the busted hearth. A group of women had turned the hearth into a shrine to the Valkyrie, and knelt before it, whispering praises to the demigoddess. Some sat cross-legged and sang softly as they sewed white goose feathers into capes, their faces smeared and blackened with ash.

She left the sticks on the table, where three old men were smoking pipes, and whittling the sticks into arrows, while watching the Valkyrie worshippers.

Ranvieg went back to the entrance.

Candles and sputtering reed lights lit the table where a dozen women trimmed fletching feathers. They shuffled a spot open for Ranvieg on the bench. She sat, unclipped a small pair of sewing shears that hung from her broach, and started to snip.

She only knew a few of the women, but she did know that none of them there had children to feed and put to bed. They worked in shifts with the women who did. Barrels of fletched shafts that the mothers had already made that day sat outside of Truda's door, awaiting the blacksmith to get around to tipping them with iron.

The chatter that had been so present through the day had quieted. It was well past Sunset Oak, a long day promising to drag on even longer. They all sensed that sleep would soon become something that would only be stolen in between tasks (each task being more important than the last).

Ranvieg was glad to help in any way that she could, before more people arrived seeking shelter, with new wounded to be tended.

She looked over at her current patients: three old farmers, sitting on pallets in the makeshift infirmary that had been set up in the hall. Wood shavings lay about them on the floor and on their laps as they carved arrow shafts and smoked.

Ranvieg licked the edge of one of the feathers she'd trimmed and carefully held it in place on the shaft. It pleased her to stitch the feathers on, a similar joy to the one she found in darning. She began to hum, and soon the younger women joined in until they were all singing together. A soft song of love and days gone by. Melancholic, yet comforting.

Grima could be heard directing work at the back of the hall.

"Yes, these ones here." She'd organised a growing collection of supplies. A lot was moving through Lutvin. Some people stayed while others continued on after trading and bargaining to support the village, and lighten their load. If a little profit was made, was that so bad?

Hildegunn stormed into the hall and made a beeline to Grima. They exchanged a few words before Hildegunn stomped off to the chieftess' office. She scowled at the Valkyrick worshippers and their broken shrine, muttering, "Don't you have better things to do?", before disappearing into the back of the hall.

Grima shook her head. Ranvieg could see how tired she was. They all were. Vigdis had also ordered stock to be taken of everything they had and Grima had taken the task to heart. She'd been out since the first rooster's crowing with a cart and helpers, collecting cloth and clothing, leather, weapons, tools, anything that could be spared.

It amazed Ranvieg how much extra could be found in drawers, trunks, and cupboards when needs were desperate.

Grima sifted through the pile of clothes.

"Like this. These here, these here..." She showed her volunteers how she wanted them sorted.

A horse-drawn wagon thundered through the West gate at full speed. They all looked up as it charged past the thinning line of peasants trudging in by the last light of day. It didn't slow, spraying dirty water , until it reached the doors of the hall.

"*Whooah!*" the driver shouted as she pulled hard on the reins and the horses stopped.

"Heyya! Bestla!" Grima called with a wave, then rushed over, leaving the women to continue sorting.

"Grima!" Bestla called, "I need help! One here is still alive!" Bestla climbed into the back of the wagon. She wore the green clothing and brown cloak of a hunter scout.

Ranvieg ran out behind Grima with another woman, as the others at the table stood, ready to lend a hand. Grima climbed into the wagon.

"Barely," Grima said, crouched over the delirious man laying there. He groaned and muttered, writhing and clawing at the bed of the cart. A pair of mud covered boots lay beside him.

"He's caught fever," Bestla said.

Three more bodies shared the wagon — along with supplies — laid on top of each other; two men, and a nearly decapitated woman. Blood dripped between the boards onto the ground. Bestla pointed at the feverish man. "He's been cut to the bone on his leg. We bandaged it, but… travelling. He's bled most of his life away."

"No all this!" Ranvieg said, looking at the crimson pool in the wagon. Bestla shrugged.

They lifted the rambling man out, carried him into the hall, and laid him on a palette in the infirmary. Ranvieg immediately unwound his blood soaked bandages.

"Wash these, Helja, and boil some water. His wounds are deep and he'll need to be stitched," Ranvieg said.

"Will he survive?" Helja said.

"I've stitched worse," Ranvieg said. Helja rushed off to the hearth.

"Who is he?" Ranvieg asked.

"He must be one of the new farmers from out east," Bestla said.

"How do you know he's not one of the raiders?" Grima asked.

"He's a farmer. His boots were outside, caked in muck from the field. His trousers and tunic, too. We found the four of them in a farmhouse near Brekkaklif," Bestla said. "Sadly, too late for his wife. He must have given a good fight though, he'd killed one. But, they were too much for him and they got her while he lay bleeding.

I was able to gut one of the pigs before he could escape. But... the farmer is raving. I had my doubts that he'd make it. He was barely alive when we found him."

"It's good you did," Ranvieg said. She washed him with a wet cloth, waiting for Helja to return.

"Who was with you?" Grima asked.

"Andras and Haldora. They helped load the wagon. Haldora's going to drive the farmer's cattle here, to Lutvin, and Andras is staying behind. She'll warn as many as she can who still don't know of the raiders..." Bestla paused, noticeably.

Grima gave her a curious look.

The scout tried, subtly, to motion with her head and eyes toward Vigdis' office, but abandoned her charades when Grima didn't catch the hint. Bestla grabbed Grima's arm and pulled her away to talk. The rest of the women returned to their work after Ranvieg politely refused their assistance.

Ranvieg placed cool cloths on the farmer's head and neck. She did her best to cut away his pants without disturbing the wound, carefully snipping with her shears. Still, he flinched when she tugged the cloth of his trousers around his mangled leg.

Some loose fibres from his pants had set in the wound. She knew she would need to be careful to remove it all, or she'd find the wound oozing in the morning.

Helja returned with the water.

"The wound is going to need cleaning before it's sewed," Ranvieg said. The younger woman nodded, and armed with washcloths they gave the farmer's leg a good wipe down.

Ranvieg lit an oil lamp to be able to examine him. He wasn't old. She estimated he still had some good years in him. Especially if his leg knit properly.

He actually fought the outlaws, she thought. He'd lost, but he'd stood up for his family and his home. That had to count for something.

"It *does* count for something," she whispered. *Something big.* Her heart swelled.

"Pardon?"

"Nothing, Helja. Thank you, I can take it from here. Go get some sleep, there will be much to do tomorrow."

Helja said her goodnights to everyone as she left the hall.

Ranvieg dipped the cloth into the hot water and cleaned the wound with careful, thorough strokes. It was deep and open, like a swollen, red flower. It would take all of her skill to save his leg.

She moved on to check the rest of him over, not wanting any surprises before she set to stitching. He had a number of cuts and bruises, all which would heal easily enough, but a dark line of dried blood on his upper arm caught her attention. She cut a slit through his sleeve with her shears.

Her discovery of a second wound surprised her. This one was older than the leg wound, not by much, but it led her to believe that his arm had been injured well before the attack at the farm.

She wrinkled her nose at the smell. His arm had swollen around the wound, pulling the crude stitches tight, and oozed when she squeezed it. The farmer flinched in his slumber, an unconscious reaction to the pain of the spreading corruption. She snipped the thick stitches and meticulously pulled each one out. They were woollen thread, which fell apart in the wound. She hoped she could clean this wound as thoroughly as she'd cleaned the one on his leg.

Ranvieg used her sharpest needle, run through a candle flame, and expensive silk thread to stitch his arm. More puss oozed when she stitched. She cleaned it all as best she could, then moved on to his leg. A weaver by trade, Ranvieg made her living with her fingers, pushing and pulling needle and thread, turning wool and flax into cloth, and cloth into silver. She sewed his wounds as though he were a child's doll.

"A few stitches to make it good as new." She snipped off the excess thread, sure to keep every spare bit. She bandaged the wounds, then covered him with a linen sheet and a double thick, woollen blanket. She watched him for a few moments, staring at his face. He'd been so fitful earlier, but now looked peaceful. The way the candlelight shone on his skin made him look majestic.

He was not a particularly handsome man, but his face was interesting. A childhood innocence had been laid upon him while he slept. She furrowed her brow when she wondered how he would react once he was told his wife was dead.

She turned and collected the bloody linens before she left.

They carried the last of the furnishings out of the anteroom that led to Vigdis' bed chambers as Hildegunn charged in, dodging two men carrying a chest out the door.

"There you are," she said to Odd, who was sitting in council with Vigdis. "Is Siv with you?"

Odd looked from her to Vigdis, who remained silent. "No. Why would she be with me?"

"She disappeared last night, after that *draugr*[11] vanished, and I had hoped—" She fidgeted with her household key ring.

"Maybe she's with Gudrun," Odd offered, with a sigh.

"She should be at home."

"Siv is a woman and makes her own choices. Perhaps she's chosen to be at her sister's side."

Hildegunn turned red and shook the keys at Odd. "Siv is too young to throw her life away... with an outlaw! I want her home, with her family!"

"If she's with Gudrun then she is with her family." Odd pointed at the keys. "Would you have passed those on to Gudrun? Thorkill's eldest daughter?"

Hildegunn stiffened. "She's an outlaw!" she snapped. "She has no interest in this family. If she wanted to earn these keys then she should have been at home, working on the farm, in the fields with the sheep. But, she'd rather be traipsing about in the woods, hunting and making silver for someone else, as far west as she can get!"

---

[11] Evil spirit

"You know, Gudrun was supposed to go with him, instead of Sigurd."

"Well now, *that* would have solved a lot of problems, wouldn't it?" Hildegunn growled.

Grima knocked on the open door. "Is this a bad time?" she asked.

"No," Vigdis said. "Hildegunn was just leaving."

Hildegunn scowled and spun on her heel and charged to the door. "Out of my way!" she shouted at Grima and Bestla, flapping her arms as she stormed off.

"It is time that I take my leave, as well," Odd said.

"Thank you for your counsel. Return when you've learned more," Vigdis said, and gave Odd a hug. The völur nodded at Grima as she left.

The room felt big and stark; only the large table and chairs remained.

"Bestla has returned," Grima said.

"Yes! Come in, take a seat," Vigdis said. Then added, "Audney, bring food and drink for Bestla."

"Yes frue," Audney replied and closed the door behind her.

Vigdis, Grima, and Bestla each took a seat. Vigdis crossed her hands on the table.

"What news do you bring, Bestla?"

"The outlaws sweep through the south, and in much greater numbers than we had first thought. The reports are that two to three hundred men vanquished Vestrijóborg, and are now attacking farms and homesteads, either in force or small groups. A number of farms have already been razed. A great many of the raiders speak in different tongues, foreigners. They are disorganised, hungry, and desperate, with little or no armour, wielding spears, axes, and stolen farm tools as weapons."

"Not an army, a mob," Grima said.

"A double-edged sword," Vigdis said. "Desperation is unpredictable, hard to plan for. Half starved and eager to find what they seek."

"*Us!*" Grima said.

Vigdis nodded, eyes cast down in solemn contemplation. "Where are they now?" she asked.

"They're already at Skald lake."

"That gives us three days at the very most!" Grima said, her eyes wide.

Too few days to get everything done, Vigdis thought. "We need to work harder," she said. Grima took a deep breath, then nodded. "All efforts to bring in the rest of the harvest need to be abandoned. Tomorrow we need everyone who isn't making spears, arrows, or armour, working on the defences."

"I will let them know," Grima said. "There are some volunteers who'll work by firelight tonight. I've had food, water, and braziers brought to the wall."

"Good. Bestla, as soon as you're ready take a small force of skirmishers out, and Loki be with you to harass the skitr out of them. Traps. Snares. Ambushes. You do the thing you do best. Slow them down as much as you can. The völur have been visiting the landvættir and offering sacrifices for them to protect us. Odd is hopeful. She is mostly concerned about the huldra, though. She says that the Lady of the Forest is agitated and refuses her counsel." She thought for a moment. "Bestla, how are Magnor's men travelling?"

"Most on foot. They've stolen some horses, but only a dozen or so, and use them for scouting. Also, they haven't crossed any lakes or fjords at all, preferring to move around them."

"Good. Travelling around the waters will slow them down," Vigdis said. "We need to keep them away from Lutvin for as long as we can. Let's use our knowledge of the land to our best advantage. Audney will have food for you in the hall and Grima will make sure you have the supplies you need. Eat quickly, then leave with your skirmishers, and may Skadi and Ullr be with you." Vigdis knew that Bestla made sacrifices to Skadi, goddess of hunting, and Ullr, the archer god who never missed.

Vigdis gave Bestla an embrace, then they left Vigdis alone in her war room.

Three days, Vigdis thought, wringing her hands. *Not enough.*

CHAPTER SEVENTEEN
An Egil Crows

A forest cat sniffed the bark of a tree before she rubbed her brow on it. She leapt up in the darkness. Sharp claws easily hooked into the bark and she leapt again, pouncing her way up the trunk to the first branch. She sniffed the air. Men were very close.

She prowled further out onto the large limb, guided by the pungent odour. The branch overhung a cliff. *There they are, below.* A ramshackle frame leaning against the cliff's base did little to keep any rain off the man sheltering beneath it. She caught the musky sweet scent of *angelikarot* smoke. It stung her sensitive nose, even in the rain and surrounded by fragrant elm. He was awake, smoking a pipe. Too wet for a fire. She crouched.

Her keen eyes cut through the gloom, revealing over a hundred similar shelters in the valley. She padded her way to another fork in the branch and lay down to watch the sprawling camp.

A small group approached.

"Egil!" one of them called out.

The man below her sat up, still puffing. "It's a miserable night, Yarri, you're not here to make it better, are you?" he said.

"No," Yarri said. "We found another one!" He held up a stick with a woven hoop balanced on the end. It swayed as he walked.

A mischievous grin spread across the cat's lips, nearly reaching from one ear tip to the other.

Egil stood and leaned in for a closer look at the hoop.

"What are they?" he asked, reaching toward it. Yarri pulled the stick away.

"Do *not* touch it!" he warned. "This is a cursing hoop. You will get nine years of bad luck if it touches you. Make your tongue turn black, too."

The cat snickered. It was doubtful anyone's tongue had ever turned black from a cursing hoop. Though, there was tell of a farmer whose wife used one to turn his manhood black, before it fell off. But, not the tongue.

"This is the third one we found here, plus the other two from the last camp. The landvættir are angry."

Egil shook his head. "I do not believe in vættir, or any other spirits."

"Then what do you call the thing that blocked our path in the gorge?"

"A landslide. Get your spears and we'll take a walk."

The group dispersed to their shelters to get themselves ready.

The cat turned, catching a claw on the bark. Egil snatched up his spear and searched the dark branches of the tree. The cat bounded away and Egil yelped.

"*Ahh!* Maybe there *are* spirits here!"

The cat couldn't stop smiling as she crept back down the trunk to the soggy ground. She slinked past a miserable sentry sitting in the darkness, coughing and snivelling. She weaved through the underbrush and autumn leaves, until she reached the horse corral; no more than a rope between two trees with the horses tied to it. She climbed up one trunk and gnawed at the line. Her sharp teeth made quick work of it, and the line fell. The horses were free, but they just stood there, staring at her.

The cat hissed at them and the horses spooked and trotted into the woods.

Once they were out of her sight, she leapt down and slinked out of the camp, into the woods. Another moonless night, yet her vision was finest in the dark.

She smelled out the grove where she'd left Haldana and Mista. She walked to the ring of trees where they were talking quietly in the dark, giving offerings to the landvættir.

With a powerful word — one of the many first spoken by the Vanier, the gods of seidr — the cat transformed into a woman: Odd.

"Volur!" Haldana said.

"Freyja's blessings upon you, sisters," Odd said, bowing her head, with grace. The trees sighed a greeting. "And Freyja's blessings upon you, as well," Odd said.

Haldana smiled. She laid a handful of tree nuts in the centre of the ring, then left with Mista.

"The landvættir of the trees are with us. They will help to confuse Magnor's directions."

"We have done well," Odd said. She crossed her hands in front of her. "A fear chafes at them, because of our efforts. If we cannot break their shields, then we'll break their minds. Now, it is late. Let us be off, sisters. Go home and catch your second sleep, I have one more visit yet to make before I return."

The three of them stood with their arms on each other's shoulders, foreheads touching. They chanted, growing the seidr within them until it roiled like a boiling pot of water.

Suddenly, the magic washed over them like a wave and the three women burst into a flurry of black feathers and fur. Odd transformed into a forest cat, Mista a crow, and Haldana a weasel, before they scurried and flew away through the woods.

* * *

Magnor huddled with a smouldering fire, under a dripping tarpaulin tied between two poles. The spear lay in his lap. The wood's patina had darkened over years of use. Even in the dim light of the flickering coals Magnor could appreciate its craftsmanship. The steel of the warhead gleamed in the demonic orange light of the embers, which accentuated the runes carved into it.

Its keen edge had been expertly sharpened after forging with a mystical alchemy. It was pristine, unmarred, even after generations of use. This could not be counted as a mundane tool for thrusting and hewing. Not a utility weapon to be thrown, forgotten, and replaced. *No! I hold a treasure! A true weapon of war, a paragon of the gods, fit for a jarl…* Fit for a true leader of men. Magnor's heart raced.

"Waylayer of ships," he whispered, unaware that he'd given voice to the words as he caressed the weapon. Providence had brought it to him, delivered by the hand of a woman. *That* woman. He gripped the shaft until his knuckles turned white, teeth gritted at the thought of her.

He'd fantasised about how he would kill her. She would succumb to his wrath and his desire to strangle away her life with his bare hands. If not that, then stabbing would do. Pummelling, whipping, branding—

He jumped up and paced, a fervent ache in his bones too much for him to keep still. It was unnatural to go this long without strong drink. He slapped the crevasse's stone wall, spraying water in his face. Who was she, to defeat a whole unit of his marines, and disable the ship? *With just this spear?*

"In a rowboat!" he shouted. "I vow this blade will not taste blood before it is quenched in Gudrun Thorkildatter's chest!"

Ander moaned, hog-tied and left in the rain, beside Magnor's tarp. Magnor kicked him in the back. "Huh? You said you know her. Who is she? Who is she to be able to destroy my ship, then dive into the sea and escape? Leaving my ship to…to…" Magnor's jaw ached from grinding his teeth. *Like waves through my fingers.* It was unconscionable! An embarrassment. A dozen men crushed by the yard and another dozen drowned, and double that number injured beyond usefulness.

The most grievous damage to Magnor remained wounded pride.

Wounds knit, bones mend, soldiers can be found and glory bought, but honour… *It never heals; it can only be changed.* The men would see it as weakness. He needed to solidify his leadership, quickly.

His father taught him all leadership is precarious; the powerful are always in peril. He needed leverage, to keep his men from wanting to stretch his neck in a noose. Only the promise of treasure protected him, for now. And, the threat of Roar's maul and wild temper helped greatly. At least he had the unwavering loyalty of that monster; a berserker who served him without question or hesitation.

They'd wasted too much time gathering themselves together and still hadn't been able to cross through the crag.

"At least I'm not being dragged by a horse, eh Ander?" Magnor laughed at the lump of a man lying unconcious in the rain.

Blocked at every turn by fjords and cliffs. Every path brings us back to the crag. Could the pimp have been telling the truth about the landvættir? How else could he explain it? Even now they made camp at the crag, all other paths blocked by lakes and fjords.

The damp cold seeped into everything, making it impossible to get the chill out of one's bones. He shared his cramped shelter with the fire, to keep the rain off it. He imagined his cup of boiled water to be thin tavern ale. He sniffed it, wondering if he'd boiled it enough. Three men who had drunk well water were poisoned, and abandoned. The water had to be brewed or boiled well before it could be drunk.

"If only I had the time to brew," he muttered, pouring the cup of water back into the boiling pot. He pulled his cloak tighter around his shoulders, but the wet fur did little to give him any warmth. A cold breeze cut through. "Fenrir's balls, it's cold!" He ignored Ander, coughing and shivering.

Magnor absently fidgeted with the golden skull broach pinning his cloak. *How? How do I turn this rabble into an army?* They were successful at Vestrijóborg, but they'd had surprise and ravenous desperation on their side.

Perhaps it's all been a test, he thought. Losing his ship; being bested by a peasant girl— he cringed. It took him a few breaths to work through that emasculation. He realised he'd been staring at the spear.

"All just the price to be paid for such a prize." Delivered by the hand of one who had wreaked so much havoc. *Gudrun.* He hated her name so much, he couldn't even say it aloud, as though it were a curse upon his tongue. She'd cost him everything.

"Everything!" he yelled at the spear, strangling it with a death grip. Spit drooled off his chin. He wiped the back of his hand over his face. *None of it will matter, not once I've conquered Lutvin. I'll kill Gudrun and be vindicated! Redeemed! To lord over this miserable...*

Wavering torchlights caught his eye, bobbing toward his tent. Fifteen, maybe twenty. *What's this, now?* he thought. "Roar!"

The grizzly-sized man emerged from his shelter, dishevelled and half naked. Even without his bear coat, he looked feral. A beastly mane of orange and white hair spanned the expanse of his chest and shoulders. He squinted at Magnor and grunted.

"Get your hammer," Magnor said, nodding toward the approaching torches. "Looks like they've brought their spears. Good. They're learning."

Roar sniffed at the air, then shook his head. He heaved the maul from his shelter with one iron arm, and draped his bearskin over his shoulders. He squatted beside Magnor, the maul's handle between his knees, and warmed his hands over the coals.

Magnor sat back and stretched out his legs.

The men strode to Magnor's campsite.

"Where are these swift feet when we're set to marching?" Magnor scoffed. It was easy to spot who was leading the small group. "Egil. Are you lost? Have you and the others already forgotten my orders?"

"Magnor," Egil said. He'd stopped in front of Magnor's shelter and the others crowded in close. "We demand answers from you, right here and now."

Roar stood, and they backed up, giving him plenty of room.

"Go back to bed, Egil," Magnor said, dismissing them with a lazy wave. "Tomorrow we have an early start and a long march to find a crossing over this fjord."

"Right *here* and *now!*" Egil shouted, thrusting a finger at the ground. Others in the back murmured.

Magnor sized Egil up. He was outspoken among the men, especially since they'd left Vestrijóborg. Magnor looked at each of their faces, scanning them carefully. The men shuffled nervously, some avoided his stare.

Magnor sighed, then stood. He drove Skera-Brynja's end into the ground with a thud. *They can all witness its glory in my hand.* "What is it that you are not clear on, my friend?" Magnor asked.

"This 'campaign' has led us nowhere. We beat and slaughter peasants and chase after rumours, all under the direction of that pathetic whelp!" Egil pointed at Ander, a mere lump, unconscious on the grass. "Gold and halls full of riches, or whatever other bedtime stories your foolish father filled your head with, when the only things we've found on these bleak shores are cow skitr, rain, and cursed forests. Another lake. Another fjord. Another farmstead, abandoned and cleared out, nothing left but rats in empty cupboards. This land is cursed, and has cursed us! Even the hunting is pitiful. The animals have been driven out or slaughtered and left to rot by the fleeing skitr-farmers!" Egil kicked a stone into the woods.

"I cannot control how the farmers leave their homes, or what their wives do with their cupboards," Magnor said, as cool as winter steel. "It's not my fault that you clod about with clumsy feet and scare the game."

Roar chuckled, a deep resounding laughter, as though he were in a wide cave. He crossed his hands on the handle of the downturned maul.

"Damn you to Hel!" Egil spat. "*You* brought us here, half starved with no provision, except fanciful promises of gold! We could be in

Albion, feasting on king's mutton! Instead, we freeze and starve in the rain, not even a shelter, for everything you've promised us! Now, you heed us, for we come to you requiring answers, and if you can't give them, then we'll replace you with someone who can."

"Hear hear!" Some of them crossed their arms across their chests. "That's right."

Magnor shook his head and grinned. Perhaps, this was the opportunity he needed to prune this tree, get the others back in line.

"Egil, you were born in Albion, were you not?" Magnor said.

"Yes, what of it?"

"We found you in the prison camp before we got there. Why was that? For poaching? Or was it theft? Murder, perhaps?"

Egil puffed out his chest. "What does that matter, now?" he hissed, through gritted teeth.

"It doesn't. You're just another forgettable, miserable thief, who will always find a way to steal and cheat your way through other's lives. You had no problem escaping Albion with me, following my lead, pulling my ship's oars. And, now you are upset at the conditions of your fate. Disagreeable to the promises that you weighed upon your own conscience. Let all here know that the outlaw, Egil Lillyfoot, is not the master of his choosing, but a bumbling follower of his fool's blind ignorance!"

Egil's eyes widened and his face was red. He leaped back and lifted his spear, knuckles white on the shaft. Roar raised his maul too late, as Egil thrust at the middle of Magnor's chest.

Magnor barely moved Skera-Brynja to deflect Egil's spear aside, as though he'd known what Egil was going to do before Egil knew himself. Egil's eyes popped when he realised he'd thrust harmlessly past and left *his* chest exposed.

Magnor jabbed at his ribs and Egil howled and fell forward. The handle of Magnor's seax protruded from Egil's side, up to the hilt into his lung. Magnor stepped aside and let Egil stumble over the hot coals that remained of his fire. Sparks jumped like glowing, ripe seeds in the wind, and Egil groaned as he stomped about, groping for the blade, until his foot pushed out from under him and he fell back with a thud.

The group jumped back, startled by the speed of the strike. Egil writhed and grasped at the handle of Magnor's seax, groaning with frustration. The handle was slippery with blood and his weakening limbs shook as he succumbed. He let out a gasp and stiffened in the dirt, shuddering his final throes.

"He's dead!" Yarri brayed. The men stared at Egil's fresh corpse, mouths agape and eyes wide, unsure of their next move.

Magnor straightened himself to his full height.

"He should not have attacked me so, without a challenge, like a murderous assassin." He spat on Egil's head.

The group took another step back. Magnor knelt beside Egil's body. He gently put his hand over the dead man's eyes.

"May the gods have mercy on this fool," he said. He used Egil's tunic to wipe the blood from the seax's handle, then wrenched the blade from his side. Egil's chest deflated with a long gurgling *hisssss*, and the men huddled together, staring at Magnor in awe.

Roar dropped the maul's head on the ground and leaned on the handle.

"Egil was ambitious," Magnor said. "Too much so. He sought for his own power and control. Even if he'd been successful, and had taken me down, then what? Where would he have taken you? What would he have you do then? Back to Albion? To starve the rest of you on a perilous, fruitless journey? Not from these shores, until *well* after winter. So, he'd have you stay here and freeze? Well, I've planned for that. Egil had no vision for what lay ahead. But, I have, every detail, inherited from my father, and his father. I swear to each of you: we are closer to our goal than you realise."

Magnor wiped the blood from his blade before sheathing it. He stepped over Egil, and squatted back under his shelter with his legs crossed. He flicked at the scattered coals with a stick to push them back together into a pile, then laid a twig on top. It hissed and crackled from the heat.

"You're wondering why we're here," Magnor said. His voice was low enough that the men had to step closer and lean in. "Wondering, what is so important that cannot be found in any other village?" He poked the coals around the dry wood.

"Before my grandfather settled his family, he answered a call put out by Jarl Mootlief, in Boddahiem, to go viking in Albion. They raided towns and monasteries all along the coast, starting in the north and attacking their way south. They had great success, and soon filled three ships until the gunnels touched the water with the largest treasure hoard my grandfather had ever seen. Enough to make every man whose family came from the Danelaw, wealthy until his sons', sons', *sons* had enough to rule as kings upon Midgard. Some of the treasure was given to the warriors who'd fought alongside Mootlief, and their families. Including my grandfather and my family.

"But, the Norns weave while weavers sleep, so while Mootlief had been away, he had his throne taken from him by his brother, Halvard. A servant loyal to Mootlief told him of his brother's treachery, and the trap that was waiting for him upon his return to Boddahiem. Halvard planned to take the treasure for himself.

"Mootlief raged! And nearly tore down his own ship, and without a thought planned to attack Halvard, trap or not. He swore he would charge through Halvard's front gate, slaughter any who blocked his path to challenge his brother to a duel of honour. His closest advisors pleaded with their jarl to reconsider, and Mootlief cut their heads off. Yet his fury grew! He swore to do battle with Halvard, to plunge his brother into war for a hundred years, if he had to!

"Then, his wife, Svanhilde, stepped in front of him, nursing their son. Mootlief raised his sword to strike her down, too, but she stepped toward her raging husband, pulled the baby from her breast and with her arms wide shouted, "Would you slice out the heart of the woman you swore oaths to, before gods and men, priests and law speakers; or, perhaps, through her belly, where your son grows? Here is your eldest! Should he learn your ways and call you father? Or would you watch your children smash upon the stones?"'"

Magnor looked up at them. The men were grey as ash, eyes wide, enthralled.

"Mootlief did not return to Boddahiem. Instead, he took his ships and sailed into the mists with a small army of men, never to be found again. Halvard was furious, of course. He spent the rest of his life, and his entire kingdom's wealth, trying to find the plundered gold, which he claimed rights to as jarl. But, as all fools do, he disgraced himself and his family, was overthrown and declared an outlaw. They say he died in a caravan tent, begging a charlatan for medicine to cure flesh rot.

"My grandfather also searched for Mootlief, until the obsession killed him. He studied every broken twig, tracked down even the most unlikely hint of a trail that might lead him to the treasure, but was never able to find it. My father also caught a fever for Mootlief's gold. The closest he ever got was to discover that Mootlief had settled somewhere in the Western fjords, with his wife and son. But, it is important to think about what changed Mootlief's mind. What was it that made him abandon his vengeance forever? Something so great, as to slake his lust for war, but not just for that day, no! It was something that satisfied him forever..."

The men leaned in, waited to hear more. Magnor revelled in it. He hid a grin as he poked at the dying embers. *They're mine again,* he thought.

"What was it?" Yarri croaked.

"His son."

The men let out a collective sigh of understanding and nodded at each other.

"Then, what happened to the treasure?" one of them asked, tentatively. "How do *you* know where it is?"

Magnor grinned. He looked up from the glowing embers at their eager faces and savoured the moment. Even Roar was leaning in to bask in Magnor's wisdom. Magnor understood it, now. *I was born for this, passed knowledge from my grandfather, to my father, to me.* It gave him a power over the men stronger than any threats that could be made against them. He revelled in it.

"In the prison camp in Albion, I made a point of getting close to Chief Gudbrand. One might say that we could have become friends, except that... he had revealed something to me that ensured that a friendship between us could never be. You see, Gudbrand was very proud of his home, and would talk about it in great detail; where it was, how they lived, on and on. Mootlief had two sons, whom he loved more than anything or anyone else. As it turned out, Gudbrand's home and Mootlief's eldest share the same name: Lutvin."

The men gasped, the final piece having dropped into place.

"I will not leave these 'cow skitr shores' until I have seen for myself where Mootlief's treasure is hidden in that town. I will tear it apart with my bare hands! Burn it to the ground, if I have to." Magnor knew he had them, but in a moment, they would be eating out of the palm of his hand. "The men of Lutvin, the true warriors, are all dead. Their corpses either lie in decay in Albion, or lay at the bottom of the sea. Only women and children remain there; farmers, sheep herders, and weavers. They are defenceless and ripe for the picking. Who knows? Perhaps each of you will be able to take a wife or two, and have sons of your own."

They looked at each other with vicious grins and nasty laughs.

That got them. The mutton heads smiled and clapped each other on the back, laughing and bragging at how easy it will be to walk in and take it all for themselves.

"Now!" Magnor said. They silenced immediately. "The hour is late and we have a long march ahead of us. Get to your beds and sleep."

They left, cheerful and laughing, praising Magnor's name. Magnor could not have planned it better if he'd tried. He turned to Roar.

"Take this piece-of-skitr's carcass and string him up on a tree at the far side of camp. I want them all to see Egil flying when we leave tomorrow. They need to know what happens when they try to cross me, or question my leadership."

Roar grunted and scooped up Egil's body. He threw it over one shoulder as though it were a sack of grain, then trudged into the darkness.

Magnor smiled. A laugh burst forth. The men were back under his control. *Even if that were to change, I have something stronger than Roar: I have their desperation.* He gave them a taste of his knowledge by serving the legend of Lutvin's treasure, which brought them back in line again. *Leave them wanting, drip out only enough to keep them dependent, like dogs in the master's kennel.*

In Vestrijóborg they were desperate for food. Egil made them desperate for information. And like all hollow men, they were also desperate for women. He turned to the unconscious man, prone beside him.

"Isn't that right, Ander? So desperate that they'll even pay for it, huh?" Magnor sneered.

He would keep them in the dark just enough that they would need to turn to him for leadership. Without him, they were just outlaws; barely surviving, like wild animals, hunted and driven off from every corner of the world. Not even a pitiful death would give them relief; never able to enter the Alfather's Great Hall.

He laughed again. He was the kind of man who only cared about gold, not his status with the gods. Some of these men did. Still, Magnor knew in the end the thing that would serve him best, that would keep his power over them, would be the particular brand of morality that he could impart onto any man: his personal, unshakable faith in greed.

"I will find your village, Gudrun Thorkilldatter. I will take what I want from you, trim the flesh from your bones, and scatter the rest to burn."

CHAPTER EIGHTEEN

Autumn Feast

T he children were being called to sleep by the wisemothers laying herbs on the fire. Clary sage and lavender smoke drifted from the hearth and the sweet aroma enriched Karl Hall. The old mothers bade the children to lay in the pile of furs by the fire and listen to their wisefathers tell the story of the first Yule, in the low firelight, as servants quietly cleared the tables and floors.

Gudrun and Siv went with the stumbling karlfolk, helping to carry them through the doors.

"Jarlhalla!" The karls waved empty skoals above their heads.

Siv laughed, charmed by their mirthful enthusiasm for more drink.

The night was crisp and fresh, and they cheered each other on, staggering through the streets.

The sound of tiny bells made Gudrun stop just inside the door. She'd heard bells like that, long ago. The wisemothers rang them over each child as they listened to the wisefathers tell their stories.

"A blessing, to keep evil away from the children while they sleep," Elli said, propping up Oskar as they passed Gudrun.

"My aunt used to do the same, until I was ten winters." Gudrun grinned and looked at her feet.

Seasoned men congregated around braziers outside the doors,

smoking pipes as they whittled with short, hooked knives. They played dice and board games using figures carved from bone. As people left the hall the men wished them goodnight and exchanged playful insults and nicknames.

A wrinkly old man laughed, saying Gudrun had a face like flatbread. "Levandlit!" he shouted. They all groaned and shook their heads.

Gudrun chuckled and made a fist at him. "This doesn't seem like a game that wins many friends."

"No, there are a lot of critics," another old man quipped. "That's why all his teeth are missing."

Wrinkly snatched his hat off his head and opened his mouth wide to show naked, pink gums. The crowd shuffling past burst into laughter.

"Well, if what's under the table is as wilted as what's above, then I'd call you 'Visna Epli' — shrivelled apples."

"Ahh! But, that one doesn't count!" Wrinkly protested. "My wife already calls me that!"

"Well, then let's leave your *visna epli* in your wife's hands," Gudrun laughed.

They stumbled up a cobbled street where the houses were so close together that it felt as though they were walking through a canyon.

"Are you going to Jarlhalla now?" Gudrun asked Oskar.

"Yes! We'll play games, dance, sing, and end the night with jarlsmead and a good fight!" He raised his arms in triumph, a silly grin on his face. The grin turned into a laugh, infectious enough to be caught by the others. Two men took over carrying Oskar and Elli stopped just outside the doors.

"I'm going to stay at Karlhall to be with the children," she said.

"I think I'll stay, too," Gudrun said.

"No! You must come with us!" Oskar protested.

"Please Gudrun," Siv said. "I want to go to Jarl hall. They make it sound so magical! And, to see it now, at the Autumn feast! Let's go see the hall, Gudrun, I don't want to go without you."

Gudrun glanced at the group ahead of the two of them, beckoning for them to join. Something one of the men said earlier came to her mind. *Could I ask the Jarl to send his army to defend Lutvin?* She realised she had to ask.

"Alright, let's go," she said.

Siv let out a happy yelp and grabbed Gudrun's arm. They said goodnight to Elli and caught up with the others.

Gudrun was glad that she'd only sipped at the cider when the skols were passed around. She'd kept a close, sober eye on Siv. It was her duty to take care of her younger sister. She didn't trust these men around Siv. Gudrun was confident that they wouldn't risk losing face in Siv's eyes by bullying her older sister away. Most of them were too scared to approach Siv, anyway.

Beauty can have that effect on some, Gudrun thought. In her estimation the men she thought might have been bold enough to try something with Siv had their wives within sight, and those women already did a good job of keeping their husbands in check. Gudrun linked arms with Siv and held her tight.

The pack of them lurched forward through the street. They'd lost one along the way — stopped to vomit and passed out right there — but they were a determined group and pushed on without him.

"The besht for lasht," they slurred, again and again. It became a joke. "You'ven't seen anythink like Jarl-all." They sang and laughed through the streets and the crowds became thicker until they came around the final bend and Jarlhalla came into view.

Gudrun and Siv stopped when they saw it, as though they'd forgotten to keep walking.

"That is... the largest hall I've ever seen!" Siv said, her jaw dropped.

Gudrun's breath caught in her chest.

Two ebony timbers, thicker than any tree Gudrun could imagine, towered over them, making up the front of the hall. The timbers had been carved from living trees, still rooted into the earth. They crossed at the top like an 'A' and held up a massive, arching roof. The roof was like the bottom of *Skithblathnir* — the mythical ship of the gods. More fat timbers along the sides held up the roof, like gigantic ribs. Two sets of double doors hung between the front timbers, set into walls that were as white as milk. Above the doors hung a carving of a monstrous wolf's head, baring its teeth. The doors were open wide and the celebration had spilled out into the yard surrounding Jarl hall.

"Valhalla in Midgard!" Siv said, breathless. Gudrun could only nod, her eyes wide.

The walls shined. The ebony timbers were carved with such detail that Gudrun had difficulty believing that they hadn't been made by Odin himself. It was intimidating to Gudrun's simple, country naivety.

Hundreds upon hundreds of people sat outdoors at simple tables and milled around braziers. They drank and ate, laughing and chattering loudly.

Within the crowded yard a game of *riðfalla* was being played — one man sat on the shoulders of another and swung a bat at other riders to knock them to the ground. Gudrun laughed, remembering a funny moment from a game of riðfalla at the lumber camp. Oskar grabbed Hugi's arm and the two of them ran to the game, like boys eager to have their turn to play.

Men were leading a group of mares around to the back of the hall, then followed with spirited stallions.

"Ah-ha!" one of the other men with them said — Gudrun couldn't remember his name — and jingled a leather purse on his belt. He pulled two others in the direction of where the horses had been taken. "I'll show you which to bet on. I always make silver at horse fights," he bragged, as the three of them disappeared into the crowd.

The group that Gudrun and Siv had come with melted away into the celebration and the sisters were left standing on their own before the great hall, its doors open wide, beckoning.

Gudrun clutched Siv's arm and they walked into the hall.

Crossing the threshold was stepping into a new world; as though they'd passed into Valhalla without having died — at least, not that Gudrun could recount. A blinding, golden light spilled over an ocean of crowds, packed in at every table, bench, aisle, and corner. The sisters stood shoulder to shoulder, shuffling along with a current of people, all in differing states of dress and undress, singing, dancing, pounding fists on tables while stomping along with minstrels.

"This *music!*" Siv cried. She bounced along with the drums and rebec, rolling her shoulders along with the tune of the panpipes and the lyre. She jumped and danced and shook her head as they followed the flow of the crowd.

Gudrun couldn't help notice the dresses that the women and girls wore; fine, white linens and shades of rich blues, yellows, orange, and green, even reds. Delicate frills and embroidery with intricate stitching adorning long sleeves. Silver and gold tassels hung from silken, braided waist cords.

The men wore their best tunics, cleaned and repaired — easier not to expect too much from men — their hair carefully combed and braided. Beards were never shaved to the skin, not like in the east, and certainly not like the Romans. A lot of the younger men cropped their whiskers; short, and shaped with a razor. It was in sharp contrast to the generations before them; salty, hard men who wore their beards thick and long. Tyr, Odin and Thor wore thick beards, reason enough to keep a blade away from the face and on the hip, where it belonged.

Gudrun had second thoughts creeping into her head. All of the women her age had golden broaches holding up their long, perfect dresses. Not a single one of them the bronze that she and Siv were accustomed to. She shuddered. She wore a tunic and trousers, like a man, and felt panic tugging at her chest from the inside.

"We have to leave, Siv," she said, grabbing her by the arm.

"Why?"

"Look around. Look at those dresses."

"They're beautiful, Gudrun. What's wrong?"

"We're too plain, I'm not even wearing a dress," she whispered. She'd turned beet red.

Siv's wide smile grew larger until she laughed. "But this is what we have, Gudrun. Should we undress? I'm sure that would turn a few heads."

"I am serious, Siv! Look how they're dressed!"

Hundreds of people, dressed in a fortune's worth of exquisite clothing, sat at wide tables that stretched out as far as could be seen. Even more food was being served here in Jarlhalla. Platters were piled high with roasted meats, vegetables, breads, and cheeses, all being gorged upon. The guests washed it all down with rivers of mead, ale, and wine. Kegs and casks were set all about the hall, each one within quick stumbling distance from the other. Those who were not eating, were dancing, singing, and laughing together.

Not an empty hand could be seen. They held either food or drink, or child, comrade, or lover; all things seemed to be as excessive as they were accessible. Even gold and silver dangled and fell from carefree hands.

Gudrun stared, wide eyed, at a large stone pedestal that propped up a golden tub, filled with coins and trinkets; a buffet of opulence to which revellers helped themselves, only to lose the treasures drunken moments later, idly slipped from clumsy fingers.

The stone floor was covered in straw, littered with empty and smashed cups, crockery, and a respectable fortune — gold and silver coins, rings, and choice treasures — lost in the chaff and trampled upon in their debauchery.

"Come on, we've seen the hall, and I've found my blacksmith. Let's go," Gudrun said, pulling Siv's arm. Gudrun turned and nearly ran into a large man standing before her. He was shirtless, with his rotund belly hanging over the thick leather belt that barely held up his trousers, and wore a metal skullcap. He had two drinking horns and held out one of them for Siv. He wobbled and swayed to keep his balance, drunkenness doing its best to tip him over.

"Mead for a kissh from a goddesshh," he slurred, his tongue swollen from drink.

"What would a faithful wife's husband think of such an offer?" Siv smiled, batting her lashes.

The man belched.

"When it comes to *fowl* drunkenness," Siv continued, "I prefer not to ruffle the feathers of that bird. And, though you are large, I presume you are not so childish as to behave like a spring bull and trample my honour."

He blinked at her. He quickly drank the first horn down, then the next. He put the empty horns to either side of his skullcap.

"*Mooorrraaww!*" he brayed and swept his head up like a bull. "Better a shpring bull, than a feast day ox!"

Gudrun and Siv laughed, and the man charged through the crowd with the horns held on his head.

"Well done," Gudrun said.

"This is all so wonderful! Please, Gudrun. We can't go yet. Tomorrow we'll wake up and the dream will be over!" Siv said.

Gudrun's mouth clamped shut, eyes wide, staring at her little sister. She looked around them, and at the dirty sleeves of her tunic.

"Our dress will have to do," Siv shrugged, "and if the Jarl won't see us because of what we're wearing, then let him provide better for us, hey?" She laughed, wrinkling her nose, and elbowed Gudrun in the ribs.

Gudrun loved Siv's laugh. Ever since she'd been a baby she'd crinkled her nose when she laughed. Now her baby sister was a young woman. Idealistic. Inspired. Everything that Gudrun wished she was, but wasn't. She would have traded her strength for just a small measure of Siv's charm. Siv looked at her with her hands clasped, pleading.

"Fine. Follow me," Gudrun said. "We'll just take a look at the Jarl's court before we leave, so you can see what dresses the gods have made for *those* women."

Siv whooped and threw her arms around Gudrun's neck.

Gudrun grabbed her hand and pushed through the crowd. Siv laughed and sang along with the music.

Thick garlands of fragrant flowers hung, billowing, from railings around the second level. Even more people gathered there, dancing, drinking, and laughing. A great wooden 'sky' above them held broad chandeliers, suspended like iron clouds. Gudrun imagined this was what Asgard, home of the gods, looked like, with rings of thick candles sparkling like stars.

Siv's right, this is *a dream.*

Four tree trunks, each as wide as a cart is long, stood as sentinels on the corners of a central square, and stretched up through a second floor to the ceiling. Giant warriors carved into the wood faced into the middle, protecting the hearths with swords and shields ready. Thick rafters sprouted and branched out from these four pillars and cradled the second level. Above that, they were the bones for wood and rope causeways that weaved through, like rigging within an overturned ship. Even more people were perched upon those shelves, voyeuristic cliff birds scrutinising the fray below.

It was as though the Tree of Life itself had sprung up among the stones and the fruit of its blossoms was this godly structure. The palatial hall was more than Gudrun could have ever imagined. She hadn't simply walked into a dream, no, much more than that. This was a sublime vision that had come to life around her.

They moved through the hall as though in slow motion, keeping with the flow of the undulating crowd. They had no idea where they were supposed to go to find the Jarl's court, so did their best to hold on to each other's hands and not get separated by the waves of people.

The music propelled dancers across a dance floor, like a wind gliding them in front of a musician's platform. Flute and pipe, harp and lyre, played well with the drum, and another instrument that

Gudrun had never heard before. It too had strings, but was played by drawing an arrowlike shaft across them. It reminded her of a rebec, but the sound was sweeter. Were all the wonders of *Miklagard* set here within these very walls? Surely, this jarl could afford to send a small part of his army to Lutvin.

A wide staircase led up, but Gudrun steered them toward the centre of the hall, where fragrant smoke rose from a roasting pit. The pit had two flights of stairs that descended on either side. *Papa would appreciate this craftsmanship,* Gudrun thought enthusiastically, then frowned. *Would have...*

Within the pit were three of the hall's largest hearths, each one was roasting an ox, carefully tended to by a troupe of servants. Set next to each hearth was an enormous oval keg.

"Look at those!" Gudrun pointed. "They must be the largest in all of Midgard!" Each keg was at least ten paces wide and stood twice as tall. Groups congregated around them, mostly young men, too green to know to stop drinking. They laughed and played the stupid games that only soused, juvenile men could invent, too often something that resulted in a broken bone or a fat lip.

A fight broke out. One thrown bucket of water stopped it, to great laughter and applause.

"Do *not* let go of my hand," Gudrun said and pulled Siv closer. Siv smiled and nodded, cradling Gudrun's hand to her chest. Gudrun adjusted the kerchief on Siv's head.

From where they stood, they had a nearly full view of the sprawling carnival. Levels above and below, the kitchen and serving tables which took up the entirety of one side, and on the other, ranges had been set up. Archery, javelin, and the most popular: axe throwing. Large crowds of blustering men and fawning women gathered to watch their kin win prizes in contests of skill; climbing, wrestling, running. All manner of folk competed, young and old, men and women, strong or agile, or simply drunken courage.

"It all looks to be more fun than competitive," Siv said.

Another fight broke out. Gudrun shook her head. "Apparently not."

In an area behind the ranges, logs had been set up for men to chop and hack through to prove who was fastest with an axe. Chunks of wood scattered across the floor as three men sent wood chips flying under the flash of steel.

"They do that in the lumber camp, too," Gudrun said.

Artisans sliced and carved logs into sculptures; a bear, a wolf, a dragon and a horse. Their skill with blades and chisels was admirable.

Siv beamed, unable to keep her eyes on one thing for too long before spying something else to marvel at.

Then, Gudrun found what she was looking for. Beyond the towering pillars a low wall had a lattice frame on it with light, billowing cloth. It cordoned off a court within the hall and obscured a procession of nobleman well-wishers. The tail of the queue ended in the farthest depths of the court and snaked around until the head of it came to rest upon a dais. There, through the lattice, Gudrun could just make out three tall chairs on a raised platform.

"There!" she and Siv said at the same time. They each pointed in a different direction. Gudrun looked to where Siv was looking, wondering what she could have possibly…

A long table on the kitchen side had a crowd of excited children hopping around it, waiting to taste the pies, sweets, and myriad of honey glazed treats and candied fruits that servants were setting upon the board.

"Ahh. Cake."

Siv's mouth was watering. "Sweeet…" Her eyes glazed.

"No, Siv. *There!*" Gudrun pointed across the pit to the other side. "That's where we'll find the jarl," Gudrun said.

"Are you sure you want to see the jarl, now?"

"The men in Karl hall had suggested I ask the jarl for an army."

Siv burst out laughing. Then her smile dropped once she'd realised that Gudrun was being serious.

"Gudrun, you can't even speak with Vigdis without getting nervous, how are you going to ask the jarl for an army?" Siv snorted.

"I'm not. You are."

"Oh, no!"

"Oh yes. And once we have our answer from the jarl, you can eat sweets."

"I thought you only wanted a spear," Siv groaned. The air was resplendent with the smoked scent of roast beasts, breads, and herbs. "Just one taste, please?" Siv begged, doe eyes on full display.

"We see the jarl first, then I promise you can eat your fill of cakes," Gudrun said. Siv pouted, which never failed to make Gudrun laugh. She put her arm around Siv. "I can't risk the Jarl thinking it rude of us, enjoying his hospitality before providing an introduction then asking for him to commit men to Lutvin's protection. Besides, you can't still be hungry after our dinner at Karlhalla."

"Fine," Siv relented.

""Chores, *then* chases"," the sisters said simultaneously, laughing at the words Hildegunn had too often repeated since they were children.

Gudrun held Siv's hand and pulled her through the crowd to the entrance gate of the Jarl's court. Siv stared longingly at the table of sweets and mourned. The table was besieged on all sides by relentless children and the cakes were losing the battle in terrible fashion to their savagry. Her stomach growled.

* * *

Prince Ormer cursed the rotten churning in the pit of his belly. The court was a lush oasis within the jungle frenzy of the hall, though occupied by top predators: sly ätt leaders and ruthless nobles, hungry for power and wealth. For the moment — within his father's court — they engaged one another peaceably; retelling tales, with bravado, of their great deeds and of those of their progeny.

Chief Ulrich stood before the court and spoke. "Lo! On the field stood I, with cracked shield and bloody spear, helpless of foot to dash, with only cursed eyes to gawk in horror as the silver prince fell..."

It felt a cruel punishment to Ormer, although fitting. The tales these jackals had been particularly drawn to were about where they were one year ago — on or off the battlefield — when his brother, Hamund, had fallen at the battle of Blood Valley.

The speech continued, "... and a great cry did arise, well above that of the men gathered in similar cause, from mine own throat..."

Ormer didn't have a tale of bravery or virtue.

Each story told, of courage, sorrow, or virtuous action, became a twisting, thorny reminder in his guts of the moment when he was told his brother had been killed. There were no lessons within these sermons that gave him any comfort. His father revelled in the sorrow, as though it accorded honour to Hamund's memory.

"... a death which brought with it such a mourning as to pale even the loss of my own son..."

Ormer wished he could take the past back, that he could have been where he'd ought, and not where he had: caught in Jorgan' Bondi's hayloft with the farmer's daughter, half naked and fully drunk on a skin of stolen wine.

"... his bravery and honourable countenance, as that of a king! Of thyself, my Jarl..."

That alone could have been forgiven, at least perhaps forgotten eventually, but Ormer had also fallen from the loft, while pissing off the edge, onto the donkey below and broke the animal's back with his ass. He had to suffer the indignity of learning of his brother's death as the donkey screamed to have its throat slit, while he was simultaneously lambasted, cursed, and threatened by the girl's father. Then to suffer it all over again from his father, grieving in his court, with Ormer as the donkey screaming inside for ultimate escape on the edge of a seax.

"...a loss too great to be carried alone. No, this burden we shoulder as one people..."

Now, he sat on the dais, exposed once more, like an animal chained to a stake to be whipped and prodded with sharpened sticks. His tunic pulled tight around his chest; the room was stuffy, with the lingering bouquet of cow manure. The prince had shuffled his chair back on the dais, little by little, just a bit more than a thumb's width, allowing him to spy through cracks in the wall and watch the games happening below. Just beyond the high back of his father's chair, and through the lattice; he could see his friends — Birger, Hermod, and Sigmund were the ones he cared to keep an eye on — laughing as they took turns throwing axes and making merry with girls who were themselves just coming of age. One of the young women caressed Birger's cheek and Ormer turned away in disgust, muttering to himself, arms across his chest. He was stuck there on a pedestal between the devil and his court.

"...and as the flames grew toward Odin's hall, within the fiery column could Valkyrie be seen, lifting the prince up..."

He prayed this would be the extent of his punishment for past behaviours, prayed that his sins would be absolved by the agony of exposure to courtly matters; a savagery entwined within the creature comforts of wealth. Gaudy and grotesque. None of it held any interest for him.

"...and none ever could, though in Prince Ormer shall we expect these noble virtues upheld..."

He couldn't listen to any more. Anyway, the pompous nobility gathered were there for his father, not him. It was easier for the Crown Prince to believe this than it was to accept the truth gnawing away at him, ingesting his childhood with an unwavering hunger, leaving scarcely a skeleton of the boy upon which he was expected to drape a man. The habits of his youth would not break overnight, much to his father's frustration. Even the past year had not prepared Ormer for the Atlassian burdens of his new station, burdens his parents expected him to carry with grace and ease.

Hamund was dead and everything was different now. Ormer hated his brother for it. Or, could that be his shame speaking? He hated himself for thinking this way of Hamund. He bowed his head and swiped at tears gathering in the corners of his eyes, horrified at how many there were. He'd expected that somehow, someway, the mantle of adulthood would simply swaddle around him once he'd completed some elusive task, and the child within would metamorphosize into something… glorious.

It was not yet so. The cipher of adulthood still remained an enigma to him. Where it might have been common for any other young man of his age, it was lost on the young prince, who had very little experience with anything common.

Ormer knew what the expectations of him were: to continue in his brother's stead as heir to his father's throne, yet he was still too young to understand what it really meant. Now that the customary year of mourning had been observed, his father's tutelage would begin in earnest. "You have fallen too far behind and will need to catch up, clearly, requiring the correct tools of motivation to spur you," his father had threatened him, through pursed lips. These days, everything his father said was a threat, unveiled and remorseless.

The recurrent, frustrated shake of his father's head became the nudge to trip the snare around Ormer's foot, rooting him to the realisation he would never be what his father wanted him to be: Hamund.

How is that fair? He thought. It was a phrase he bounced around his head more often, of late. He looked up at the lord who was currently kissing his father's ass — Hafleikr the Deaf — by trying to pawn off his daughter with a promise of unity and strength through marriage, and on and on… Ormer stole a lingering glance at the boys, then down at his feet. He had no interest in Hafleikr, or his daughter.

"…to solidify our alliance of prosperity and peace."

Prince Ormer was now one of the most eligible bachelors in the western kingdoms, and his mother made no secret of the fact that they were entertaining offers of marriage. It was clearly written within the layout of the court. Representatives from far-flung ätts — claiming nobility and influence — were present to reinforce their allegiances to Jarl Ulfer. Most by invitation and some not.

Those who had them, brought their daughters along, though few brought their wives, Ormer noted with curiosity. They'd dressed the young ladies in elegant gowns, trimmed in gold and sewn with fine stitches from exotic, imported silks. Gold and silver jewellery were hung, draped, clung, and clipped to the girls, making them a showcase of their family's wealth (in truth, a wealth much greater than each family's value) to catch the eye of the Jarl; their daughter's noble upbringing to catch the eye of the Frue; and to show off accentuated breasts and bottoms to catch the eye of the young prince.

Ormer sneered. This was how they made their alliances: through marrying off their children. "Remember this, boy," his father had told him once, "sons are useful for extending power through conquest; daughters ensure you keep it through marriage and children."

"*Sit up straight!*" Ulfer hissed, gripping the arms of the throne until his knuckles turned white. "Sitting on your hands, shuffling your feet like a child, more interested in peasant's games and the style of your hair than with matters of the court you would inherit!"

Ormer rolled his eyes. He took in a deep breath, straightening his back, chin up. *Why does he do this to me?* He wasn't a child, required to endure the embarrassment of being chastised by his father. He didn't want to be there at all! Ulfer quickly turned away from him.

"More wine!" the jarl bellowed, and shook his golden cup as though ringing a bell. A servant rushed in with a jug and the goblet was quickly refreshed, as the next nobleman in a long line stepped forward to present his gaudy, prepubescent daughter.

CHAPTER NINETEEN

The Den

The herald, a short man with a thin, black beard and moustache, and wearing a floppy brown hat, sat between two guards just inside the small gate to the royal court. He held up his cane of office to bar entry to the two young women who'd approached.

"This area is off limits," he said. He looked back and forth between Gudrun and Siv, his eyes narrowed with suspicion.

Beyond, the walls of the Jarl's court were decorated with banners, shields, and spears. The court had a large hearth with the carved remains of a cow on a spit raised high, warming over top. To each side lavish tables were set for the noblemen and their entourages. Each had a healthy showing of men and women representing their ätt, all in their finest dress. Velvet, supple leather, and more silk than an Eastern caravan, had been made into dresses and lined long fur coats and brightly embroidered vests.

A never-ending flow of servants dressed in white linen trimmed with golden thread carried silver platters. They were piled with thinly sliced meats, cheeses, fruits and other delicacies, which the guests picked through. Wine, ale, and mead were brought to each table in jugs so large they each needed two men to carry and yet another to pour.

"More wine!" the Jarl bellowed.

Gudrun bristled at the thin bearded herald. *Angry, petty little man.* He reminded her of a scrappy little dog she knew back at the camp, who didn't know its size and would yap at the bulls until someone rewarded it with a kick.

"We're here to see the Jarl," Gudrun growled. She wanted to shove him onto his ass.

"I was not talking to you, *thrall!*" he snapped at her. The guards leaned in, eyeing the sisters.

Gudrun's vision turned red and she straightened herself up to her full height and looked down at the herald. She had one fist on her hip and the thumb and forefinger of her other hand pointed at his chest, like the beak of a rooster.

"What did you call me?" she demanded, through clenched teeth, giving him a hard peck to the shoulder. "You think I'm a thrall? You *oaf!*" she jabbed him again and he shrugged her away. He raised his cane to strike, but her fist was already cocked, level with his nose. Siv jumped in between them.

"Stop this!" she hissed at Gudrun, then turned to him. "We are here from Lutvin, to see the Jarl on a matter of great importance," she said, locking her eyes with his.

He couldn't help but grimace and imperceptibly shrank back. He cocked his head sideways, and looked her up and down, as though she were a threat.

"Thin Beard!" one of the guards said, then whispered into the herald's ear. Thin Beard lowered his cane and slowly turned away from Siv before breaking her gaze. He gave a quick glance toward the dais, then with feigned indifference looked out toward the farthest rafters.

"Names," he barked, turning up his nose. He furiously wiggled two fingers, signalling "give them to me". The only thing Gudrun wanted to give him was a solid punch in the face.

"I think this is a bad idea—" Gudrun said.

"Gudrun and Siv Thorkildatter," Siv interrupted, stepping

forward.

Thin Beard gave a displeased grunt. A nobleman had just finished his audience with the royal family and received a polite round of applause.

"Wait here," he snapped, viciously pointing his finger at the ground. Thin Beard spun on his heel, and made his way around to the dais.

"Gudrun, we're here to *ask* for help, not beat it out of them," Siv whispered.

"He called me *thrall!*" she hissed through clenched teeth.

Siv leaned against her and let out a deep sigh. "I know. It's not fair."

As Siv pressed her shoulder against Gudrun's, her tension dissolved away.

* * *

Frigga was becoming impatient. All of this was taking too long. There was still no report of the 'war-bringers' from the west that the Warloga had babbled about. *Perhaps the wicked creature was wrong? Perhaps the curse has been... The Grey Wolf... in its den...* She shuddered, knowing the firekeeper's curse was still upon her.

She'd given orders to certain staff to quietly report anyone who might have arrived from the west, and report it to the herald. The firekeeper, too, was to be arrested on sight. *What if these treacherous slaves betray me?* Frigga thought. Her narrowed eyes darted about the room at the servants. Years of experience and training made her aware that she was holding a grimace. She relaxed immediately. *Breath in,* she tapped her foot. *Breath out.*

She looked about the court for her 'war-bringer' while feigning interest in the speech being given by— she really didn't care who it was. She glanced at Ormer, his brow furrowed and lips pursed. His father must have upset him, again.

All of her children were dead now, save for Ormer, her baby.

The youngest. Smallest. Neglected by his father for his older siblings. There was nothing for it now; blame would not change Ormer's destiny. He *was* destined to be thrown to the wolves and grow stronger. Or die. It was the way of things. She knew there was little comfort that she could give him anymore; she didn't want to be seen as coddling. Her husband was now responsible for turning the boy into a man strong enough to be the next jarl.

But, the expectations, those that would have been Hamund's, were being placed upon Ormer, and they were… immense. And she knew her son. She knew he was ignorant of what it all meant — what it really meant — even though the signs of it were laid before him. He was not like his brother, Hamund. Ormer needed to touch fire before he believed it would burn. Foolish youth occupied too much of his mind. *Better as a boy than a man,* she thought. *The Grey wolf in its den —*

She shook her head to dismiss the damned words. *This is going to work, this is going to work!* she repeated in an effort to convince herself. Movement at the court gate caught her eye. *What is that idiot doing?* she thought, watching the herald in heated discussion with two women, servants perhaps? No, not dressed right. *What is that idiot doing?*

Frigga's eyes darted back and forth between him and the women. *They must be the servants of one of the lords,* she decided idly. She turned back to the speech. It would be over momentarily and she would need to display a big smile. *Oh! Lord Sigurd,* she thought, only then noticing him and his family. *I like him.*

She felt a hand on her elbow, which startled her. It was the herald, suddenly at her side.

"Frue," the short man whispered, "those two women, Gudrun and Siv Thorkildatter, say they rode from Lutvin, with an important message for the Jarl."

Frigga's heart leaped, almost out of her chest. *Western shadows blanket the sun —* Could those be them? Were they here? She felt it in her bones. She hadn't expected it, but wasn't surprised that the agent of her doom had turned out to be a woman. *But one who seems so… naive?* One wore the cap of a married woman, though neither of them carried the keys of their household, nor any other indicators of any status. Just two peasants. *The warloga's magik is already at work!* she thought. She knew exactly how to play this.

She couldn't help but stare at Siv. *Beauty is plain…* She hadn't really understood that part, until now; this girl was plainly beautiful. The woman with her, Gudrun, was nothing to speak of, but was tall and strong, sturdy enough to one day make a farmer happy as his wife. *Her champion?* Frigga could hardly count these young women among her enemies; they were simply casualties, whose only purpose was to be the perfect bait for her husband, to break the thread of destiny.

Thin Beard cleared his throat. "I-I would not have brought it to you, but Lutvin is West—"

"Did they give you their names?"

"Yes, my frue, they are—"

She raised her hand to stop him. *She can't be the champion.* Frigga kept a stone-faced expression and gave a slight nod. Thin Beard bowed, then left back to the gate. She'd given him instructions earlier in the night; he knew what she wanted him to do.

Like a spider watching flies hover above its web, she kept her eyes glued to the young women. She fought against restlessness; she just wanted to reach out and grab them. They were so close, nearly in her trap.

Sudden applause startled Frigga when Sigurd's speech ended. She forced a smile and nodded approval, lightly clapping as Sigurd and his family left the centre court. Servants carried a chest and deposited it against the wall, where a collection of gifts and treasures had been piling.

Frigga watched the herald lead the two women to the back of the court, closest to the open cattle doors and the cool night air. They were all that Frigga could focus on; two young women from Lutvin, come to steal her husband, destroy her family, and her kingdom.

The Grey Wolf in its den, she thought. *Do not think it so easy to slay the Wolf in its den!*

Then, Ormer stood and sauntered across the court to the back, where Frigga's flies sat, waiting. *What is that boy doing now?* She gave a stern glance to her head manservant. The man returned a slight nod, then followed the prince.

* * *

Thin Beard had led them to the very back of the court, to a spot just around the corner from the cattle doors. The air coming in was cool and refreshing, but it also carried the pungent reek of dung, left over from the gifts of livestock presented by the noble families. Thin Beard left in a huff.

"What a funny man," Siv whispered.

"I don't like him," Gudrun said. "Not his clothes, or his cane, or his dumb hat, or his thin beard." She watched him strut back to the gate. He took a fresh cup from a passing wench, gave her an unkind word, then sat on a tall stool like a perched crow.

Gudrun looked around the court. It was just as she had suspected: the noblewomen wore garments and dresses worth more than what could be made in an entire year from any farm in Hoddlund. Silks imported at great expense from the farthest corners of the east, had been made into dresses with needless trains, gloves, and hats. Coats and cloaks made of velvet in red, blue, and purple, lined with fur and adorned with gold thread, were draped to show off wealth through the excessive use of fine cloth.

Gudrun had thought that the karls in the main hall wore a lot of jewellery, but here the amount of gold, silver, precious jewels and pearls that were worn around necks, arms, and as headpieces was breath-taking. It all sparkled with thousands of points of light, like sunlight dazzling off the ocean.

She was glad the two of them were at the far back of the court. It was perhaps the only dark corner within the entire hall, even hidden away from brazier light, and most importantly hidden from judging eyes. Their clothes were so plain. Siv's dress was dull and straight, one that had been given to her by her mother. It had been her grandmother's before that. Freyja, why couldn't it have been pleated?

Why does this bother me so? she thought. It had never been an issue for her before then. In fact, she had little use for fashion, pomp, or public display. But, here she felt different, felt as though it mattered a great deal. She prayed that it would not make a difference to their mission, that they would not be dismissed for their plain dress.

She looked at Siv. Beaming as she took it all in, munching on a piece of—

"Hey! Where did you get that bread?" she demanded.

"It's so good! Made entirely from wheat flour. Look!" Siv said. She showed off the soft, doughy bun. Siv took a cursory glance around, then plucked another from the table next to them.

"Siv!" Gudrun gawked at her.

"Try it."

"No!" Gudrun pushed Siv's hand away.

"It's bread, Gudrun," Siv grimaced. "At a feast. No one loses a hand for eating bread at a feast." Siv held it out for her, again.

Gudrun snatched it away and hid it in her lap. "Stop waving it around for them all to see," she hissed. She picked at the crust. It was so soft. She took a small bite. Then another.

"No seeds," Gudrun said. "I like seeds." She hated how good it was. And, especially how much she wanted another, after she'd finished that one.

Gudrun stuffed the rest of the roll into her mouth, just before she felt Siv squeeze her arm. Hard.

"Ow! Siv! What—?"

Then Gudrun saw him. A young man, strolled toward them, dressed in more silk than Gudrun had ever seen on one man. White fur with black dots trimmed the collar of the blue cape that hugged his neck. The cape swished as he walked and Gudrun could see flashes of the cape's white, silk lining. It was pinned with a wide, gold clasp that sparkled as it caught every bit of light in the room, and even more gold twinkled from his wrists and fingers. A circlet of thin silver adorned his head. Behind him, a stern man followed closely, dressed in ätt Vargr's silver and blue livery.

"It's *him!*" Siv whispered.

"Who?"

"Prince Ormer, son of Ulfer," he said, and bowed. Gudrun tried to swallow the huge ball of bread in her mouth, but choked.

"My lord," Siv said, her face flushed. She curtsied, then slapped Gudrun on the back. She coughed out the dough ball and it launched from Gudrun's mouth to land with a splat between the prince's feet. Both women stared in horror at the ball of pasty mush. Though, Ormer hadn't noticed (or pretended not to). His eyes remained locked onto Siv.

The servant came up beside Ormer and cleared his throat, "M' lord—"

Ormer held up his hand, silencing him.

"What is your name?" Ormer said, holding a hand out to Siv as though his fingers caressed the petals of a flower. "Or, perhaps I should guess." Siv looked up and their eyes met. She shivered, but straightened herself up to hide it. "Perhaps it is Beauty. No? Or Sunrise. No. Peace Upon My Heart. Yes, you are Peace Upon My Heart."

"Siv Thorkildatter, of Lutvin," Gudrun said, flatly.

"Siv... Of course it is..." Ormer said, a dreamy look on his face. "Siv: most beautiful of all goddesses; even silver in sunlight pales before such silken hair; even Thor himself — the stormy god of thunder! — is known simply as 'Siv's husband' when at feast with his ravishing wife, so torrential is her beauty."

The servant stepped closer to the Prince and persisted, "M' lord, your mother requests—"

"My mother can wait!" Ormer snapped. He waved the man away with the flick of his wrist. The man bowed, then rushed off.

"I apologise for my mother's servant. He is a loyal pest." Ormer smiled and Siv looked at the floor. "I— uhh—" Ormer stammered. He took in a sharp breath. "I could not help but notice when you entered."

"I am flattered, my prince, that your attention could be stolen from important courtly matters by such a dull and insignificant maiden, as myself. I know the jarl and frue seek for you a wife, and there are many beautiful women here, each more pleasing than the last."

"And you do not count yourself among them?" Ormer cocked his head and smiled. Siv dropped her gaze for a moment, then smiled back.

"I must disclose, my prince, that you are the only man at court who has approached me. Perhaps, I assumed, it was on account of my plain countenance," Siv said.

Gudrun groaned and rolled her eyes. *Not again,* she thought, *first Erich...*

"Some men's hearts can be cowed by a woman's grace. It is because they do not understand beauty. Some are loath to admit that they wish to possess it. Such men regard a woman's charms with terror; a thing to be chained and conquered. I am not such a man. I regard beauty as a delicate and fragile blossom, requiring careful, deft attention to bloom, lest it be undone by the fumbling grasp of a brash fist."

Eww! Gudrun thought. She looked at Siv, shocked to see her melting at Prince Ormer's words. *What is happening right now?*

Just then, the servant returned and whispered to the prince. Ormer started from the man's appearance at his ear, but quickly calmed as the servant spoke. The nobles were settling back into their seats and Thin Beard stood in the centre of the court, waiting for the prince to take his place on the dais, ready to announce the next speaker.

Ormer cleared his throat. "I must return before I am missed by my father."

A strand of hair had fallen across Siv's cheek, and Ormer gently brushed it over her ear, too seductively for Gudrun's liking. Worse, she caught the moment and felt a shift. It was subtle, yet profound, like a breath on a candle's flame that plunges a room into darkness. She caught the look in Siv's eye and the rapture in which it entangled Ormer's attention. *She's smitten!*

Gudrun took a deep breath. The air felt dry and stale, yet her lungs ached for more. The prince spoke with Siv a moment longer, although Gudrun couldn't make out what they were saying. *What is happening to me?* Her head swam and her belly seethed.

Gudrun suddenly found herself sitting, not remembering having sat, nor the prince excusing himself and leaving.

Siv chattered nervously. Reality slowly settled, yet still revealed itself to be turned on its head. Gudrun was barely aware of the hawkish stares from the nobles seated at the other tables. She couldn't decide if they seemed too far away, or not far enough.

Nothing here was real; lavish furs, silk, finespun wool, gold and silver jewellery. Her fingers lingered on the horse blanket lashed to her rucksack. She looked at Siv. Her sister was absolutely radiant, glowing. Fine hair like milk, draped over the front of her dress, which she stroked absently as she spoke. Her delicate features barely contained her elation. Siv turned to Gudrun and nearly burst.

"What do you think of him?"

"I'll be right back," Gudrun said, standing up before Siv could object. "Stay here. On this seat. Don't go anywhere, or steal anything. Do you understand?"

"Where are you going?"

"To get the Jarl his gift." Gudrun spun on her heel and marched to the gate where Thin Beard sat guard. She strode past him without a glance.

"Stop! No! Where are you going?" Thin Beard protested. He jumped off his stool and leaped between Gudrun and the gate. She looked at him, doing her best to hide her contempt. He made no attempt to hide his.

"I'm going to get our gift to present to the Jarl."

"You can't leave now, you are soon to be announced. What is... this gift? I will have it fetched for you."

"A horse," Gudrun said, crossing her arms. Thin Beard raised a dubious eyebrow.

"And where is this horse kept?"

Gudrun described Embla and the stable boys and the half silver coin she'd given them. Thin Beard sent her back to her seat with assurances that the horse would be fetched in time for her to present to the jarl.

"I really hate him," Gudrun growled. She plunked down on her seat.

"This is so exciting, Gudrun! Can you believe we met Prince Ormer? And this court! Have you ever seen anything so fine?"

"Nope." Gudrun shook her head.

Siv gushed about the prince and the court and everything that crossed her vision, with as much poise as her excitement would allow.

"Be careful not to piss yourself," was the best that Gudrun could muster.

"... and the food looks and smells so good! I want to taste it all." Siv's squeaky whispers felt strangely harsh in Gudrun's ears. Her head ached and she still couldn't take in a full breath. She looked over at Thin Beard. He hadn't moved.

"Did he send someone already?" she mumbled. *He better bring that—*

"What?"

"Horse!" Gudrun blurted. Her face got hot and she tried to hide it. Siv's smile disappeared and she furrowed her brow.

"Gudrun, what did you do?" She thrust her chin at the herald. "What did you say to him?"

"Why, so you can flirt with him, too?"

Siv's jaw dropped. "You're jealous that the prince said those beautiful things to me!"

"How do you know those words were for you? I'm sure they were well practised for another one of his court trollops."

"Why would you say such a thing?"

"Why would you invite Erich to stay with you for Yule?" Gudrun snapped.

Siv's eyes went wide. Gudrun knew that Siv would be able to see her pain — she'd always been able to — and had become quite adept at hiding it from her little sister, but this time...

"I didn't—"

Applause in the court interrupted her and the sisters politely, grudgingly, clapped along. Jarl Olvir 'One Ear' finished his speech and bowed. The herald stepped to the centre again.

"Gudrun and Siv Thorkilldatter of Lutvin!"

The announcement of their names caught Gudrun off guard, and her anger was drowned out by nervousness.

Thin Beard indicated where the sisters should stand, a stern, serious look on his face.

The sisters stood, each taking a deep, anxious breath.

"I didn't invite Erich for me," Siv whispered. They began a slow march forward. "I invited him as *your* guest, Gudrun. He's coming to be with *you*."

"You did what?" Siv's words hit Gudrun in the chest like a sledge. She hadn't even realised she'd been carrying this burden which had made her think such poisonous thoughts — about herself, about Siv, and Erich — though it was never real.

Siv tenderly held Gudrun's hand.

Gudrun put Siv's hand to her lips and kissed it. *I love you, too. I've been such a fool!* Her heart was racing. *Erich is coming... to see* me! Her head swam as tears welled in her eyes. It was all too much for her to take, and *here*, of all places, just as they were about to be received by the Jarl and Frue. She suddenly didn't want any of this, she suddenly wanted to be home, waiting for Erich. She wiped her eyes quickly with her sleeve and snorted a sharp breath in to clear her running nose.

Siv held her hand as they walked past the hearth and the dismembered cow to the spot where Thin Beard stood. Gudrun was glad for the moment of warmth from the roaring fire. She couldn't remember having walked the entire distance. Within a few beats of her pounding heart, they were standing in the clear area of the court, before the royal dais. Thin Beard stood beside them.

Gudrun clutched the talisman under her tunic, fiddling to soothe herself with the carved stone, cold and hard against her skin. *May the power of the Valkyrie be with me and not consume my heart!*

The gaze of the court fell heavy upon her, as the weight of an entire castle; expectant, demanding, wanting of an explanation as to why these two peasants would dare request the ear of the Jarl. Gudrun's clothes felt tight and thick, though she shivered with cold. They clung to her skin, making her fumble her steps. Thoughts disappeared from her mind, taking with them any memory of why she was there, what she was going to say. *Oh! Odin help us! Huginn and Muninn give me words,* she prayed.

Upon the dais the royal family sat on gaudy, high backed chairs. Frue Frigga sat to the Jarl's left and Prince Ormer to his right; the hierarchy clearly on display for all to see. It read like a children's story: papa-wolf, mama-wolf, and pup.

"My lord Ulfer, Frue Frigga, Prince Ormer, lords and ladies of the court," Thin Beard announced in a clear voice. "If it pleases m'lord, may I present Gudrun Thorkildatter and her sister Siv Thorkildatter of Lutvin, in Hoddlund. They claim to have come on a matter of great importance, my lord, and wish to address you in your court." He bowed and stepped aside in one, well rehearsed motion.

From the dais the Jarl and Frue scrutinised the women where they stood, like sheep before ravenous wolves. Ormer sat on the edge of his seat, his gaze fixed only on Siv.

Gudrun couldn't stop shivering. It wasn't the cold, but her uncontrollable nervousness. She wanted to run, to scream, to break the tension pulling from her gut like the string of a tight, new bow.

She felt vulnerable, exposed, as though everyone could see

through her to the fear she hid; this naive, simple farm girl from the hills. It hadn't even begun and all she wanted was for it to be over. Siv gave a low curtsy, prompting Gudrun to follow suit. She made a stiff curtsy-like bow. They glanced at each other, and Gudrun gave Siv a nod. *Go ahead, please. Pleasepleaseplease...* she thought.

"My lord Jarl," Siv began, her voice shaky, "we have ridden from Lutvin to tell of raiders from Albion who have ransacked Vestrijóborg, and even now make their way to our village, under the false belief that they will find hidden treasure there. Lutvin is a community of farmers, sheep herders, and fishermen. We are not wealthy. We do not have more than our meagre allotments, and we are not warriors, lord. We humbly present ourselves before you, this sacred night, to request your protection. We are your people, Jarl Ulfer."

Ulfer looked into his cup. He swirled what was in it and investigated the dregs.

CHAPTER TWENTY

Webs Upon Webs

It was too easy for Frigga to manipulate the dull, predictable minds of Ulfer's men with honey, and tonight she'd drizzled over them the hive's entire, dripping comb. No thrall served the noblemen that night, she'd made sure of it. Tonight, the nobles and their men would only be served by young women, eager to carouse with wealthy men for silver, or the opportunity to gain position within a household — invariably from their sponsor's bed.

For Ulfer, on the other hand, Frigga had given strict instructions that her husband's servants were to be male thrall only. They were to keep their demeanour stark, with hoods up and heads down, forbidden to stand in his line of vision. On the last point she was very clear, threatening to flay any who broke her command. The cook had assured her, with great enthusiasm, that she would take care to ensure her orders were followed to the word, while caressing the bound leather cords she used in daily floggings. The cook's assurance was so earnest, one of the thrall men shook and wet himself.

Frigga couldn't afford to have her husband distracted by anything which might take his concentration from what she'd planned. She couldn't believe her good fortune — or, perhaps it was a testament to the warloga's power — when she'd seen this woman,

Siv.

The radiance of the young woman; her flawless skin, like taffeta from the farthest corner of the orient; blonde-white hair, flowing like corn silk; delicate features that she held high and proud, boldly presenting herself before nobility, which only enhanced her sensuality. The girl was surprisingly well spoken, contrasting her sister who proved, predictably, to be a simple country brute.

Inside, Frigga was suspended within an insanity that only wanted their destruction. More than anything else in the world, she wanted these two to burn. *All the king gives… repaid with blood…*

Her heart beat out of her chest. *The Grey Wolf in its den does laze.* She looked at Ulfer. The Grey Wolf might laze, but the spider could not. She needed to remain calm as she weaved her web. The firekeeper's prophecy was coming to pass. *They are sisters… but, the warloga only made one broach. Which one do I pin it to?* She looked to her manservant to be sure he was ready with the cursed jewellery. Armed men stationed throughout the court quietly awaited her signal to spring the trap.

The Grey Wolf in its den does laze, the Grey Wolf in its den does laze… This was Frigga's destiny, it was as palpable as an ache in her bones. If only she could stop fidgeting with her hands! Her world began to swirl; the intoxication of the moment mixing up reality until her perception became completely distorted. *I must test them to know which one gets the broach, then give Ulfer his cup of the warloga's wine.*

Patience.

No need to rush into disaster. She forced slow, deep breaths to try to relieve tension in her neck.

She couldn't help but stare at Siv. *Beauty is plain… It really is too bad,* she thought, a sardonic lament. *If this one has even half a brain, with beauty like hers she could have become empress of all Asgard.* She looked at Ormer. He was ready to burst out of his seat. *Plain as yearning. Perhaps…*

Everyone else looked at the jarl, awaiting his response. Thin Beard patted a linen cloth across his beading forehead.

"My lord," Frigga said. "Your kingdom is under attack from the west and your people require your protection."

Ulfer grunted, still unable to take his eyes off his cup.

"Tell me once more where is it that you hail from, girl?" he said.

"Hoddholm, lord. We are within the stewardship graciously bestowed upon the Chief of Lutvin."

"Ahh! *Now* Lutvin comes to me! And, sends little peasant girls to do the work men of office aught, no doubt," Ulfer bellowed.

The noblemen snorted and snickered. Frigga took a deep breath. *Perhaps Ulfer will do the work for me? No. I can not afford complacency. The prophecy will come to pass, and I must guide it.*

The sisters exchanged quizzical looks at Ulfer's words.

"You are perplexed," Ulfer said. He took a careful sip from his cup. "Then let me enlighten, and let this be a lesson to you all! Chief Gudbrand went raiding in spite of the order to observe a full year of mourning due Prince Hamund after his death. My sweet, sweet prince..." He and Frigga each made a reverent sign to Odin — three triangles across the breast — as did Thin Beard. Ormer absently touched his chest. The nobles made a show of it as well.

"This was foolish of Gudbrand," Ulfer shouted. "Disrespectful! To me and my grieving household. To my noble son's memory, and a blow to the kingdom! Punishment is required, you understand." Ulfer was incensed, sitting on the edge of his seat.

He stared at Siv and licked his lips.

A suggestive murmur rolled through the court. One nobleman laughed outright and rubbed his hands together.

"Y-yes, lord," Siv replied. Her face flushed.

The air in the court held a chill and servants placed more wood on the hearth and stoked it.

The Grey Wolf in its den does laze... he does this to keep them off of their guard. Ulfer always looked to press any advantage. Frigga had to admit that she loved watching Ulfer command power. He never left any doubts he was the alpha, no matter who was in the room. He'd inherited such confidence from his father.

She smiled watching the young women squirm on their feet. *They know they're in a trap now*, Frigga thought. Gudrun looked around nervously. *It dawns on her that they are surrounded.* Drunken, burly men watched the sisters with hungry eyes and wolfish grins.

The jarl's words still hung in the air, his expression blank.

"Th-the transgression against your lordship is clear," Siv said. She curtsied low, with exceptional grace. "If it pleases my lord, your servants may be able to offer some news of the raid, which I believe to be unknown to you, and may be considered in your wise judgement."

Frigga caught the look Gudrun shot at her sister; eyes wide, betraying herself. *Revealing no truth... She hides something*, Frigga thought.

She watched in amazement as Siv dared to look straight into Ulfer's eyes. He relaxed and slowly settled back into his seat. *The little bitch!* Frigga had to keep her jaw from dropping open. Had another woman just tamed her husband?

Ulfer turned to his son. Ormer was transfixed by Siv.

"Ormer!" Ulfer snapped, startling the prince. "What might this news be, do you think, that has prompted two young Hoddskin maidens to travel unescorted to Vargr and present themselves before their jarl?" Ulfer snorted, and threw back the lees in his chalice.

"*Wine!*" he bellowed, slamming his fist against the arm of his throne. Servants rushed in to refresh the jarl's cup.

"Wine!" the nobles echoed with mirthful glee, as servants scurried about from table to table, ensuring every cup was filled.

Good. The nobles still enjoy themselves while Ulfer rages, Frigga thought. *I must ensure that these two eels do not slip from my fingers.*

Ulfer stared at Siv, his eyes glazed and as wide as the moon, mouth agape. He seemed to have lost his ability to think of anything else. He raised his cup to his lips and took another deep drink.

"Come closer," he bade the fidgeting young women, red liquor dripping from his beard. "I would hear what this news is, and will *then* decide what is wise and what is not."

The sisters took a step closer to the dais, looking to the jarl for more direction.

"Well?" Ulfer snapped, startling them.

"My lord," Siv said, choosing her words with careful consideration. "Chief Gudbrand had, indeed, left Hoddlund and gone viking without your blessing. It was clearly a mistake which cursed the campaign, for Gudbrand and his army were slain in Albion, and Hoddlund is in mourning for our loss. But, it is well known that Gudbrand's dedication to his Jarl was absolute, and out of respect for the prince's death he had declared any plunder collected would be given freely to your lordship."

Ulfer smiled, slowly nodding his head with his brow furrowed. He was studying her closely, as though trying to glean an insight to the truth.

"As it should be. I am not concerned with losing Gudbrand's plunder, for it would all have been mine by right!"

"Father," Ormer spoke up, "these ladies have travelled to your court with, hopefully, more than simple promises of openhandedness." He turned to Siv. "Speak now to your lord of the 'matter of great importance' you wish to bring to his attention." Ormer kept his eyes on Siv. He leaned in to hear what she had to say, a warm smile slowly spreading across his lips.

Siv caught his gaze and trembled. She took a deep breath, and focused on the Jarl.

"My sister, Gudrun, and I have been travelling for many days, and we come to seek your help. We ask for your majesty's aid in dealing with the army of outlaws who are threatening to plunder Lutvin, and all of the farmers and good people who live in Hoddlund—"

"Outlaws?" Thin Beard shouted. "Lutvin's chieftain is the one who is responsible for dealing with outlaws. It is *your* chieftain's duty to uphold the Jarl's law, and capture those who are outside of it. If he does not then *he* is breaking the Jarl's law! You cannot expect Jarl Ulfer to—"

Ulfer held up his hand for Thin Beard to stop, then waved him away.

"Presumably, now Chieftess Vigdis presides over Lutvin, not Chief Gudbrand. Did you not hear that Gudbrand is dispatched?" he chided Thin Beard.

Ulfer leaned heavily on one elbow and motioned Siv to him.

"Come closer, that I may see you properly," he said. She curtsied, then flitted to the dais. Gudrun stepped forward, too, but Thin Beard blocked her path. Without any acknowledgement of his presence she dodged around him. He put his arm up and blocked her path again.

Gudrun paused for a moment, scowling, then knocked his hand away and continued. He threw his other hand up and grasped the collar of her tunic. He pulled, but she was solid. In one sharp motion she had him by the throat. He squawked and thrashed as she squeezed.

"Enough!" Ulfer snapped. "Let her pass!"

They ceased and grudgingly released the grip they had on each other. Thin Beard stepped back and rubbed his throat, his red face barely able to contain a pronounced grimace. Gudrun straightened her clothes, then took her place beside Siv.

Ulfer carefully studied Siv's face, as though she were some rare object he'd just discovered. She fidgeted and darted her eyes about as though following a fly.

"My lord—"

"*Shhh*," he interrupted her, and placed a finger on her lips. Siv froze, terrified. Gudrun took another step forward, but the Jarl shot her a glance which stopped her dead. She stood ready, alert.

"My lord," Gudrun said, trying to grab Ulfer's attention away from Siv, "with Gudbrand dead we are defenceless. Mostly women and children remain there now, and still recovering from last winter's plague. Lutvin is vulnerable to attack from these Albonite raiders, and we are asking for your protection. Lutvin is your last western stronghold, and should it fall, all of Hoddlund goes with it."

Ulfer glanced at Gudrun, his eyes glazed. He nodded, pensively.

"Albion? Well…" he whispered, only loud enough for Siv to hear. He threw his head back and finished the wine in his goblet. "Wine!" he shouted. Once again, servants came out from the shadows to refresh empty cups.

Frigga waved Ulfer's servant away and motioned for her own manservant to come forward. The man brought the cursed bottle and filled Ulfer's goblet with the warloga's blood red brew.

"What is this?" he said.

"A rare gift," Frigga said. "A Greek vintage retrieved from Miklagard's fabled imperial cellar. It is said to be able to bestow godly visions of wisdom."

She looked at Gudrun, fiddling with her talisman.

"What is that, girl? What do you play with? Show me," Frigga said.

Gudrun thrust her hand to her side. "N-nothing, my Frue, a simple pendant." She looked down at her feet and her face flushed.

She lies, Frigga thought. "Show me."

Gudrun tentatively pulled it from her tunic.

"It is a warrior," Frigga said. "Perhaps, a guardian?"

"Yes, Frue. It's my champion."

Frigga froze. *Revealing no truth…*

"And what do you call your champion?" Frigga held her breath.

Gudrun vigorously shook her head. "No, my Frue, I do not dare— uh, no name."

It's her! Frigga thought, her heart racing. *Revealing no truth, nor a champion's name!* "Charming," Frigga laughed. She turned away, unable to look at Gudrun anymore, and caught Ulfer's eye.

Ulfer looked at her in a way he hadn't for many years.

"We need wine for our guests," he announced, calmly. "You have charmed me, and my wife. It appears my son as well, judging by the idiotic look on his face. In the spirit of the feast we shall toast together."

Gudrun and Siv gawked at each other.

Servants brought golden goblets for the sisters and filled them with a dark red wine from the large jars.

Frigga held her breath as Ulfer stood, holding his cup containing the malign brew up above his head.

"Your request is granted. We shall sweep these outlaws out, and send them back to Albion, or send them to see Hel! *Skol!*"

"*Skol!*" The nobles pounded the tables, drank and nodded their agreement.

Gudrun and Siv toasted, then carefully drank from their cups, trying not to cough on the unfamiliar libation.

Frigga prayed Ulfer would find whatever the evil, mysterious liquid the warloga had concocted to be palatable. She became queasy and tried not to think about the truth of it.

Ulfer drank the entire cup without pause, then let out a loud belch — a sure sign of satisfaction — which allowed Frigga to breathe easier.

Now is the moment, she thought. Her head ached. She signalled her manservant once more, then walked over to the women with all of the grace she could muster.

"Honoured guests," she announced. "Please accept these gifts, tokens of our commitment."

She waved forth her servants, who brought out two white cloaks, each made from finely woven wool and lined with silk, their hoods trimmed with fur. The servants laid a cloak on each of the sister's shoulders and fussed over the drape.

So close, Frigga thought. A bead of sweat ran down her forehead. Her heart was pounding so hard she was sure everyone could hear it.

Her manservant handed Frigga the warloga's broach, safely wrapped in cloth. Then Frigga removed her own cloak pin, letting her royal garment drop to the floor. She held hers out for Siv and the cursed one she presented to Gudrun.

The sisters hesitated.

Just take the fucking pins! Frigga thought and thrust them at the women. Her head was pounding. She feared the women would see her hands tremble and expose her.

Gudrun took hers first, and grumbled a low "thanks", then unwrapped it and turned it around in her fingers to admire the piece.

Siv smiled and accepted the frue's gift with unparalleled grace, displayed by her low curtsy. Frigga watched Gudrun with an intensity she found difficult to hide. This only worked once the pin was installed. *This last piece, and the trap is set! The Grey Wolf in its den —*

"May they be a symbol of our bond," Frigga blurted, trying to tame the tremble in her voice. She nodded encouragement to the sisters to put the pins on, *now.* They smiled sheepishly as they admired the luxurious fabric and fumbled with the pins.

Curse their clumsy fingers! Frigga's stomach began to gurgle and churn. *Breathe,* she soothed herself, refusing to mentally travel down the path which she knew would lead to her losing her bowels.

"These pins hold the royal cloaks around you, a symbol of the safety and protection which Jarl Ulfer's kingdom surrounds you with." It was happening, nothing would interfere now. In a moment, they would be hers.

Gudrun hesitated with the broach in her hand. She looked at Siv and mouthed the words, "We did it."

Siv grinned and nodded, barely able to contain her excitement.

Gudrun took a deep breath, then pushed the silver pin through the thick fabric, turned the hasp, and locked it into place.

It is done! Frigga thought. *The Grey Wolf in its den does laze.* She looked to her husband. Yes, but not anymore. He blinked and rubbed one eye, as though it were infected with dust.

"Something still niggles at me," Ulfer said, his voice dramatic and loud. The Warloga's wine stained his greying beard a deep maroon, like fresh blood on a hound's maw. "Chief Gudbrand knew I had forbidden raiding because of Hamund's death." He looked at Ormer and sneered, a look of disgust on his face. A darkness had taken hold of him.

The warloga's elixir is quick! Frigga thought, pleased with herself.

"My lord—" Siv began.

"*And yet!*" Ulfer shouted, shocking her and the entire court into silence. "He left regardless, in open defiance of my order. A slap to my face while I was still fresh in my *mourning!*"

Tears streamed down his face, and he frothed at the mouth. He began to tremble.

Did the wine poison him? Frigga thought.

"And then, two little girls are sent to beg for my mercy! Not a delegation, but *children!*" He was snarling.

To Frigga's amazement something strange was happening to Gudrun's cloak. The flawless white wool began to stain a bright red, as though Gudrun's neck were gushing blood from the cursed cloak pin at her neck.

Frigga could feel something growing within her, a power building up.

"Gudrun! You're bleeding!" Siv cried, gawking at Gudrun, horrified by the growing red stain.

Gudrun grabbed at her throat and tried to wrest the broach open, but it was firmly locked into place. The blood red seeped over the entirety of her cloak, and try as they might, neither of them could remove the garment.

Gudrun pulled out her seax to cut the fabric, but stopped short at the sound of an armoury of swords being drawn, all in the same moment.

"Siv, stop!" Gudrun said. Siv was still struggling to remove Gudrun's cloak. Only then did she notice the men surrounding them with swords drawn, closing in.

"We have to go," Gudrun said. She shook her head, as though trying to clear it.

Siv pulled on her arm, but Gudrun was rooted to the spot and wouldn't move. A dull look paralyzed Gudrun's face.

"You two are not going anywhere," Frigga said, through a wicked smile. She grabbed Gudrun's arms. Gudrun didn't resist.

The jarl stood, grabbed Siv and pulled her close to his chest.

"No!" Siv struggled against him, shocked at his boldness.

Ormer leapt up and put himself in their midst.

Siv beat against the Jarl's chest, but her blows did nothing to assuage him, his hands tight around her waist.

"Father! What have you done? Stop this!" Ormer shouted. He grabbed his father's arm and pulled him off Siv.

Incredulous, Ulfer wrenched his arm away from Ormer and threw Siv to the ground.

"You dare lay a hand on your father?" Ulfer shrieked, foaming at the mouth like a wild dog. "You *dare* to raise your hand to your *jarl?*"

"You are not in your right mind, father!" Ormer shouted. "These are guests in your court and allies by your decree! What evil has taken a hold of you?"

"Ormer! *No!*" Frigga shouted. It was nearly done. *Stupid boy! You're going to ruin it!*

"You will not lecture *me* on how to be jarl! Unless..." Ulfer's eyes went wide. "You are looking to challenge..." A new darkness crept over Ulfer's face and twisted it into something otherworldly. It was a snarling visage which terrified both Ormer and Frigga.

In one swift motion Ulfer had his sword drawn, and swung it down on top of Ormer to split him in two. Ormer wrenched his own sword free at the last moment and parried the blow.

A woman's shriek and a smashed pitcher grabbed the attention of the men. Frigga dashed in to halt the fight, but stopped short as their swords sliced past her face, grazing her nose.

Their weapons clashed again. Then again, and smashed down onto a table, sending splinters of wood and smashed crockery flying.

"Stop this!" Frigga screamed. She turned to the guards. "Do something!"

The guards hesitated, too intimidated to intervene against their jarl. They backed away, clearing a space around the two royal combatants.

Ormer stabbed through Ulfer's tunic, nicking his arm and drawing first blood. The two of them paused as Ulfer felt his arm. Blood covered his fingers.

"Father, stop it! You must come to reason!" Ormer pleaded.

But, Ulfer's mind remained in a place well beyond reason. He bellowed and shrieked as he lunged at his son.

Guards rushed to the gate to keep the crowd from spilling in from the main hall.

All eyes were on the duel between the jarl and the prince.

"The jarl's gone mad!" Someone shouted.

"I've unchained a beast!" Frigga cried.

An old man was crouched by the hearth, ignoring the chaos around him. He held up two smouldering cedar bows and blew on them until they issued forth thick, white smoke. It billowed out rapidly from his breath as he mumbled an incantation. It was an unnatural vapour, which crept across the floor and billowed in the air as though it were alive.

Within moments it had filled the entire court and all there were enveloped in the fog — not choking, like smoke, but a thick cloud of mist.

It happened so quickly, that none had the opportunity to shriek in terror, until they were completely enveloped in it

"What is this evil?" Frigga cried out. She couldn't see past her outstretched hand. She clambered through the fog to find her throne.

Men shouted, but the haze even distorted sounds, making them echo in unnatural ways. The garbled clash of Ulfer's and Ormer's swords split the air once more, at once here and then over there, with more shouts warbling in Frigga's ears.

"Ormer! Ulfer!" she called. *Is this one of the warloga's tricks?*

Out of the corner of her eye she caught the movement of a strange shape. There! In the mist she could see a glowing red light moving. *The magic of the warloga's pin!* she realised. Then it dawned on her.

"The women are fleeing! Guards! *Guards!* Where are those idiots? Must I do *everything?*" She'd hidden a bow behind her throne and three arrows, each with a poisoned tip. "I did not get this far in life without a 'cow dung plan'," she muttered.

More shouts in the mist; Ulfer slashing at Ormer; the clatter of silver dishes crashing to the floor.

The glowing shape moved quickly, Frigga had only moments! She drew the bow and loosed an arrow, then shot another and the third as the shape retreated.

* * *

"Come with me," was all that Gudrun had heard, an old man's voice from within the mist.

All else was distorted to her, distant, as though she were trapped beneath a frozen lake. Yet, that simple command had been clear. She no longer found herself rooted to the ground, but felt a great need to obey his commands. She'd turned and saw an old man in a long leather coat and a grey woollen cap. He walked ahead of her, leading her through the mist. Siv followed, too. The thought never crossed Gudrun's mind to ask him who he was, where he was taking them, or why.

A sharp pinch on Gudrun's neck made her yelp and she slapped her hand on it. It burned, like acid. A moment later, Siv groaned before stumbling sideways. She grabbed Gudrun's arm and leaned on her with all of her weight.

The old man guided them through the mist as though his vision could pierce it.

Around them was shrouded chaos; the angry shouts of men and

cries of women; the clash of swords in fierce combat.

But, the old man was calm as he led them to the cattle doors.

They broke through the mist, out into the night air. A mule-drawn cart stood only a few steps away. The bed was lined with cedar bows and on top lay a large bundle of sticks strapped to a pack. The old man rushed them to the cart, and Siv crashed to the ground.

"Siv..." Gudrun mumbled with all of her strength, tears streaming. She wanted to jump, to dive, to catch her sister but her body was stuck inside a nightmare where her limbs were unmovable stones. She could only watch, with blurry eyes as Siv collapsed into an unnatural heap on the cobbles, the protruding shaft of a black arrow pierced through her ribs.

End Part I

Part two, **Daughter of the Valkyrie: Web of Destiny**, is being prepped to launch for Christmas 2024!

For progress updates, free stuff, your chance to have a vote on insider design ideas for the series, and exciting behind the scenes information, visit **daughterofthevalkyrie.com**.

Another way to support your favourite author is to leave a book review. Reviews really help a book, and an author, to thrive in a competitive market. I appreciate all of my fans and how you've stuck with me through my crazy process, and I appreciate you taking the time to review my work and let others know your opinion. Thank you!

—Kevin Saul

Kevin Saul lives in Ontario, Canada, with his family and their cat, Cleo. Kevin has a varied background, which includes having been a proud serving member of the Canadian Armed Forces, and learned a handful of different trades.

He has been creating and sharing stories since childhood, writing and running role-playing adventures with friends, such as *D&D* and *Warhammer*. He is a continuing, enthusiastic student of the written word.

Visit tritale.ca to send Kevin a message and for exciting exclusives on upcoming books!

Manufactured by Amazon.ca
Acheson, AB